TRAVELERS' REST

This book is a novel.
IT IS NOT Travelers Rest S.C.
The writer is from Pickens County S.C.
The Writer wrote another book
he entitled Red Hills and cotton
This book in history about life
in Pickens County in the 30's + 40's.

TRAVELERS' REST

BY BEN ROBERTSON

Introduction by Beatrice Naff Bailey and Alan Grubb

CLEMSON UNIVERSITY PRESS

Published by Clemson University Press in Clemson, South Carolina

Editorial Assistants: Teneshia Head and, Charis Chapman

Cover image: George Caleb Bingham, *Daniel Boone Escorting Settlers through the Cumberland Gap, 1851–52*. Oil on canvas, 36 ½ x 50 ¼". Mildred Lane Kemper Art Museum, Washington University in St. Louis. Gift of Nathaniel Phillips, 1890.

Cover design by Charis Chapman

To order copies, please visit the Clemson University Press website: www.clemson.edu/press

CONTENTS

To Dorothy

"The land shall not be sold forever; for
the land is mine."

"The land and the dream and the mystery."

FOREWORD

The high valleys of Central Java are far from home for me but toward the end of a rainy season I was there—with two other restless Americans, spending a few days in the cool of the green coffee groves and the quinine trees. I remember the remote and curious feeling we all had, sons that we were of the Puritans and Pilgrims—wonderfully excited by so much strangeness about us yet homesick all the time and lonely for another land. Southward from the house where we were, between us and the Indian Ocean, loomed a great jagged mountain called the Kloet, a volcano which until the Dutch cut tunnels through its vast crater walls used to fill every seventeen years with water, then explode with terrible convulsions taking thousands of lives. Northward rose other volcanoes, one fuming with yellow sulphur smoke.

Between these sinister ranges of tropical mountains, running east and west, lay our valley and several other valleys, the whole forming a deep cup which was used every day by the immense Java clouds as their miracle place. These clouds would pile above us, higher and higher, until the clock struck four, then they would come down in roaring rain, always and exactly on time.

This was a fascinating picture but it was not Carolina, nor did this Kloet cut the sky like Pike's Peak; this was not the kind of rain that fell on Chicago. It was a foreign, alien, faraway scene and like all Americans who are forced by their business to live long abroad—we grieved. We were exiles from home and we knew it.

So we read old New York newspapers and old letters and I, being lonely, homesick and recovering from a foreign tropical illness, began reading "Leaves of Grass." It was then in faraway Java, engrossed in those lusty and delicate and living American pages, that I for the first time saw the vision of our people—the long dead line of our fathers, succeeding, failing, crying in the night, singing hymns and drinking, glorying in life, longing for death, "lovely death." I saw them all moving through American time and the vast territories of American space, homesick themselves and lonely, an American exodus, a long westward search for a way of living, for spiritual rest. I heard the cry in the wilderness, the voice of anguish which Americans have always known and still know in their secret heart. It was the way of the wind for us, the winding road, the star.

And suddenly I saw myself, my own generation, and our place in America's procession. We stood on a high hill in a peculiar position. For behind us, still in sight, lay the early valley of the past, and there ahead of us stretched another mighty valley—the field of the future. It was into our lifetime that the division of time had come. The paved road and the automobile and other things such as adaptive necessity had cleft tomorrow so swiftly from yesterday that I saw our own succeeding generation would be more distantly removed from William Jennings Bryan and maybe the kerosene lamp than we were from the ways of Priscilla Alden. We alone lived at the high noon, an end and a beginning.

So there in the tropics I decided to look backward and inward while time and the back valley lay before me—for I had heard from my Carolina grandmother what her Carolina grandmother had said about the redcoats; also I had flown to California. I wanted to catch the glimpse I had of a plain family making its way in America—through the whole 300 years of the venture, changing as America changed, keeping the step, constantly renewing itself, finding new strength, and at the same time holding to its original belief, remembering still the dream. I wanted to show a group of Americans as they had been from the beginning, as their children were, as surely their children's children would be—a people almost living for the future.

So I began and I have worked on this whenever and wherever I found the time—on board ships in the Indian, Atlantic and Pacific Oceans, in a little hotel opposite the railway station in Stockholm, at Elsinore in Denmark, at Senora Teetz's pension in Caracas, on Riverside Drive in New York, on Thirty-first Street in Georgetown, in the basement of No. 1 Great Smith Street in London, and at last and mostly in Keowee Valley which is where I belong.

I have used the pioneers of my own family as inspiration, Daniel Boone and James Robertson, founder of Tennessee, and Horseshoe Robertson and the blacksmith-scout; also that more powerful line called here the Caldwells who into the fourth generation have left their dual and conflicting qualities of nullity and strength—but they are not the actual figures in this fable, none of them, nor are any actual persons here depicted; these characters and their scenes are emotional fictions.

I have drawn on old letters at our house and old legends and on my own lonely reflections when far from home—for I believe in the clarifying word of loneliness, it lies at the base of our national character. Emotion flowing through New World space has been my concern—the building up and handing on of an American attitude and in attempting to show this, I have tried deliberately to write a novel as though it were a mythical history. And as for the delineation of the characters—lost in genealogy, lost in time and space, names now only on a stone, they are all and they are nothing for it is the procession that counts, the peculiar idiom and its mood, the costly national flower that blooms above the grave. It has been the cry, living still, that I have tried to deal with, the love Americans always had had for America, the long never ending search for a home.

B. R.
Clemson, South Carolina

INTRODUCTION

BEN ROBERTSON, JR.'S *TRAVELERS' REST* (1938)

As we open Ben Robertson's 1938 *Travelers' Rest*, we realize, just from reviewing his Table of Contents, that Frederick Jackson Turner, whose "frontier thesis" fostered the idea of American exceptionalism, had some significant sway in the author's understanding of American history. Over two-thirds of the pages within his historical fiction saga are within a section named "The Westerners." The rest are fairly evenly split between the other two sections: one called "The Southerners" and the last called "The Americans." This one structural decision may be a bit jarring for many readers who will choose to delve into this re-issued book because of Robertson's reputation as South Carolina's upcountry author, but Robertson was a deep thinker with a wide vision who spent most of his adult life trying to make sense of who he was as an American who was also deeply rooted in South Carolina's upcountry. In this his only extended fiction, he traces one Scots-Irish family's migrations from eastern Pennsylvania through a series of "westward" migrations that eventually take some of his characters all the way to the Pacific shore while others slowly work toward building a family home-place within the Keowee Valley, nestled within the Blue Ridge Mountains of South Carolina's northwest corner. To help us find our way within this expansive, multi-generational story, the author also offers within his opening pages an essential reader's guide to the convoluted genealogical lines of his fictional family (see chart on pp. xiv–xv), which is modeled, in part, on one strand of his own family's history. Through the use of various family letters, artifacts and oral histories as well as his deep understanding of American literary and intellectual history, Robertson crafts an American epic, not just a Southern one, that evolves from his growing understanding of how his own particular family story is part of, and even a reliable exemplar of, a much larger American story.

When Robertson spoke to Clemson College cadets at his alma mater in February of 1941 (while on leave from covering as a war correspondent the Battle of Britain), he explained to aspiring writers, just a few years after *Travelers' Rest's* release, that the great American literary tradition was very much about "defining ourselves to ourselves."[1] He believed that the literary efforts of Hawthorne, Emerson, Thoreau and Whitman were focused on one essential question about American character—who are we? He also found that various contemporary local-color writers were following in this same tradition as well. He noted specifically Sarah Orne Jewett, Sherwood Anderson, Ellen Glasgow and Thomas Wolfe, contemporary American writers who had wrestled with the nature of American identity by examining it carefully from within their own local communities. His *Travelers' Rest* was certainly influenced by this strong regional literary tradition, since he focused it around one specific American family and one place that he knew so well—his own kin and his own upcountry South Carolina.

In his conversation with the Clemson undergraduates, Robertson gave a nod also to the up-and-coming journalist Ernest Hemingway (who, like Robertson, was working for the New York daily *PM* at the time) and John Steinbeck (who had been covering international affairs long before Pearl Harbor). Like these modernist writers who had examined the nature of American character as they covered the news in international contexts, Robertson too grappled with America's coming-of-age as he continued to cover—and at times recommended thoughtful responses to—current foreign affairs.[2] By the time he completed *Travelers' Rest*, Robertson had written about communities in Indonesia, Australia, New Zealand and Hawaii while he also considered America's footprint within those places. He also covered the 1935 Naval Conference in London as United Press correspondent for the United States and Great Britain and was putting the finishing touches on his lead article for *The Saturday Evening Post*, "King George Strives to Please."[3] Defining America's character within an international context became an incredible but important challenge for these writers. What role should the United States play upon the world's stage and why? How should we respond to the Japanese aggression in Manchuria or the Fascist imperialism in Spain or Hitler's violence toward Jews? How were America's actions rooted in the larger world's evolving nationalistic and imperialistic tendencies? These were challenges that were foremost in the minds of Robertson and other American intellectuals and writers who had lived and worked abroad—and that Robertson was thoroughly conscious of as drafts of *Travelers' Rest* began to evolve.

By alluding to a selection of America's established writers in his conversation with young writers, Robertson was in no way trying to suggest that he was already among them, since *Travelers' Rest* was his only full-length fiction (and remained so, because of his tragic early death in 1943), but he did want them to appreciate the literary tradition that he had come to respect and the essential question that continued to perplex reflective, literary U.S. citizens and himself: how can we best explain ourselves to ourselves? Robertson probably wondered aloud with them: how should they, as young Americans, respond to current world crises? Would they bear arms? This was certainly a focus of Robertson's keynote address at the college that following evening. How should Americans respond to the escalating Axis aggression during the months before Pearl Harbor? And, as Carl Becker, a former student of Frederick Jackson Turner, explained in his 1931 American Historical Association address "Everyman His Own Historian," Americans needed to use their understandings of their past and the value it had for them to anticipate their future.

Repeatedly, throughout Robertson's various writings, he suggested that he and the American people were a part of a much longer tradition of ideas and beliefs that had made its way across the Atlantic and into their ways of being and seeing. He clearly thought the stream began to evolve early within the Western tradition and that, in addition to the Enlightenment ideals that had inspired Jefferson and the founding fathers, it surely included the wellsprings of Judeo-Christian thought as well, since he opens *Travelers' Rest*, as just one example, with his colonial family's excitement about the prospects of yet another promised land within their New World wilderness:

> There was passionate earnestness about Carter. He rolled out his words like a religious fanatic, obsessed with redeeming the lost. He became grim. "Down this valley, folks, runs a rocky river that is shallow and low with easy fords; out of it flows two roads for produce—the first and nearer, to the head of navigation on the Savannah River, and the second along an old savage trail clear to Philadelphia…"
>
> Bowing her head, the old woman wanted to scream out: "Lord God," to shout, "I've lost everything, I'm lost." But all she did was to whisper, "Do something. Heavenly Father, save me."

Fair rich lands, more bountiful game, cooler winds, a brighter flower—it was the same old story. For eighty years old Narcissa had heard it and now her sensitive upper lip, full and expressive, quivered; she began bitterly to weep. For this was the fourth time one of the restless men had brought into a home of hers the enchanted fable of a new land that flowed with Bible milk and honey.

The fourth time!

Tragedy strode always into the Caldwell family with the telling of that story. Abandoned cabins followed it, a caravan moved deeper into the wilderness, then there was murder, starvation, finally cabins no better than the ones the pilgrims had deserted.

"Lord God, Lord God."[4]

Robertson keenly understood that the American experiment that he knew was a part of a much larger historical story. It did not begin within Winthrop's New World covenant community. The errand into the wilderness began long, long ago. He was proud of, and strengthened by, this extensive life-giving heritage that went all the way back to his family's Old Testament liberation stories and days. He does, however, suggest that the Caldwell story swerved toward the British Isles of Western Europe as a result of the Roman Empire's expansion, and that Thomas à Beckett, from the Middle Ages, ranks within this family's tradition. Robertson brings us to Canterbury via Caldwell Crossing's leave from his World War I Western Front. Caldwell, yet another kinsman within the Caldwell line, honored the memory of Thomas à Beckett in a letter home to his mother who was eager to hear from him back in the Keowee Valley:

Up early and off from Victoria Station to Canterbury to see the beautiful yellow cathedral with fine windows filled with stained glass…I came to a plain stone chair standing on stones before a great stained window—the chair in which all the heads of their church have been enthroned for a thousand years—since St. Augustine's time, and standing there I felt that through this rock flowed the spirit from Calvary and the Cross, straight from here across the Atlantic. I looked down the narrow aisles…it was the anniversary of the murder of blessed Saint Thomas à Becket. And in the evening I sat far in the back, in the dark, listening to the choir and the chanting of the mass, the organ pouring its divine song through the centuries of time…beautiful, it was beautiful…the deep purple and the green of the windows in the north transept built for pilgrims who could not read, telling them in great pictures the story. "Pilgrims," said the sign where Thomas was murdered, "pray for peace." And I prayed. The choir came down the steps as Thomas himself came that winter evening…when the sun was setting. They sang, "Ah, St. Thomas, pity our helplessness, rule the strong and lift up the fallen…" the voices rose, "pray for grace that we may be better men, guide our going in the way of peace!"[5]

Again, we see the theme of the pilgrims down through time and the trans-Atlantic spiritual connection that Robertson would make foundational in this and his subsequent work.

As Robertson explained in his foreword to *Travelers' Rest*, he wanted to capture a sense of emotion evolving through time within the New World. While recovering from a tropical illness within the American Consulate in Java in 1928, he became enthralled with Walt Whitman's *Leaves of Grass*, an American epic in verse form. Following Whitman's lead and encouraged by the literary influences he alluded to in his discussion with the Clemson student writers, he, too, chose to use the classical epic genre of the Western tradition; and like Whitman, he, too, added his own modernist touches that he found useful in the contemporary American literature he valued and encouraged.

As Whitman surely understood, the epic has typically been used to serve a civic purpose by helping a community or culture think about who they are and what they value. Since Robertson had devoted his entire adult life to civic service and since he was personally obsessed within his own identity struggle, he may have felt that this genre would best serve his inquiry purposes. If he was going to spare the time to write fiction, it had to offer more than just entertainment or aesthetic pleasure. It had to serve a civic as well as a personally meaningful purpose. It had to matter.

Like other epics, *Travelers' Rest* is grounded within a good-versus-evil structure. As we begin to read, we slowly begin to see that the evil Other is what helped tear apart the American Union. The evil Other is an evolving American tendency that found currency within the slave-holding aristocratic South. It was also found lurking with the industrial North that Thoreau and other writers before him were able to hunt down and expose. This evolving American way of thinking found little wrong with exploiting others for the sake of material gain, social standing or outright political power if it aided individual pursuits of happiness. This expedient means toward happiness, no matter what the cost, was at odds with a somewhat opposing fundamental belief that Americans were also somehow bound together within a covenant (and increasingly contractual and law-governed) community that honored the dignity and the rights of human beings—no matter what the cost. Within Robertson's epic, these two strains of the wilderness errand and our country's founding ideals were variously interpreted in different ways throughout the depicted family's intergenerational journey and would clash in almost every plot development until the final family hero discovers his way to secure his personal happiness without having to exploit others in the process or deny them their dignity and rights.

Travelers' Rest also contains highly stylized literary language in keeping with the epic tradition. The opening lines of his story set the tenor of his tale:

> Over the low plains of the Carolinas, across great marl lands and marshes, a wild western gale was blowing—the wind of a new spring and it filled the long-limbed pines about the Caldwell cabin with deep and restless soughing, a lonesome song. And all the Caldwells heard it. The sound of this raging music gave to them, resting about the fire in their house, a feeling of secure strength and peace, but also it disturbed them. For there was nothing like a high wind to dissatisfy a Caldwell with the present.[6]

Robertson's use of alliteration with the "marl lands and marshes," his hyperbolic description of the "raging music" and his use of polyvalent symbols like "a high wind" all suggest a poetic flair. We get the feeling from this opening paragraph that a natural rather than a supernatural spirit is somehow miraculously calling the Caldwells onward, making them feel restless and not quite comfortable with the present. The wind, a natural spirit, aroused them, making them yearn for something more.

In addition, Robertson's story unfolds within a massive geographical expanse and over an extended time—"it sprawls" as did Dante's *Divine Comedy* or Homer's *Odyssey*. He traces the exploits of one family over more than five generations. Although many of the kin settle within the Keowee Valley in hopes of building a family name and home place, others go on to realize their dreams throughout the wild West, while others eventually turn, within the twentieth century, toward the Northeast after World War I began to bring various American regions back together through a common cause. Robertson's tale begins in the early Colonial Era around the 1750s and ends just before the Great Depression within the late 1920s.

Interestingly, Robertson's more modernist epic still includes a cosmic struggle. The whole Protestant theology of the Great Awakening permeates this pilgrim family's multigenerational journey. In Robertson's New World story, people pay for sins and pray for salvation. People are held accountable and continuously think about the proper path in a seemingly unceasing cosmic drama that somehow seems contained within history. The just yet merciful God that permeates the tale is one that the faithful have chosen to adopt. They believe in that Spirit's influence and response. They find it at work deep within them and among them.

Furthermore, as in most canonical epics, Robertson's omniscient narrator enters into the thoughts and feelings of multiple characters. Because of this we can feel the needs of motherly pioneers as well as the young in search of romantic love. We can get a sense of the needs of the worn-down elderly and the yearning of younger generations eager to build their names. We can try on African American feelings as well as Scots-Irish ones. We are able to enter into the provincial clashes between South Carolina's upcountry and her low-country neighbors and kin. We can even sense some of the changes and enduring continuities within emotions as the generations wrestle with problems and possibilities. This yearning for a better way of living seems to endure, but the nature of that better way seems to slowly but surely change down through the generations.

Finally, Robertson's epic serves as an encyclopedia, a teaching tool, for readers who are new to America, for the young, or for those who continue to search for understanding about the nature of American character, even as it is expressed within a single family story. The author offers a splendid cultural bible that vividly portrays some of America's abundant flora and fauna as well as its rich natural resources. We learn about remedies and folkways and what to eat and drink and which songs to sing. We learn what not to do and how to get along—what works and what does not within this New World Caldwell family.

⁂

[The character genealogy that follows (on pp. xiv–xv), entitled "An American Family: The Caldwells of Forest Mansion," is adapted from a long, 21-by-9-inch figure of the same title that was tipped in after Robertson's Foreword in the first and, until now, only printing of the book.]

⁂

CHARLES CARTER CALDWELL, settled originally in Pennsylvania.

└ STEPHEN JOHN, murdered. Married Narcissa the First of Forest Mansion (also murdered).

    └ CARTER, a restless wanderer, moved to Virginia, was murdered.

      ├ CARTER,* the most famous of the Caldwells, married Clarissa, went on to Tennessee.

      └ SILAS,* the founder in upcountry S. Carolina of Forest Mansion. Suffered apoplexy while hunting rustlers. Married Lucinda.

        ├ SILAS THE SECOND, killed at Kings Mountain.

        ├ STEPHEN JOHN, renounced the world.

        ├ CARTER THE SECOND of Forest Mansion. Was forced to marry Caline Lott; became the Senator. Struck by lightning.

          ├ STEPHEN JOHN THE SECOND, married Unity the first, became rich, was known as the Congressman.

          └─────────────────────────────→

          ├ LUCINDA THE SECOND, died of cholera morbus.

          ├ ARTEMISSA THE SECOND, married a Roper, moved to Alabama.

          ├ CARTER THE THIRD, bitten by a mad dog, he died of hydrophobia.

          ├ SILAS THE THIRD, went to Texas and on to California.

          ├ TEMPERANCE, married a Riggins and went to Texas.

          ├ UNITY THE SECOND, she died.

          ├ FRANCES, married Eilas Caldwell, her cousin. Became mistress of Red Hill Plantation.

          ├ PISGAH, went to Kansas where the Caldwells lost sight of him—he disappeared.

          ├ JESSE, once in Arkansas, he escaped injury in a tornado.

          └ LUCY, her mother died bearing her; Lucy, being a Caldwell, lived on.

        ├ NARCISSA THE SECOND, died in infancy on the wilderness road.

        ├ NARCISSA LUCINDA, called Narcissa the third, was murdered.

        └ PATIENCE, married Philip Carr, a rough old bachelor twice her age; went West.

FRANCES THE SECOND, became an eccentric spinster.

CALINE THE SECOND, married Habersham Wyatt and went to Texas; Habersham later went to California during the gold rush; they didn't get rich—neither he nor Silas the third.

UNITY THE THIRD, became an eccentric spinster.

LOTT, killed at Gettysburg by the Yankees.

LAFAYETTE, murdered at New Orleans.

WARREN, died of yellow fever at New York and had to be buried among the Yankees.

JAMES, died of alcoholism in North Carolina.

RICHARD, killed at Lookout Mountain by the Yankees.

SILAS THE FOURTH, married Patience Noble, his cousin. Almost ran for Governor.

LOTT THE SECOND, married Naomi, granddaughter of the stepdaughter of his great-grandfather Carter.

THE LAST STEPHEN JOHN, went to Harvard.

THE LAST LUCINDA, went to Goucher.

STATES RIGHTS, died in infancy.

SUNSHINE, died in infancy.

NARCISSA THE FOURTH, murdered. Married Miles Crossing, son of Sue Crossing, the herb woman.

CALDWELL, killed at St. Mihiel.

THE LAST CALINE, ran away, was deserted afterward with two children.

---

* CARTER and SILAS were cousins of Patrick Caldwell, for whom living became unbearable, and of Artemissa, his wife. Their son Oliver was an idiot.

Regrettably, as international events unfurled in 1938, perhaps the only redeeming return Robertson himself received from his ten-year *Travelers' Rest* project was the personal strength he gained from wrestling with the history of his family and country. He did not earn any fortune or fame or a place within America's literary canon. In fact, he had a tough time getting his epic published. While Robertson had connections to publishing venues in New York through his past work within *The New York Herald Tribune,* the publishers he sent his manuscript to had little interest in his story. Harper did offer suggestions for revisions and was willing to work with Robertson, but he had other pressing responsibilities as a journalist and wanted control over his narrative. Instead of going with a major national press, he finally chose to publish the book himself. For the price of a few bales of cotton, he jokingly noted, he and his friends issued a small run of *Travelers' Rest* through The Cottonfield Publishers.

Unfortunately, this was only the beginning of Robertson's problems with this particular literary endeavor. Upon release of the book, many upright citizens within his upcountry community and the state were troubled by the realism within the tale. As one lady put it, "You have smeared mud all over us." And when the Governor's wife was asked to comment on the book, to share whether she felt the story was worthwhile reading material for young people, she did her best to dodge the question, while another leading lady within the state publicly declared that "*Travelers' Rest* is full of 'eagles and swine' and our red cotton hills have suffered an 'inexplicable tragedy.'" "I am tired," she added, "of so much unhappiness and so much lack of courage. I am tired of reading so many bad things our people have done. I want to hear about some of the good things once more." Robertson had written *Travelers' Rest* for a national audience, but it was readers within his own South Carolina who ended up reviewing it. Many in his hometown remained embarrassed and unappreciative of the tale that realistically and sometimes shockingly revealed challenges that his forebears had faced. Many within his family also thought that the epic was too thinly cloaked, revealing way too many family and community secrets. Only his closest of kin rallied in support.[7]

Although censorial concerns about specific passages within the text do not exist in the surviving written records, we can make reasonable guesses about what may have shocked many of Robertson's readers. Just for starters, Robertson failed to offer his readers a "moonlight and magnolias" version of his southern family. This is particularly a grave fault in that *Gone with the Wind* was published in 1936 to the thrill of the South and nation at large, becoming a best seller by 1937. Robertson's story, in contrast, in no way resembled Margaret Mitchell's saga that honored the traditions of the old slave-holding aristocracy. When talking to the student writers at Clemson, Robertson did not include Margaret Mitchell in his litany of the American writers that they needed to know even though she had just earned a Pulitzer Prize in 1937 for *Gone with the Wind* and was from their own region. His saga was filled with struggling frontier farmers who had worked for several generations just to build a fine farmhouse (not a plantation) that was decidedly free of white columns. Yet, these yeomen's undoings begin to take shape not as a result of something as momentous as the Civil War but as many of their own head West in search of gold and get-rich-quick schemes—not a flattering portrayal.

Closer to home, the Caldwell family fights internal demons in a narrative that could have unfolded in Hawthorne's *Scarlet Letter*. A brother, for example, kills his sister for bringing dishonor to her kin because of her single act of sexual passion. Then, in a bizarre twist, this half-crazed murderous brother works without ceasing to prepare her coffin:

> In a furious rage, Carter pointed one of his lean fingers at her, began shouting. "What do you think folks will say when they hear about this?" He grabbed her roughly by both arms, shaking her. "You've disgraced us, that's what you've done—you've disgraced the Caldwells."
>
> Carter's words were instinctive, shouted out without the slightest reflection. His sister had broken an obligation that extended beyond her right to break, shown a lack of discipline. "Disgraced us," he shouted, 'brought us to shame." All the merciless cruelty of the Caldwells flamed into his brain. Like someone crazed, he grabbed Narcissa's throat, pressing his brute thumbs into her windpipe, calling out all the time, "Who was the bastard?" Pressing harder against her throat and shaking her and continuing his shouting, he kept repeating, "Tell me his name, you hear me?" Harder still he pressed and Narcissa reeled senseless, there was a blurred yellow sun setting in her mind and a river flowing and a bursting flower and there was a great whirring through darkness, it was coming toward her, like a tornado, roaring closer...nearer. Her fine ascetic face was swollen purple; she collapsed.
>
> Carter placed her still body carefully, most tenderly upon a patch of briars. Then raising his own eyes and high cheek bones and sensitive, sensual lips, he was about to address a statement of his own to God. But he changed his mind. Instead he walked away slowly, and going into the cabin, began to hew a coffin from a cedar slab.
>
> While he worked, half-dazed, one of the Hunter boys rode away on horseback, at full speed, to bring McKay, the preacher, to the Caldwell cabin.[8]

This scene, like others in the epic, while perhaps truthful and realistic, was surely too much, or too removed from the self-images of Robertson's pious reviewers.

Another concern for particular readers of the time may have been the author's generous portrayal of an African American slave named Queen Elizabeth (even as the narrator warned readers that her arrival represented the arrival of the sinful institution of slavery that would lead to the upcountry's demise):

> It was at this time that Queen Elizabeth came to Forest Mansion. Tall and proud and black, she was standing in the old slave market in Augusta when Carter first saw her—an immense figure poised beside a white column. Among a group of frightened Negroes, cringing and uncertain, Queen Elizabeth loomed triumphant. Seemingly an ageless being, above destiny, she broke into fine singing when the time came for her to climb the block. Her shoulders were flung far back and very white in her jet face were wide eyes and brilliant teeth. "Lord," she said, "I'll fall upon my knees and I'll face the rising sun." The fearless physical beauty and the courage of this black woman entranced Carter. At once he began bidding, raising the price higher and higher. After a quarter-hour of haggling, she was his. He had bought her.[9]

Generation after generation of the Caldwells—who had strong Puritan leanings that permeated their Baptist tradition and who had followed the Wilderness Road West in search of their promised land—would wrestle again and again with the powers and values of their state's Low Country, as the South itself did thereafter with its "peculiar institution," slavery. But this was not something many readers wanted to read about or contemplate. The Caldwell family's desire to acquire more and richer lands or greater social stature, which they considered legitimate pursuits of happiness, somehow enabled them to justify their need to employ slaves and to put their faith in one staple and lucrative crop, no matter what the costs to the enslaved or the depleted soil.

In 1938, many within the American South who chose to read Robertson's tale were still partially unreconstructed. Many were still mourning the Lost Cause.[10] Few leading Southerners or readers of *Travelers' Rest* would have found the decision of Stephen John (the character who completes the family saga) to travel to the North with his black kin for the opening of the New York gallery that was to feature the Caldwell family's old weathervane, a noble or appropriate one. Clearly, Robertson did not seem to be currying favor with the general reading public in South Carolina. His purpose seemed to have been to explain the ongoing moral and emotional struggles within one American family, which was grappling with ways to live in accord with their country's founding, but often confounding, principles.

Robertson's idea of a Travelers' Rest, then, was not in accord with the ideals of some of his South Carolina readers. Indeed, for some it perhaps proved the polar opposite and another reason for their angry disgust. Robertson offered a revolutionary possibility for Americans in his last, lone scion, Stephen John, linked as he still was to the family's long search for "freedom." Through his inner guidance, this still-searching remnant could now shake off the trappings of excessive materialism and worldly power and head instead to a free wilderness sanctuary, a public place preserved for his and the free world's rest and restoration.[11] The emerging Americans did not have to spend their entire lives accruing their own landed estates, as the Caldwells had done, in order to be free. They could turn their backs on conspicuous consumption and focus instead on preserving their finest and real American treasures within artistic expressions or cultivating their talents and gifts, not only for their immediate families, but for the larger common good. Ben Robertson himself had traveled with President Franklin D. Roosevelt when he dedicated the Shenandoah National Park in the 1930s. Details of the region's flora and fauna throughout *Travelers' Rest* are fine expressions of the author's love of the land and its natural beauty, which was quickly giving way to American dreams of excessive profit.

Thankfully, a few other reviewers in 1938 did leave their impressions of Robertson's first foray into fiction; and Robertson himself responded to the public outcry within columns of the newly minted *Clemson Commentator*, a newspaper that Robertson helped launch to encourage political dialog in the upcountry and to prepare aspiring journalists at Clemson. Alester Holmes, a former history professor at Clemson and a historian who crafted a biography on Thomas Green Clemson, the founder of Clemson College, suggested that Robertson was far too generous in his assessment of the inner strength of the upcountry people, and hence the American people they represented in microcosm: "Reality is in Robertson's book in its sordidness and in its beauty, but the book is none the less idealistic in its portrayal of the hopes and longings of American life." In contrast to

Robertson's severest critics, Holmes believed the young author was way too idealistic and gave the upcountry people, and Americans in general, way too much credit. Holmes could not accept that most citizens were that concerned about America's wilderness errand or the country's founding ideals. Earl Mazo, who had recently graduated from Clemson and who worked for *The Commentator* during the summer of 1938 before launching a career in journalism, found *Travelers' Rest* "easy reading" and "really interesting" and felt that it "could have been made much longer." He seemed to be countering objections that the book was too difficult, long and boring.[12]

Responding to the mixed reviews, Robertson offered the following explanations in *The Commentator:*

> There is no place for me like the foothills of the Blue Ridge. I tried to define them in my book—their beauty. I tried to write of the hills, the cotton fields, the looming mountains so that people far from Carolina could be able to see them as we see them—the valleys within the valleys, the mists and the great white clouds, the storms. I have tried to write of the flowers and the birds and I have tried to write of the people who have always lived in the foothill country, and in writing of them, I will admit I am open to criticism.[13]

He shared his deep love for the beauty of the upcountry—both of its natural beauty and the beauty of its people. He went on to share that he could understand and still believe in his people who had "a strange conflicting dualism" that he himself must have surely felt within his own being. He indirectly addressed specific critics' concerns by alluding to "eagles" and "swines:"

> I believe in the people I have written about and I believe they had deep within them that strange conflicting dualism that is the secret of America. They had the strength and divine weakness of the people of the United States—they were "eagles" and they were "swine," and in the swine there was a lot that was swine. They had those dual qualities that have always confused Europeans when they consider Americans.
>
> The Pilgrims and the Puritans were in these people…They were strong, vigorous, violent people and they had an ideal and a dream for a continent and they thought in terms of their children's children. And they were lonely as Americans still in their secret hearts are lonely, and they had a goal.
>
> Their hearts were willing even if their flesh was weak. But their hearts never forgave the flesh. I have tried to write of them as this kind of people—fierce people who did things. And I have exposed them as I would my secret thoughts. Writing, to me, is a most intimate thing—the written is far more intimate than the spoken…
>
> I wrote of people who, like David and Paul and blessed St. Mary Magdalen, were imperfect.[14]

Here we begin to see, in this long-neglected story, a point Robertson was also to make in his better-known nonfiction work, *Red Hills and Cotton: An Upcountry Memory.* He felt that his southern upcountry people were representative Americans, that many Americans had this dualistic sense that seemed to stem from the sometimes conflicting ideals of America's original errand as understood in their founding ideals. Perry Miller, Edmund Morgan and Cambridge University's American literary critic Sacvan Bercovitch believed that many Americans, as documented within our literary and intellectual history, have had an abiding sense of being involved in "a wilderness errand."[15] Robertson, writing before their works had currency, tapped into this American sensibility as well. Perhaps what Robertson failed to deliver within his epic was his belief that the Caldwells were representative Americans versus representative Southern Americans. *Travelers' Rest* should be read alongside his *Red Hills and Cotton: An Upcountry Memory*—and not just as a story about the South, but as an American saga and a representation of American character.

Notes

1   Ben Robertson. Personal Journal, 1941. Ben Robertson Papers.
2   See, for example, these published articles: Ben Robertson, "Australia's Sons of Perdition," *Travel* July (1929): 35; Ben Robertson with McCoy Hill, "At the Heart of Desolation," *Travel* February (1929): 38; Ben Robertson, "No Sunday School Town," *Asia* August (1929): 612–617; Ben Robertson, "The Mattress-Stuffing Tree," *Asia* August (1931): 492; Ben Robertson, "Hawaiian Melting Pot," *Current History* (1930): 312–315; Ben Robertson, "That Yellow House in Surabaya," *Asia* May (1933): 314–316; Ben Robertson, "A Follower of the Prophet in Australia," *Asia* January (1934): 60–61.
3   Ben Robertson, "King George Strives to Please," *Saturday Evening Post* 4 February (1939): 5–7.
4   Ben Robertson, *Travelers' Rest* (Clemson, SC: Cotton Field Publishers, 1938) 4.
5   Robertson, *Travelers' Rest*, 248–49.
6   Robertson, *Travelers' Rest*, 3.
7   Local Newspaper Clippings and Family Documents. Ben Robertson Papers.
8   Robertson, *Travelers' Rest*, 104.
9   Robertson, *Travelers' Rest*, 123–124.
10   Walter Edgar, *South Carolina: A History* (Columbia: University of South Carolina Press: 1998).
11   Ben Robertson, Personal Journal, Ben Robertson Papers.
12   Local Newspaper Clippings and Family Documents. Ben Robertson Papers; Earl Mazo, *Clemson Commentator* July, 1938, n.p.; see also the biography of Thomas Green Clemson that Ben read and alluded to—Alester Holmes and George Sherrill, *Thomas Green Clemson: His Life and Work* (Richmond, Virginia: Garrett and Massie Incorporated, 1937).
13   Ben Robertson, "Clemson Twice a Week," *Clemson Commentator* July 15, 1938, 2.
14   Robertson, *Clemson Commentator, n.p.*
15   Perry Miller, *Errand into the Wilderness* (Cambridge: Harvard University Press, 1984); Perry Miller, *The New England Mind: From Colony to Province* (Cambridge: Harvard University Press, 1953); Perry Miller, *The New England Mind: The Seventeenth Century* (Boston: Beacon Press, 1954); Perry Miller, *Roger Williams: His Contribution to the American Tradition* (New York: Atheneum, 1965); Perry Miller and Thomas H. Johnson, *The Puritans: A Sourcebook of Their Writings* (New York: Harper and Row, 2001); Perry Miller, *Transcendentalists* (Cambridge: Harvard University Press, 1978); Edmund Morgan, *The Genuine Article* (New York: W.W. Norton and Co., 2004); Edmund Morgan, *Inventing the People: The Rise of Popular Sovereignty in England and America* (New York: W.W. Norton and Company, 1988); Sacvan Bercovitch, ed. *The American Puritan Imagination: Essays in Revaluation* (London: Cambridge University Press, 1974); Sacvan Bercovitch, *The American Jeremiad* (Madison: University of Wisconsin Press, 1978); Sacvan Bercovitch, *The Rites of Assent: Transformations in the Symbolic Construction of America* (New York: Routledge, 1993); Sacvan Bercovitch, ed. *The Cambridge History of American Literature* vols 1–8 (Cambridge: Oxford University Press, 1995); Sacvan Bercovitch, *The Puritan Origins of the America Self* (New Haven: Yale University Press, 2011).

PART ONE

The Westerners

CHAPTER ONE

Over the low plains of the Carolinas, across great marl lands and marshes, a wild western gale was blowing—the wind of a new spring and it filled the long-limbed pines about the Caldwell cabin with deep and restless soughing, a lonesome song. And all of the Caldwells heard it. The sound of this raging music gave to them, resting about the fire in their house, a feeling of secure strength and peace, but also it disturbed them. For there was nothing like a high wind to dissatisfy a Caldwell with the present.

Down the rubble stone chimney and right into the cabin swept one of the powerful gusts of this gale, bringing ashes from the fire and so much sharp smoke that the eyes of all began to smart.

"Carter," said an old woman in a tired low voice, "pull open the door a minute."

A lean man, lithe and eager, with an ascetic face brightened by the fire, moved to obey this request. He held open the heavy beamed door until the small room was pure, and then banging it shut with one casual shove, returned to his place before the burning logs. In a passionate and highly emotional way, calculated deliberately for effect, he was telling of a new country he had come upon forty days to the west. In a granite region covered with gneiss and bordered with primitive limestone was a fine fertile valley lying among misty hills, this valley was watered by bursting clear springs and had soil so deep and rich that two hundred bushels of corn could be produced on every acre; there were wild strawberries the size of walnuts; and so numerous were the buffalo that three or four men with dogs could kill from ten to twenty in a day.

Turning toward the dark corner where the old woman was sitting. her thin hands clasped in her lap, addressing her for the moment, Carter said wild turkeys were as common in this new country as jaybirds, and sugar canes grew twenty-five feet long and six inches round. "I have seen them," he said, raising his powerful voice, speaking above the sound of the driving wind which now was being strengthened by the beat of a rain. "With my own eyes I have seen them," he shouted breathlessly, holding his fine head a little higher. He had become exultant.

Bitterly, the old woman observed all this and, listening to the excited flow of Carter's words, allowed her warm heart to swell with the great pride of the Caldwells—this was her son's son, strong as he was and stern, a leader, and she loved him. O she loved him! But his words were more bitter to her than the sound of the wind. Silently, she continued her watchful listening.

"Folks," said Carter, "I give my oath that a common hunter in this new country can kill in one season as many bears as will make three thousand weight in bear bacon." He spoke of the days there, they were warm, the nights were dry and cool, and toward the west, forming a perfect protection, soared a range of mountains which the savages called the great blue hills of God.

"It's a paradise," said Carter, "a garden."

There was passionate earnestness about Carter. He rolled out his words like a religious fanatic, obsessed with redeeming the lost. He became grim. "Down this valley, folks, runs a rocky river that is shallow with easy fords; out of it flows two roads for produce—the first and nearer, to the head of navigation on the Savannah River, and the second along an old savage trail clear to Philadelphia..."

Bowing her head, the old woman wanted to scream out: "Lord God," to shout, "I've lost everything, I'm lost." But all she did was to whisper, "Do something, Heavenly Father, save me."

Fair rich lands, more bountiful game, cooler winds, a brighter flower—it was the same old story. For eighty years old Narcissa had heard it and now her sensitive upper lip, full and expressive, quivered; she began bitterly to weep. For this was the fourth time one of the restless men had brought into a home of hers the enchanted fable of a new land that flowed with Bible milk and honey.

The fourth time!

Tragedy strode always into the Caldwell family with the telling of that story. Abandoned cabins followed it, a caravan moved deeper into the wilderness, then there was murder, starvation, finally cabins no better than the ones the pilgrims had deserted.

"Lord God, Lord God."

His eyes glistening with faith. Carter said, "This valley is within our grasp." And as he talked, a new expression came into his lean face—a look of hunger that instantly changed him, gave him a prophet's look, of power. "This is the place we've been looking for," said he. "Yes, folks, there's no doubt about it this time. We'll get rich out there—we're bound to get rich in Keowee." He waved his long woodsman's arms, a pleading gesture. "Aw, come on with me—won't you take a chance?"

At this, burning tears formed in the blue eyes of Narcissa; with her hard fingers she gripped the rungs of the hickory chair in which she was sitting; then the room reeled. At that spinning moment, she lost all earthly hope—the hope that had lived through love and grief, the desolation of four decades on the frontiers, it died in her heart. At eighty years of age, a grandmother and a great-grandmother, a veteran of savage massacres and wilderness wars, a tired wanderer in the forests—how could she leave this twilight peace, this last hour of rest, and at her age start once again racing for the promised land. As the tears fell, Narcissa said to God, "I can't stand it, I had rather die."

Ashamed of being caught crying, she leaned low over the wide hearth, brushing away some light wood ashes with a broom made from the feathers of wild turkeys; then she settled back, tilting the old chair with her long legs and resting the knot of hair at the nape of her neck against one of the logs of the wall. In desperate anguish, she waited for Carter to complete his wild tale and for what was to follow—the kinsmen, all excited, would vote to leave the home they had cleared and founded after so much work; they would try for a richer, easier living in this newer place. Narcissa waited, for this was a wilderness drama that she knew by heart. Always this story of a new land acted upon the Caldwells in the same way, like a mad raging fever; it was the great temptation against which they never could muster resistance. Always it was the same, it set them half crazy; filled them with the wildest excitement and yearning. Narcissa knew what the Caldwells secretly believed in; they believed in El Dorado.

The fire light flared brighter, lighting the room with new glow, higher lights and shadows played upon the fresh strong faces of the family, all of them upturned now toward

Carter, toward their leader, the strong man in whom they could trust. The wind and rain were forgotten. The only sound for them was the sound of his voice.

So watching the great fire, Narcissa retreated from the present. Refusing to listen any longer, she drifted away into memory. The far past rose before her, the far away and the long ago, and she was running from a stone house in a green valley in Pennsylvania across a wide yard through flowers; she put a foot upon a wagon wheel and a clean, strong young man lifted her into a wagon. And she smiled and waved and off she started, off toward the wilderness of wild upland Virginia where melons grew as big as oak buckets. All was hope then and faith, soon they would be rich in the new country—rich and free. Bitterly now she reflected, for she had believed it all. She saw herself again a bride and her fine understanding husband was standing again beside her, so strong, a man with manner, with the air about him of command; and Narcissa saw herself waving to her frail old mother and touched by this sorrow she called out to her; she still heard the words echoing through all the years, "We'll be back soon—in a year or two for certain." In a year or so—and that too she had believed. She had waved and then a whip had cracked and their long and endless procession had started, a journey of sixty years, taking her on and on, never allowing her once, not once to retrace a step.

The fire flared and a log burned through, the ends fell. Dreaming on, Narcissa began to think of that old Pennsylvania house with its flower gardens and bees; dreaming, she thought of the pond where a man had drowned and there before her rose the gravestones of her little sisters, so long now among the angels. And next in her mind loomed the cabin she and Stephen John had built in Virginia—a little low house in a cornfield and with roses and finally a lilac. And then there again was Stephen John, nervous and restless; he had come rushing to take her in his arms. For he had found a better place, a richer valley in more southern Virginia. That day he had wanted to pick up and leave, that moment, but she had protested. "We can't leave our home," she heard herself saying, "It's our home, we've got to stay here and take care of what we have already." "It is all very well," she remembered saying, "to strike out once into the unknown—when one is young, but we oughtn't to strike out twice. Why, Stevie, we'd become adventurers and you know what happens in the end to adventurers—they get killed or they starve to death." And what had her husband said to those words? He had kissed her and away they had started, deeper into the woods. Frantic in their haste over an entire section of southern continent. Relentlessly Narcissa traced her story. Well, before that next settlement had been stocked with smoked hams and wheat flour against winter hunger, her Stephen John and two of their sons had been buried, scalped by the savages, and dead also was a small daughter, gone on, taken by a form of wilderness dysentery known as the cholera morbus.

She knew what wandering meant. A violent life, lost always in remoteness and solitude and sorrow. Never had there been quiet nor rest, not even in death. For hardly had the songs over the graves of her husband and her sons been sung than the old issues again had risen, revivified, between those who would keep what they already had and those who would risk everything for the new paradise, the garden. And what had happened then this third time? Again the strongest minded, the most determined had forced their way. They had roved on, bringing the Caldwells into eastern Carolina, deeper still into the wild forests. To the brooding and silent marl plains of North Carolina, half drowned in swamps. And here now was this grandson singing in a brilliant manner a strain of the same old song. Freedom and riches in a newer country. And about him were sitting a row of the kin completely fascinated by the sound.

Lord, lord, the strangeness of her people, driven wanderers, never at rest! Bitterly Narcissa reflected—if only they knew themselves as she knew them; realized that in all their strength they were peculiarly weak for they lacked the will to endure the monotony of routine existence and in that characteristic lay the deep secret of all their tragic failures. Simply they found it easier to move on than to stay; rather than fight the lean years through they preferred to run away. But also this was the secret of most of their triumphs. All of them were the same—just a wandering clan of wilderness people, given to brooding and to melancholy, a family of idealists. They were mist dreamers who in listening to the full music of living invariably turned a fine ear to that high wailing clef which to ordinary men lay buried in the depth of the other whirling notes. She recognized in them the poignant strain of poetry; it made them long for some quality in living they were never able to find.

Thinking of all these things, reflecting, Narcissa suddenly was overcome by all the lost rapture, the secret despair which she knew was hidden deep in. the hearts of her children. She thought with deep pity of their loneliness and yearning, their peculiar inability to accept the present. And again, sitting in the hard chair before the fireplace, Narcissa wept great tears. This time she wept because she loved the Caldwells; she loved them because they were what they were. Not even she, she said to herself, would change them. But again raising her eyes, she said to God, "Father, we are lost in the wilderness, looking for a cloud, for a pillar of fire; give us a sign, Heavenly Father, show us the way."

Brushing away these last tears, the old woman returned her attention to Carter, still standing there, still talking. The rich land of Keowee, she heard him say, generally was uneven, gradually became more hilly as it approached the range of western mountains, the lands were covered with thick green canes affording excellent pasturage; the lands most level and valuable were situated near the water course which never had been known to fail; and near the looming mountains, the river that flowed through the valley was so limpid, so pure, that a stone, pitched, could be seen to a depth of six feet. There was a wild flower in Keowee like fire; a bird that sang the sweetest, the most restrained, the most lilting of bird songs.

Lightly, Carter moved forward a step, shifting the weight of his great agile body, and with one of his quick gestures brushed from his glowing face a tuft of hair—fine yellow hair that all the Caldwells inherited as a family distinction, thin and never falling unless from bouts of fever. Having finished his descriptions, made his plea, Carter turned hawk-like upon Lucinda Caldwell, wife of Silas Caldwell, the oldest of the Caldwell brothers, head of the Caldwell house. Fiercely, he asked her personally and directly if she were willing to start at once for this Keowee.

Excited and a little frightened, Lucinda was not prepared for so direct and immediate a question. Unconsciously she looked to her husband for some hint—but it took only an instant to disregard what she saw on those violent and hard features; her glance told her that already Carter had convinced her husband; Silas was ready to pick up and move on. But not Lucinda. Lucinda did not want to leave this cabin home any more than did old Narcissa. She too belonged among the meek, the gentle ones who wanted to stay, the undaring. So she hesitated.

Annoyed by this hesitation, Carter shouted again his question, he demanded an answer. Still Lucinda waited. A woman nearing middle age, a compelling person in appearance, she was sitting a little forward in a straight hickory chair, exactly across the fire from Narcissa. Her lips, parted in excitement, gave a look of intense eagerness to her expression. Lucinda was a large woman with eyes as blue as Narcissa's, her hair was of the same yellow as Carter's and as fine and thin. For Lucinda had been born a Caldwell before marrying one. Her nose was too long, her sharp face of the hatchet type but her general features were touched with beauty by a solemn spiritual aspect which many of the Caldwells possessed, a lonely sorrowfulness that—no matter how soiled the possessor—seemed nearly holy.

"Well," said Carter, irritation in his deep voice. He turned to scuff the fire with his heavy soled shoe. "What do you say, Lucinda, speak up, speak up."

"Maybe we could consider going this fall," murmured the harassed woman, very timidly. "The spring crop is in the ground, perhaps we ought to wait until the crop is gathered."

"I have more seed for sowing," said Carter sharply. Then he ignored the gentle, motherly Lucinda. For Carter knew as well as she did that she objected with all her character to any sudden leaving of a secure home on the chance of finding better conditions at a distance. Carter took advantage of Luanda's timid fear and of her not speaking her mind openly. He ignored her and turned to Patrick Caldwell, sitting next in the family circle—between Lucinda and Artemissa, Patrick's stalwart wife. Patrick was a cousin of Carter Caldwell and of Silas.

"All right, Patrick," said Carter, looking directly at him, "How about you, do you want to go?"

Patrick who was the finest man physically of all the giant men in that section and also the most handsome answered this question with another question. Turning his sunburned, almost perfect face to one side, looking away, Patrick inquired, "What will happen if we fail?" This was characteristic of handsome, slow, plodding Patrick. He dreaded decisions, and too he wanted to stay where he was, neither did he care for long journeys through new wildernesses. He liked to plow "deep furrows in cleared fields, plant corn and watch young sprouts grow; he liked the little things, preferred to observe the change of the seasons in one place rather than to dash off toward far mountains and valleys. spending oneself like a wild goose, always hunting for summer. He liked to listen to the sound of winter dying in the wind, to hear the mourning dove just before day. He was gentle; but he was a passionate man—he liked to lie in a soft bed, warm with his arms about stout Artemissa. Also he was a man that had to fight a deep fear of violent things—often he would awaken startled in the night, listen intently for sounds; he kept a rifle and an axe by his bedside. This fear made him cautious and, because of the gigantic size of his fine body, this caution made him misunderstood by many men. Some thought he was a coward.

"We ought to consider the risk of failure," said Patrick. This enraged Carter, caused him to flush with wild anger and thrash his long arms, to stride backward toward the blazing fire. Also he sensed that he was not succeeding in his appeal and realizing this he instantly changed tactics. For by instinct he was a general, he knew the exact moment for retreat. More excited than ever before, Carter now began over. He began exhorting his kinsmen in nobly worded abstractions which as a method of arousing his family, he knew, was as effective almost as telling them about a country that would make them rich and free.

Glaring at Patrick's powerful face, Carter began scornfully to recite an austere creed, poured upon Patrick a sort of catechism, a doctrine he had learned from the vast and lonely forests where, alone with the unfathomable, the mysterious and the silent he had sensed the infinite being. From a lifetime of wandering in desolate continental space, this pioneer had come to know renunciation; journeying towards an end now more precious to him than reaching the end itself.

"Failure," said he, staring intently at Patrick, "failure is our fate—it is the only goal." In exasperation, he shouted that at the end of every road lay failure but that started once on a way there was no turning back; no rest, he said, with a nod of compassion toward old Narcissa (he had seen those bitter tears). Then turning again upon Patrick, Carter spoke with furious exultation of their fortune. For the Almighty Himself had set them on their forest path; for them to live in the wilderness was his will and hard work and privation were his burden on their shoulders. But there was divine compensation. "We are doing something with our lives," Carter said with triumph, genuine triumph shining in his face. "We are do-ers, not sitters. It has pleased the Lord to give purpose to our existence, a pattern to our efforts. We are not destined just to be born and lie down and decay as most men are—and we are not just living for ourselves alone. There is something nobler for us. We are here to create—in a great time in a great country, we have been sent to open a wilderness." Carter's rich voice soared. Again the shining gleam came into his eyes. "Such a time will never come again and when we come to our time of trouble—God will not fail us. I know God will not fail us. We are his servants. We were not sent here to fail."

Lowering his voice, calm and sure, Carter told the Caldwells he had rather be living at that time in that place than at any other period in any other country in the whole of time and space. It was a moving appeal and it had its desired effect. So touched was Artemissa that without waiting to be asked she jumped from her chair, saying, "Brother Carter, I'm ready."

Like Carter, Artemissa was a westerner born—one of the first, she came into being with the faith, believed from the time she could remember in the power and hope that lay in the country beyond. The far things were always her dream and whenever she went walking about with Patrick—while Patrick watched the little beautiful things close by, she used to keep her wide eyes trained on the most distant hill, the remotest and most lonesome beacon. Artemissa never knew what it meant to rest, she was a pilgrim, and no matter where she was, she also was a stranger.

"I'll go," said Artemissa. Then Silas Caldwell stirred.

"What about this road for produce from Keowee to Philadelphia?" He spoke cautiously but his question caused Carter almost to shout, a wild flutter throbbed in his heart. For understanding this silent, brooding brother, Carter knew this was Silas' way of making known his decision. Silas who did unexpected things for strange reasons had been persuaded.

Quickly, the excited words flowing, Carter told of the trail along the foot of the mountains, of how it was watered, provisioned with grass, a road along which cattle might be driven half a thousand miles into the Pennsylvania market; also he told of the shorter way to the broad waters of the Savannah, less than ten days from Keowee—using glowing, exaggerated words, playing without conscience upon Silas' favorable mood, strengthening it while it lasted. Carter had not expected the head of the Caldwells to be convinced so quickly, with such ease. "Hides can be transported easily—so can corn and at greater profit if it is distilled first into spirit." This last was injected deliberately, intended to arouse the ire of Lucinda.

And Lucinda instantly rose to the bait. "You all don't make corn liquor," she said, pointing a reproving finger. "No, sir," Carter only smiled. Long ago he had learned how to confuse an issue.

Now came the critical moment. It was old Narcissa's turn to speak. "Grandma," said Carter, moving toward her nervously and indicating by a curious jerk of his fine head that her word was awaited. It was apparent that Carter was uneasy, that he expected opposition from this old woman, strong opposition. And to resist she surely intended.

While listening to Carter's outburst, Narcissa made ready in her mind to bring an old woman's full wisdom down against this wild dream and fancy; to recall from the prestige of her many years that the story Carter was telling with such feeling was a bright color on a bubble, a thing like a mist, a picture in a still pool; four times in her eighty years it had been spun in her presence and always it was the same old cobweb—a fine rich land in Virginia, well timbered with ash and wild cherry trees, a valley still to the south of their first Virginia homestead, a marl meadow in North Carolina, watered with a great number of little streams and full of natural forage, covered with wild rye, pea vines—empty, immense lands waiting for the white man. The race for those treasures, she intended saying, had carried her down the face of the continent, occupied sixty years of her lifetime and what was there to show for it, what monuments had she left behind—tombs of her loved ones scattered across six hundred miles of frontier clearings, a small yellow creek bearing her name, a grove of cedar trees she once had planted, and memories, a host of them of terrible troubles, of a carder on the fringe of civilization, of a woman working, doing without, facing the scalping knife and the tomahawk, always in such dread of the present that her thoughts either were of the distant past or were cast into the remotest future; there had been so little of love, of quiet or rest, so little peace—the safeness that a woman wishes. She would tell them that sometimes it seemed she had given her hard life for nothing more tangible than a thrush's song, than a scent of pennyroyal.

And fully did Narcissa intend to reveal to them the true nature of Carter—he was strong, marked with assurance and command, a man with a warm heart, but he also was ready to make selfish use of the dearest of their hopes, the finding of a land rich enough to free them from all masters—he was ready to take advantage of that dream to further the force of his own inner hunger. Narcissa had learned from all these years in the deep wood that Carter was of a forest type, his yearning was to explore, to travel, not to settle; the legacies were combined in his secret being so that ever so often he had to move, to go on, to see. Narcissa knew—the cold evening star, green in space and trailing into the western sky, a wild bird flying, these were enough to drive Carter from home. She would predict to them that if they followed Carter to this Keowee that the time would not be long coming before some night he would rush in to urge them on to some newer paradise and this time it would lie beyond the Blue Ridge Mountains. Old Narcissa recognized the vast nature of her grandson's ambition—the great waters of the Mississippi flowed in his dreams, the wind blew over western deserts, there was even the Pacific Ocean.

And then over Narcissa, old and tired, discouraged, there swept the greatest weariness of her long life, a sudden questioning, a realization of what's the use, why raise a tired voice, who among them would listen to the experience of an old woman—and how could she fight a man who when asked for a fact would turn for answer to fancy, pick a tale from the sky. What good to warn them that savages would harass them in this Keowee, that their lives would be passed in constant fear, with the fall of every acorn, the hoot of every owl a potential alarm; that there would be wolves and panthers and wildcats. Suddenly Narcissa knew she could not resist this grandson, this dreaming inspired Carter. He was too like her own Carter, the son she had left behind in the Virginia uplands—and what had this son said when once she had inquired if a country he had told of were infested with panthers: "Oh, panthers, the savages admire panthers for their wonderful stealthy step and for their leaping; they made their sons sleep on panther skins; they call the panther the cat of God." What kind of answer was that for a woman who lived in terror of the cruel beast that screamed like a little child!

O son of Carter and Carter, the father's son, fallen angels! Their weapon was the flame of enthusiasm, the power to set the hearts of men on fire.

So, an old woman, she realized—there in the straight chair beside the flaming logs. The magic set against her was too formidable. Sometimes it seemed a power stronger even than the instinct of her kin to wander was pulling them, drawing them like a magnet deeper and deeper into the wilderness.

Well, since she could do nothing else, she too would bow to the inevitable. She would accept and obey. Her strength would be the strength of Israel and henceforth she would make her home wherever night found her—heaven was her only home, sweet beulah land far beyond the sun. She would live for the day, rise like the winds, accept all things as she endured the daily weather.

Thus did Narcissa, no longer with hope, turn at last to dreaming; about her old body she drew another vestment and retired into an inner universe, fantastic, whirring with wings, set with whatever illusion she chose. She accepted Carter's exalted definition—indeed defeat was their lot, as was sorrow; so not only accept it, expect it. For what was an individual's life—one more ant, another bug, a butterfly, a leaf on a tree and it was the tree that lived on, not the crop of fluttering leaves. A vision came to her of the wilderness as a great barren rock upon which millions of settlers would have to lay down their lives, like the leaves, one upon another. The flower they hoped for—when finally it would bloom—would grow from the very dust of their bodies. So why resist the lying down? There was this comfort, they would make it an easier place for the children and the children's children.

Still Narcissa was bitter. She was lost in the wild forest and there was nothing she could do about it. Her desperate feeling was she had utterly failed. None of the things she had wanted to achieve had been won. More than anything she had wanted to settle, she had wanted a house in a safe place, had wanted to hear bells ring and choirs sing, to discuss with many women such things as syrups and roses, to sit still and listen to the voice of God. Narcissa folded her spotted brown hands, she surrendered. It was her weakness, she told herself, that she never had learned to express the secret cry in her heart, had never made known her opinions. In private behind shut doors, she had comforted the weak and gentle and meek but she had not learned to organize their voices.

So it was when Carter finally put the question to Narcissa. She replied that she was too old to make an answer. She bowed her head, again clasped and unclasped her hands. But Carter shouted. Rushing to her, he kissed her thin sagging cheeks. In another moment, he was asking all who were willing to take the chance, to go with him to Keowee, to raise their right hands. A solemn silent moment followed. Then up went the hands of Silas and Artemissa and Patrick. Narcissa and Lucinda refrained from voting. Patrick did not possess the courage of his conviction. Often in matters where his will clashed with Artemissa's Patrick would allow her to have her own way if she were firm—it was the easier thing to do, things went smoother.

"We'll start at daybreak," said Carter exultantly.

"Daybreak!" cried Lucinda startled. "Leave home on a night's notice?"

"Sure," replied Carter, laughing at his sister-in-law.

"No, sir," she said determined. "It's impossible, beyond reason to expect us to get ready in such a hurry."

But Carter insisted. "We haven't a minute to spare—not a minute, Lucinda. There are other settlers breaking their necks to beat us into Keowee." Lucinda was preparing for further protest when Silas, firm and dour, sustained Carter's decision. It became a command.

Carter smiled, slowly he turned his firm lean buttocks before the fire, now blazing high; he rubbed his broad, strong hands—a picture of a leader at a time of victory. "Well, girls," said he in a tone almost singing. "Let's eat." Even the sound of his voice was powerful and commanding and deep.

Chapter Two

In preparing the supper, Lucinda moved lightly about the warm, bright room. Carter, watching her, thought her grace was like a bird's, like a mallard landing in winter on a skim of ice—ready at a moment's warning to break into flight. Very soon the meal was ready. Hot hunks of cornbread, red fried ham, thick cream gravy, hominy that had boiled in an iron pot swung from a crane over the log fire.

After drinking a second cup of China tea, Narcissa said she must pack her things. She rose and went to her room, a second cabin joined to the first and raised above it one step. But she had no more than entered the place than in came Lucinda. Closing the door, resting her hands upon the latch, Lucinda began to cry. She wept bitterly and silently, the tears flowing freely down her red healthy face. Calmly Narcissa sat down on the edge of a beautiful maple bed, absently smoothing a coverlet with her knotted hands. It was a heavy woven counterpane; she had brought it all the long way from Virginia over the wilderness road. Falling on her knees, Lucinda put her head in the older woman's lap. Anxiously she began to speak of her baby daughter. "How can the baby stand such a trip," she said. Then Lucinda began uncontrollably to sob.

Bursting into spell after spell of violent weeping, Lucinda said to Narcissa, "I can't stand it—I can't bear to face the wilderness again." Soothing the grieving woman, old Narcissa offered words of encouragement. "You can stand it, Lucinda; we can bear anything we are obliged to." She said there was no end to the pliability of human emotions in emergencies. "Besides, it is God's will." Together they remained in that room for a long while, Narcissa quoting odd bits of scripture. "As the sparks fly upward so is man born unto trouble."

"It is tragedy," said Narcissa. "So ennoble it by the brave quality of your acceptance."

Lucinda wiped her face. Narcissa began to pack. Quickly she gathered together her personal possessions that she could not think of leaving behind, an Arabian Nights, a bottle of bear oil for snake bite, volatile drops for the heart, peach stones, hollyhock seed, seeds of melons and roses, two spun dresses and knitting needles. Finally she wrapped a shawl about a sugar bowl—this was a piece of yellow crockery with a gold band that was a miraculous thing to the old woman. For starting out with her, a bride from Pennsylvania, it had survived all the hazards that she had, murder and oxcarts and covered wagons and flatboats. It was a symbol to Narcissa.

Into another tight bundle she put with careful hands the herb and dye book she was compiling for her granddaughters, a small docket inscribed in her wavering handwriting with such secrets as: "Blue—derived from the inner bark of the ash tree; yellow very pale— from the roots of the nettle; yellow beautiful and deep—from yellow root; red—from the bastard saffron blossom, from the juice of nightshades, from poke boiled in rainwater and set with alum." Narcissa had experimented for fifty years, searching for richer, more living dyestuffs for the Caldwell homespuns.

Last of all she picked up her old hand Bible, turned for a moment to the Book of Job, letting her eyes wander through the tenth chapter, "My soul is weary of my life... Remember I beseech Thee that Thou hast made me as the clay and wilt Thou bring me into the dust again; hast Thou not poured me out as milk and curdled me like cheese." Then closing the book, she placed it beside the sugar bowl.

Her packing finished, Narcissa took up a goosequill to perform the last of the rites that she never forgot when about to move again deeper into the western forests. She began writing a letter to her sister, one of the Pennsylvanians, telling those at home of the newest development in the ceaseless journey. At the close, she added: "We have learned to endure hardship, to suffer affliction and to brave the dangers of the wilderness with no more prospect of notice or reward than that promised by the Divine Master who himself had not where to lay His head." This completed, Narcissa lay down upon her bed and that night was the only person in the household who was able to sleep. There was no illusion left for Narcissa; she had given up, renounced the world. Nothing mattered to her now, she was waiting for her time to come.

In the other cabin, the others also were busy. Lucinda and Artemissa began gathering their things together, sorting and discarding, while about the fire sat Carter, Silas and Patrick, making plans, At midnight, Carter stood up. "Folks," he said, "we better get some rest, we'll be too tired starting if we don't get some rest." Soon they had retired.

And Silas put his big arms about Lucinda, passionately grasping his wife. He was a zealous man, hardworking, a strange Puritan of the spirit; he liked to preach sermons on Sundays but he also was a man of powerful passions. Tonight as he lay with Lucinda on a mattress of shucks, there was a shuffling sound in the room; the shucks rustled.

Long living in cramped quarters, in wagons and cabins, had robbed the Caldwells, as it sometimes does bands of traveling actors, of a certain shame. So long as there was darkness and those about them also were married, they said there was no reason for personal embarrassment. So this night, the only effect of this rustling was to arouse in Patrick's withers a similar lust. Artemissa whispered "no" when she felt the arms of Patrick closing about her but there was nothing Artemissa could do; she had the stronger mind but Patrick was the stronger body.

Pre-occupied and indifferent, Lucinda at this moment actually was thinking of the faraway future, as she often did, of her children's children's children—living in a great American country with a fine settled look upon it, where there would be no savages, no wilderness. She saw them moving among fine stone houses with flowers in gardens and about them were streets filled with processions and gatherings, near neighbors. Lucinda sighed. Theirs would be the victory. Even the thought made her calm.

But Artemissa was not calm. Entirely different for her were these dreaded moments. Anxiety gripped frantically at her heart as it always did for her at such times. Silently and awfully, she pleaded with God to spare her from bearing another child. For child-bearing was a problem which she and Patrick had never been able to solve. The pall over their married life was that two of their children had been afflicted from birth with "queerness," they were not "quite right." And as Artemissa and Patrick were first cousins, daughter and son of Caldwell brothers, Artemissa believed in her deepest being that God was so punishing them for the closeness of their blood relation. Being a determined woman, she was willing to renounce all possible chance of having another child, and once they had lived for two months holding to her decision; then Patrick who in so many things was so gentle, usually so obedient to her will, had forced her again to run the risk. Sometimes the inner urge of his powerful body overwhelmed all his other instincts. Artemissa loved Patrick—for his sensitive moments, the exquisite secret things of his mind; but sometimes also she despised him—for his inability at certain periods to control himself, for what she thought was the weakness of his discipline. Once when their younger idiot child was very ill, burning with a fever, Artemissa had dropped on her knees at the child's bedside, praying for deliverance. And deliverance had come. Soon after, while she was out of the house, a large pillow that she had placed above the child's head had fallen over its face and on her return to the cabin she had taken the idiot in her arms and had wept, and that evening when Patrick had come in from the fields, she had said "The child is dead." And that was all that she had ever told him. Not even now did he know. There was no doubt about it—Artemissa had will.

So fervently she prayed and after a time Patrick relaxed his hold upon her and she heard him whispering, "Forgive me, Artemissa, I am sorry." He was such a tender and kind husband, Artemissa kissed him. "It's all right," she said, reflecting, "After all, he is a man."

In the same cabin with Silas and Lucinda, Artemissa and Patrick, there also was Carter. Stretched on the floor on a pile of skins before the fire, Carter was this night satisfied with the things of the spirit. Victory was his comfort and as he lay on his pallet, with the dull roar of the gale about him, he went over in his mind the hazards of the way over which he was so soon to lead the Caldwells. Gradually he drifted in the spacelessness of the mind into regions far beyond Keowee; he saw himself crossing mountains, coming to a long sloping land of plains, watered by rivers flowing west, always west; finally he came himself in that distant land, beyond the plains and the canyons, to the very walls of Cibola itself, the golden cities of Cibola. He dreamed.

Silently, after a time, he aroused himself and rising quickly he placed another log on the cabin fire.

⁂

Long before the spring morning broke, they were up and about in the cabin, storing an ox cart backed to the door with iron pots, pewter dishes, a supply of fish hooks, awls, hoes, an axe and plow shares: also with provisions and various small treasures such as the leather-bound Shakespeare book from which Silas would not part and the roots of the lilac which Lucinda insisted must be taken. Into a second cart they piled clothing and quilts, a bag of salt and a bag of hominy, a bit of sour dough. The furniture they decided would be returned for later. Such was their plan but they knew that the curly maple bed, the corner cupboard, would never appear in Keowee. The bed and the walnut table and the hickory bottomed chairs, all home-made and carved with fanciful and careful attention, were being abandoned. But nobody would admit this, they all were very fond of their furniture.

So in the east the sun rose, clear and hot, and the Caldwells turned their back upon the east: their caravan had formed. First there was Carter and then Silas, both riding horses; then there was Artemissa driving the first oxcart followed by Patrick driving the second in which rode old Narcissa, carrying Lucinda's baby. After them followed a drove of cattle, herded by the older children. And bringing up the rear, also upon a horse, rode Lucinda. With her in the same saddle rode her oldest son, who bore the family name of Silas after his father. This boy was weak, recovering from a fever.

Uncovering in the early morning sunshine, Silas opened the Bible and read. To all of them this was a half-religious occasion—not only because of the need they felt for heaven's protection on their perilous way but also because they sensed deep within themselves that somehow their country with its boundless future was intimately dependent on this particular journey. Actually they believed they had been sent by the Almighty.

This feeling at this time made Silas regard himself as a prophet. He read the twenty-third psalm, lingering with emphasis over the passage about going without fear through the valley of the shadow of death. Then he prayed. Silas enjoyed praying. "Have mercy upon us," he cried, lifting up his face, "guide us and protect us on the way, strengthen us to meet danger, to face death—receive us finally, Father, into thy bosom."

Soon after there came a loud cracking sound; Carter had swung a long leather bull-whip, jerking the end. In another few moments they had started, the Caldwells were moving into deeper and more solitary forests. Wheeling about on his horse, Carter shout-ed, "Follow me, boys—we're on our way."

Far ahead rode Carter, moving quickly forward, facing the west—the only road, the only way. He actually sang for this was the time of his happiness and triumph, his secret joy.

But for Narcissa and Lucinda it was the final sacrifice. Alone of that little group they gazed backward steadily, seeing everything they had ever hoped for fading away—it was home they were leaving; they saw the blue smoke still sifting upward from the high rock chimney, desolate and deserted and filled with dignity and quiet—they saw in this scene the symbol of all their frustrated living. There was the letter in the crack in the door, ad-dressed to the old sister in Pennsylvania with its accompanying note to passersby: "Please post—we have left for South Carolina."

"Pity us, God," said Lucinda, and the procession moved into the deep woods and the cabin was lost from sight.

So they went on, the Caldwells. It was a fine southern day with an old wind blowing and the soft sun of the south shining. They wound among deep half tropical swamps, over a marl roadbed, a soft calcareous clay that sometimes was quaky. For a long time tall cypress and glaucous pines, like green ice, green with long needles, rose around them. Deep and dense was the gloom of this region, a dominion of the molds, hardly lighted ever by direct rays of the sun. There were tracks of swamp animals in the narrow pathway which curved among dark-growing briars and elder bushes, the tangled vines of the bitter foxgrapes. Later Carter led them onto higher ground into a white drift of plum trees, all in a burst of blossom, among budding dogwood and yellow jasmine and jewel weed and Indian pipes and turnips. Sometimes in this region, patches of radiant sky crept into sight through the trees—deep southern splotches of blue with whorls of soft sensuous cloud. Often there came the hidden song of the woodthrush, four notes rising, four falling, lyri-cal like a flute. Riding through these scenes, down dark aisles amidst luscious flowers and passionate southern odors even old Narcissa was aroused and the old excitement stirred within her—for like them all, she was on her way, moving again into the unknown, wheels were rolling; in her old heart there rose a momentary recurrence of the old time confidence. Perhaps Divine God would again see her through—were not the hairs of her head numbered, was not her strength become as the strength of Israel. But this revival of spirit was only faint and it soon vanished. Narcissa had a deep feeling about this trip, she had a premonition.

The child she was carrying in her arms stirred, it was fretful. Putting one of her old hands on its forehead, Narcissa noted it was a little feverish. For a time the elderly woman sang to the child—in an old frail broken voice. And the child slept. Studying its tender innocence, Narcissa suddenly said aloud, "What chance have we got on a journey like this?" Long did she wonder—"A helpless old woman and a baby?" As for the child's chances, she finally came to an uncertain decision, perhaps it would be tough, belong to the breed of Artemissa, maybe it would survive the hazards of the frontier. But as for herself—she knew; like some old soldier, she felt she was tempting the fates one time too many. "They'll scalp me," she said, "this time for sure."

Narcissa lifted her bright old eyes. "God," she said, "I am not afraid—but when the time comes, be Thou with me, hold Thou my hand."

That afternoon later they were drenched to the skin by the first thunderstorm of the season; there was oppressiveness and a stillness and quiet, even the yellow air seemed to hang motionless in the anxious sunshine, the cardinal bird disappeared into the deep thickets, a fleet of small lemon colored butterflies fled under a milkweed as the clouds gathered. Crashes of blue lightning came, swift booms of thunder, soon a new gale arose from the west with the heavy driving rain. And that night the baby cried and could not sleep. "It's got a touch of the iliac passion," said Narcissa, brewing some herbs.

"The dry bellyache," said Carter.

They moved on at dawn, traveled hard that day and the next and for seven days more. Once they smelled burning woods and one night wolves howled. They crossed a clear crystal stream and, leaving swamp country, Carter shot three turkeys. The caravan was following a crooked creek with high clay banks on that same day when the dogs roused a large buck elk. During the chase a blaze-faced hound called Tumbler was killed. Tumbler was their oldest dog, loved by all the children, and his death was a great blow to them. They wept bitterly.

"I tell you what we'll do," said Carter, moved to pity. "We'll name this creek Tumbler in Tumbler's honor." Carter was accustomed in his travels about the continent to giving names to streams and mountains according to his own whims and fancy. The suggestion appealed instantly to the children and they watched Carter with intense interest as he carved in a great beech tree: "This creek is named Tumblers Run after our dog." They felt better after that.

At night around the glimmering light of the fire, the children persuaded old Narcissa to tell them stories, their favorites being the tale of the flight through the eastern wilderness of Mary the Mother of God, and Joseph, and the tale of the three wise men. Also they liked the stories Narcissa remembered about Pennsylvania where people lived in houses and had barns for their horses and cows—bigger than cabins. Also Aladdin was another of their favorites, and the forty thieves. Narcissa had a gift for story-telling; she shrouded her tales in great wonder and gave to them the feeling of remoteness and deep mystery. "Aladdin," she whispered, looking into the heart of the fire, "was a very careless fellow; he was disobedient to his father and mother and would go early in the morning into the street and stay out all day playing with the idle children of his own age."

Thus did the great figures of the ages make their appearance on this fringe of a new world—between sunset and bedtime, introduced by a great-grandmother to a band of children who listened with rapturous attention. This journey was a delight and joy to these children—Artemissa's idiot boy Oliver and the younger Silas, also Luanda's boy called Stephen John and the second Carter, his younger brother, and to a half dozen more. They loved the wild life, eating around a camp fire and hearing in their wagons at night the spring winds blowing in the pine trees like the soft sound of sleet falling in winter. From their beds they could see the bright western star which Uncle Carter said the savages called Nagoochee.

On the tenth day after a pushed march they arrived in the early evening at Carter's cabin; it was a small house set in a grove. There were several chickens and some pigs and a cow in the yard, a few fruit trees in full bloom. Hurrying to meet the travelers came Clarissa, Carter's wife, a big woman like Lucinda.

"I thought you all never were going to get here," she said, drying her hands on an apron as she crossed the hard yard, half running. There was a worried, fretful look on Clarissa's face. She shook hands with the men, kissed the women and children. She began at once to complain; complaining was her habit. "We haven't much on hand to feed you— looks like we never have much on hand," she said to Lucinda. "You'll have to make out on plain fare here, but what could you expect at a house where the man never stays at home." Clarissa looked viciously in Carter's direction. "Carter's never here—always off somewhere enjoying himself, running around, seeing the country." Then she began to complain about having to give up her home; she had got settled in this cabin, she liked it.

The pilgrims halted for three days at Carter's house to let the oxen and cattle rest. On the first night, the travelers went to bed soon after sunset; they had come a long way and after ten days on the road they were tired. But Clarissa was not tired. She put an arm about Carter. Soon it was the shucks in Clarissa's bed that rattled. And wide-awake on a pallet in the loft, a growing boy listened. It was the second Carter.

"I'm a grown man," this boy said the next morning to a group of the children who had gathered in the dense darkness of a scuppernong arbor. "I'm old and married—I'm Uncle Carter."

Grasping a red-faced girl with yellow hair in plaits, with young forming breasts, Carter said, "Temperance, you're Aunt Clarissa."

"I want to be Uncle Silas," said Oliver the idiot, lolling his heavy head.

"All right," said Carter, "and Annie can be Aunt Lucinda." Annie Caldwell was cross-eyed and freckled, she laughed.

For the role of Aunt Artemissa, Carter quickly selected from among the smaller children a cousin called Ella. Stephen John was to be Uncle Patrick. Stephen John already was developing extraordinary traits—a moodiness and withdrawn dreaming and a secrecy intense even for a Caldwell. He said nothing.

"Now," whispered young Carter, "its night time and we've already eaten our supper. It's time to go to bed." So they fell upon the vines—young Carter and lusty Temperance and Oliver and little Annie. They huddled together. But Stephen John forced away the thin arms of his eager companion, slapping the startled girl's face. Angry and ashamed, she began to cry. "I'm going to be a trapper when I grow up," said Stephen John frowning. "I'm going to live by myself like Mister Tirzah." Mister Tirzah was a shiftless character of eastern North Carolina, a beaver trapper, whom all of the children liked.

"Aw, shut up," said young Carter.

Suddenly Stephen John broke into tears and he rushed from the arbor. The older Carter was sitting under an oak by the well, mending a cart wheel, and he saw Stephen John leave the scuppernong arbor. Wondering why the children suddenly had become so quiet, he put the wheel aside, deciding to investigate.

"Temperance," said he, pushing aside the mass of vines, "put down your dress." He ordered all of the children to follow him to the house. With averted eyes, they followed; all expecting a scolding and a round of whippings. But Uncle Carter surprised them.

"Sit down," he said when they had reached the well. Quietly, he picked up the wheel, beginning again to fit one of the spokes into place. After that job was finished, Carter began in his quietest way to tell them a tale—one of the stories he had remembered from the Indians. He had learned many legends from the savages during his wanderings. A long distance beyond the mountains which the savages called the great blue hills of god, he said, there once was a place called Klausuna after a magic turtle. Here two gleaming rivers joined and in the old days, long ago, it was the home of this turtle which was the most wonderful turtle in the world. It was warm and sunny at Klausuna and the old turtle liked to lie there when he was tired and wanted to rest and nap. But the bad people who lived in the world in those days would not allow him so much even as five minutes of peace. They had learned that the life of this old turtle was charmed—he was beyond harm, nothing could hurt him, not even a hurricane nor a tornado nor a bolt of lightning. So they tried in every way to learn if they could not find some way to kill him. They built fires about him in an effort to break the charm and they hit him with rocks and poured boiling water down his neck. They made life miserable for the poor old turtle who was one of the quietest and best creatures that had ever lived. One day they shot arrows at him and this so disgusted the old turtle with the world that he burrowed his way into the center of the earth and remained there ever after. "The moral of this story," said Carter, "is that folks and especially boys and girls oughtn't to be so mean, they ought to try always to be good, for if they are bad, there is no telling what magic turtle they may drive away forever." The children understood.

Sometime later—behind some bushes near the spring, old Carter found Stephen John with his sensitive face buried in leaves; the boy for some reason still was sobbing. "Don't cry," said the uncle. This was why Stephen John so loved his Uncle Carter—so strong, he always was so gentle with a troubled boy.

※

Joined at Carter's cabin by another group of Caldwells, the caravan was more than doubled when it put out from Carter's house on the long western road, which was not well cleared from now on nor beaten. They moved through the solitude, through the silence. The sun rose, the long west winds blew, the sun set. Hurrying on, they camped and broke camp. The wild yellow azaleas were in bloom, so was painted trillium in low places and Solomon's seal. Rain came on suddenly several times, falling heavily, terminating at once, again leaving a clear and settled southern sky. At the end of the ninth day following the second start, they came to a low ground belonging to an Adam Beard, an ignorant, impudent, brutish fellow from whom they bought some hominy, a few beans and sweet potatoes (Carter bought also a jug of brandy). On the tenth day Lucinda rode in the oxcart with old Narcissa as it now was becoming quite clear that Lucinda's baby was not of the breed of Artemissa. The child was sick and as they traveled on that day it became worse. It was restless, refused all nourishment. In mid-afternoon, Lucinda sent for Carter. "We can't go on," she said in a sort of panic.

Carter looked for an instant at the infant; he touched its burning cheeks with one of his brash hands. "All right," he said to Lucinda, then gave orders for a halt, commanding quiet in the camp. Old Narcissa made several hurried trips into the woods, returning with fresh herbs and roots from which she soon had boiled a syrup. But neither she nor Lucinda could get the child to drink it. Toward night, they poured heated milk down the child's swollen throat but this did no good. It caused violent vomiting and profuse perspiration. They had done all they knew to do. Realizing this, Lucinda retired into the oxcart, holding the baby close to her warm breasts. Giving up further attempts at remedying, the mother turned desperately to the Almighty. "Hear me, Heavenly Father," she said weeping, "Just this one time—hear me." But even as Lucinda was beseeching, there came a convulsion, a sudden jerking. Lucinda screamed, a terrible cry of anguish that pierced far into the wilderness. Three times the echo was repeated.

Silas came to offer comfort but Lucinda refused to have him near her. She looked at him with a bitterness, a look of accusation in her eyes, that he never forgot. Silas knew of what Lucinda was thinking—that if they had not started out on this journey their child would still be living. He knew she would add this to the list of things for which she would never forgive him. There was a sob and again for a moment a mask was lifted. Here was a human soul, a mother lost in the night, sorrowing without pretense. She cried over the dead child's body and the cry in the depth of the forest died but in the heart it did not die. It lived on.

They stood uncovered the next day before a grave dug at the foot of a three-forked pine. Opening the Bible, Silas read what he could find of the burial service; there was prayer and singing. Wild flowers were strewed and a cross made from two branches of an alder. The cross was stuck in the earth and piled about so that wolves might not find the body. Then they went on. The child was left behind in the long western procession.

The hearts of the vast multitude who died in the wilderness and passed on and gave no sign! The lost in the wilderness whose dreams came to nothing, whose prayers were never heard. O the bitterness of the lost cry. "God, must it come to this—all the things we had hoped for, to waste ourselves in a desert, just to be born in obscurity, to yearn and hope and then to die."

They wept and the wilderness sun set, wild and lonely and desolate, and the lonely wind rose in the pines, and they died and were forgotten and so were their children also forgotten,

The waste, the tragic secret sorrow.

A panther screamed and Carter listened, estimating the distance, noting the direction. Carter seemed always listening now as they were in higher and wilder country—entering the Indians' land. Seldom sleeping, he watched and wheeled about the caravan on his horse; sometimes he rode far ahead, scouting, guarding his family army—the band of tired men and women, marked by travel, their hard, sensuous bodies firm like marble, seasoned beings with beautiful hard faces and hands, beautiful buttocks and breasts.

One evening Carter sent the boys after firewood. While cutting down an oak sapling, the cattle passed them, grazing. Suddenly the cows returned in a state of panic, running at top speed, their heads high and their tails higher. Frightened also, the boys ran. Later they discovered by a trail in the grass that some savages had been near.

"These cattle," said Carter, "were the means in the hands of Providence for saving us—God is with us, watching over us, these cows are his witness." On another night while sitting alone in the darkness, guarding the camp as the others slept, Carter heard something like a man moving. He cocked his rifle, placing a finger on the trigger, determined—for he believed a savage was approaching—to wait until the enemy touched the muzzle of the gun and then to shoot. "It came pretty near and then ran off," he said the next morning. "Maybe it was a wild beast." Maybe so but Carter did not think so; he became more cautious than ever. All this enthralled Carter; sometimes his spirit soared to the point of ecstasy. It was a glorious thing to be riding at the head of a column moving deeper into this great country, to lead the exodus,

Lord, Lord! he loved this vast lonely land—its sweep, its deep forests, its wild American jorees and restless chicadees and cardinals and wild blue anemones and strong blackberry flowers and its free swift rivers; he loved its space and depth, even the sun that shone on it—and there was the west wind. There was no other land for him but this land, no other sun, no other wind. "It is home," he said often to himself as he marched on, "it is ours."

Also this was success and this was action; Carter was doing what he wanted to be doing.

Old Narcissa, when she spoke now to Carter, referred to him to his face as Moses. She used the title in sarcasm, bringing it from the depths of her bitterness. But to be called Moses pleased Carter. He cut himself a staff and over and over he felt the secret feeling that he was leading his people on their way as surely as the real Moses had led the Israelites; this journey was destiny, reason for being, guiding them was the Almighty. Carter never wavered, he knew he was bound, bound "unto a good land and a large, unto a land flowing with milk and honey, unto the place of the Canaanites and the Hittites and the Amonites and the Perizzites and the Hivites and the Jebusites." Carter began to regard himself as God's right hand. Exulting one day in his secret soul, he muttered, "I don't give a damn if it takes us forty years to get there."

So Carter and the Caldwells traveled on, lean and lanky westerners—for the most part proceeding on their way in silence, brooding, each keeping his own counsel, looking to different goals—Carter equipped for adventure; Silas beginning to turn over in his dark mind a plan that was to fill the rest of his days; Lucinda, inconsolable in grief, watching a wedge of shellrakes, a cloud drifting in space; Narcissa, contemplating ultimate quiet and heavenly rest; Patrick, living in the present, enjoying the feel and look of the things about him; Clarissa wishing to God they would turn back; Artemissa, dreaming of a better land for herself and Patrick out there in the west.

They traveled.

And the suns rose and set.

They crossed great hills, forded wide yellow rivers, gathering dewberries and early purple blackberries, resting at night in dark groves of oak, hickory, chestnut; moving on through a rich, various south country, seeing the big-eared bat, cottontail rabbits, red squirrels, sometimes glimpsing a fierce lynx, a panther, a swift-fleeing frightened chipmunk. And in the moonshine at midnight, the brazen mocking bird, a tout, sang its mimic song. Another night, it rained, wolves howled and there was thunder; huddled in the wagons, the travelers waited in wet clothes for day to break. The water of a stream ahead of them rose three feet in an hour and continued to rise, halting the oxcarts for the better part of a day—which fretted the Caldwells. Nothing through the generations of time ever taught them patience, not even high water.

While they were waiting, Silas sat down on some straw beside the sorrowing Lucinda; he took one of her hard, work-worn hands in his, saying "Lucinda, I'm tired of adventuring." For a few moments, he was silent. Then continuing, he said solemnly, "Let's settle down." Turning over on his back and resting his body on his powerful elbows, Silas looked intently into his wife's sad face. Lucinda smiled slightly; she was tired. Becoming intensely earnest and serious, Silas announced a determination to build a home. "We're going to build a house, Lucinda—not just a cabin, a great strong house, a refuge. This wandering about is all right up to a certain time but when a man reaches a certain age, he ought to stop it. I've got to stop it. I'm going to take root." His manner became more excited and enthused. "Lucinda," he said, "we're going to found a family—we're the first of the Caldwells of Keowee." Again Lucinda smiled but only vaguely; just then she was concerned with a problem that was more immediate. Her caked breasts were aching and she was wondering if she might not take one of the babies from one of the other Caldwell women to suckle; perhaps she might borrow Cousin Sarah's little William to nurse; Cousin Sarah wasn't very well; she hadn't much milk .

"We'll plant flower gardens and clear great fields and plant many crops," continued Silas, "and when roads are opened up, we'll have a carriage—and we'll educate the boys. Lucinda, no amount of money must be spared on educating the boys."

"Where will we get the money?" said Lucinda, turning to look at Silas.

"We'll get it," said Silas, a grim new look spreading over his face. "We're going to give the boys the best education money can buy. They must know the things we've never been able to know." At this moment, their conversation was interrupted. Darting in on them came Stephen John, their son, tugging at their clothes and crying happily and hungrily, "Supper's ready." Smiling at the boy, Lucinda said, "All right, son." She brushed Stephen John's hair from his forehead. Then Lucinda suddenly was overcome with love and pity for her husband—for a man dreaming in an oxcart of founding a dynasty. She kissed Silas lightly on the forehead. "You go on to supper," she said, "I want to speak a word with Cousin Sarah."

Having settled the matter satisfactorily with Sarah Caldwell, Lucinda joined Silas and the others a short while afterward at the camp fire. Watching Silas dig up a great hunk of bear steak from the common bowl and sop half a hoe cake in gravy, she said to herself, "Well, his appetite hasn't changed anyhow."

But in the secret life, Silas had changed. Luanda's cry when little Narcissa had died and the look he afterward had seen in his wife's eyes had changed him. Qualities within him that had never stirred now were stirring; he was a man with a purpose. Like his brother Carter, Silas had found a cause.

‿

By the firelight that night as Silas kept watch about the camp for savages, Carter brought out his fiddle, playing jerky, scratchy tunes full of lively melody and Patrick and Artemissa sang. And in her herb book old Narcissa scratched with a quill: "Use birch for baskets and hoop poles, ash for plows, wagons, spokes of wheels, tool handles; use chestnut whenever possible for building purposes—many of the oldest houses in Pennsylvania are built of it; it is good also for tubs or vats for liquor and never shrinks after being seasoned; a decoction of the bark of the candleberry myrtle is good for dropsies, use a decoction of the root for restraining uterine hemorrhages; use dogwood bark as a substitute for Peruvian bark in the cure of fevers and mortifications; a decoction of bark of black cherry is very good for dysentery and consumption."

On a warm Sunday afternoon soon after, with great clouds looming, warm and moist, they rested. The oxen were shackled and the cattle turned to graze. Suddenly Carter climbed on a pine log, announcing, "Brothers and sisters, I feel like preaching a sermon." No one was surprised as Carter often had such a mood. First he flung up his hands, leading them in a hymn, then he prayed—for it was his habit to stir the emotions of his listeners gradually, to prepare them for whatever it was he wanted them to hear. Quietly he now began but he gradually raised his voice until the woods began ringing with his roar. So morbid was his theme that Stephen John hid his face, and Clarissa, always fearful in her soul of hell's terrors, determined to do more good in this world, to think more of others. This was about the only quality in her husband that she boundlessly admired—his ability to preach a whacking sermon.

Pointing a lean finger directly at Clarissa, Carter shouted, "If you have not been made to loathe and abhor yourself, to repent in dust and ashes—if you have not laid your hand on your mouth and your mouth in dust and ashes, crying out, unclean, unclean—if you have not, my sister, it is a certain sign sin reigns in your mortal heart and is unto this day bringing forth fruit unto death." The finger shook directly in the face of Clarissa. She had never put her hand over her mouth crying out unclean; she was uneasy about her soul.

Carter turned now lo Sarah Caldwell and Artemissa. No one could tell, could make absolutely sure of their redemption; hell fire yawned for all. "Lord have mercy," called out Sarah, Carter then spoke about renting the caul of the heart, wearing sackcloth. "But imagine not you are secure because you acknowledge yourself to be a sinner." He shouted, "Oh, no." And his laugh was high and sarcastic, his look still upon Sarah Caldwell. "Oh, no, my sister…" Seeing the attention of the older people so absorbed in pictures of corruption, the younger Carter slipped away from the rapt circle, a bucket in hand, making as if to fetch some cool water. Soon in a cluster of alder bushes, he found his Cousin Temperance, the ruddy faced girl with the two plaits of yellow hair and the forming breasts.

"…Oh it shows you are a stranger to the operation of that spirit whose office it is to convince men of sin…" Amidst shouts of hallelujahs for redeeming love and converting grace, Carter rolled with Temperance into a pile of leaves. Scorpio the loins was their sign, they were born for extraordinary pleasure and trouble.

Carter led the column a long way on that Monday; also on Tuesday. Then on Wednesday the Caldwells reached one of the peaks in the long fable of their story. Climbing that day to the top of a high rise, they saw for the first time the blue ridge of mountains, the long powdered pure blue hills which for two centuries to come were to form their chief symbol, their principal charm. They gazed, rapt again and silent, upon a violent and beautiful country as little given to moderation as they were—a storm-blast region of droughts and whirling rain, livid glaring lightning and trembling thunder and silence and deep and desolate snows and tropical summer. Before them lay deep valleys, strewed with ancient hornblende, granite, gneiss, shale—soil tinged with iron. They had reached the promised land.

They saw for the first time the haze which spread away in every direction making this a perfect world for dreamers—home of the sumptuous cape jesamine with its deathly sweet odor, a flower that corroded on touch, home of the passion plant, the rattlesnake, the bald turkey buzzard that fed in secret on carrion and floated like an angel in the sky. Home now for the fierce, gentle, unpredictable Caldwells. On a high ridge looking into the west, they had reached in the rugged west the land of their bourne—here they were to stay through the centuries with this landscape of old mountains and quiet valleys as the picture to be carried deep in their feeling, their memories to fill here with immense vastness and remoteness, here a south sun shone and here were snakedoctors, and the sound of whip-poor-wills crying in the lonely sunset, and screechowls in the woods, and the high rasping wind, bringing old western dust. Here were many other things. Even the signs of spring were to change for them—the mourning dove in a pine tree and a cardinal singing in a wild cherry were to bring to them in their future the sign that new life was returning to the world—their evensong was to become the shy melody of the wood thrush.

In this wild windy country, under this rough and ragged sky—this was their America. As they looked, seeing the growth of the land as far as the sight could reach, Carter began telling them the names of domes and crags and peaks, pointing to Glassy Mountain, small and glistening with igneous rocks, long Pine Mountain and Hogback and Rabun Bald beyond swift Tugaloo River.

"And that one," he said, indicating an immense rounded promontory, looming in front, "that's called Bald Mountain—just plain bald." He explained that once it was covered with a thick forest, though it was barren now, a great waste of rain-streaked granite. Once in these mountains, he said, there lived a dreadful bird, foul smelling and very large, much like the green-winged hornet. This vulture got to carrying off the children of the savages who lived in the valleys. There would be a swoop of wings and down the bird would come upon the boys and girls who happened to wander into the woods. Soon a great number of the children had disappeared, and to destroy this creature all the Indians were gathered together. They schemed and made plans but had no success. So the matter was referred to the wise men summoned in special council. The wise men decided a savage should be posted on the summit of every mountain and when any one of them discovered the bird he should cry and his cry should be taken up by his neighbor on the next mountain and as the vulture passed everyone was to shoot. This they did, loosing arrows for an entire day but the creature flew too high for harm. Toward evening they found his hiding place—a cave on the eastern slope of the Blue Ridge near the head of the Tugaloo. On reaching this place, the savages found it was inaccessible to mortal feet. So they prayed the Great Spirit to bring out the great bird from its den and place it within range of their arrows—if the Great Spirit would do this, they would slay their enemy themselves. This courage pleased the Great Spirit who sent a great thunderstorm. In the midst of the tempest came a crash of white lightning which tore away a half of the mountain. Screaming, the green-winged creature rose, only a few feet above the heads of the savages. It was killed by the first arrow. As a reward for their courage, the Great Spirit then ruled that all the highest mountains were to lie barren in order that the savages might have an opportunity after that to watch the movements of their enemies.

Looking uneasily toward Bald Mountain and the long range of granite peaks, Stephen John, wild-eyed and frightened, asked, "Are we being watched?" Carter gave the boy a truthful answer. "Yes," he said, "we are." He had heard sounds, had seen signs, and one night he had felt an eye.

On the afternoon of this invasion of Keowee by the Caldwells, the valley was filled with wisps of mist—drifting low clouds were turning into showers of rain, melting sometimes into yellow sunlight, a world of yellow. It was seen by the tired travelers from the crest of a final hill up which Carter brought them, announcing with a proud sweeping gesture—"This is the valley I was telling you of; here we are." Their hearts pounded their ribs as they gazed, at first half in fear of disappointment, upon a clear river flowing through a deep valley, patient and varied and as old as the world—a country now quiet and calm, resting after a thunderstorm. It was as beautiful as Carter had said it was and it looked as rich.

"Let us pray," said Silas, new authority in his voice. And from that time on it was Silas who was their leader—Silas who watched for them for the pillar of fire, had the sight on a star. Silas, the builder, relieved Carter, the explorer and soldier.

Leaving Patrick to watch the camp, Silas and Carter went off to select a site for a home. Two days later they returned, having chosen a piece of high ground at the conflux of Visages Creek with Keowee River, a rise that commanded a noble view across miles of valleys within valleys and deep forests—a far-flung sight which for generations was to stir up in the Caldwells the sense of being free.

"This is the place," Silas whispered that night to Lucinda as exhausted they lay stretched in the oxcart. "We're going to build a house here that will live on and on into time—it'll be a rallying place for all of the Caldwells forever, we'll see to that. And it'll be a house the world will know about some day. For we're going to turn out great men, lawyers and doctors and farmers, send statesmen to the parliaments. We're going down in history, Lucinda—Silas and Lucinda, the first of the Caldwells."

Silas slept.

CHAPTER THREE

Silas was always fond of ceremony and show. So on the morning the Caldwells were to begin the actual building of their first house in the wilderness of Keowee, he again gathered the family about him. Taking an axe scrubbed clean and polished, Silas symbolically cut down the first tree—not for the great house that he had begun to dream about but for the cabin they were to live in until the time would come when he could start on his dream mansion. He swung the broad blade and in all that vast and lonely world on that fine spring morning, the only sound anywhere was the song of a catbird and the ring of that axe. It gave the Caldwells a powerful sense of independence and a feeling of being their own masters. Silas knew it would have this effect, it was how he wanted them to feel. It would be a thing to remember too—cutting where no one had ever cut before. They did not consider the Indians.

Then Silas took a spade and turned the first earth. "Folks," he said, "this is our home and we've come here to stay. Some of us, I guess, will be living on this very hill from now on until the end of time. This is our land," Silas swept the spaces with a gesture. "We've won it by the oldest right in the world, the right of conquest. And we don't intend to give it up to anyone. It has been given us by the Master." Silas wiped his forehead. "Well, folks," he added, "pitch in, let's get started with the work. It looks like there's a good deal needing to be done." They laughed. Then all of them, women and men, began to cut down trees.

Until they had built a cabin, which was intended more as a fort than a home, they worked through the days and far into the nights without resting. These first days and nights were followed by weeks of the hardest labor. More trees were felled and rung, patches of land were cleared, brush was burned, the first corn was planted.

Now it was great strong-limbed Patrick who set the pace. Neither Silas nor Carter cared much for tree-cutting and they lacked the patience to clear a piece of new ground, to grub among roots. Silas spent much of his time surveying this new land, also he would stand for hours at a time listening to swift water pour over worn granite ledges, looking into the misty valleys—a mansion was taking form in his mind. Before even the first cabin was roofed Silas had chosen a site for the house that he intended to outlast the ages. He had selected the top of a high hill, a commanding view. While the sound of axes still echoed within the hearing of an Indian tribe, Silas was planning gardens and fields and even roads and bridges.

"Lucinda," he said, "we'll call it Forest Mansion."

And like Silas, Carter also was dreaming. Carter kept the camp guarded and supplied with game but this did not engage his full time. Carter already was turning an eye toward the rim of the looming mountains, wondering about the country beyond; he was thinking of another expedition. To both Carter and Silas all this present activity was only a means to an end.

It was the end itself to Patrick. Patrick swung a double-edged axe and sang. He was slower than the husband of Cousin Sarah Caldwell, lacked the easy skill of young Will Caldwell, another of the cousins, but Patrick was the steadiest workman among them all and with his loud singing he brought rhythm into the work of wood cutting. He made them all feel the deep beauty that lies in the regular swinging of an axe. Things moved more easily when Patrick set the pace. Sometimes he would look about him and laugh. He was a sight to see, his strong arms moving through half arcs, his broad back bending. "My," said Artemissa, proudfully to herself, "nobody has a handsomer man."

Sometimes the wild meat brought in by Carter was all they had to eat. As they lacked salt, the Caldwells were weakened often by a form of dysentery. But they did not mind much. They saw clearings growing wider and cabins rising higher; they felt they were getting somewhere, getting something done. This buoyed their feelings.

Old Narcissa planted a half of her hoarded stock of peach kernels and hollyhock seed, a quarter of the seeds of the roses, keeping the others dry in a buckskin bag as a reserve—Narcissa no longer dared risk all of anything at one time, too many things had happened to her. "I'm waiting for the Father to call me home," she said one day to Lucinda. "But in the meantime I might as well occupy my time." So she perfected a new scarlet dye from the Indian fig and took over the care of the younger children. "Mind your manners," she told them, "never walk between anyone and the fire and always say ma'am and sir to older people and never speak when older people are speaking." She had them memorize psalms and urged them to keep the Lord's commandments and to have faith in God and to love their neighbors as themselves.

"Are the savages our neighbors?" Stephen John inquired one day as they watched water boil in an iron pot swung over an outdoor fire. "No," answered Narcissa, hard lines forming about her old mouth, "savages have no soul."

The children were advised to do what was right and what was good and to remember they had to make something of themselves when they grew up. "And don't always be running around the country looking for bigger and better places," said the great-grandmother more than once, "settle down—become a credit to the Caldwells. You've got to amount to something, be somebody." She was always harping on this last theme. Hardly a day passed that Narcissa did not caution these children against yielding to the lure of distance.

"It ain't true," she said over and over, "the pastures beyond these mountains aren't one bit greener than the grass right here in Keowee Valley. That's always been the trouble with us," she spoke wistfully. "There's not one of us in the whole Caldwell connection that is willing to enjoy the thing at hand. No, sir—we're either way back in the distant yesterday or else we're grieving in our hearts because tomorrow hasn't come. That's our trouble—restlessness. And if you don't remember anything else your great-grandmother ever told you, remember this: Guard against traveling, children. It doesn't get you anywhere in the end."

One morning, Narcissa attempted to prove this theory to the children. "Today," she said, "I'm going to teach you all a great lesson." Each child was given a big cup. "What's it going to be?" inquired the boys and girls, all delighted and excited.

"You'll find out," said Narcissa. She led them to a small stream where blackberries were ripening on the banks. "Now for two hours," she said, "we'll pick." Quickly and carefully, Narcissa began filling her bucket. "Pick the berries clean as you go," she cautioned. Before they had been there ten minutes, old Narcissa began to smile, ruefully. She had observed that young Carter was almost out of sight. Soon the boy came back, running and shouting, he had found a patch with berries big as his thumb. "Come with me, grandma," he cried, "let me show you." But Narcissa shook her head. "You pick there if you like, Carter, but the rest of us will stay here." Again Carter drifted away and after a time he returned with word of another discovery. The berries there were even bigger than those in the other place. "Come on, grandma," begged Carter. "No," said Narcissa, firmly.

At the end of the two hours, Narcissa called all the children together. "See," she said pointing gleefully at the buckets and cups. All of them were full or nearly full except Carter's. Carter's was only half filled. "See what comes of running around," she said.

"But grandma," said young Carter, an earnest frown on his forehead, "my berries are bigger than the berries in your bucket and maybe if you all had come with me—maybe you'd been able to fill your buckets a lot quicker. You all pick faster than I do." Narcissa never forgave young Carter.

That afternoon the children begged Narcissa to tell them again about Pennsylvania and for the hundredth time they listened to the story of the house that had glass windows and curtains. Once more they heard about the painted barn and the pond and the burying ground with the three stones in a row.

"All of them were named Annie," said Narcissa, folding her thin spotted hands. My mother was that determined to have a girl of that name in the family. It was her own mother's name. The first one was just Annie but after she went on beyond, my mother gave to the one that followed the name of Mary Annie and called her Annie. And after that one had left her, she called the next one Annie Eleanor. That one died of the milk fever." Narcissa looked far away. "I was the next one. My mother decided to call me Narcissa and here I am today."

It was time now for the children to graze the cattle and while they were away, Narcissa wrote in her herb book about the new scarlet dye. Suddenly in the midst of this, Narcissa had one of her original inspirations. There were no schoolbooks in the wilderness for the children; she would write some schoolbooks. Instantly she began. She started the composition of an arithmetic. "Arithmetic," she wrote, "is the art of computing by numbers." This work engaged her spare time for seven weeks and at last when she had written as far as she could remember, it was over a hundred pages long and besides addition, subtraction, multiplication, division, vulgar fractions and decimals, this remarkable arithmetic contained many other things included in no other arithmetic in the world. For often in the midst of composing a page, Narcissa would grow tired of the stern mental discipline of figures and would rebel. Thus the pleased children in their arithmetic would discover that "a family of well-regulated children is a charming sight" and that "good breeding is often a surface without depth but politeness is the sunshine of the soul." Queer and delightful indeed right after "the distance from Philadelphia to Trenton is 30 miles, from Trenton to Princeton 12 miles, from Princeton to Brunswick 18 miles, from Brunswick to New York 30 miles, how many miles from Philadelphia to New York?

Through all those pages Narcissa never referred once to the wilderness or its problems- her arithmetic was a Pennsylvania book written by a Pennsylvanian. Here revealed in its fullness was her secret tragedy.

Narcissa still was an exile; after a full half century, she was sick yet for the rock house in the Pennsylvania which had become an imperishable thing of her own creation—it was security and peace, settled existence. That step she had taken sixty years before in mounting the oxcart north of Philadelphia now was regarded by her as symbolic of all the steps she since had taken. "The first one," she said to herself, "also was the last." During the first ten years after that first step she had come down with child six times, three times bearing the children entirely alone and fearing every minute to hear the wild whoop of a savage. During those ten years she had never left a cabin door that she had not expected to meet a dart or an arrow, she had known the fear of the constant threat of death, of being always exposed to attack. She had never taken a trip that she had not prayed, "Have mercy."

One springtime while the corn was being planted, Narcissa had herself sent her eleven-year-old boy to catch a horse; he had never been seen again. They supposed he had been taken by the Indians but there was no absolute certainty, there had never been any trace. A few years later another of her sons had been scalped, then the death of her husband had followed. Seldom were those days spoken of but in the old house in Pennsylvania were her letters:

"Dear Sister:

"Sam and Wesley Clements and a Mr. Whistler and us made a new settlement on Liberty Creek. After the construction of the new cabin, Mr. Whistler returned to the old home for provisions. On Christmas morning, Sam and Wesley went to work not far from the house to cut logs for another cabin. It seems the Indians had discovered them and were ambushed in the morning ready to attack them. Sam was shot down and instantly killed. Wesley escaped and got within 40 or 50 yards of the cabin when he was confronted by two Indians who had crept up—doubtless with a view to attack the women and children. Stephen John rushed forward and while engaged with these savages in a hand to hand conflict a pursuing party arrived—they cleft Stephen John's head with a hatchet. Mrs. Clements had started to his assistance with a rifle when he fell. Seeing Wesley overcome a few minutes later, she returned to the house, pursued by the Indians. On her entrance, the other Mrs. Clements slammed the door and they presented the gun at the Indians through the crevices and between the logs. From this cause or fearing help might be near at hand, the savages after scalping the dead men quickly disappeared.

"Before the attack was made, I had gone to the spring for water. As soon as I heard the shooting and the screams of the women, knowing it was an attack and not doubting all were killed, I jumped into the spring-branch with a view of preventing the Indians trailing my footprints, and followed the stream to the creek. There I found the backwater from the creek had formed a drift of wood. At that moment, I heard a bell coming toward me and realizing they were in pursuit of our cow, I hastily hid myself beneath the drift with only my head above water. I saw the Indians catch our sow not twenty yards away. They took the bell. Hearing no other noise and still fearing I might be pursued, I attempted to follow the bed of the creek in order to make my escape, but the waters were too deep and I was compelled to make my way through briars and dense thickets. Late in the evening I reached Throckmorton's settlement, almost entirely destitute of clothing, and bleeding from many wounds made by the thorns and brush in my wild and reckless efforts to get through.

"The two other women remained at the house for some time after the attack and then took the children, theirs and ours,—with a gun, and an axe, and followed the road we had made in going into the place. At the creek they met two gentlemen camped on the banks of the stream. These men cut down a tree to enable them to go over and then brought them in their wagon to the settlement. There, to the surprise of us all, we met. But it was but poor comfort. We were so overcome it was quite some time before we could tell what happened.

Next morning, several of the menfolks went for the dead and our household effects. Burial was on the day following. Stephen John's coffin was of hewn slabs split from a cedar tree.

"We are going back in a few days—we are not going to let go of our land."

The spring passed in the high wilderness valley of Keowee and the south summer began. Everyone was busy. Carter had made several short scouting journeys, traveling once to the foot of the mountains. Silas had been often to the hill where he planned to build the great house. "It must be plain and severe," said he to Luanda. ' It must have character." Patrick had helped Narcissa start a garden. For no matter where Narcissa found herself, she always planted trees and started gardens. "A flower," she said to Patrick "will grow where a weed will—if you put it there."

Then came the day that the trouble began. It was late in the afternoon and Narcissa at the time was teaching the children about ciphers and decimals. She was squatting on a stool before the fireplace in the cabin, not long finished, conducting the lesson and at the same time watching some bread baking over coals spread on the granite hearth. "Ciphers connected to decimals," she said, "neither increase nor decrease their value" Before a table in the middle of the room sat Lucinda, knitting and idly listening to Narcissa's voice, and to the responding voices of the children. All at once, Narcissa saw Lucinda jump. Lucinda slammed the door, which was ajar; instantly she bolted it tight.

"Why, Lucinda, what's the matter?" Narcissa said, regarding her granddaughter intently. "I thought I saw a shadow pass," whispered Lucinda, her face very pale. Lucinda turned her back to the wall and put her hands to her throat. Seeing how really alarmed the younger woman was, Narcissa suggested that perhaps a bat or an owl had flown by, attracted by the light.

"No," answered Lucinda, "it wasn't a bat."

Narcissa got up. Cautiously she then pulled back the strong iron bolt, which was one of the things they had brought in the caravan. She edged the door open about two inches, then slammed it as quickly as Lucinda had. and dashed the bolt again into a holding position.

"Lucinda," she said, her old face quite composed, "get down the rifle, give the alarm." Lucinda ran across the room; soon through one of the loopholes went a cracking sound, another followed, then another.

"What did you see?" whispered Lucinda, quaking but again reloading the musket.

Narcissa lowered her voice. "There's an arrow buried in the door."

The sound of the rifle shots brought the men running to the cabin; they had been working that afternoon in the furthest bottom land, along the rocky ledge of the river— under heavy guard. Soon Carter was sent off down the valley to warn other settlers and that night the Caldwells waited through the darkness, expecting at any moment to be attacked; they waited through the whole of the next day and through the following night but there was no disturbance. On the second morning, they grew more bold and being by this time forced to replenish their water supply and to kill a little meat, they sent out several sorties from the clearing. It was during a mid-afternoon lull with all the household busy pouring bullets that Narcissa decided to slip down to the spring to bring in the wooden buckets, which filled with milk, had been left in the cool water. Narcissa had faced so many Indian raids, she had lost her original caution.

At the pool she bent over to lift the buckets from the water. Suddenly in the still surface of the spring as she leaned down, she saw a reflection. Instantly she knew what was happening; she knew that the time had come. Turning about, Narcissa was struck on the ear. The next blow knocked her flat on her face among some ferns. In another moment her back was pierced with darts. Then she was scalped. After that her head was severed. High in the air rose Narcissa's thin gray hair and through the woods a warwhoop rang.

Heard in the cabin, the cry frightened the Caldwells with its wild, terrifying fury. Bars and windows were bolted without a second thought. Silas this time did not wait to pray. He yelled a command, "Take your places." Sarah Caldwell's husband and Will Caldwell and Taylor Caldwell did take their places—instantly they manned the loopholes.

But Patrick—it was now that Patrick had to face the crisis of his life. This was his moment, one of those flying instants which in a pendulum's swing can suddenly burst upon a human being and glorify or devastate an entire life. In that fraction of time, with the forests about the cabin roaring with high pitched yells, gigantic and strong-limbed Patrick had revealed to him the exact nature of his courage.

"Take your places." Silas' command swept into Patrick's consciousness; he heard the words spoken but they left him without the power to move; the brain in his finely moulded head suddenly lost its control over the strong arms that dangled by his sides; his legs seemed to lie far away, paralyzed, in another world. Patrick heard his name called, felt an angry jerk—a rough hand pulling at his shoulder. But he was powerless, iron chains bound him, blocks of ice were about his body, he was a heavy form, a stone. Then the whole world seemed to crash, worlds within worlds wheeled, and the left side of his smooth high-cheeked face began to twitch. His passionate loose lips opened and Patrick too began to scream—wilder, louder, more crazily than the savages at the door. He fell down behind a loom. He lay there shivering with fear until the fight was over. All this happened within a few moments but it was long enough to ruin Patrick's life. There could be no place for him after that, his role had been taken from him.

Artemissa took over Patrick's role. She grabbed the long rifle that fell from his hands. Rushing to the loophole which was Patrick's to guard, Artemissa looked out with a steady blue eye and when she saw a savage form creep forward, she aimed and with a steady finger squeezed the trigger. She saw a Cherokee collapse in the dry short grass. The savages swept four times against the side of the cabin defended by Artemissa and each time the bullets that sang out from her loophole turned them back. After the final retreat, her quarter of the battlefield was strewed with four Cherokees, two of them dead, two wounded.

Nobody said anything in the cabin after the struggle was over. They waited dazed for another attack. When it did not come, Silas opened the door. Commands were given to Sarah's husband and to Will Caldwell to clear the yard of corpses; Taylor would go with Silas to look for Narcissa. Nothing was said to Patrick.

Within a few minutes, Sarah's husband and Will had dragged fifteen Indians down the steep side of the hill to the river. One after another the bodies were dumped into the swirling water, the living along with the dead. Silas and Taylor soon found the body of Narcissa. The spring stream was dyed with her blood, it ran a pale vermilion color for a dozen feet through green banks of moss into a patch of wild lilies of the valley. Silas sent Taylor to the cabin after a counterpane.

While the other men were away on these missions, Patrick dragged himself from behind the loom. He crept into a corner; like a dog, he sat there; bowed to earth, his spirit completely broken. Patrick hid his fine handsome face in his strong hands. Throughout the rest of that day everyone ignored him—even Artemissa, who alone might have saved him. But it was only afterwards that she realized that. At this time Artemissa was not thinking of Patrick; her thoughts were of herself and her own humiliation. She spent the day lying face downward on Lucinda's bed, pitying herself and her little children. Occasionally she sobbed aloud. This stung Patrick like fire. That night, Artemissa fed her husband as though he were some animal in, a cage. Without speaking to him, she set a plate of fried hominy and ham on the floor at his feet. Patrick did not touch it.

This was the family found by Carter on his return a little later from his journey down the valley to warn the other settlers.

Silas and Will made a coffin for Narcissa from fragrant slabs of cedar. Then through the night they sat up with the corpse, burning candles perfumed with pine and balsam scent. Burial took place the next day in a deep grove of pines on the very top of the high hill beyond the cabin—on the hill beyond the hill which Silas had selected as the place for Forest Mansion. It was a meditative spot, full of repose and rest, and brightened with yellow mullein and saw-briars and wild eglantine roses. It was a free place for a free spirit. Patrick followed the procession, walking apart and far to the rear. He too loved Narcissa. Standing away from the others, he heard Silas deliver the eulogy. "She met life with calmness, resignation and the firmness of a Christian philosopher." Then Patrick listened to Carter who spoke with more emotion than Silas. "Disappointment did not change her," said Carter. "No matter what happened to her, she still looked and listened; she heard the birds singing and saw the beautiful wild flowers." Patrick remembered that once Narcissa had told him these were the eternal exquisite things, these were the pleasures that would never desert them. They sang Narcissa's favorite hymn, "Bye and bye, when the morning comes." Silas prayed, "Have mercy upon her, pardon all her transgressions, shelter her soul in the shadow of thy wing. Make known to her the path of eternal life." Patrick wept, he could not help it.

Thus in the midst of tragedy did Narcissa enter on her last and longest journey, among strange mountains. Her name, Narcissa Caldwell, was chipped into a piece of granite by Carter. Beneath it was the verse from St. John, "He that believeth in me though he die, yet shall he live." That evening as the sun dropped behind the blue ridge, Carter gathered the children about him in the chimney corner of the cabin as the old woman would have done. To ease their grief he decided for that once to try to take her place with them. Very gently, childlike himself in sorrow, Carter began quietly talking. He told the children that once in a far country there lived a girl named Nagoochee, who was distinguished for her beauty and for her attachment to all the flowers and wild birds of her native valley. But this young girl was not strong. She was delicate and frail and one day she died—at the twilight horn of a summer day in her fifteenth summer. "And on the evening of her burial, what do you think happened?" Carter looked intently at the cluster of children about him.

"What?" asked Stephen John, excited.

"A new star was born in the sky," Carter said it was the most beautiful of all the stars in heaven. The Indians called it Nagoochee. "It was Nagoochee gone on to join the angels."

"Will there be a new star for grandma?" the children cried.

"Why, of course there will be," said Carter. Opening the door, Carter pointed to the western horizon. "See," he said, and looking in wonder, the children saw in the dazzling magenta half-light of the southern evening, above the last red and purple of the sunset, a gleaming green star.

"Grandma's star," they whispered, holding their breath.

It was the glorious evening star, the planet Venus.

In such little ways did Carter enrich the way of living in the wilderness. He was determined the memory of wistful old Narcissa should not die and so did Lucinda likewise determine.

More than any of the others, Lucinda wept over the death of Narcissa. She was overcome by the pitifulness, the disappointment of this life, lived so far and so long from the great world and so filled with secret hope and suffering and brought in the end to such brutal defeat. Frantically, Lucinda determined Narcissa's spirit, her nobility, her hope, should live on. Somehow these qualities must be kept alive, the memory not just fade away into the wilderness. She would tell her children's children—that was her plan and they perhaps would tell the children of their children of an old woman who helped found a country she did not want to found and who was scalped. Weeping, Lucinda determined Narcissa should become a great and noble martyr, living on in legend, a source of courage to a race. She began to compose the story.

⁂

That night the Caldwells were so tired they did not even keep a guard. Chances and risks had to be taken often in the wilderness and they now were taking one. They slept the deep sleep of exhaustion, their emotions as worn out as their tired bodies. Only Patrick remained awake. Sitting quietly in his corner, he waited until he was sure all were sleeping; then quickly he slipped across the room, lifted the bolt and opened the door. Once out in the open, he silently pulled the door behind him. He disappeared.

He had been on his way six hours before Artemissa awoke suddenly, instantly wide-awake and filled with a warning of disaster. Something told her, even though she could not see well in the dim firelight—she knew that Patrick was not in the cabin. Jumping up, she wakened Carter who was laying full length before the fire. Carter grabbed his rifle, "What's wrong," he whispered.

"He's gone," said Artemissa. She was a wild sight, her long hair hanging loose over her large shoulders.

"Maybe he's just stepped out; he'll be back in a minute." But Artemissa shook her head. "He won't be back—I have a feeling," she said, beginning to cry. "He'll never be back—he's left us." Lifting the bolt from the door, Artemissa dashed into the dark clearing. She ran faster and faster, falling over a log and stumping one of her bare toes.

"Patrick," she screamed desperately. "Patrick." The words came back from the valleys beyond the river, terrible and vast echoes, mocking her. She was dragged an hour later into the cabin by Carter and Lucinda. Lucinda bathed her bloody feet. "He didn't even take his rifle," said Artemissa, pointing to the long weapon that Patrick had dropped at the start of the fight. It was hanging now in the gunrack.

"Did he take anything to eat?" Artemissa inquired. She shook her head, knowing the answer to her own question. Patrick had gone without provisions. At the breakfast table next morning as the family sat down to eat, Artemissa turned savagely upon them. "You didn't know him like I did," she said, pointing her fingers accusingly. "You didn't know how kind he was and how good he was. You didn't know anything about the beautiful things he thought." Losing control of her emotions, Artemissa screamed out, "You have driven him away."

Nobody said anything and Artemissa soon became quite calm. "I'm sorry," she apologized. After that Artemissa remained perfectly composed and she never in the presence of any of them was ever again heard to mention Patrick by name. Taking no further part in the long search, she sat listlessly in Narcissa's chair in the chimney corner and sometimes for days would hardly budge from the cabin. When Carter or Silas came in, scratched and tired and hungry, she did not ask them where they had been nor if any traces had been found. She just sat and looked into the burning pine fire. Once she asked God to give her a second chance but she knew that was a prayer that would never be answered.

The men searched the hills for many miles in every direction. Armed and traveling in groups, they moved up and down the river, then, branching they circled into more distant areas, hunted the gullies and hollows along Crow Creek, Mile Creek, Chump's Cabin behind Six Mile Mountain, Walnut Creek, Little River, Crooked River, Cane Creek, west as far as the wild muddy waters of Chauga. Travelers on the wilderness road were asked to watch for Patrick, northward on the Philadelphia trail, southward along the swirling Savannah. Hurried expeditions were made at considerable risk into the Indian country. But nowhere did anyone find a sign, not even so much as a footprint. Patrick had vanished—like the wordless winds in the soughing pines. Finally Carter had to tell Artemissa that they had done everything they could, there was no point in looking any longer. He took her aside one noon after dinner. Weeping, Artemissa held his hands. "Thank you, Carter," she said, "thank all the others."

Artemissa pitched away the light shawl from her shoulders and that afternoon began the acceptance of her long sentence of sorrow. She spun and wove until there was nothing left in Keowee to spin and weave. Then she began plowing corn in the new ground and she cut down trees, working like a man. But Artemissa was not able always to keep to her rigid discipline. Often she would drop whatever she was doing, leave a hoe, an axe where it would fall, and she would rush away. Sometimes during these bursts of despair she would visit the grove where Narcissa was buried. There with her hands clasped, she would pass entire afternoons, her eyes on the infinite and faraway. Artemissa's devotion to her idiot Oliver now became extreme, she completely neglected her other children. Sometimes taking this simple one by the arm, she would wander far off into dangerous country. Sometimes the mother would walk ahead, and behind her about two steps would come the child, his thin arms dangling and swinging. Without Artemissa knowing it, Carter began to follow her. Hidden among brush and vines, rifle in hand, he would keep a watch. Often he heard Artemissa and crazy Oliver talking to God and frequently they spoke to the angels. Many times they fell on their knees. "Pity us," they would say, "have mercy."

The southern summer bore its crop and sad autumn moved into the Blue Ridge, preparing the sorrowful woods for the exultant victory of death. So still and magnificent, the killing frosts crept upon yellow hickory leaves, the soft poplar, the dogwood's red, the red sassafras, and sourwood, the sweetgum's tarnished chrome—swarms of brown and sea blue and little yellow butterflies drifted among the last flowers, primroses and foxgloves and sundrops. Then a thick mist rose like a shroud from the river and there was ice in the shallow pools. One afternoon the whole world was brilliant and when the morning came everything had perished. Artemissa knelt in the cold light, joining in the mourning.

At the cabin, a hickory nut falling on the roof would cause her to rush to the door, a falling limb would bring her running. Her ears ceaselessly were alert for a sound beyond the sounds, her tired eyes strained for a vision. She rarely slept before midnight; there were long nights when she got no rest at all. Lucinda would hear her, turning and moving and twisting. Then the cold northern winds came down the bleak valley, with the leaves—the dead leaves of the year—and one morning snow covered Mount Pinnacle and Pine Mountain and far in the Indian country the mighty sides of Rabun Bald. Sometimes at night the wolves howled and Artemissa would grip about herself the bed quilts, her heart pounding from fear—perhaps out in that cold it was Patrick they were trailing. So lived Artemissa, restless and waiting, hoping for a sign.

But Patrick was not to return.

From the cabin that night he walked straight toward the Indian country. He climbed sharp hills, thrashing his way through creeks and thickets for six days without food other than berries. Sick at heart from the start, he was so tired and starved by the end of a week that nothing mattered any longer except the final rest. He was almost senseless when captured by six savages returning from a buffalo hunt.

They burned him to death over a pile of sticks. Fed by pine faggots, the smoking fire rose, slaked rich with resins. Patrick was clean and young again, lying naked, he was lying on a smooth rock among vines, above him a woodthrush was nesting, and beside him was a dark flower turning its petals—the flower faded, it was Artemissa. "Artemissa," he cried and the power of his great voice commanded awe even among the savages. "Artemissa," he pleaded. Then as human grease trickled down his burning legs, Patrick's scalped head fell forward.

❧

This wilderness which had cost them Patrick and Narcissa left also its secret mark on the mysterious and ecstatic soul of Carter. For during the excitement, he committed a theft. He stole from the Taylors, a poor family of settlers, closely related to the Caldwells. It was not a great crime in itself but Carter regarded it as such. "It was such a sorry and low-down thing to do," he told himself. He let it trouble him greatly.

Rushing into the Taylor cabin to warn them of Indians, Carter found the place already deserted, so recently that smoldering ashes, quenched with water, were smoking on the hearth. Evidently the Taylors had fled in great confusion, for no attempt had been made even to conceal provisions that could not be carried with them—several smoked hams still were hanging from the rafters, there were barrels filled with flour and in one corner lay a pile of fine beaver pelts. Quickly Carter gathered the skins in his arms, slung them over his horse's back and an hour later stowed them under a ledge of granite in a rhododendron thicket. Long after the Indian troubles had been stamped out and the Taylors had returned to their cabin, Carter came back to this thicket and crossing the mountains with the furs traded them to a Frenchman for a new type of rifle. No one ever thought of suspecting Carter.

Afterwards he was tortured by remorse; he knew these skins were all the Taylors had and that they were depending on trading them in at the settlement at Ninety Six for tea and sugar and other necessities. He knew that without these pelts they would have to do without for another year. Yet Carter did not make amends. Sometimes the sight of his new rifle would bring him moments of the most poignant regret. But he kept the gun. It was very powerful, its bullets sped so far.

This was a great time for Carter—a general Indian uprising followed the scalping at the Caldwell spring and in the action Carter rose to the occasion, became a well-known frontier leader. As the trouble became more general and alarming, he ordered all settlers in Keowee to abandon their cabins and under his direction they began to build a fort, a few miles above the Caldwells' place on Keowee. Neither he nor Silas objected when at the suggestion of the Taylors it was decided to name their rising log bastion Fort Prince George after the vain, vindictive, lethargic, and sulky son of the British Prince Frederick who died without coming to his faraway throne.

Soon Carter had become a noted scout and after the trouble was quieted, he never did spend much more time sweating over a hoe or driving oxen to plows. He did not even make the pretense. He took up a thousand acres of land, next to and north of Silas' holding, and helped to raise a cabin for his family but he seldom was there to sleep more than a night or so at a time. This led to gossip. Peter Garvin, a boy with a loud vulgar voice and pimples on a fuzzy face, said Carter had women among the Indians. "How about it, Carter," he shouted one Sunday in a grove where the settlers had gathered for a church service. Slapping his knees and bellowing with laughter, Peter cried, "I hear more than seventy little savages call Carter Caldwell pa." In a rage, Carter turned on his banterer. He grabbed the youth in both hands and flung him into a brush heap. "Aw, take a joke," said Peter. "A Caldwell is not one to joke with," said Carter in a fury. Because of the intenseness of Carter's anger, a number of people believed Peter's jest had a basis of truth.

Carter was absent sometimes for months at a time—scouting, trapping, making expeditions. These habits of his extremely annoyed Clarissa, who more than almost any of the younger Caldwell women wanted someone to support her—someone on whom she could depend, a rock, a pillar, a tower. "I know Carter's a good man and he means the best in the world, I reckon," she grumbled to Lucinda. "But I wish he'd do a little more for his family. He's a mighty poor provider." It scandalized Clarissa that Carter should ride off in the spring on a horse, leaving the heavy plowing and the corn planting for her and the children. "Sometimes I think he doesn't love me at all," she whimpered.

But Carter rode on, memorizing the physical geography of this mighty region, learning the place names—Sticoe Mountain, Kings Gap, Oolenoy—place of tubers, where turnips grow; Nantahala—the middle of the sun; finding his spiritual home in the silence and vastness, waiting wet and patient through gigantic storms. He climbed the steep sides of mountains for no other reason than to look into new valleys. One of the sweeping moments of his entire life came the day he gazed down from a crag of worn granite onto a stream that flowed in a western direction. "By God," he burst forth, talking to the clouds and the bright sky, "'that's the most beautiful sight in creation." The shining water of that torrent, dashing into western distance, was the precious road to freedom, dangerous and full of peril and worth the risk of dying. Carter believed in the wilderness. "It's our hope, the future," he said. Striding that granite mountain, contemplating that vast valley, rich, remote and protected, Carter sensed the time to come. It was a sweet land; to him the wilderness was an epic. He lived among passions more frigid and by far more complex than any of Clarissa's.

Soon after this a strange thing happened to Carter. He crossed into the Indian country with two young men of the Hunter family, settlers on Twelve Mile, a yellow river running through a valley eastward of Keowee. The three men had forded Tugaloo dividing upper Carolina from Georgia and in several hours of hard riding had gathered together a dozen wild horses—wild was their name for them although they knew the mounts belonged to the Cherokees. On their return, Carter and the two were overtaken by the savages on the banks of Chauga Creek and seeing no chance of escape by flight, Carter sprang from his horse, lying concealed in a sink among weeds. The savages scalped the Hunter boys and butchered them, cutting them into hunks. But Carter lying still escaped. Often in the past he had outwitted the savages but this was the narrowest of all his adventures; he regarded it as a miracle, directly an act from God. And together with the sound of the cries which came to him from the dying Hunter boys, it changed him. Making his way back to Keowee a few days later, Carter strode into the cabin. The family had gathered at the table, eating. "Brothers and sisters," Carter said, "I have been called of God as was Aaron." The Caldwells laid down their knives and forks; they listened.

"I will go into all the world and preach the gospel to every creature," he said, a wild and intense look coming into his eyes. At this Clarissa burst into tears, attempting to dissuade him. "You're needed at home," she said. But Carter replied, "I covenanted in my heart if the Lord would keep me from destruction, I would go and labor in his vineyard." Soon afterward Carter entered the itinerant connection as a Baptist minister. This enraged Clarissa; she was a Methodist.

The suddenness of Carter's conversion became the talk of the whole Carolina upcountry. In explaining what had happened to him, Carter adopted a manner of mystery. "As in the time of Saul of old," he said, "there shined about me a light from heaven and I heard a voice."

"We don't know yet all about it," Lucinda wrote to another Lucinda, one of the cousins in Virginia. "It's just the Caldwell in him coming out, I guess—queer and sort of half crazy. He who used to roam for weeks hunting without a word, now speaks of braving exposure and the fear of the tomahawk and scalping knife to carry the word…amidst din of war and terror of deprivation, he says he is carrying on the holy work and many have been the subjects of Carter's saving grace…a surprise to us all…"

Taking his new duties very seriously, Carter rode hundreds of miles visiting settlers whom he tried to convert to his own type of frontier faith. His preaching was sound, it had both method and motive. For he reminded his congregation of their high destiny as settlers of the wilderness. "We have hope for a better world in our western country, for a finer place for our children to live in." He told them they must learn to endure, must believe they would be rewarded. "We must not fear danger nor death, we would not be worthy at all." Upon men and women spiritually hungry, Carter poured his spirit…"Risk everything, folks," he shouted, "be willing to take chances." As text for his favorite sermon, preached oftenest and with greatest fervor, he took the second, third and fourth verses of the first chapter of Joshua:

"Moses, my servant, is dead; now therefore arise, go over the Jordan, thou and all his people, unto the land which I do give them, even to the Children of Israel. Every place that the sole of your foot shall tread upon, that have I given you as I said to Moses. From the wilderness and this Lebanon, even unto the great river, the river Euphrates, all the land of the Hittites, and unto the great sea toward the going down of the sun, shall be your coast."

Inspired by these deep words, Carter soared in spirit in his pulpit in the oak groves—like a prophet. "As Jehovah is my witness," he would shout, almost weeping from earnestness, "That is the Lord God himself speaking to us in this passage—to us here this minute." Thrusting the open Bible before his congregation, he would demand of them an answer. "What does the Book mean by that Lebanon, what is that great river, what is that great sea toward the going down of the sun?" Without pausing an instant, he would cry out his answer. "What could be plainer, my brothers—verily, it is our Lord speaking of the Blue Ridge Mountains, the Father of Waters, the great Western Ocean. It is the promised land, folks—our own land of Canaan."

Carter was able always to find in the Bible whatever he sought. What he was about now in reality was to wage a holy crusade. God was promising settlers a new continent and the savages inhabiting it were no more deserving of notice than were the old Hittites. This sermon always had devastating effect. In the name of the Almighty, it stirred the wanderlust in a people given by instinct to traveling, a people looking for any kind of excuse to move on.

Carter favored another subject in his pulpit—repentance. "Man is born of woman to sin and in sin...it is the fate of us all to struggle in this sin...to fight, even to kill...to commit the seven deadly things...so do not bow yourself forever because of your troubles. Repent, my friends, ask Jesus to forgive you, start over..." It was this doctrine that led Carter into theological difficulty. A heated controversy arose between him and the Reverend Alfred John Noble, another itinerant minister, over the doctrine of general and limited atonement. The whole wilderness rose up, took sides with the two preachers and the two principal characters themselves became enemies for life. At the height of this quarrel they met face to face one day in the road and Noble shouted out at Carter, "Good morning, you despot, you tyrant—lording it over God's creation."

"You are one of the horns of the seven-headed beast spoken of in the Revelations," replied Carter.

"You're a damned liar," shouted Noble, getting down from his horse.

"Don't you call me a damned liar, you seven-headed beast," yelled Carter.

"You heard me." Rushing at Noble, Carter hit him a hard blow in the right eye, and Noble being as experienced as Carter, being himself a former blacksmith, struck back. His hairy big fist landed in Carter's teeth, knocking out two. Reaching home that evening, his head aching, Carter startled Clarissa with the announcement, bitterly made, that his preaching days were over. "What is the matter," Clarissa said sarcastically, with her usual nagging way. "Has the novelty wore off already?" Carter said nothing; that scotched that conversation. He never was able to say many things to his wife, never talked with her of his problems, never told her of his secret dreams.

"For a change," goaded Clarissa, "why don't you try a little work?"

"All right," said Carter, furiously angry, "all right."

So Carter, the wanderer, the restless promoter of endless frontiers, remained at home for a season, plowing in the green corn in the Keowee bottoms, stirring his great muscles over tough weeds and grasses. He enjoyed for a time the deep joys of the man who plants, he felt the beauty of a straight furrow and the quiet rapture of seeing a crop growing stronger and higher under the broiling sunshine—there was a small fraction of Carter's being that appreciated the beauty of farming, but it was very small. Sometimes dropping his light blue shirt, he would sing—almost as another race of field hands was to sing in later days in these same bottom lands, chanting his own mind. "O, I'm going to raise more corn than Silas Caldwell...yes, law." And he would raise his tired, sweat-streaked torso and turn his wondering eyes to the mountains, hallowed with eternal quiet, beyond rest and work. The spell of this sight would quiet Carter. Sometimes coming as close as anything ever did toward bringing him content.

The boys laughed at the sight of their father bathed in sweat. "Pa, the monkey'll get you sure as living—he's wrapped his tail around you already." They made him rest, then restraining the hand on the water gourd, they cautioned, "Now don't drink too much water, pa—it ain't good for you—too much cool water in this heat." But Carter gulped anyhow. Carter was prouder than any of the other Caldwells of the corn in his fields.

Before long laying-by time came—August with Sirus the Dog Star in conjunction with the sun. One night a great storm broke over the valley, a torrent of rain fell and within six hours the flood waters rose, sweeping with them the entire crop—in six hours Carter saw the work of a whole year disappear. "It's God's will," mourned Clarissa, accepting the disaster as sent upon them upon divine purpose, but Carter was deeply bitter. "What's the good of this blasted country," said he. He rode off the day after the waters subsided, crossed the mountains, returning two months later in a great nervous hurry, with an inspired account of new prospects.

"Clarissa," he said, kissing his wife, "I've found it—I've seen it at last, I have been in the Promised Land." He told her to get ready, they were moving to the Tennessee country. Quietly Clarissa listened, without batting an eye, rendered mute. Frantically she wanted to scream, to protest with all her jaundiced force against any further wandering on, but she said nothing. So overcome was she that she did not move until Carter had left the cabin; then falling on her feather bed, she wept the bitterest tears of her life. "O God," she cried in despair, "everything is over for me—there is nothing left."

Outside in the fine southern sunshine, Carter was striding one of the Keowee hilltops, triumphantly happy and completely unaware any longer of earthly surroundings. Again he was a prophet, seeing a vision. "God is with us," he said, "it is his will; we go to open a new land for Him; he will call us blessed." He called out to the Almighty. "I am delivered, God," he said, "I am free." Carter began that day to tell Silas of the land beyond the Blue Ridge; in his old vivid way, he told of a great yellow river, winding through deep silt valleys, there were great mountains and fields of marble. Carter whispered a crazy glint in his eye, "Maybe there is gold."

But this time, Silas was not stirred by Carter's tale of wonder and promise in the western distance. "It's no use wasting your time on me, Carter," he said, "this time I'm not going, I'm staying at Keowee." "You're the judge," Carter replied scornfully accepting the decision. "But take my word, brother, someday you'll be sorry." Silas was not persuaded, but Taylor Caldwell was and so was Henry Caldwell. By sheer personal power, Carter went among them, fanning into being a new epic in the fable of a lonely land. "I have seen the country, I know," pleaded he, "…and besides it is the will of God, it is our duty to do this." He spoke with definiteness and a certain awfulness, with conviction and driving force. Within a week, Carter had organized his expedition, a new procession was ready to start out over the wilderness road on another stage of the endless journey.

"We're on our way," shouted Carter as this new caravan gathered to leave Keowee Valley, "We're bound for the Tennessee."

There was the rasping sound of the long land wind, it sustained a strong melancholy note, the wind blew and the sun shone, and Clarissa saying good-bye to Lucinda said, "Will it never end—always moving on, will there never be any rest?" Lucinda put her arms about the other woman. "We'll pour out our red blood in that savage country," Clarissa wept, placing her head on Lucinda's shoulder. "We'll stain the very earth.".

"All aboard," shouted Carter. A frightened look came into the blue eyes of Clarissa.

❧

Carter left his land in South Carolina in Silas' charge—a thousand acres of rich fields and hills covered with primeval forest, strong upland country, rapidly increasing in value. It never occurred to Carter not to trust his own blood brother.

CHAPTER FOUR

Silas in those days was filled with plans and hopeful purpose. Long before now he had worn a path from the cabin on the hillside to the hilltop where already in his mind the house of his dreams was standing. He spent many hours there, brooding, planning rooms and stairways and porches; often accompanied by Silas, the oldest of the boys, he made long trips through the woods searching for the biggest and strongest trees—timber for this mansion.

"It's to be a great house, son," he said time and again to young Silas. "And you must conduct it in a great way and so must your son and his son." Sometimes Silas shook his head, deeply bewildered. "It's a great responsibility." It was this that bothered him—how could he project this idea into the future, force his dreams on the sons of his sons after the years had taken him on the journey. "How?" Silas spent many hours seeking for a way; for he was determined his house should become great, grow and last. He was determined before he died to leave it in the midst of so many rich acres of cultivated land that its economic independence would be assured; but how could he force his son's sons to keep it so, keep it free from debt, keep it ever from being divided or sold? For a long while, Silas considered drawing up a will forbidding his heirs forever from borrowing money or selling an acre of Keowee. But he rejected this—both life and the future were too uncertain, he would not bind his sons in any such manner; it would be the way of force, and force would not be the way. Silas realized that if Forest Mansion was to live on and become the home of a strong family, it would have to live from generation to generation on spirit.

Silas set out to create this spirit. He began to talk long and often with young Silas. Also Silas began to drive everyone about him, forcing the Caldwells to work from daylight to dark. There was so much delay, it took so long to get anything done and he was no longer young; Silas would rage and shout; he got more impatient every day. But there were forces in the wilderness that not even Silas could elude or order. There were Indian troubles and there were hard times and sickness. Also there was the vast problem of the wilderness itself. It took the Caldwells three years to clear enough land merely to supply themselves with hominy and meal and flour. And after Silas' field had been cleared and his cabin raised and caulked and covered, he and his sons had to give their time to Carter and Will Caldwell and the other cousins, helping them cut trees and build their cabins. Ten years passed and still they were poor, living still in log houses. It almost drove Silas crazy.

And then the flood came, sweeping away the corn in the bottoms. It was on this night that Silas finally admitted the first of his defeats. "Lucinda," he said, raising his voice above the hurricane sounds, "It's too big a job for any one man—we can't do everything. We'll never be able to educate the boys as they should be—we'll have to give up our dream for their culture; they'll have to make out the best they can with what they can pick up. Culture will have to wait until the fields are cleared and the house built—it'll have to be for our children's children."

Silas was very discouraged.

Looking the next morning across the swollen flooded valley of the Keowee, Silas went for a long tramp over the hills, taking young Silas with him. He would create the spirit.

"Son," he said, "never sell a foot of the land—never mortgage an acre, no matter what. If times are hard—do without. Remember that nothing in the world can ever budge us if we hold on to the land—we'll be above everything. We won't divide it either. Oldest sons will have to succeed oldest sons. Younger sons and daughters will receive what ready money is available and, whenever they are in trouble—a seat at our table must always be set for them."

So, believing in the strength of owning land, Silas walked on. Climbing once again to the hilltop where the house was to stand, the father pointed out to the son the exact location he had chosen. "It must be a plain house with plain trimmings," he said, "the very simplest form of building—no white pillars nor plastered columns." Belonging to the plain upcountry, the frontier—Silas scorned the plastered columns of the great houses of Charleston. Columns for him were a symbol. Houses with gleaming porticos were too much like palaces to suit his backwoods taste. "Don't ever let anything change your simple ways and your plainness, son," said Silas, continuing his flow of counsel to his silent boy. "Remain a common man—always belong to the common people."

Switching his talk again to Charleston and its people, he said suddenly in a blaze of fury that Charlestonians should be driven from America, "They're an alien race." Then Silas sat down on a rotting log at the very top of the hill in the midst of a tangle of black-berry briars and foxgrapes. "The central room of Forest Mansion," said he, "will be here." It would be an immense room with splendid mantels of Carrara marble and large open fireplaces at either end. The walls would be panels of white pine eighteen inches wide, and overhead the beams would be 'of heart of cedar. The wide floorboards, hardest oak, would be polished until they glistened with beeswax; all woodwork would be hewed simply and squared; and about this great central room, extending the circumference of the house, there would run, one-story high, a series of smaller rooms with space in the middle of the west elevation left open for a small piazza. Above the central room and of the same dimensions would rise a second floor but here instead of one room there would be four rooms. The roof would be pitched and shingled in wide cedar and there would be no eaves—the roof would rise from the walls of the house even. It would give a more severe appearance. Stones from the fields would be used for the chimneys and the outer walls would be of pine clapboard; the posts for the porch would be square and small, almost like spindles, and for doorsteps—long slabs of split granite would be piled, piece on piece.

Suddenly Silas quit speaking. Staring away into the mists over the valleys, he said to himself—how could he make this son feel as he felt, explain to him the yearning, searching, restlessness of the spirit that was within him, make him feel about this great wilderness house as he felt. O how! He wondered and young Silas watching his father, also wondered—of what was his father thinking?

That afternoon, the father and son cut down some fine cedar trees which they hauled back to the cabin, piling the logs under a shed with other choice woods that Silas was gathering to go into the house—white and red oak from the slopes beyond the burying ground, heart of pine from a ridge farther north, holly and sycamore from the river banks.

"This is the ceiling in the big room," Silas said of the cedars.

That night, Silas worked by firelight on a weather vane for Forest Mansion—a rooster on which he had been carving for more than two months. It was a rooster with a long flowing tail and long spurs, all colored with chrome and ochre. It was a fine rooster and Silas knew it. Silas had a gift and feeling for carving. Also he could make fine furniture; the cabin was beginning to fill with the beds and chairs he had fashioned for the future Forest Mansion. After coating the rooster that evening with a new tint of the chrome, he worked for an hour on the first leaf of a dropleaf table. It was something that Lucinda wanted.

As Silas tinted and carved on these things and cut down trees in the woods and raged because so many things happened to delay his purpose, Lucinda cooked over an open fire on the hearth and baked bread from sour dough and spun and wove. She pieced quilts—the May Apple, the Cartwheel, the Rising Sun being her favorites; she cared for old Narcissa's hollyhocks, peach trees and roses, most of which had grown luxuriously in the rich dirt about the cabin. Often in mixing dyes for staining new homespun, Lucinda would refer to Narcissa's herb book. And also during these early years at Keowee, Lucinda became the mother of two more children—daughters, the first of whom she named Narcissa Lucinda and called Narcissa, third of that name—for Lucinda was as determined to have a Narcissa in the family as the great-grandmother in Pennsylvania had been to have an Annie. In a burst of pity for frontier women, Lucinda called the second girl Patience.

Lucinda on the surface was quiet and meek; she asked no questions, seldom expressed her will. She seemed prepared to follow her husband, ready to do what he wanted to do at his convenience. She was a home-maker, whether in an oxcart or in a cabin; her character was as a still pool in the midst of rushing waters, and whether happy or not, she usually gave the appearance of being so. Silas never knew really what went on in his wife's inner mind, she never told him. Lucinda liked to sit in the sunshine when there was time and read the Bible aloud to her children. Usually the psalms were her favorites—she too like old Narcissa could lift up her eyes unto the hills to receive strength and her favorite images were the green pastures and. the still waters.

"God," she said one day, talking to the Deity as there was no one else to talk to, "I hope heaven will be like that—a quiet, safe place, filled with rest." Desolately lonely, Lucinda on that day was overwhelmed by a sense that she and her family were the only living beings in the world; she was not Lucinda—she was Eve, the only woman. Looking over the great southern valleys about her, she felt this might be the garden—man had never lived and here was she and here was Silas to leave the mark of their hands forever. Then she felt exalted. It was a wonderful thing to be alive in the clean morning of time, so little had been done, there was so much to do. Lucinda raised her voice, gloriously sang, "O I feel the fire burning in my heart."

Lucinda often sang with Stephen John the simple songs of the backwoods—"Jesus shall reign where'er the sun," "Our God our help in ages past." There was a deep unexpressed understanding between this wilderness mother and this dreaming son.

> "…I am a pilgrim bound for heaven,
> and a stranger in this land…"

These hymns were very real to them both.

Lucinda's children were the only concern now of her life—she taught them after Narcissa's death, told them stories of the wild highlands of Virginia where she had been born and reared. Often she went with them on their little journeys about the valley. She thought they were happy.

When they were not working in the new ground, the children liked to fish in the back-waters of Keowee and in the still pools; for days at a time they would watch red-headed woodpeckers and nuthatches walk downward on trees, pecking bark; they followed crows and buzzards to their roosts but they ran away from the buzzards, afraid they would vomit on them; they fed green flies to spiders, tied threads to the frail legs of junebugs, imprisoned lightning bugs in an old iridescent bottle that had been brought over the wilderness trail, and they listened with endless wonder to such things as the clear two-note song of the katydids. Lucinda told them the first katydid always sang sixty days before frost. In secret the children wondered at the odd habits of tumble bugs, living in dung, and they studied the birds, the way they flew, and they came to know the birdsongs. There was the howling of the wolves to listen to in winter, the screaming of the panthers.

And there was the stale of polecats, and the southern sun, and the autumn fog and snow, and corpse flowers and watergliders, suspended on top of water, and the cities spiders hung on a weed, and always dominating everything, there was the granite rim of the mountains. For these children, time itself became timeless in Keowee. For already this was home and the only home—a cabin on a steep hill and a white cloud and a swift river and mica and the taste of cornbread with chittlings and the sight of sorghum molasses pouring from a jug in January and a red haw and a red field and a chinquapin and a red bird, feathers ruffled, in a swamp in December and a mocking bird singing in a wild rose hedge at midnight and the smell of cape jesamine on coffins and the blue skim over the eyes of the dead, and the songs. And there was the song their mother sang…"Hallelujah."

Brooding home in the south! It was a sorrowing land these children loved, moody and often melancholy, and these children reared within its hollows reflected its somber, ecclesiastical, wild power. Inclined naturally to the solemn, they received as they grew older a still deeper tendency to silence. They walked where there was no one, lay upon the old gray outcrops of granite, smooth and worn by all the great forces that beat and wear down and overcome—the oldest strata of rock in the universe and there was the feeling of eternity for them in the far blue shadows—they too seemed weary, hanging there on the edge of the world, silent and still, as though waiting for the end of time. They listened to old dusty winds blowing in from the west; they passed whole days alone, living dreams of their own, consulting their own fancies. The great clouds of the south hung over Keowee and on the mountains the thunderstorms broke, violent and vast and free, and in their hearts these growing children longed and yearned and passionately sought for something beyond.

One morning at breakfast, Silas turned to the boys, all busily eating hominy and red gravy and ham. "Boys," he said, "get out the horses, the oxcart, and the ox."

"What for, sir," said young Silas.

"You all are going to Charleston," said Silas. Young Silas dropped the fork from his hand; Stephen John looked up, his mouth wide open. "Charleston!" repeated the younger Silas. "Pa, you're fooling."

"I ain't fooling," said Silas, "you all are going down there to fetch the marble mantles for Forest Mansion." The boys dashed from the cabin, delighted. Charleston, the great world! "We'll hear singing and see dancing," said the younger Silas. "And lots of sights at night…and…" The boy's experience was so slight, the sphere of his worldly knowledge so bound by wild rivers and lonely mountains, that for a moment he could think of no other city pleasures.

"And wild women," added the younger Carter. He had learned from listening in lofts, from lying in bush thickets—he knew. Stephen John said not a word. Following his brothers, close at their bare heels, running toward the barns, Stephen John seemed to walk on air—dizzy Icarus, just about to fly!

They left in the half-afternoon—first the younger Silas, driving the cart at father Silas' order and made responsible for the delivery in Broad Street, Charleston, of eleven packets of furs and pelts and for the safe return to Keowee of the costly Italian marbles. Behind the cart on horseback followed the younger Carter and Stephen John—the first, broad and powerful with a capable face, marked by will power and passionate desires; the second, somewhat slighter, with an appealing wistfulness in his look, a boy still as innocent as an angel. Bringing up the rear of this expedition rode the younger Will Caldwell and Wade Caldwell, the cousins.

These boys rode down through the hills, dusty travelers in a new part of the world, their mountain garments red from the dry clay dust of the uplands, the red rich soil which at twilight lay like a robe of velvet over the earth. They chose the way by Pendleton, a town about a square, and Corner Creek to the settlement at Ninety Six. Fifteen days from home their cart and ox and their four horses crossed the band of yellow sand which like a stone wall divided the Carolina hillmen from the lowland men and the sea. They left the red hills and suddenly entered a strange land within their own borders—crossed immense still rivers, stained and brackish; they rode for miles around deep swamps.

"This country seems like it's asleep," said Stephen John.

"It smells like it's dead," said Carter.

One day for the first time in their lives they saw magnolias in the full burst of bloom. "I despise them," instantly said Stephen John. Those sensuous cream petals, so close to putrefaction, seemed to him brazen and unblushing, they had no sense of shame. They moved on over the flat earth among great pine trees with long needles, among ancient cypresses and live oaks, tangled with moss; slowly they traveled mile after mile over long flat lands, watching the sun rise, circle and set on the edge of a flat world; at night unconsciously they kept a brighter fire burning, crept a little closer together, for the deepness of these strange swamps at night made them uncomfortable; they were not accustomed to such black darkness; the night in the flat country seemed to close them in, hem them about, stir their forebodings. Strange cries rose from these unknown forests, sounds they had never heard, and over there in the murkiness, something sinister was moving.

So they piled the logs on their fires and slept closer together—strangers in their own country, in Carolina; the far hills of Virginia and savage Tennessee, even the rolling western lands of the Mississippi would have been more familiar by far to these mountain boys than these marshes and salty swamps. Within them stirred the uneasiness that highlanders have always known when crossing the border—this was not their country, theirs lay northward and toward the west; this was the south, ocean country, and they were invaders. So they were cautious, on their guard.

Soon they were among great clearings; immense fields stretched before them and there was a new smell in the air and new birds flew through the soft air. They had entered the region of the great plantations. Sometimes they saw the great white houses, lying miles away at the end of long avenues bordered with trees—vistas creating the impression of vastness and space commanded, as impressive, as free to the sight as the view over the mountains. This was not their country.

One morning the Caldwells were overtaken by a group of gay young men and women, all wearing the finest clothes that the youths from the upcountry had ever seen, all saddled on the finest horses. They were laughing and talking, their ringing voices sounding happy and carefree, and the boys drove their bullock cart far to one side so that there might be room for the strangers to pass.

"But why must you go to such a place as Camden," they heard a young woman saying to a young man, evidently a visitor and planning this trip. It was a rich, stirring voice, immensely exciting to the Caldwells. "I must—I absolutely must," said the young man, speaking his words in a drawling way, very strange.

"It's the end of the world," said the girl, riding forward rapidly, still with a laughing, note in her voice. "Nobody lives there—nobody who is anybody at all ever came from Camden. No one, really. So why bother?"

"The Richardses came from Camden."

Again there was the rich sound of the girl's quick laugh. "Oh, yes—the Richardses. An old house but NOT an old family." As the group neared the boys, they reined in their fine horses; then galloped swiftly by. One of the young men nodded but the others—the girl with the laughing, teasing voice, the visiting young man—they did not even look at the boys; quickly, they rode on.

The Caldwells, sensitive and proud, realized what had happened; they knew they had been ignored and no one had ever ignored them before; it made them very angry. "Damned cavaliers," said Silas, furiously watching the gay young men and women riding away. "They might at least have passed the time of day—not that we care but they at least might have done it. You'd think we were oxen or something—that we didn't even exist." He determined after that to keep his oxcart in the middle of the road. "I'll show them," he said. All day long, he planned to block the path of the riders as they came back but his fury came to nothing—they did not return.

This was not their country, these were not their people.

Two days later the boys were traveling along the edge of a rice field when Carter's horse, shying suddenly, lost its footing and fell. Pitched forward, Carter landed on his left shoulder. He was in great pain. The boys spread down a heavy coat and placed Carter upon it; they thought of riding away for a physician but they did not know in which direction nor where to go.

"Where does it hurt worst," said Silas, rubbing the injured shoulder with bear oil. Carter winced and groaned. They were wondering what to do next when a stranger, also driving an oxcart, appeared.

"Howdy," he said. Without waiting for an answer to his greeting, he swung himself from his cart and walked over to Carter, beginning to make an examination.

"Shoulder's dislocated," he said. Soon he had the bone in proper position, gave it a sudden jerk, and after a wincing stab of pain, Carter was comfortable. "I learnt that in the campaigns," the stranger said, grinning. "A man picks up some good everywhere if he's a mind to—that's my observation." He was a hungry looking man, middle-aged. Again he licked his loose lips and grinned. He was lonely and anxious for companionship. His oxcart was loaded with swamp liquor.

"You boys headed for Charleston," he said.

"Yes, sir," said young Silas, directly and in his friendliest manner.

"Then how about joining bands?"

"Fine," said Silas, and the stranger grinned. "My name is Parkin," he said. "John William Parkin." He held out his awkward hand and Silas shook it. That night after supper, John William brought out a jug of moonshine, a heavy brown jar. "Have a swig, boys," he said, rubbing the unstoppered jug neck with his dirty hands. The eyes of the boys sparkled with excitement. For none of them had tasted whisky. But they were anxious for the experience. Whisky was one of the mysterious things of the great world and they wanted to know the ways of the great world, to taste everything for themselves and to know the different feelings.

"It's A1 good liquor," said John William, "Guarantee it myself."

"Thank you, sir," said Carter, holding the jug with his uninjured right hand and arm. Carter took a deep swallow of the powerful fierce glowing liquor. It burned like fire. "You act like it was poison," yelled John William, nudging the boy. Carter laughed, but he knew then he liked this taste, this searing fire. Then Silas drank and Wade and Will. "Sure is good," said Wade blinking, hardly able to keep back the tears.

Wiping the jug with his fingers, John William handed it now to Stephen John. But Stephen John looked sternly at the wild laughing man who was licking his thin blue lips savagely. "No," said Stephen John. "Well, God A'mighty, son," said John William, "don't bite me."

So Stephen John who wanted more than any of them to taste the fire of liquor, whose secret spirit was craving, starving for experience—he turned away; he refused and blindly, furiously he cursed himself for not taking the risk, for not daring. Also he turned upon his brothers and cousins for their possession of a fearlessness which he did not possess. And he was angry with John William.

Around the circle the jug went again and Stephen John got up and left. Why not, he asked himself bitterly in the darkness. What difference would it make, who would care? He determined to force himself to drink of this powerful mysterious whisky; he returned to the campfire for that one purpose but when the jug came round again he passed it on, untouched—some tragic, restraining sensitiveness, buried deep within him, would not release him, he could not put the bottle to his mouth.

Humiliated and ashamed, defeated, Stephen John sat back in the shadows, listening to the easy friendly talk of this strange man, whose home seemed to be this campfire, whose friends these chance acquaintances of this evening—this restless wanderer, one of the wilderness dreamers, always moving, always on the go. John William had traveled far, had seen much; even his talk was a traveler's talk, far away and touched with wonder and magic. Fascinated, Stephen John listened.

"...When a man has got to fight," said John William, his hand on the handle of the jug, "it's a natural sort of thing enough but when he has got nothing to eat, it's an unnatural state." Now he took another drink. "I have heard of men who said they would rather fight than eat but, boys, to tell you the truth I never met one." The bright fire blazed and John William, his face glowing, talked on. Far away in the long ago, he was a soldier, fighting the French and Indians. "They began to shut us in, every day a little closer—first they closed a door on one side and then on the other, till at last they were at our back door and they shut that up and double bolted it. They had us. We were shut in and had nothing to do but look out and we had nothing to eat. Well, boys, we got taken at last and surrendered because we were starving. I shouldn't have minded it much, it was the fortune of war but they insulted us—as soon as they got our arms from us, they tried to wean us from our cause. It was a blasted cowardly trick in them." John William kicked together the burning ends of the blazing logs of the fire. On he wandered through his lonely memories…"A soldier's a soldier no matter what side he is on…and they are the naturalest people in the world for fellow feeling. One day a soldier's up and the laugh is on his side and next day he is down and then the laugh's against him." Up went the jug again—up and down and around; heavily John William laughed. Getting drunker, his tales sank lower, became more coarse. He flung his long legs away from the fire. "Women and whores," he shouted; he began gloatingly to talk of them, all the beautiful couchant whores who lived in houses along the waterfront in Charleston, pink and fat, soft as goose feathers, he said, scrimpy, dumpy, lean and lank ones, thin as a rail. "Any kind and ever kind, boys—Charleston has got them." His dark eyes glittered, he spoke of brothels with the same ecstasy that some preachers of the gospel use in describing Zion. Scorpio the loins was also John William's sign.

He was drunk now. So were Carter and Silas drunk, so were Will and Wade. "Ah God," said John William, "Charleston has got fine women."

"Hurray," said Carter who had never been more excited in his life. "Hurray," he yelled.

Looking up suddenly, John William saw the fierce stern eyes of Stephen John on him. "Don't look at me like that," he said. Stephen John did not move a muscle. "Don't—I tell you." John William's drunken voice was pleading. Then something caused this strange man's whole expression to change, a quiver passed over his face, a mask was lifted and there, bare and unprotected, was revealed a lonely, desperate, desolate human being. "I ain't the only one, son that has been spoiled in his religion by these wars and wild ways of living." He spoke quietly and there was a note of earnestness in his voice, filled with infinite sorrow and regret, "I had both politeness and decency until we got to squabbling over our own chimney corners." Impulsively the jug was raised and John William drank. "When a man's conscience begins to get hard," he muttered, "it does it faster than anything in nature." John William began to weep a drunk man's tears; then his head flopped, one of his hands fell like a dead man's to his side.

It was midnight before the yelling and roaring and vomiting was over. Wide awake, Stephen John lay still, listening to the frogs in the deep pools—the solemn night sounds; miserable and unhappy, he was thinking.

"Damn us all, God," he said bitterly, "damn us all."

They rode in the late afternoon through the narrow streets of the rich city of the south, awed as poor shepherds reaching Jerusalem from the edges of the Sinai deserts. Slowly they moved, staring, gazing upon lacquered carriages, harness shining with damascene metal, sky blue silks brought round the world from China, plum brocades and laces, the great town houses of the cavaliers of the plantations with their marble doorsteps, leaded glass, carved doors, grilled gateways of wrought iron. And there were the luxurious half-hidden gardens bursting with indigo crepe myrtle, the red oleander, flowers the boys had never seen. It was so very strange and bewildering and rich. Charleston frightened them, there were so many people, moving in so many directions, carriages and wagons and carts dashing through the streets, there seemed no purpose to all this wild movement, no order; several times they only narrowly avoided a collision. But it was the great world and here were they—riding through it, happy and wildly exhilarated by the intenseness of their new experience.

"My," said Carter, "it's exciting." He rode on, his fine head held high.

The din of the city interested them, the sounds of carriage wheels and horses' shod hooves against the stone paving blocks, the many voices, careless and low and high-pitched and loud, the laughing—the songs of the street hucksters with honey and ears of corn and green beans in baskets. And Negroes—black and big, glistening broad and tall and bright yellow, they had never seen so many Negroes. From somewhere Stephen John heard a tinkling sound like water falling on rocks. Never in his life had he even dreamed of a sound so liquid pure. Rushing his horse to John William's side, he cried, "What is it." John cocked an ear. "It's a harp," he said. It was a wonderful thing—for the first time to hear a harp.

A beautiful girl in a pink satin dress stood on a street corner, talking to a handsome young man, who was looking at the girl and laughing. They looked so fine and friendly that Stephen John, when the boys drove past, smiled too. "Hello," he said. The boy and girl did not return this greeting. Looking for a moment at the young man who had spoken to them, they turned their backs. They did not recognize Stephen John

Carter, who was watching, laughed at his brother and Stephen John blushed.

"It's a sinful, wicked city," said Stephen John, gazing with northern reproach and anger on these scenes of splendor.

"Stevie, for Jesus' sake," said Carted, "for one time have some fun."

John Williams showed the boys the way to the inexpensive well known inn where they were to stay, the Wooden Whistle in old Meeting Street, an old time place with piazzas extending over the sidewalk. A little man with white hair and a broad red face rushed out joyously to greet them. "Are you all the boys of Silas Caldwell," he asked, smiling and warmly friendly. He took the bridal of Carter horse which he had become frightened.

"Yes sir," said young Silas.

"Well, come right in boys, welcome—I've been expecting you." The little man, proprietor of the inn, was one of those men who like everyone and who never forgot a name nor face. He began talking to the boys about Silas the elder. "Used to stop here every time he came in to trade—that was when you all lived in North Carolina." Still smiling, he led the way up some creaking steps. This friendly greeting pleased the boys, giving them a reassuring feeling among so much that was strange and chaotic; is pleased them to know that someone in Charleston who knew who they were—someone knew they were the Caldwells.

"How is your father?" asked the innkeeper. "He is fine, sir," said Silas. "And how is your Uncle Carter—he's one of my oldest customers; many a night your Uncle Carter has slept in the Wooden Whistle." Silas said that his uncle had gone on West, on to Tennessee.

"On to the Tennessee, well, I declare," said the innkeeper.

"And how's your Grandma Narcissa?"

"She's dead."

"She's dead, well, I declare. Well sir it's the way of the world. You don't see nor hear of a dead body for a year or two and then you see somebody and how is so and so and they say—oh, didn't you hear, she died. Yes, sir, it's that way, boys." The proprietor flung wide a door, opening into a clean room with two big beds. "Here is your room—it's your home in Charleston." A window was raised, cold water poured in a basin, then the innkeeper turned to go away. "Soon as you boys are ready—you just come downstairs and we'll have a big hot supper ready."

In a few minutes, the hungry youths were eating gumbo soup and flaky steamed Charleston rice and turkey hash and fried chicken; later there were large helpings of apple dumplings, sweet with honey and brown sugar. They ate enormously and the innkeeper laughed; it pleased him to see the customers enjoy their rations.

Later that evening, John William came by the inn. "Boys, he said licking his blue lips and grinning. "Let's go for a little walk—what do you say." Enthusiastically, the group agreed. Slyly the fat hand of the proprietor was waved in their faces. "Now you all be careful—don't you get into any trouble."

Laughing and feeling fine, the boys hurried into the street—into the great mysterious streets of a city at night for the first time in their lives. And the experience filled with wild happiness; in the cloaked city night, they sensed a promise of endless adventure. They started.

"Well boys," drawled John Williams, "what would you all like to see first?" John William licked his lips, looking at the radiant faces about him.

"The women," said Carter, unhesitatingly

"Ah," he protested, "I was a little drunk I guess when I was talking."

"But we want to see them," Carter insisted. He had not forgotten a word. "Some that are pink and fat and soft as goose's feathers."

A frightened look came into Stephen Jon's face. "I'm going to look at the ocean," he said. John William glanced for a moment at Stephen John. "All right son," he said, pointing southward with one of his dirty fingers. "Hit's that way, keep straight ahead."

So Stephen John walked away; he started out alone through the lamplight and again was that strange bitterness within him. He started off toward the sea, the boundless waters, but before he reached he sea, Stephen John came to St. Michaels. He slipped into the chill, stately place, into the gloom, stood there before the gold cross and the burning candles, the stained windows. He listened to the diapason notes of the great organ, and the deep song stirred depths in his soul that had never before been touched. The cornopean sounded, and he wanted to shout aloud to God. Here at last was glory.

He fell on his knees and after a time began to pray. He did not know why nor was he conscious of what he was saying. The boy knew only that there was a great unsatisfied something burning within—some great unexpressed longing, an intolerable yearning. Suddenly, he began to weep. "I want to go," he said, "But I was afraid."

Rushing back to the inn, he talked for a while with the friendly innkeeper; then he wrote a letter to his mother. He did not tell her of the glory he had sensed in the church nor of the anguish that had made him burst into tears. He did not know how to put that feeling into words and would not had he been able; he lived a secret life; Stephen John did no confiding. He wrote of other things.

"...I saw some of the ugliest folks in this world. Their heads are about a foot behind their shoulders and their feet turn in and they are bow-legged. But I saw one or two that were all right. The man that runs this inn would do first rate if he would just let me have some thread—I wanted to mend a hole. But he said he had no thread. He told me about the wicked people over in London that he had heard about; he said when they went to church the preacher would pray for the soldiers and for peace and the men would say amen. But when he would pray for the soldiers' wives that they might have the comforts of life, and that the men might open their hearts and give them these comforts—why, the men were all still as death, no response at all. He does not believe there is any Christianity in the world at present but that the people have gone plumb crazy."

Stephen John stood the next day looking over the celebrated harbor of Charleston, toward the thunder of the sea, toward the small island far off in the distance, the far low shores of the bay, smelling the iodine and the salt, watching the waves break and the floating lightness of the sea weed. Long did he stand there, dreaming, filled with loneliness, utter and immense.

And inspired, he determined for the first time to make something important of his life. "I'm going to be somebody," he said to the ocean, "I'm going to amount to something."

※

While he was there, dreaming and making his promise, his brothers and cousins were forming a plan. The plan originally was Carter's but they all had their part, they laughed a lot about it—it seemed the funniest scheme they had ever thought of. Eating more fluffy steamed rice and more turkey hash that night at the Wooden Whistle, they hardly were able to keep their faces straight, they all were that excited. Then John William suggested that they walk to St. Philip's to look at the lantern hanging in the tall tower of the highest steeple in Charleston—a guide for ships far to sea. At once, the boys agreed.

"Come on, Stevie," said Carter.

"All right," said Stephen John. So they hurried out and soon there rose before them, looming above a narrow street, the form of this soaring church. "It is beautiful," said Stephen John, looking in wonder upward at the spire looming against the night. High up he saw the gleam of the yellow lantern.

A moment later he turned with the others into a cobbled alley behind the church, to look with them all at the beacon from another angle. Then suddenly his arms were pinned to his sides; a door was beaten upon and Stephen John was pushed into a house that had a worn turkey red carpet on its sagging floors; thick red curtains covered the windows and there was almost no furniture. John William and the boys bellowed, pointed their bullying fingers at Stephen John. Several women, worn looking and tired, came into the shabby room through an open back door. "Here he is," cried Carter, motioning toward his brother. The women looked at Stephen John without changing their expression—these were seafront women, accustomed to the attentions of teamsters and deep-sea sailors. They had been eating supper of turnip greens and fatback bacon. One of them was picking her teeth.

"Well, here he is—the virgin."

The boys held Stephen John by his arms and legs, stripping him of his clothing and then they tied him to a post in the center of the big bare room. The woman who had been picking her teeth removed most of her clothing and without any show of mirth began moving about Stephen John. In a hard voice, she began singing a song. Carter and Silas laughed. "Ain't it the funniest sight you ever saw," said Carter, "ain't it?"

For Stephen John, this was the crucifixion.

※

It was early morning, dark and chilly, before the boys returned to their hotel in Meeting Street; there waiting for them was the old inn man, still wearing his day clothes. He rushed to Silas, grasping at his hands. Worried and showing his distress, he said, "I don't know what has happened, but the young gentleman, your brother—he's gone."

This frightened the boys. Already they were ashamed of themselves, their intention had been to go straight to Stephen John and to ask him to forgive them, they were sorry.

"He came in here and got his things and rushed right out again." said the anxious publican. "I did everything I could to stop him but it wasn't any use; he said he was going home."

Sheepfacedly, as though telling some secret that should not be told the proprietor said, "He was crying like a child."

❧

Stephen John rode hard, and at first his mother and father were too frightened even to speak when they saw their son, dusty and worn from hard travel, come riding into the clearing alone. Both parents thought the same thing at once—there had been an Indian ambush.

Finally, Silas Spoke. "Son, where are your brothers?"

"I left them," answered Steven John, wearily.

'Why did you leave them?"

"I didn't like it at Charleston"

And that was all that he ever told them. What he had not liked, what he had seen, what had happened to him, whom he had met—to all questions about those things, Stephen John shook his head.

Silas shook his head. "A strange child, Lucinda."

Leave him alone, Silas," Lucinda answered. Lucinda loved this wistful boy more than her other children together. 'Gentle Savior," she prayed. 'If you can have no mercy for any of the rest of us—have mercy upon Stephen John."

Several weeks later the other boys returned, bringing safely in the oxcart the costly Italian marbles, and it was not long after this that the family, one windy day, was gathered about the dinner table—Silas and Lucinda and all the other children and Artemissa and Oliver her idiot boy and her other children—and Silas was reading from an almanac, saying soon the pathway of the sun would lie in the middle stars of Taurus, he was saying this when there was a commotion in the cabin yard, a dog barked and the chickens cackled. Suddenly, a figure in torn linsey-wood appeared at the door, gaunt and ill. It was the older Carter Caldwell, back from the Tennessee.

"Silas," he cried, utterly exhausted. "We're starving." Running to his brother, Silas held Carters arms and helped him to a chair by the fire; Lucinda brought him a glass of milk.

"Times are awful hard beyond the mountains," said Carter, "and I've come to ask you to help us." He was very weak and thin, his wasted condition alarmed Silas. Sipping the cool milk, Carter began quickly to tell of Indian attacks and smallpox and the ague that had followed that and after that there had been fever. Carter had himself been sick for six weeks with smallpox and complications and on recovering had been sick for another two months from fever. Conditions had become so perilous with the Caldwells that Carter although just able to sit on a horse had decided he would be obliged to return to Keowee for assistance. On the way, the fever had again attacked him, and burned by these attacks, and weak, he had fallen one day off the horse and had lain for a long time beside a road. He had wrapped the reins about his wrist and then had fainted. On coming to his senses, he had found himself unable longer to stand alone.

"Getting hold of a stirrup," said Carter, "I urged the horse to pull me to a creek at the foot of a hill, and drinking water I was revived and able to continue on." The telling of these experiences brought on a spell of hard coughing, and Carter complained of heavy pain in his chest. Leaning forward, he spat blood into the fire.

"You're tired," said Lucinda like a mother, "You'd better lie down and get some rest." Putting the ill man to bed, she whispered to Silas with foreboding in her voice, "It's the congestion."

"Well, you attend to him," said Silas, "I'm going after Cousin Tom and his boys—we've got to send help right away to Clarissa." All that afternoon and night as Lucinda and Artemissa sat beside Carter, who only at times now was conscious, Silas rode up and down the valley collecting supplies—hams cured in hickory smoke, fine yellow meal and jars filled with soft white lard and bags of hominy and whip-poor-will peas; also powder and lead for bullets. Early the next morning, young Silas and young Carter and young Will and Wade Caldwell and two of the Hunter boys from the lower river were ready to start west with the provisions. It would be a dangerous trip, they all knew, the road lying through the Cherokee country, they having decided to take the shortest cut, the pass through the Great Smokies at Clingman's Dome. Just as the boys were about to depart, Lucinda rushed into the yard with the roots of a lilac bush in her hands. "Give this to your Aunt Clarissa," she said anxiously. Lilacs to Lucinda were a symbol.

So again at Keowee there was waving of farewells to Caldwells on the way to the west.

Carter at the time was out of his mind; despite the dogwood tea and black cherry decoctions fed him by the two women, he was growing weaker. In his fever, he still traveled, and through his mind floated brilliant visions. Through that day he called many times for Clarissa. "Clarissa...Clarissa...it won't be long...we'll settle there..." He came worn and weary to his senses in the late evening. Looking up at Lucinda, he then grasped one of her hands as though by so doing he would be able by force of will to cling on a little longer. "Lucinda," he said, with that profound and knowing look which the dying often assume, "I'm going."

Lucinda tried to be reassuring. "It's not that bad, Carter." But he ignored the reply, making a sort of benedictory sign with his freehand, a helpless wave. "Yes, it is," he said, "I'm dying." Slowly he tried to swallow. Lucinda held a glass of water to his dry lips.

"Lucinda," he said, "I have tried to do good. I have been baptized twice. I have kept the faith... I have entertained the preachers." This brought from him his last burst of laughter. "Everything is straight but one thing...there's one thing I wish I hadn't done..." He wanted earnestly to tell of his stealing the beaver skins, but Lucinda would not allow him. "Whatever it is—it doesn't matter," she cried, placing her hands over his mouth. "Everything is all right, Carter—the Lord allows every good Christian one blot on the record." She could not bear to hear this confessional—a curious trait of hers, she later in a somewhat similar manner was to enforce silence upon both Silas and Stephen John. "Don't say it," she commanded. At this time, Carter did not mind; soon again he drifted into the flame of fever, forgetting the beaver skins and all the rest of his troubles. He was far away traveling in the bright world of disease, into the far land which in reality he had never been able to reach. "What is that high mountain?" he cried, gesturing splendidly. "What is it that I see?" Then for a few minutes the old Carter reappeared. His head sank into the pillow. Plaintively and with effort he said, "I had dreamed of so many great things—there were so many things I had planned." A splurge of phlegmy coughing that did not clear his lungs wracked him. Desperately the dying man cried out, "I've got almost nothing done— Lucinda, I've been such a failure."

Then Lucinda became majestic. "Only little men with little aims ever succeed," she said. "Always the men with great visions are failures." Again Carter took her hands and smiled; Lucinda was comforting to him during the last moments of his consciousness. Toward midnight, he drifted back into the realm of the fantastic; in his delirium sometimes cursing, sometimes talking of the far country, shouting he would carry the news of redeeming love, plant the stand of the cross and gather into the fold of Christ, scattered and perishing souls. Just before the day broke, Lucinda heard death approaching; calling Silas and Artemissa to the bedside, she said, "I can hear the death rattle."

In worn homespun, patched and fresh washed, not a penny at hand, Carter's wasted body was buried on the hill beside Narcissa. He went, he passed on, but in that vast land of the west, among all those great mountains and lonely valleys, his spirit lived on; Silas said at the funeral that his spirit lived on.

"The dead do not die."

So did Carter pass, and in dying left in Carolina a thousand acres of land—those rich fields and that mile of primeval forest which on his first departure for the Tennessee he had entrusted into the hands of Silas.

Silas spent many hours walking in the woods and fields that belonged to Carter. He dug his feet deep in the soft dark earth of the river bottoms, caressed the great trees with his hard hands. This was his madness now—gneisses bordered with primitive limestone, clay tinged with iron.

Land!

He owned a thousand acres of his own and he wanted another thousand. A thousand to a thousand—two thousand acres of land. "It would mean freedom itself," said he to himself. "Freedom for Forest Mansion."

At first Silas did nothing, he waited. He went about his work, hewing timbers for the mansion, gathering the crop and at night carved on the furniture. For months after the boys returned to Keowee from their journey over the mountains, this was his absorbing routine.

A light fall of snow was lying over Carter's grave before Silas did anything about the land that belonged to his brother. Then by hand one day came a letter from Clarissa who having been skilled at complaining as a wife now as a widow already had expanded the habit into an art. "Dear Brother Silas," wrote she. Her letter told of nothing but trouble. Pox and ague and more fevers were plaguing the Tennessee wilderness, there was starvation and sorrow. In a fine indelible ink, Clarissa covered seven pages with the detail, not omitting even running sores and diarrhoea, "the back door trots," as she called it. Concluding, she authorized Silas to help her, a widow, by selling the land in Carolina, naming the figure she would expect him to realize—a sum three times the property's value.

This communication had not been unexpected. Lying in bed at night, sitting by the warm fire, walking through the fields, Silas already had memorized word by word, the answer that this letter would receive when eventually it would appear at Keowee.

"Dear Sister Clarissa," wrote he. "Surely Brother Carter told you; Surely he did not keep such an important thing from you...did you not know that Carter sold the property to me, the whole tract...that I paid him in cash the day you all departed for the Tennessee..." In these few sentences was Silas to make shrewd use of a brother's knowledge of a brother, of Carter's dreaming, his improvident unconcern for money, of the way he frequently misrepresented financial facts to his wife, withheld sums, never telling. Also he was taking advantage of Clarissa's lack of faith in Carter's word, of her knowledge of his concealments. And should worst come to worst, Silas had decided to stake all, to risk his reputation against his sister-in-law's. Whose word would it be? His or hers? The wilderness was casual, seldom were family documents drawn up or recorded—everyone knew that and did not everyone know of his concern, his constant anxiety, often expressed, for the welfare of the family beyond the mountains. Had not he sent them help? And then there was Clarissa's own reputation—it was caustic. Had she not always been filled with criticism and accusations. And finally there loomed between himself and Clarissa two great ranges of mountains—he was in Carolina, she on the Tennessee. Silas felt safe; there could be nothing very effectual that Clarissa could do.

So Silas put on paper the letter he long had planned and he dispatched it. But that night he was unable to sleep. "I have done wrong," he admitted to himself. "But it has been for a great purpose—the end justifies the means." Thrashing about, restless, getting up several times to pile logs on the fire, Silas through that night searched his mind for further justifications. "This land will make Forest Mansion rich—it will mean economic independence, it will set free a long line of Caldwells, in the long run will benefit many people—it'll free them, allow them time to study, allow the Caldwell family to take a place at the councils of the great—they'll be able to direct their energies to the public welfare, stand up for all the ideals and causes the frontier has fought for—they'll be able to work for a better world."

"I must be strong," Silas told himself, "I have a mission and I must take this step because of my mission—I must assume the responsibility." But in spite of all this, Silas worried; often now he was unable to sleep at night and when he did sleep he was tormented by monstrous dreams—he became bad humored and sullen. He drove the Caldwells harder than ever.

Clarissa on her side of the mountains began writing to everyone she knew in Carolina to tell all that Silas had robbed her; soon there were rumors going about and this enraged Silas. He became self-conscious and took insult easily—at church; he imagined people were talking about him, which they were, and whenever he saw a group of people together, he accused them of accusing him of taking something that belonged to his brother. Finally,

Silas could not bear his burden any longer. So one evening, when there was no one in the cabin but himself and Lucinda, he began to weep.

"Lucinda," he said, "I have sinned." He told her what had happened.

"Well," said Lucinda, thoughtfully regarding her husband, "what are you going to do about it?"

Silas' expression changed and he jumped to his feet, transforming himself again into the stern figure of the man that liked to preach sermons on Sundays. "I'm going to stand up next Sunday at the meeting house and confess everything in public and I'm going to give the land back to Clarissa." He pointed his long, mountain fingers at his wife, "I'm going to save my soul."

"No," said Lucinda, suddenly becoming sterner and more forbidding than he had ever known her. "No, Silas, you're not going to do that." Lucinda took charge of this situation. "A man has no right to save his soul at the cost of the good name of his children. A father has not himself to consider alone. If he sins and the sin cannot be proved in public—he must do privately what he can to make restitution but after he has done that, he must bear the rest of his burden." Calmly and coldly, Lucinda declared there was to be no public confession, neither was the property to be returned to Clarissa.

"The damage has been done," she said, "the sins committed."

This made Silas look in astonished amazement at his wife, the gentle, tender, hymn-singing woman from whom he had never heard a stern word. At this moment, Silas realized for the first time that there was a hidden depth in the character of his wife about which he had known nothing.

"There are sins that are worth committing," said Lucinda, exhibiting that tinge of ruthlessness which so many of the Caldwells possessed in the secrecy of their complex characters. "The Lord permits us under circumstances to break any of his commandments. What the Lord demands is not strict obedience—what he demands is atonement. He permits us to do anything if we are willing to take the consequences. So prepare to accept your punishment and don't whine." Then tenderly she added there were dark alleys of sorrow in every human heart. "Everyone carries his burden of secret regret."

Now it was Silas' turn to act as consoler; for Lucinda broke down; she began to cry as she had not since the night on the wilderness road when the baby was about to die. Silas also was moved to tears. Together with their arms about each other, they wept. For both of them loved Carter; they still loved Clarissa, and they knew in their hearts she was in need of the money.

They sat for a long while, staring into the dying fire. "He will chasten me with the rod of men as he chastened David," said Silas, reflecting moodily. He knew then what his punishment would be. Raising her head and looking into Silas' eyes, Lucinda read his mind. "God," she said, "will not let you build Forest Mansion." Bitterly, Silas got up and walked into the darkness. It seemed that he could not bear to give up this greatest hope of his life. He walked for hours that night; he avoided the cemetery where Carter was buried.

Lucinda in her years in the wilderness had learned deeply of the inner ways of men and women. As she was determined to face this issue through, she forced Silas against his will to attend the preaching service the following Sunday at the old stone meeting house. Sitting close beside her husband, she gave a fierce tug to his breeches when the Reverend Mr. McKay, the preacher, announced the congregation would be led in prayer by Brother

Silas Caldwell. As Silas rose, Lucinda gave another tug. A moment later, she heard the deep voice of her husband, mechanically reciting his regular prayer, "Be with us—guide, guard, and protect us." After Silas had taken his seat, the minister in a high flat mountain voice gave out the words of an old hymn:

"The worst of all diseases
Is light compared with sin;
On every part it seizes
But rages most within."

Resolutely, Lucinda raised her voice and sang. She wanted Carter's land even more than Silas did.

Silas was silent as they rode home that afternoon on their horses. In a dejected and beaten mood, he ate very little that evening. "Lucinda," he said, as they sat again before the fire, "we've lost the way." Trying to comfort him, Lucinda began at once to defend their action. "We've given our lives for one ideal—one purpose. There has been reason in everything we have done. What we have done represents progress and we must expect progress to be cruel—it demands victims "She talked rapidly."We have compromised but compromise is inevitable for all who live lives of action—we have done what we had to do. We can't expect to get something for nothing…"

Silas was not listening and Lucinda, looking at him, realized it. Suddenly there swept over her the feeling of unutterable loneliness and infinite remorse. She was tired, and for the first time in her life she felt she was old.

CHAPTER FIVE

Silas did not completely abandon his hope of building Forest Mansion—he still made attempt after attempt to begin work on the house but invariably something happened. First there was the revolution which broke out the year after the death of old Carter; this struggle thwarted his plan for eight years, the boys being seldom at home for any lengths of time. They came and went, serving enlistments in the continental armies. These were anxious times at Keowee as there were many Tories about, old Will Caldwell's youngest son among them, and the savages again were hostile. All of Silas' time was occupied.

Once he thought of hauling some of the finest hewn and sawn beams to the settlement at Ninety-Six for safekeeping but this idea was soon given up; Silas had no assurance that Ninety-Six would prove any securer a place than Keowee. Once Keowee was saved in the nick of time. An army tramped into the valley from the south, fought the savages in a fertile bottom not far below the cabin. Joining in this fight, Silas helped defeat the savages and rode with the Carolinians as they pillaged, ruined Indian women, burned Indian towns, trod down green corn and scattered corn meal for miles through the uplands.

Silas stood one day on a high hill west of Keowee and watching a cloud of dust saw the Cherokees, beaten by longer cannon and swifter bullets, retreat for all time from the valleys of Carolina. It was a moment of exaltation for Silas. It was triumph. He raised his hand in wild salutation as the last of them disappeared from sight. Keowee belonged to the Caldwells now-the lonely land stretching away; they had taken the land as land always had been taken-by force They had taken it from the Cherokees who had taken it from the Creeks who centuries before that had taken it from a tribe forgotten except for pieces of pots. There on a hill in the wilderness, alone in the immenseness, stood Silas and a spirit filled him that was to last in the Caldwells. At that moment all that had been in him that was European, a part of the Old World, was forgotten—he forgot the old centuries, their wars in cramped little countries and their worries, Silas forgot the ocean. He stood in his own land in Keowee—the lineal descendant in spirit of the Cherokee and Creek.

❧

Returning to the cabin from this victory, Silas made one attempt more to build his house—young Carter was at home at the time. But just as they were ready to start the digging of the foundations in the red plutonic field at the hilltop, Silas decided to send a herd of cattle to Philadelphia—he was in need of some money. It would be a long trip, a great risk to run—driving cattle up the face of the continent in war time, but the chance was worth the taking; the price of cattle was very high in the north.

So away in a whirl of red dust went Carter and Will Caldwell's son Wade, and one of the Hunters, the lean one named Tom, quiet and dull but strong, a good hand with steers. Cattle lowed, dogs barked, and the three young men, feeling their strength in the fine morning, sang, "Oh, the downward road is crowded, crowded." Carter turned at the foot of the hill as he always did, waving to his worried mother.

"Boys," cried out Lucinda, "take good care of yourselves."

"Yes, ma'am," shouted Carter, smiling. The boys had ridden off so often they were confident now of coming back.

But this time it was the hound dogs that came back—old Star and Blazeface and Red, ten days later, yelping about the door in the early morning. Hurriedly a searching party was formed and Silas and Will Caldwell and four of the wiry, lean Hunters dashed away on the old north trail, following Oolenoy Creek and crossing the south fork of the Saluda at Douthet's ford. Farther on, in a bend, they found traces of butchered cattle and broken arrows and beside the dead coals of an old campfire—there they found the charred legs and chest of Thomas Hunter. They knew it was Thomas because a scar was on his left breast and he had a partial sixth toe. It was the old frontier tale again for Carter and Wade—they had disappeared, gone on as Patrick had when he left behind lonely Artemissa.

Gathering together the hunks of Thomas' body, the men brought them back in a sack to Keowee, and poor Lucinda, frantic with worry, fainted. Reviving her with volatile salts, Artemissa whispered to her, "Don't give up hope—they may have escaped; they're wilderness boys—their chances one way are as good as another." Artemissa who always hoped, remembering Patrick in the night, believed the boys had escaped. But not Lucinda. Carter her son was dead, she mourned him as dead. She began even to speak of him in the past tense and was making ready to raise a stone in the burying ground to his memory when one day Carter returned. Like one raised from the dead, he stood at the door.

"Hello," he said, laughing at the sight of his mother's consternation. Lucinda wept and praised God. Artemissa also wept but there was a new bitterness in her heart. "Why," said she to herself, "must some folks have all the good fortune." She still grieved in secret for Patrick.

Explaining quickly what had happened, Carter said they had fallen about night into an ambush, the savages had risen yelling from a thicket of wild laurel and the first arrow had killed Tom Hunter.

"A chief took Wade and me," Carter continued, "he and a party of six braves led us for four days through mountain valleys and passes and on the fifth day they brought us to a large camp where four more chiefs received us. We were told these chiefs had decided to learn the white man's language and we were to be their teachers." Lessons then were held in a camp in Hiwassee Valley, lasting for hours, with the old Indians pointing to objects and repeating their English names after the youths. "The old boys were pretty smart," said Carter, looking slyly at his mother. "Only we fooled them; you should have heard the words we taught them for tree and stick." One night during a thunderstorm, Carter continued, he and Wade had escaped; slowly they had made their way across the mountains.

"You don't seem very much disturbed about Tom Hunter's death," said Artemissa coldly.

Carter's manner changed quickly. "I have seen men die before," he said, "I have been in the army."

Carter left the next day to join a new force being recruited. And after his departure, his mother and two sisters and Artemissa returned once more to spinning. "It's women's contribution to the cause of liberty—spinning and cooking," said Lucinda to her strong young son as she had kissed him again and again and told him, "Take care of yourself." As the wheels whirred, Lucinda revealed herself as still another and stranger Lucinda, about whose existence none of the men of her family knew. In that cabin, spinning and weaving,

Lucinda became a woman who was a mother of daughters. She was calculating and shrewd and cunning; she wanted to show her daughters a way of avoiding hardships; more than anything, she wanted comfort for them and security.

"Be careful," she said, whirring the wheel, "avoid risks—beware of taking chances." She preached to them in the secrecy of the cabin a doctrine at exact odds with that creed with which old Carter had stirred so many in the family into action. Lucinda's counsel was passionately selfish and stingy. "Women must learn to make the best of bargains—so always think twice." She warned her daughters against men with the words and ways of poets. "Pick out a hard, steady worker—even if he is ugly and old, it doesn't matter. You don't want to spend all your lives in cabins."

Patience listened to Lucinda but not her sister—not the third Narcissa. Patience was meek and retiring, she always permitted others about her to impose their will upon hers. But Narcissa was different. Narcissa possessed an eagerness that was never suppressed; she was unable to accept anyone's word about anything, not even her mother's. She had to find out for herself; like her Uncle Carter and like Stephen John, her brother, she was filled with moods. Often in the midst of spinning, she would run away for an hour or so to look at the old blue ridge and listen to the whip-poor-wills, watch the mysterious unfolding of a day, watch the sweat bees and the quivering humming birds and the carrion beetles, which also were a part of life.

"Mother," she said, "I don't want a safe life—I want a full arid exciting life. I want to live in a great way."

"Well, it isn't worth it," said Lucinda, greatly provoked.

Narcissa laughed and this was the first time that her yearning for lightness and variety clashed openly with her mother's secret passion for soundness and comfort and money.

So the summer passed at Keowee and in the fall, the women went into the field to help Silas bring in the corn to the high ground, safe from rising waters. They were in the most distant bottom one day, piling stalks, when Artemissa appeared, screaming.

It was death again. This time it was Oliver who had been taken; Artemissa's idiot boy.

Oliver had died, and he was buried, and after the funeral, Lucinda sat down to write the news to the Caldwells in Virginia, Pennsylvania, and on the Tennessee. Then to her own sons in the armies she wrote: "Oliver hadn't been feeling well for sometime, suffered from swelling, but we let him alone for a few days. Then we commenced giving him medicine which acted like a charm and the swelling was nearly all gone out of him, but unfortunately, he got to a dish of boiled beef and took a founders. By next morning he was swolled so he could hardly move.Artemissa commenced upon him again but the medicine did not have the same effect, took more for a dose. Swelling though disappeared again, got so he could sing, whistle and go about considerably. But again in spite of the utmost vigilance on our part he got to three squirrels which were cooking and took them from the pot and nearly ate them up—this was in the morning and by night he was so badly swelled about the face he could not see his way. And then we put a watch over him all the time.

"Artemissa again commenced giving him medicine which acted finally, causing him to make water almost constantly, and he again improved fast as you ever saw. One day he was sitting in the yard, Artemissa told him to go into the house and as he started he snatched a biscuit from Patience's hand and Artemissa did not see him but for Patience's crying out she would never have known it at all. Oliver was then so much better he could be about very much and set up all day and said he would go meeting in a few days, singing all the day. But all the time he told Patience he intended to show Artemissa he would eat—that he had tried eating too often to believe that it would kill him. Artemissa was feeding him very little and his appetite was voracious.

"Well, Artemissa was gone to the field a Friday last and Narcissa was watching him closely, as she thought, but there was a good many persons coming in and during the afternoon her eyes were thrown off him about five minutes and he got to a dish of baked potatoes and eat them all. I then said to Narcissa he is gone sure. After this he went into the back cabin and was caught broiling on the fire some guts of a chicken that I had killed a short time before. These he got in the piazza as he was on the way to the back cabin. I think he eat about half of the chicken guts before he was caught.

"Well, sure enough a little after dinner he was taken and died Saturday afternoon at 2 o'clock with a congestion of the brain from overcharge of the stomach. We had him buried in the burying ground. I am sorry it has turned out the way it has, but I think we did the very best we possibly could."

Finishing this letter, which was sent by one of the Hunter boys to Pendleton to be mailed, Lucinda went again into the cornfield.

And again there was death. Within less than a week, they were awakened one night by a courier, pounding on the door—a tired young soldier from the Continental Carolina Rifles.

"I have bad news," the trooper said, quietly. They all knew what this meant.

"Which one of them is it?" asked Silas, his voice weak. He put one of his arms about Lucinda.

"Sir," came the answer, "it's Silas."

Among the blue gentians and the goldenrod on the rocky granite slope of Kings Mountain, young Silas was dead—killed by the redcoats. Quietly, the father and mother began weeping.

"He died bravely for the cause of liberty," said the young soldier, who hated to see parents grieve. "We were all proud of Silas." It was all that he knew to say.

Again alone, Silas walked in the darkness. "God," he said, "I can't stand it." All his plan had centered in young Silas. "My son, my fine son." A long time afterward, Silas returned to the cabin and sitting down before the fire he began that very night to attempt to re-create in Stephen John the burning sense of obligation and ambition he had tried to fan into the heart of young Silas.

"My son," he wrote by the firelight, "It will fall upon you now to build Forest Mansion and to direct the life of our family—it is a great responsibility and I am growing older and my way is uncertain. If it should happen that something should happen to me before we meet again, remember you must never sell a foot of the land nor mortgage an acre." Silas poured his soul into that paper. "Eventually five hundred acres must be cleared and put into cultivation on the lower place, and four hundred on the upper place—Forest Mansion must become self-sustaining, we must be free—and spare no expense in giving your children a first-rate education, they must be taught Latin and Greek and classics…"

Unable to communicate quickly enough with Stephen John by letter, Silas the next day started a diary for his son in which he included on the first pages diagrams of every room in his plan for Forest Mansion. Next he filled pages with minute instructions. "In the first shed behind the cabin you will find thirty-nine cedar beams—these are for the ceiling in the big room. In the second shed there are one hundred and nineteen panels of pine for the side walls..." Every day Silas wrote, sometimes despairing of ever being able to breathe onto paper the deep emotions stirring within him, to hand on unmutilated a dream, but he kept writing in the book until the war finally ended and America was free and Stephen John and Carter came back to Keowee.

"Now," said Silas, rejoicing, "we'll start soon to build the house."

Silas began to talk to Stephen John as formerly he had talked to young Silas. During long walks through the fields and woods, he outlined the Caldwell future. "We must build a powerful house, give the family deep roots, and provide it with land and money, and we must do more than that—we must build up a code that will be handed on, set up a sense of discipline that will make our sons' sons feel us still living with them, that will make them feel the unborn and unbegot still to follow—we must create something within them that will make them yearn more than anything to make something of themselves; they must want to become somebody."

Silas was intense and earnest and his words were not without effect upon Stephen John, but somehow the father was unable to pervade the inner depths of this second son as he had that of the first. Often Silas had a deep feeling that Stephen John was not listening to him at all. "Confound the boy," said Silas to Lucinda. "Sometimes I don't think he hears a single word I'm saying—half the time it's just like he was a thousand miles away." The old man blew out his breath hard, a way of his when exasperated. "I would he would develop some interest."

"You leave him alone," said Lucinda, siding always with Stephen John. Physically, the years in the army had changed Stephen John. Burned by open weather, he had come home as tall and gigantically broad as his brother Carter. His stride was free and easy, his face radiant and cheerful; he was friendlier than formerly; laughing often, he was gayer. But beneath these new mannerisms, there still lay the old character, melancholy and brooding. Watching Stephen John in repose, Lucinda saw there still was the sadness in the blue eyes, the wistfulness. This worried her greatly, she spent many hours wondering about this son.

As much as Silas would let him, Stephen John spent his time alone, going for long walks by himself. In the secret life, he had come at this time to a crisis, was diligently, passionately in the depths of his soul seeking a way, fighting within himself, seeking some solution. Sometimes he climbed the highest hills beyond Keowee, sometimes he slipped off his light clothes, swam in the clean clear river; often he sat in the burying ground, thinking of old Narcissa and old Carter. And there were other things Stephen John thought about—the war, the war memories. His life in the army had been vigorous and many of these recollections were filled with joy but not all of them—there were the moments of great regret. One day Stephen John was disturbed by the arrival at Keowee of a letter addressed to him in a firm hand on fine white paper. The letter had come from Charleston, was sealed with a heavy daub of vermillion wax.

Glancing hastily at the handwriting, Stephen John walked off into the distant woods with the letter in his hand unopened. Hurrying sometime later back to the cabin, he said it would be necessary for him to go to Charleston.

"It will delay our plans for starting the house," said Silas, impatiently anxious.

"I must go," said Stephen John.

"All right," said his father.

Without giving his family any other explanation, he left early the next morning. At the foot of the steep hill, he stopped to wave to his mother. "Hurry back," she called, tears coming into her eyes.

"I will," cried out Stephen John. Lucinda waved her long mountain hands and the boy rode away swiftly. "What is it that troubles him," wondered Lucinda. But that worry was something about which she never spoke, Lucinda never inquired.

Stephen John was absent that time for six weeks, and on returning to Keowee, he went immediately to Silas. "Father," he said, simply and bluntly but deeply moved, "I have something I want to say to you." Speaking then with hesitation, he said, "I am not equipped to make the family a strong leader. I have thought it over for a long time and I have decided Carter would qualify a great deal better than I ever would—I want to give up all my claims in favor of Carter."

From the pages of the open Bible which he had been reading, Silas looked up, consternation showing in the depths of his blue eyes. For some time he said nothing. "My mind is made up," said Stephen John, and there was anguish in his expression. Quietly, Silas accepted the decision. "All right, son," he said, "tell Carter to come here."

Carter came in. Patiently, Silas began for a third time to try to educate a son. Desperately, all that day, he talked to Carter and long into that night, he talked, trying to create quickly and intensely within another of his sons the feeling he carried within himself. It was a hard and wearisome task, but Silas did not tire; he seemed to sense he was working now against time, that he had much to do and little time in which to do it. Over and over, he repeated his code, his instructions—about the house, about the land, about never mortgaging the property. Midnight had passed before he retired to his bed.

Up early the next morning, seeming full of strength, Silas left immediately after breakfast to meet a posse of valley hunters. He was to lead them after a band of horse thieves that had been raiding Keowee ever since the close of the revolution. Carter accompanied his father but not Stephen John.

"I want to talk to mother," explained Stephen John.

Silas continued during that day to give hurried instructions to Carter, talking almost constantly as they rode along the trail. An hour before noon, reaching the store at Horseshoe Crossroads, they were joined by the posse, the Hunter men and a dozen Caldwells. Silas complained to Richard Hunter, a patriarch with hard black eyes, about feeling a little ill—"sort of stomach upset"—but neither of them thought much about it; Silas galloped on, took his place at the head of the posse. Riding hard for two days after that, he led the men finally into a wild ravine, filled with deep thickets of splendid laurel and rhododendron—at the foot of Stump House Mountain. The rustlers were camping there, Silas had trapped them. Stepping ahead while the others protected him with drawn rifles, Silas moved into an open space. "All right, boys," he shouted into the thicket. "Come on out, we've got you." Silas shifted his fingers, fleshy and spotted with seed warts, along the stock of his rifle. "Come on—give yourselves up."

There was a brittle rustling in the laurel. A moment later, out from a mass of pink flowers and glazed green leaves, symbols of victory-out stepped a giant man, gaunt and weary in appearance, his eyes blue as the sky, his hair fine and yellow and thin, like a young corn tassel. Behind him were three hungry looking men, dirty and bearded, strangers in the upcountry.

But their leader was no stranger. "Well, I'll go to hell," Silas said, astonished. "It's Cousin Tobias." And Cousin Tobias it was—Tobias Caldwell. He had come into the up-country a dozen years before, a wild young man, seeking adventure; had settled miles north of Silas' place in a cove on Whitehorse River, one of the roaring mountain headwaters of the Keowee.

Silas leaned his rifle against a tree and sat down on a rock to think. "Tobias," said Silas after a brief reflection, "Tobias, do you know what we had in mind to do to the head of the horse thieves?"

"What did you intend to do?" asked Tobias.

"We intended to brand him, face and behind, with a red hot iron and we were going to strip his shirt off his back and lay on thirty-nine lashes—one for every horse stolen—and we were going to rub salt in the welts—and we were going to cut off his ears."

A frightened look came over Tobias' face. "God A'mighty, Cousin Silas, you wouldn't cut off his ears?"

Silas' face seemed to become as worn as the side of one of the granite mountains. "But you're a Caldwell—sorry, low down, no account as you are, shiftless and a horse thief, still you're a Caldwell, the grandson of the grandson of old Charles Carter, the same as a lot of these other boys here." A relieved look came into Tobias' expression. Seeing it, Silas blew out his breath, snorting hard.

"Get out of my sight," he yelled, "clear out and take these sorry rascals with you." He pointed to the three other men. "And if we ever catch sight of you again in Carolina—Caldwell or no Caldwell, by holy Jesus, we'll hang you."

Silas felt a sickening dizziness.

That afternoon as the posse hurried homeward, riding into one of the wild storms of the region, Silas suddenly felt a great helpless numbness begin to creep over him. In spite of himself, he could not keep his seat. "Carter," he cried; and he fell into the trail. A great frenzy seized Silas as he realized how ill he was. He was about to die and he knew it and he could not die—there was Forest Mansion. He had yet to build it, the house—there was so much yet to tell Carter. He could not die yet dying he was; he felt the grip upon him.

"Carter," he said, taking the hands of his son, "I guess you will have to build Forest Mansion for me." Bitter tears welled up. "Promise me you will build it?" Fearfully, he searched Carter's face, gazing deep. Carter promised. Soon after, Silas lapsed into unconsciousness, and in less than an hour, in the midst of a great thunderstorm with lightning bolts crashing into trees along the mountainsides, he died.

So they made a litter for him, slinging his body between two of the horses.

※

At Keowee on the hilltop, Preacher McKay lifted his oratorical voice, preaching Silas' funeral sermon, crying out about his meekness, his love, labors, prayers, tears, his own sermons and exhortations that would not be forgotten. "There are hundreds of men living in this wilderness," roared Brother McKay. "Hundreds, who have a pleasant recollection of this holy man—his pathetic addresses, his patient suffering. The last, loud, lingering trump will call him forth to the resurrection of life and this worn mortal body will come up all immortality, all divine."

Over the grave, throwing in the clods of red clay as ashes, McKay again shouted, "He was a pattern of piety, humility, and patience—in his life and in his death."

The Caldwells listened reverently, with great respect, but if they had not known about whom it was that Preacher McKay was speaking, they would never have guessed it was Silas.

Tobias fled northward and then west.

His fate was recorded from the Tennessee country by Clarissa, who wrote this to Artemissa:

"After you folks caught him that time up at Stump House, Tobias went to live by himself on Rabun Bald. A few months after he had taken over the mountain the government sent an agent to demand of him a poll tax of seventy-five cents, but instead of paying, he said it was a free country, and shot at the agent and from then on he shot at everyone coming on the mountain. He killed a man named Higgins, said he found him prowling on his land. He was tried for that one at one of the Georgia courthouses—I forget which one. But the jury acquitted him on the ground he was crazy. So old Tobias went back to his cabin, cursing and carrying on. A number of attempts were made on his life and it was a common thing for him to be waked at midnight by balls passing through his house. Then suddenly he gave up his hermit ways and came on over here. He worked here in an iron forge but one day he got into a dispute with a fellow workman. He swore he would shoot this workman within five hours and started off home after his rifle. The offended fellow was a party by the name of Tompkins and after consulting friends about what to do he was advised to take the law in his own hands. He took this advice and as old Tobias was discovered along the road with a rifle in hand, this fellow Tompkins shot him through the heart—a good shot, clean as a whistle. Public opinion was on the side of Tompkins and he was never summoned to account for the defensive murder he had committed."

CHAPTER SIX

On the very day that Silas was buried, the family walked straight from his grave in the burying ground to the site on the next hill that Silas had cleared as the place for Forest Mansion. There they sang a song and knelt in prayer, then standing again, they were told by Carter, "This is where he wanted the house built and by the Lord I am going to build it."

Young Carter sealed a Bible and a coin and a wild laurel flower in a block of granite; he placed this rock into the foundations of a chimney. This was the cornerstone for Forest Mansion. Twenty long years had passed since Silas first whispered of this home, a great house that would last through time, a refuge for all their children-whispered to Lucinda in the oxcart on the wilderness road. At last it was to rise—exactly as he had planned it.

Four of the Hunter boys, skilled carpenters, and three of the Caldwell cousins, stone-masons, began to help Carter with the building. Soon the first beams, hewn and numbered by Silas' hand, were fitted together with the round locust-wood pegs that Silas also had whittled—dove-tailed, the grooves were knit together.

Before long a month had passed, a long day of work was drawing to a close, the sun flaming beyond the mountains. "Wham " said Carter, driving in a peg with a short-handled mallet. " We're getting alone boys." He wiped his salty sweating brow and grinned, and the cousins and the Hunter boys grinned. "By God, it's beginning to look like progress."

Carter worked hard through these weeks, getting up at daybreak, leading a full hard simple life-working, eating, sleeping, getting done what he wanted done. There was a magical evenness to the days and weeks and he was happy; for this often is what happiness means to a man. Every day he saw a great thing growing under his hands. In him, wide awake, also was the feeling of work as a form of beauty

Something was happening in the depths of Carter's secret existence. In his way he quickly was becoming his father living again—there was a new pride swelling within him as the beams of this strong and honest house rose surely in their places; a deep love for this house was springing into life within Carter, growing as the house grew. Without knowing it at first, Carter was becoming. like Silas before him, a man with a purpose in the world, a duty to perform—Forest Mansion was becoming his mission.

He swung the mallet hard with a will, driving wedges into the timbers with all his great strength. So did Carter pass the mystic weeks of a fine southern autumn with the tart tang of muscadines and persimmons in the air and the sun shining and the stars clear in the flawless nights. This was what he liked. He knew that he was happy.

Carter was happy, but not Stephen John. On the morning that Silas and Carter rode away to join the posse, Stephen John sat down before the fire in one of the walnut chairs his father had made for Forest Mansion. Talking intimately and quietly with Lucinda there came as he continued to unravel himself, that note of weary rest about him, that quietness that always comes over men when they have faced a crisis and have decided. He skipped entire passages of thought in this conversation with the one with whom he had never to be on guard. "I am not what I seem," said he, tired and deeply moody. Lucinda sensed this feeling completely. "Neither am I what I seem—neither is your father. No one is. There is the body in us all and there is the spirit." Dropping the stocking she was pretending to mend, she rested her hands in her lap, backhand to palm in the way of old Narcissa.

"But we have to pay for everything that our body does with our spirit," continued Stephen John, becoming more despondent. "And very high is the price—so much for so little." The firelight flamed over his high-boned face, playing with its glow upon all the ascetic qualities of the Caldwell expression. "I think our lives are like the moonblossoms on the arbor at Charleston—thousands of them are produced for the darkness of just one night. It's such wasteful extravagance but nature doesn't care about the waste."

"Most lives are wasted," said Lucinda, concerned at seeing her son so filled with deep sorrow. "All of them are strange, we're all looking for something that we never find. So weep and pay the price—don't keep on grieving. Weep and pay the price and start over." It was the curious creed she had developed-part hers, part borrowed from the older Carter, the doctine of one who looked to the universality of sin in all life to sustain her in the lonely bending of her own will to her own conscience. "We carry within ourselves our salvation and our destruction. We must do what we must do."

Finer and stronger and at the same time coarser and weaker than Lucinda, Stephen John at once contradicted his mother. "We must not do what we must do," he answered, "We must do only what is good and right, discipline is the thing." Then he cried out to his mother, "O I have tried...I have said to myself that I am a superman, stronger than ordinary men, I have told myself that custom was local only and changing, but I've failed. I'm too puritan, my heart knows too well what is shameful and what is sin." Leaving off further argument, Lucinda leaned sidewise and placed a hand on Stephen John's shoulder, saying "What are you going to do?"

"I'm facing myself," he answered, "I'm putting the best against the worst and instead of running away I'm going to stand against myself and fight—I'm going to live alone in the cabin on Gingerbread Mountain."

This decision was accepted by Lucinda. She watched the blazing firelight, reflecting. Strange indeed and alone and self-tortured were her people. Then she turned again to the universalities for her comfort, trying also to hand over to her son these same convictions as a comfort for him. "Well, remember this, son—no matter what your cross is, no matter how heavy is your burden, remember it has been borne before by thousands. There is nothing new—not even in trouble. What others have withstood we can withstand."

They sat there for a time silent; finally Stephen John kissed his mother and with the fine sound of the rainstorm on the roof, he began to pack his things. It did not take him long. Soon he was on his way, walking by the side of his horse. As he started off down the hill, his great shoulders back, he took with him an appearance of determination that Lucinda was never to forget.

"Stephen John," she called, "keep your troubles to yourself."

It was her farewell word. Looking back and waving, Stephen John said, "All right," a grin on his handsome and weather-burned face. So he began the strange and voluntary seclusion that he was never to break. In the cabin on the side of the mountain, Stephen John nailed a cross over his fireplace and, in time, became a complete hermit, but by strength of will and surrender he controlled that vast spiritual defect which, he always said, sought to destroy in one way or another all the men and women of his gifted and troubled family.

Once a great box filled with expensive leather-bound books came to him from Charleston, on another occasion books came for Stephen John from Philadelphia, afterwards some came from Washington, the new federal city. Nobody ever knew from whom they had come; Stephen John never said. On the mountain, he read these books, began to observe the habits of the birds and wild animals. Also he began in the midst of the wilderness to raise a flock of gorgeously decorous peacocks—the Pavo cristatus and the lustrous blue Pavo nigripennis—symbols, he said, of pride.

Lucinda brought him woven coverlets and clothing and gifts of good apple jelly and dried apples, marble and pound cakes, and Carter became a frequent visitor. But when others called, though received with chill civility, they were asked politely not to come again and the fence rail over which they had climbed was burned on their departure. Carter one time asked his brother what had troubled him, why he had retreated. "I ate the forbidden fruit," replied Stephen John, turning to allegory. For a long time, Carter sat staring into the fire; then greatly troubled himself, worry and grief on his own face, he said, "So have I." Both of them then were old.

On Gingerbread Mountain, Stephen John kept a journal, strange and beautiful notes which he set down during the long, lonely evenings, filling page after page in old ledgers with observations about birds, flowers, chipmunks, mountain lions; and there sometime would appear fragments of poems, fleeting thoughts, confessions that were not confessions. "Remember the lonely, the lovely...the fragrant and hot...O the longing that I have, watching a star, shining by itself in space, in immensity alone...one cloud and a single star." Often he would record passages of the always moving effect the cold light of the stars had upon him, under this spell he seemed to feel some magic. There were passages in the books about peacocks and butterflies and the muted singing of the wood thrush. "I have listened to that sad song in the deepest thicket, restrained...the loneliest of the songs and I have heard it." There was a hymn to the wild beauty of flying geese, motion without question...flying, flying, accepting fate. In those pages were prayers, notes on "the deepest passions," the need for self-control. "Hear me, St. John; blessed St. Francis, hear my cry." And there was deep remorse. Lines also on the immense and lonely ocean over which lonely men sailed and left no trace; troubled pages, revelations of his tortured soul, a spirit in sackcloth. Once he wrote of the ponds which in their still, unruffled shallowness carried the image of all depth—skies and clouds, all space. He wrote too of the cardinal sin, the sin for which the Bible promised no forgiveness, the sin against the Holy Ghost. And there was one sonnet..."to this vast continent...sad, vast and silent...like me, like the thrush, born under a star."

❧

And so, as old Narcissa brought martyrdom to enrich the tradition of the Caldwells, so did Stephen John bring them mystery. The family at Keowee poured over his letters and as they read his chill music, they wondered. Again and again they wondered and so did everyone else on the frontier wonder. They called him names according to the searching they found in their own hearts—crazy, a saint, a grieving poet. But in the end they all had to give up their guessing. They could never be sure.

❧

Busy about another sort of work that autumn after Silas died was Lucinda. She was interested only materially in the building of Forest Mansion The house itself was not her dream, never had been; it was Silas'. It was land now that she wanted—always, it was land. And despite the scornful way she had of saying to her daughters, "Do you want to spend all your lives in cabins?" Lucinda did not herself mind living in one. But she lived for her children and it was because of them that she was interested in the progress of the house. She was ambitious for her children and Forest Mansion, she well knew, would help them in their prospects for marriage. Matrimony now was constantly on Lucinda's mind—she must find settled working men of prospect for Patience and young Narcissa; also a hard-working, thrifty, plain woman for Carter

At home, at the meeting house, in the field—this became her obsession. Every eligible man and woman in the upcountry was counted off by Lucinda on her brown lean fingers. But marryings have a way of caring for themselves, especially on frontiers—and how was Lucinda to know that already a shrewd woman had in mind a secret plan to make herself Carter's wife, and how was she to know about the fate waiting for Narcissa. Lucinda for all her effort was to succeed only in forcing a husband upon Patience and she never could consider that much of a personal victory; Patience would have married anyone, a Tory, even an Indian, had Lucinda insisted.

But Lucinda did not know what she so soon was to find out. So she busied herself with plans. At the stone meeting house, she began watching a man named Philip Carr—gawky, big and brutish, a man with shaggy eyebrows and stained teeth. He was as old again as either of her daughters; also there were stories told about him—but he had land, a thousand acres, and a clapboard house and he was a settled man. That appealed especially to Lucinda—not only did he have land, he also was settled.

One Sunday after the preaching service was over, Lucinda spoke to old Carr. "You seem a mightly lonely man," said she, in the manner of a woman looking for prospects for a daughter. "Come on over with us to Keowee and eat dinner; we'd be mighty glad to have you." So Carr. being no fool, came to the Caldwell cabin, where he sat down heavily, ate with his mouth open and drooled milk over the curly mat of his whiskers. He bellowed at everything that was said. And he was invited to come again to dinner on the Sunday next. "There's no use staying over there at your place all alone—lonesome on a Sunday" said Lucinda, adding, "We're always glad to add another plate at our house."

All that week Lucinda prepared her daughters for the proposition that was foremost in her mind. "Limit your wants," said she, whirring the spinning wheel, unconsciously setting up a defense against the fact that Mr. Carr was not the handsomest of men. "Wish for few things, take what you can get, and you'll be less disappointed in life. Don't set your heart on any one thing that's too great, don't count on any dream too much—the road is too hard and there are too many disappointments." The wheel whirred and whirred and she talked. "A woman hardly ever gets what she wants—but there are compensations." Lucinda spoke a great deal about the compensations.

"What are you driving at, Ma?" asked Narcissa, suddenly interrupting one of Lucinda's apparently casual talks. "Do you want one of us to marry old Philip Carr?" Lucinda's face flushed. "Well, I hadn't exactly put it that way." Narcissa laughed, rudely, boldly. "Not me" said she, shaking her hand at her mother. "He's dull as a dog."

After that Lucinda concentrated entirely on Patience, talking much to her in private. As Carr called more and more often at Keowee, folks began talking; then they all were invited to a wedding. This was a great time for Lucinda. "He's settled, child," she said to Patience, a hundred times, "and he's so comfortably fixed."

Lying quiet and frightened the night before she was to marry, Patience could not sleep. Outside the cold winds of late autumn were blowing, freezing a world that waited for snows and great hoarfrosts and December storms. "November," she whispered to Narcissa, "is a poor time to be getting married."

❧

"Well," wrote Artemissa to Clarissa, "poor Patience is married, Lucinda has married her off to a tough, ugly old bachelor about forty-one years old, entirely uneducated but he has very good property, a home and a horse and sheep and some cows and stands very fair with the male portion of the community, but has been held in perfect contempt by the weaker sex for some time. Several years ago he went to live with a widow, a cousin, and under promise of marriage, seduced her. She gave birth to a child and died. I can only think for myself but I never thought Patience would have married old Philip Carr. I would have been poor Patience Caldwell forever in preference."

And poor Patience! She was mild and good and meek. And she and her husband had planted and gathered only one crop when Philip grew restless. For some reason (it was pure cussedness, Lucinda said afterward), he broke into open rebellion suddenly in one day. One morning he rode off to the field, moody and brooding, and that afternoon, completely dispirited, he returned to the house, asking, "What the hell good is this country?" He flung his cap on a peg on the piazza wall, doused his grizzly face in cold water. "Nothing ever happens here." That night he ordered Patience to pack. "We're leaving here," he said, "We're going out to the Tennessee where things are happening. Things out there will be more free."

"Yes, sir," said Patience. She closed a door and wept.

So leaving behind the fine walnut furniture that Lucinda had given them and most of the cows and sheep, Philip and Patience started in a new caravan, a caravan that included Samuel and his wife, Eliza Caldwell, who was a daughter of Will Caldwell, a girl of strong character, possessing all the determination that Patience lacked. Also in this procession went almost all of the upcountry Ropers and a large section of the Temple Clayton connection, and several of the Patricks and Garrets.

"The going fever has got us," Philip said to Lucinda the day the settlement folks gathered at the old stone meeting house to tell the travelers good-bye. Lucinda could have struck him, so filled was she with fury. There was the usual prayer and singing:

> "I'll go where you want me to go, dear Lord,
> O'er mountain, or plain or sea..."

Lucinda waved as bravely as she could. "Come back soon," she said, kissing her daughter.

"Sure, we'll be back," said Patience, her voice trembling. "If not next year—then the next one, sure." Then the whips cracked and drivers shouted; there was a general commotion with everybody excited; again there rang the cry, shrill and exultant, "We're on our way." Patience had started off toward the west and the new wilderness. Another pilgrim had gone on.

"They'll get along all right," said Lucinda, waving a handkerchief.

"I'm sure they will," said Narcissa, for once allowing herself to speak sarcastically to her mother.

Patience at first wrote back to Keowee about hardships and savages and later her letters recorded the lonely and lively life of a struggling settlement. Some of her notes were malicious gossip, but through them all ran quiet undertones of homesickness, a mood weaving everything together. Always Patience revealed herself as planning next season, next year to come back to Keowee. It was Carolina always that was home, always in the west she wrote as a lonely exile.

"...Narcissa, I want to see you all bad...Ma, I sure would like to be back for the camp meeting...we have better crops this year than we have since we come to Tennessee. Everything is looking fine as we have been having rains lately. If things work out, maybe we can get back..."

"A freshet has ruined our crop..."

"Ma, Cousin Joe Garret's wife had a young one before they had been married six months. Old Cousin Polly was very mad about it. Joe gets drunk all the time. Our camp meeting comes on next week. Our crops look very well. Cousin Temple has quit the worst of his drinking but he is not working like he ought to. He has made friends with Mr. Carr; they are very friendly.

"We stayed at Eliza Caldwell's last night. Eliza's health is so bad she can hardly tend to her things. Her boys have been sick, too. They are looking poor and pale. Eliza went and stayed a week with Cousin Temple's folks and while over there ate too much green fruit. Eliza says she wants to come to Carolina this autumn the worst kind. But she has to stay through and help gather in the crops. She has her own cotton to pick and her goobers to dig...

"Ma, maybe we'll get over the mountains next year. No hope for this year. Temple Caldwell is talking of going on to Alabama soon. What he is going to do is unknown, but if I was a man I'd try to be a man; there is plenty of land among the kinfolks if he would take up farming for a living...I can wish him but well. They put off the communion and foot washing at Yellow Creek on account of the bad behaviour of Sarah Caldwell, a granddaughter of Aunt Clarissa. I hate to tell you all but that girl is a wild one. And you ought to have seen Cousin Temple walking about barefooted, crying, with a flowing duster on—coming down on his knees. Old Jim Kelly that used to live below us on Keowee preached the sermon.

"Ma, I certainly would have enjoyed being with you when you all found that bed of arbutus. I think of our hunts for it—the walks we used to take on the lovely Sabbath mornings when I was still there. How delicate arbutus is. I have never seen any of it but once since...

"Ma, I stopped at Aunt Clarissa's and she was crying; she told me Sarah Caldwell was in a family way. Said she had been put in such a fix by one of the sorriest, no account scoundrels in this country. She said also one of Wash Smith's girls was big, also a Miss Tucker living in a settlement known as Poverty Flat...

"Ma, wheat is a complete failure, oats is a failure, killed by the rust. Times are very hard but not so hard as they are going to be this fall. Some people are going to suffer..."

And then a long time later.

"Brother Carter, the day is very cold. I am sitting in Mr. Carr's blacksmith shop and the fire is low. I am not well but I am inured to sad changes and disappointments. During the summer we had made preparations to move to Alabama where Mr. Carr says there is more congenial prospects than here—Mr. Carr says he don't like it in Tennessee, says the country is all right but the folks are rude and uneducated, they live like dogs. We were all ready to go but the news came of Eliza Caldwell's death and my own bad health prevented our doing so. Life is full of bitter days. When the news of Eliza's death came to us, I thought I couldn't stand it. Kindred affection will naturally cause us to weep for dear Eliza but no one except Eliza's husband can at present feel her loss so deeply as I. I do not like to write upon such a subject, it is too painful and has cost many a tear to write what I have already written. Since her death I do not feel near so satisfied to live in the West. I would now gladly change my home in the West for any kind of a cabin in Carolina. 'Life is but a day at most, then why not spend it among one's own.' I hope you will write me as soon as you get this. Nothing delights me more than to get a letter from home."

After that, Patience wrote only one letter more. Written from a district then being settled in wild northern Alabama, this one concluded: "Brother Carter, I express doubt whether I will ever see you any more in this world as God permits the barbarous enemy to slay the righteous along with the wicked—I have learnt to eat coarse fare with gladness and singleness of heart, praising the Almighty..."

When at last Patience did return to Keowee, she was brought in feet first in a coffin, paid for and her transportation paid for by Carter. On the high hill among the wild winds and the blue skies of eternal hope and the immortal green of the pines, she was buried beside the second Narcissa. The epitaph which far away from home she had composed herself was cut into a stone by Carter:

"I rest in thy bosom, Carolina, thy skies over me, thine earth and air above and around me. Among my own, in my own country, I sleep."

It was the only rest Patience ever knew—the grave.

Patience got no sympathy from young Narcissa. Narcissa the third was strong and confident, able to defend herself, and she had no understanding of people who lacked such qualities. Such traits as meekness only irritated Narcissa. "Have some get-up and go," she said often to Patience, "Say no."

Throughout their childhood, Narcissa ruled Patience; also she protected her. Often Narcissa was thoughtless and sometimes she lacked tact but she was affectionate, of a generous spirit; she was buoyant, the lightest hearted of all the Caldwells—gay by nature and that was a rare characteristic in this family. Lilt and lightness lived even in the thin herb-scented pages of her diary. "It is a fine day, a lovely day, not too hot, not too cold, and I feel fine." She wrote those words the Sunday Lucinda first invited Philip Carr to Keowee. Ten days later she recorded, "I have been to a singing followed by a brush arbor dinner—bacon and beef, pork, light bread, chicken pie, peach pie, pound cake, honey, preserves, fried ham—tables covered over with victuals, and conversation was lively, some of a melancholy nature, some of a religious nature, some very common. I tell you, I enjoyed myself."

Narcissa had breathlessness and verve and energy and mischief, all of which she wrote about in her secret journal. "On Wednesday, I packed up and Carter, Will Caldwell and myself went down to the Hunter place. Soon after I got there I bid them good-bye, mounted and rode off, eleven miles to the Hendersons', stopped there and had dinner, then came on five miles this side of Charlie Daniel's and stayed the night with the Gadlocks—sewing, cornshucking, I talked and eat to the full. Mr. Henderson has got the fever and Cousin Amanda is taking it so I hear. But Fred O'Dell is coming on a visit and I think it will cure her fever or make it worst, one…" And there was guile and nonsense. "No marrying nor giving in marriage, everything quiet…I was invited to several parties, went to none but I expect to get married as soon as anyone will be content to be mine, which I hope will not be long. I have just lived single long enough—that I am getting old by any means, but I never saw the use in staying single until one is so old she cannot marry to advantage…if God forgive me for living single this long, I will promise Him faithfully I will take one of his best gifts to women to my own self in the very near future." The morning she wrote that down, she deliberately left her diary open on her bed, so that Lucinda would be certain to see it; Narcissa knew how anxious Lucinda was for her to find herself an acceptable husband. But that night, Narcissa added this: "I am having too fine a time to think of marrying for at least a year—let the gentlemen compete a little, it won't hurt them any and I like it."

But there was more depth to Narcissa than this: aloofness and solemnity were hers also, legacies from her stern fathers and a continent which by its mystery and vastness, by sheer space alone commanded reverence from its own. Nature was too imminent on the frontier for her to be entirely flippant. There were the wild summer storms and the lightning and who knew in April when tornadoes might not sweep away the whole of Keowee. This was America that Narcissa lived in—not a gentle bit of county land like little Britain. The soughing pines were here and the blue mist over the ancient hills and the curling jessamine and the red fields. The violent spirit of the pilgrims and puritans lived also in Narcissa's heart and this too tinged her like the iron tinged the red clay. The hard life was her life—Massachusetts and Pennsylvania and the savage Cherokees were her heritage, and a continent was her home.

"O I live bound," wrote Narcissa the day Patience left for the land beyond the mountains. "But so is a tree bound, so the wild rose. I sit still and watch the light falling through the thick leaves, water whirling in a pool, the river flowing, a spider spinning a web. O I wish I were a bird—I'd be an eagle, a strong bird of prey!" This was the deep part of her character that checked and remembered, called her to account, the solitary side that regarded nature, rapt, and contemplated death.

Narcissa enjoyed solitude, like all the solitary Caldwells. Like them all, she went to wild places for comfort, sought hilltops and thickets when she wanted to think. And like them all, she was restless.

She was restless and one June morning when the passion of summer was upon her, she lay in a stack of cut wheat in a field, reading:

"Dark was the night and wild the storm.
And loud was the torrent's roar;

And loud the sea was heard to dash
Against the distant shore."

Narcissa was in a yearning mood. And along in a cart came the clock man, one of the journeymen of the frontier—young and healthy with clear blue eyes and black hair and a good straight Irish-American face. Smiling and waving at her—it was Jimmy O'Reilly. He made his living peddling the fine wooden clocks of Connecticut, wonderful time pieces with engraved and silvered brass dials. They were driven by weights. Some of them with chimes told the day of the month, the moon's age and seconds. They came in mahogany and cherry tree cases. Also Jimmy sold cow bells and dinner bells, weathercocks, buckles and pieces of pewter.

"Narcissa," shouted Jimmy, "howdy—this fine summer morning." Smiling, he waved again at the girl lying in the wheatfield. Quickly, he stopped his horse. Narcissa also smiled, waving at him with both hands. And he came across the field. The sunshine was warm and the wheat pile was clean and fragrant and in the hot wind there was the sweet smell of mimosas, also a mocking bird sang. Jimmy touched the girl and she quivered; he put his long arms around her and they lay down in the strawstack. For the tide was at its full within Narcissa, demanding and mysterious, making her yearn for this need of love.

Jimmy was a clean young man and he was honest; his reputation too was good; he was the best peddler in the country. He was a dreamer also, an idealist, and the act of love with him was physical and natural, an exercise and a nervous release. "It's all right," he said, talking to himself as afterwards he drove through the upper end of the valley that was as old as the world. He had omitted the call he had intended making at the Caldwell cabin with his bells and clocks. Jimmy was not brazen enough to go from a wheat field direct to the house.

At Deep Creek, Jimmy washed himself in the swift water, scrubbed his red hands with fine sand as there was a lingering scent on them of lavender sachet and that now was obnoxious to him. He dried himself in the bright sun and the sharp wind, thinking how peculiarly direct, how odd was Narcissa. This was her first time with a man, at the moment he was certain. Yet she had received him as an experienced woman would have, very knowing. There had been no pretense, nor asking, "Do you love me—do you love me only?" Nor had there been that question often asked him in the after-quiet, "Have there been any others for you before me?" It had been casual as a cloud, they had lain down without a word, like the sweet fragrance that just happened along in the breeze from mimosa trees.

"Ah, well," Jimmy said, whacking the rump of his horse with a hickory switch, "Get along, old Liz, we got clocks to sell."

But with Narcissa, this was not a physical event. Even at the moment of the flesh's victory, she had to begin dealing with the spirit; she could not dismiss such an occasion from her memory. There was remorse and she felt she must punish herself. At first, she was so repulsed by what she had done that she vomited. Stephen John vomited and so did Carter when they felt repelled by the weakness of their flesh. And Narcissa was like them. Narcissa ran down the steep hill to the horse branch and there in a deep pool of pure water began violently to wash herself—it was symbolism, a rite, and then there began the fear that was to grow more gripping, hour after hour, day after day, without relent.

Sometimes she ran, wildly desperate, through the woods, up the sides of the steep hills until she thought she could not put one foot forward again, then she would run once more, trying not to think any more about what was there to be done. Should she send for him—if so, whom should she send and where should whomever she should send be sent. She decided to write and hurrying into the house composed one frantic letter after another, none of which she ever mailed; she destroyed them all. She did not know where to address them—at first, she considered Waterbury, Connecticut, where the clocks were made, but that would take too long, it would be too late; she thought of Augusta, Georgia, and Hamburg, South Carolina, and Ninety Six. But he was at none of those places either, he was far away in the wilderness. Months might go by before he would return again to those places. So in the end, Narcissa did nothing. She simply trusted and had hope. She trusted that somehow Jimmy would know. "God," she prayed, "make him have a vision-speak to him; whisper to him just a word." Narcissa passed many desperate hours in the burying ground, keeping the company of the cedar trees and the stones. The feeling of profound rest that sometimes came to her there quieted her and she liked to smell the trees, the cedars and the pines, the trees growing about the graves of the other Narcissas—the fragrant pines. One afternoon while watching a storm gather, she saw a sheet of heat lightning strike and shatter a cloud and the stroke terrified her—it seemed she was watching her own life disappear. Terrified, she cried, "I'm trapped; there's nothing I can do."

Next Narcissa went through a period of deep melancholy brooding during which she sat for hours on logs and rocks; sometimes by the river, she stared in the pools, deciding she preferred to watch the reflection of the sky there than to watch the sky itself. She could see so far and so deep in a pool.

Then there came a cold winter day when Narcissa, looking up from the chair in which she was sitting before the fire, found Lucinda staring steadily and angrily at her—in a way that was entirely hostile and new. Narcissa flushed crimson, and frightened and ashamed, she suddenly jumped up, running into the hard, wind-swept yard. Grimly then she saw Lucinda reach for a bonnet and shawl and stride from the house, heading up the hill to find Carter.

Bareheaded, his blue shirt open at the neck, Carter was pitching bundles of wide home-split shingles to one of the Hunters, whose big feet covered the width of a twelve-inch scaffold. "Carter," she called, hesitating at the edge of the clearing, "Come here." Carter stooped for some loose boards that were scattered on the ground about him, answered, "I'm busy, ma, we want to finish the roof this week sure."

"Come here," said Lucinda, speaking sharply this time. And across the yard of the new house came the son, wiping his wide forehead with his forearm. "What is it, ma?" he asked, decidedly annoyed.

"I think," said Lucinda, a look of deep fury on her face, "that you had better have a word with your sister Narcissa." "What about?" inquired the young man.

"What about!" replied Narcissa, raising her voice to a shrill sarcastic pitch, "haven't you noticed?"

"Noticed what?" replied Carter, frowning and adding impatiently, "I haven't noticed anything."

"Well, if you haven't—you're about the only one in the settlement that hasn't."

"Ma, what are you talking about?"

Bluntly then Lucinda said, "Your sister is in a family way."

Carter was stunned for a moment, then a great surge of fury swept over him; he cried out in angry surprise.

"You'll find her down there in the holly ravine," said Lucinda, pointing down the hill. Her gesture sent Carter off down the hill, running wildly. He almost tripped over an exposed oak root growing across the path, catching himself in time to avoid sprawling headlong. He found his sister waiting for him in the grove, calmly and composed as her own crisis, the terror within herself, had passed.

In a furious rage, Carter pointed one of his lean fingers at her, began shouting. "What do you think folks will say when they hear about this?" He grabbed her roughly by both arms, shaking her. "You've disgraced us, that's what you've done—you've disgraced the Caldwells."

Carter's words were instinctive, shouted out without the slightest reflection. His sister had broken an obligation that extended beyond her right to break, shown a lack of discipline. "Disgraced us," he shouted, "brought us to shame." All the merciless cruelty of the Caldwells flamed into his brain. Like someone crazed, he grabbed Narcissa's throat, pressing his brute thumbs into her windpipe, calling out all the time, "Who was the bastard?" Pressing harder against her throat and shaking her and continuing his shouting, he kept repeating, "Tell me his name, you hear me?" Harder still he pressed and Narcissa reeled senseless, there was a blurred yellow sun setting in her mind and a river flowing and a bursting flower and there was a great whirring through darkness, it was coming toward her, like a tornado, roaring closer…nearer. Her fine ascetic face was swollen purple; she collapsed.

Carter placed her still body carefully, most tenderly upon a patch of briars. Then raising his own eyes and high cheek bones and sensitive, sensual lips, he was about to address a statement of his own to God. But he changed his mind. Instead he walked away slowly, and going into the cabin, began to hew a coffin from a cedar slab.

While he worked, half-dazed, one of the Hunter boys rode away on horseback, at full speed, to bring McKay, the preacher, to the Caldwell cabin.

🦎

Old McKay, when he heard, did not blame Carter for what he had done. "Having sowed the wind it was but just that Narcissa should reap the whirlwind." So he spoke to the Hunter boy. But the journey he had to make that day to Keowee was filled with its distractions. This was his anxiety—what under the circumstances should a minister of God include in his funeral sermon. Should there be a eulogy, should there be only a prayer? "Which, which, this, that?" McKay asked himself as his horse jogged over the great hills. Strictly speaking, said he to himself, there should be a prayer only, but even so, Narcissa was a Caldwell and a Caldwell had power even in the clothes of the grave. The horse's gait shifting, the preacher began wondering what would the Caldwells expect from him; fording the river an hour later, he resolved the matter by putting everything into the care of God—he would be moved by the spirit when the time came. That very night in the cabin he raised his ghostly hands over the cedar coffin, and observing the true and deep grief of both Carter and Lucinda, McKay chose the eulogy.

"Now that death has come," he said in the gloom of the dark cabin—for they buried Narcissa at night—"All is forgiven; wiped away are all mortal sorrows. She was too fair a plant to grow long upon this corrupt soil. She has been transplanted into a region more congenial with her pious soul to mingle with angelic forms and inhale a purer atmosphere."

Then Lucinda fainted, she did not think Narcissa had been prepared to die.

A wide slab of granite, smooth and a foot thick, was laid over the grave of Narcissa and with a mallet and hard tempered chisel, Carter set to work, chipping:

> "A brother's sorrow dedicates this stone
> To the memory of his sister.
> Beneath this slab are
> The remains of
> Narcissa Caldwell, third of that name,
> Whose spirit has Returned to
> Heaven."

Carter planted a scarlet myrtle at the head of the tomb; then he walled the grave with a fence of stone, seven feet high.

Jimmy O'Reilly made the long north circuit that year with his clocks, twice crossing the main range of the granite mountains in the far reaches of the wilderness. On that journey, he slept where sundown found him, deep in the woods alone, sometimes in the cabins of the wild and unorthodox men and women who were his patrons. Eccentric and individualistic, many of them were able neither to read nor write; they welcomed the young man to their bare houses, engaging him in great discussions, eating and drinking with him and all the time talking about democracy and its dream, its hope for the world, and about the rights of common people and the duty of governments to the poor. In their mean cabins, with burning logs the only light, they talked of liberty and equality, and they burst forth into violent opinions on religious doctrines—the form of the Lord's supper, the Biblical authority for total immersion, the apostasy. Some of these men wore clothes made from animal skins and some wore linsey-woolsey, a few were trying their best to get rich quick, but there were many who seemed not to care at all about money; some liked to lie down in the sunshine, flat on their backs—they were hairy-faced trappers, traders, lean hunters, farmers, all different. Some of them kept cowpens; one toothless old fellow in a remote spur of the mountains ran a general store. No one lived within ten miles of this man's cabin but that did not bother him; he wanted to open a store, so he opened one.

Freedom was their idol—its burning flame flared high above their mountain altars. "Hell, brother, do what you want to—do it when it suits you; raise peacocks, strip naked." They gave a hearing to any man so long as he was not a Roman; they all hated the Pope. Their restraint on conduct was to forbid horse and cattle stealing; and they held also a man ought not to do too much shooting unless really provoked. Beyond that they believed in leaving every man to God and his own conscience. "It's a free country, boys; we aim to keep it free."

Besides buying Jimmy's cowbells and clocks and talking to him, they sat him down to big bowls of hot hominy and creamed gravy and broiled red ham and plates of hot biscuits and they broiled squirrels for him, and they told him their troubles. For they had learned that Jimmy held his tongue. Also this itinerant had a way. When the lonely Widow Allen, pausing over a dough tray, poured for him a glass of pale corn liquor, Jimmy told her it was the first drop he had had in two months and that he had rather drink that fine moonshine than step into heaven that minute. The widow shuffled her awkward feet and half coughed and said, "Law me alive, boy, pshaw," but those words put her in a pleasant frame of mind for a whole evening, and although a strict Methodist, she bought a silver buckle.

And Fanny Bowen, who lived in the wilderness near the Saluda River in a two-room cabin—she showed Jimmy her carriage, a great aristocrat's coach with wheels five feet high and heavy iron axles. Swung on double springs, the body rose four and a half feet from the ground; there was a long tongue with a bolted ring and seats for coachmen and footmen. It already was famous on the frontier as "Fanny Bowen's folly." "They say I'm crazy to live in a cabin and keep such a carriage," said the lonely woman to Jimmy. "But all my life I have wanted a carriage—so when I got the money, I got one." Jimmy solemnly said it was the most beautiful carriage ever seen. Mrs. Bowen bought a set of pewter.

One night, a lean little man with a weasel face, piercing blue eyes and a long white beard told Jimmy he had worn out five women, fathered thirty children, that he had kept a count of, and that he had killed in his time thirty-nine savages with one gun. This man believed in the portent of ruling days, and Jimmy listened—the twelve days between December 25 and old Christmas each ruled the weather for a month of the coming year; there would be as many snows in winter, many or few, as there were fogs in August; the first thunder in spring came to awaken the snakes and lizards. He bought two bells and a clock.

Sometimes in lonely cabins he would find lone men and women sick, and Jimmy would nurse and feed them. Once he came upon a man dying of fever; was told by the man that his wife had deserted him three days before, leaving him there helpless. "She's run away to Tennessee with another man."

These strange men and women, inexhaustible in energy, their great appetites and hope unbounded, were Jimmy's real friends. He liked them, knew what they wanted, carried letters and messages for them, carried gifts—onions and red pepper and wove coverlets, smoked hams, flower seeds, new varieties of fruit, the Persian melon and the Chinese quince. New quilt designs made their way through the backwoods "by courtesy of friend Jimmy"—the pinwheel, the fruit basket, the star of Lemoyne, the road to Indiana.

Moving on his way, Jimmy made the circuit, the weeks lying timeless and spaceless in his mind—sometimes on this trip his thoughts were of God and good things; sometimes they were obscene, for things came into his mind that never found verbal expression. Sometimes he remembered postures, poses, smells, the feel of a hand, and sometimes he sang to the free sun, the long wild wind, to the evening star; he talked to old Liz, his horse, and to himself and once inspired by the infinite wisdom and mystery of the old granite mountains, he stood up in his cart and shouted "hallelujah." He was singing then to his country, wild and solitary land—he loved it. It was so young and full of adventure and unrest, and those were the things that counted. Sometimes on this long ride, Jimmy thought of Narcissa.

From the Waxhaws, he crossed Carolina's mighty rivers, the sweeping Catawba, wide and slow and deep, the tortured Salude struggling through rocks, the Broad, bound by canes; he came on over the rich red hills into the quiet, water-oak, shaded square of Pendleton. It was an old place for the upcountry, with a settled look upon it, very sedate. Pendleton was one of the places to which Jimmy's clocks were shipped, a district center; they were received there and kept for him by Aaron Gadlock, the storekeeper, who like Jimmy himself was one of the characters of the frontier, a round-bellied, hearty, democrat. Aaron knew everyone and everyone's business, for all the people sooner or later passed through his wooden store on the square opposite the white-pillared Farmers' Hall, "the oldest in the U. S."

"Well, God rest me, brother—look who's here," Aaron said, halting in his greeting to spit some tobacco juice and wipe his grinning mouth with his spotted sleeve. Then he stood up. "If it ain't James himself." The older man shook hands enthusiastically. "Where you been so long, boy? I got orders for you from here on through to the Tennessee." Jimmy smiled, saying, "I been to hell and gone this time, Mister Aaron—all the way to the French Broad River and up the side of Grandfather Mountain. Sold a clock to a man there that said Grandfather Mountain was the highest mountain in the world. You know why? Because he said all the other mountains sloped away from it, far as the eye could see. Sure, looks like times are booming in the clock business."

Aaron grunted, settling again in his bottom-sprung chair, and slowly edging himself into a comfortable sitting position; he had a great affection for this hard-working, smart young Yankee peddler, was glad indeed to welcome him again to Pendleton. He began telling the local news and gossip to the boy—it was his custom. Old Emma Landrum was dead, "whether she was worth telling about or not." But Emma was worth telling about and old Aaron knew it. Emma had lived in her day, raising a bastard boy without loss of all of her good standing; she always told everything on herself before anyone else could grab a chance, and the place she chose for her confessions was the Baptist Church. "I've sinned, folks," she would shout, "and I'm sorry." Always the Baptists felt under the circumstances, they would be obliged to forgive her.

Aaron bit off a dark hunk of pressed tobacco, filling half his mouth with this cud. "The Masons are planning a big performance for the fourth of July—fireworks from Charleston. Old Miss Hunter is right sick—chilling." It was pleasant there among the calico bales in the rear of Mister Aaron's store; Jimmy half listened. There had been a big public debate at the schoolhouse. The question: The cat and the dog. "The dog side beat us," said Aaron. "Bill Hunter was the dog captain and I was the cat." He bellowed. "We got another one scheduled for this Saturday next—the question is: Powder and the sword."

Quietly, Mister Aaron in the midst of this small talk leaned forward, saying without a change of expression, "Jimmy, Carter Caldwell was in here the other week, said he sure was mighty anxious to see you." Instantly Jimmy was alarmed; he felt a violent throbbing within his ribs and an involuntary flush creep over his face. "What did he want?" Jimmy asked, trying to seem calm. Jimmy had a moment in which to collect himself as just then the store was filled with ringing sounds—the fine clocks, all kept in running order by Mister Aaron, began striking an hour. "He didn't say," said Aaron after waiting for the vibrant Connecticut music to die away. "Maybe he wants a clock for Forest Mansion—he's building a fine house." Old Aaron leaned still further forward in his chair and, lowering his voice, asked Jimmy, "Have you heard about Narcissa?"

"What about her?"

"Somebody knocked her up," whispered Aaron, troubled, "and Carter choked her to death."

Jimmy was haunted—from that moment he was a criminal in his own conscience, watching, guarding, never trusting. His eyes, stung with terror, were kept trained on the fresh-scoured floor as old Aaron spoke. He hardly heard the words, the rest of that story, and yet he heard them, every single word, and was to keep on hearing them for the rest of his troubled days. He heard the easy, soothing, worried voice of Aaron saying that the strange thing was nobody could find out who was Narcissa's "goodtime" man. "There ain't nobody that knows—and that's a fact." And now there actually came from Aaron the soft sound of laughing, his fat stomach which was one of the few paunches to be seen on the frontier, was quaking. "Everything in pants," he said, "is suspected—even Preacher McKay."

Then Aaron, a keen man, noting many things, prized himself from the chair and hobbled to the front of the store to wait on Floride Elk, a stooped little woman who had come hesitantly into the place, asking for a spool of thread, some goods for a petticoat, and a package of needles. Jimmy ran through the back door, crossing a dry dusty street and into a green corn field, rushing on into a pine grove where he flung himself on his arms, burying his face. Beginning to sob, he said to himself, in a burst of remorse and regret, "God damn me—I'm a scoundrel." Jimmy lay for hours on the fine needles of the pines; they were as soft as velvet cloth. By turns he was filled with anguish, fear, suspicion, with all those great emotions which seek to destroy the soul of human beings.

Why had Mister Aaron told him that Carter Caldwell had asked about him—did Aaron know, did he suspect, had he meant it as a warning. Did Carter know—what did Carter want with him. Jimmy decided he would leave the country; he would give up his clock business, start that night for Kentucky, perhaps for Southern Indiana, there was a country that was opening up, the richest land yet, a young man could forget the past there—start over in a young country like Indiana. But he soon abandoned that idea. "No," said Jimmy to himself, "I won't run away like that—I'm not that kind of a coward. And what would it solve?" Next he decided he would drive at once to Keowee, confess everything, stand up to the consequences; but soon that was dismissed also—it would be foolish. Either Carter, with things gone this far, would have to kill him or he would have to kill Carter—and what good would that do Narcissa? Late in the afternoon, he got up and walking, aimlessly, still thinking, he drifted through fields. In a clean stream, he dipped his hands, recalling the lavender scent that had been upon them; he climbed a bank of moss, made his way through blackberry briars and alders into a cotton patch; a thunderstorm broke, with hard blowing rain and furious wind, drenching him to the skin.

"There's nothing I can do now," he said to the lightning and the sky. He decided to make a bold visit to the Caldwell cabin, calling as usual with his buckles and pieces of silver and his clocks. Then if Narcissa had told them, as God knew she should have—then he would soon find out; if not, if she had not told them—well, that much at least would be settled. He felt so desolate he did not much care at this moment what happened, but starting next morning from Pendleton, red-eyed from lack of sleep, Jimmy found himself packing a rifle in the fresh yellow cart straw; he did not want to die. As he climbed into the wagon, he felt suddenly weak, his heart pounded wildly and he was frightened, so frightened that for a moment he considered giving up the plan, of turning in the opposite direction and running. But he overcame this temptation. He rode toward Keowee in a daze, forcing old Liz to walk slower than she had ever walked; he wanted to make the journey as long as possible. Jimmy felt a great surge of terror come over him as the horse started finally to climb the hill to the Caldwell cabin. He tried to say a word to old Liz but there was a fierce dryness in his throat; for the moment he was speechless. Soon the horse was trotting into the hard, brushed yard, and in the doorway appeared Carter.

A flush came over Jimmy's face; his hands trembled. In the first flash Carter seemed to him old and marked by trouble, his grave look was alarming; with an unconscious gesture, Jimmy reached into the straw, groping for the rifle. But in the next instant, Jimmy saw Carter smile; heard him saying, "Well, Jimmy—come in, I'm real glad to see you." Slowly a smile came over Jimmy's face; in fact, he laughed—a loud, nervous, mirthless laugh. He knew what he wanted to know.

He walked with Carter through the empty and splendid rooms of the new mansion, listening to descriptions of timbers and dimensions, and he watched Carter's strong hands lightly touching beams of pine and rich cedar, polished with beeswax until they were glowing. In the great room in the center of the house, Jimmy saw the glistening Carrara mantles, and in the windows he saw the clear blue tint of the leaded panes—the first glass in windows in that section of the wilderness. He heard Carter say, "Soon it'll be finished." Carter then became gloomy again, shadows appearing in his unhappy face. Looking Jimmy full in the eye, he said, "Jimmy, boy, I've been through hell since I saw you." The young peddler felt a sudden urge to leap head foremost through the nearest window; he could not bear to have Carter confess anything to him. Desperately, Jimmy looked about, trying to think of something to say but there was no necessity for him to say anything. Carter's mood had changed. "Pick me a clock," he said, and Jimmy chose a narrow waisted grandfather in Honduras mahogany with an engraved dial framed in twisted pilasters, and there was a chain of wheels with bells and hammers to strike the quarter hours; it was a wonderful timepiece.

"All right," said Carter, leading the way into the yard, "I'll take it—now find me a place to dig a well." From his blue shirt, Jimmy pulled out a y-forked twig of dried peachwood. For in addition to peddling clocks, cowbells and silver shoebuckles, this half Irish-Yankee also was a water diviner, so famous that no one dug for water in the up-country without seeking his advice. One of the topics of talk that endlessly fascinated the hill people was this great gift of Jimmy's—was it secret geological information taught him somewhere by someone or was it a magical power? Jimmy said it was magic and his searches for water always were conducted with so much mysterious ritual that many were convinced. Jimmy put on a show. His divining rod seemed only a peachtree stick, an ordinary piece of warped wood; to hundreds who held it in their hands with awe nothing ever happened. But in Jimmy's fingers, it became a wand—the fork suddenly would turn downward, and struggle as he might, Jimmy would be unable to stop the turning. That was the sign, there was water to be dug. Once an old man at Pendleton laughed at Jimmy and to show him what he thought of water divining he sank a well by himself. This man dug through clay for fifty feet but at fifty-one feet, his diggers struck solid granite. He tried again under a tree and this .time was stopped by a wall of gneiss. Then Jimmy came with the peachtree stick; soon a trance came over him; he began walking like a man sleeping and soon he came to a spot that was exactly between the two dry wells; he began struggling with the magic twig. "Dig here," he commanded, and the man, digging, found cold, clear water in forty-three feet. This tale was told everywhere along the frontier, establishing Jimmy's reputation for certain.

Looking carefully about him, Jimmy walked downward a considerable distance below Forest Mansion, in a grove of honey locusts, and there he found the spot for which he was looking. "This is the place," he said, marking it with a stake. It was noon now, the sun shining hot upon them through a ragged cloud. "I must be on my way," said Jimmy, but Carter insisted, "You must eat dinner with us." Jimmy protested, he was in a great hurry, but Carter was persistent. Not daring then to refuse, Jimmy nearly choked eating fried chicken and boiled rice and gravy and pound cake with all the Caldwells sitting about him—he swallowed hard, almost ill, wondering if his place had been Narcissa's; had she ever raised this cup from which he was drinking; had this knife cut meat for her dinner.

Driving finally in the quivering half-afternoon through the high hills, blue that day with a blueness unexcelled in the southern spectrum

Jimmy knew that his secret was his own, safe in his own secret keeping; but also he was lost in the depths of his own being, and that also he knew. Only the dark forests of night were ahead for him, the ghosts that haunt the conscience. A little ill, feverish, he saw a deep river flowing underground toward a secret sea, and into those black waters he saw himself flung; in that darkness, he was unable to struggle—he was overcome, he quit trying to hold his own against the heavy current, he began drifting, slowly he approached the inevitable. Jimmy groaned in new anguish. "God, if only we could live over a life." "What would you do with it, for Christ's sake," he said to himself, sneeringly. "I'd do plenty," he replied to himself, great earnestness in his manner. "I'd plot a different course and I'd steer it."

It was not long afterwards that he began a period of drinking. He began to drink himself into unconsciousness, and this frightened him for he was afraid now of his tongue. Always on recovering from one of these debauches, he would inquire anxiously and cautiously, "What did I talk about—what did I say." Once when he asked that question and old Aaron happened to be in the room, the older man looked intently and squarely into Jimmy's face, said, "Jimmy, you are trying to hide something." The boy's face burned with shame and fear, and seeing this, Aaron whispered, "Whatever it is, be careful." And right there in the presence of his old friend, Jimmy wept, and then he cursed himself for although he felt very sorry for himself, he also hated himself—his irresolution. He would not confess what he had done nor would he forgive himself for not confessing. "Jesus Christ," he said, "If there is anybody that has ruined a good life more one hundred per cent completely than I have—well, God, help him, the poor bastard."

"Well," said old Aaron, "there is Carter Caldwell."

⁂

In the early days, working hard on Forest Mansion, Carter was happy just to be alive; there was so much to be done and he was so sure he could do it. Stopping work twice during the building of the house, he made trips southward with wagons loaded with tallow and hides for the dusty markets of Hamburg, proving himself shrewd at bargaining. Once again he sent a wagon train over the mountains with provisions to keep the Tennessee people going through another winter that was hard. Very soon he had become the head indeed of a growing family of pioneers, directing interests and property and advising people across five hundred miles of continent, all the way from Keowee to the Father of Waters.

He was happy and young, refused to permit the moods to down his exuberant spirit. "Hell, Stevie," he said once to Stephen John, "don't let a little thing like trouble get you down. Turn your back on trouble, boy, forget it." When Carter felt one of those melancholy moods creeping over him, he would pick up an axe, swing it for half a day hardly without stopping. Action was his refuge, hard, back-tiring work. He knew what a blessing work was, it was a wonderful thing to come into a cabin at dark so tired he could hardly walk; then rest itself—just simple rest would take its place among the exquisite pleasures. And so did eating become plain delight—the fine taste of bread when he was hungry, and cool butter on the bread, and a cold melon, and cold milk in the pitcher. And then there was sleep.

Carter liked to walk, to tramp alone over the hills, to think, adjust himself to nature. He was sensible to the ruddled beauty of his red fields; the primeval woods touched his emotions, so did the quality of Keowee sunshine, steady and clear, and the feel of the wild western wind and the sound of the pines. Gradually there came over him a feeling of responsibility to the past—to old scalped Narcissa, to his father, who tried for twenty years to build a house, to all the hardship, the spiritual hunger, the fear of the savage, the never knowing what tomorrow might bring, the readiness to face that tomorrow. Carter came to bring himself as a living link between the wild forest life of his father and the rich future, for surely the wilderness some time would fulfill his father's dream, his Uncle Carter's dream he never doubted. He was a fragment in the immensity of time—this stirred his pride, also it kept him humble.

One thing Carter had not done was marry and this was a subject people gossiped about in the valley. "Why," they asked, "has not Carter Caldwell married?" The reason, he always said, was simple. During the war he was a wandering soldier; returning from the war he had found few unmarried women in the wilderness who approached him either in experience or in age. "And I'm going to marry for companionship," he explained once when Equal Sue had brought up this subject. "To hell with youth and beauty."

Carter was in no hurry to marry. His celibate state did not bother him. In his inmost life he still was Carter the passionate, the adventurer, but matters were arranged for him at Equal Sue's. He was managing his secret life well enough until Narcissa died—it was so that he regarded her death; she had "died." For a time afterward, he had managed well enough. Narcissa's dying had been a blow to him but not a shattering one; he was a rough wilderness man, strong and with a frontier will. He had done what had to be done and, having done it, there was no turning back. Carter brooded more trying to find who the man was who had known his sister than he did about his own taking of her life; he spent hours considering the men of the foothills—man by man. His greatest worry was that he could reach no sure conclusion; it angered him.

Carter would have gone on his way determined enough had it not been that he allowed himself to be seduced. He permitted himself in the moral sense of that term to be seduced. The experience was fraught for him with threats of disaster; it nearly destroyed him within, crushing the unquestioned justification of his right to take his sister's life.

The girl's name was Caline Lott, and in her way she was a kind of genius, born with ruthless shrewdness. For at the age of sixteen she had discovered that the armor of men's love is not perfect, and without older advice or suggestion she made a plan, picked a man, and violated him successfully.

It happened so.

After a lonesome week in the high valley, working hard on the house, Carter straddled his fastest horse and rode at a swift gait towards Pendleton to do the trading of the moment—there was a little indigo to be bought, a packet of green china tea, a pound of syrupy Barbados sugar, several light plowshares. Also he intended to stop at a cabin that green canes hid on the bank of Eighteen Mile Creek. This was the home of Equal Sue, a prostitute of considerable strength of character and knowledge, who regarded herself as a sort of missionary in a wilderness with few unattached women for unattached, wandering men. She came into her name after a declaration that one man was as good as another to her. Time was her money. So economy was arranged on the length of what was called "the divertissement"—ranging from three dollars for "a night's lodging" to twenty-five cents for a "scat call." For this last, Equal Sue did not bother to take to her bed, merely raising her skirts and standing behind the door. "Personally," she said once to Carter, for he was her confidant as well as she was his, "Personally, I'd like to do away with the scat call, but poor men have their rights."

Riding on this day through the steep hills, Carter was thinking to himself of the insolent and honest wit of Sue—he had almost reached the narrow-muddied creek which his own family had decided years before to name Eighteen Mile, he was nearly at the house in the canes when in the middle of the red clay road—there stood Caline Lott. She was holding a crude hook beaten into shape by some clumsy blacksmith. Raising up her curious sweet face—an always surprised face, flaming with wild beauty, she said to Carter, "I'm going fishing." Eighteen Mile Creek was too shallow, too muddy for fish to live in, everyone in that country knew that. So swinging one of his great legs over the narrow back of his horse, Carter stepped lightly to the ground; he knew adventure when he came upon it. He pretended to be gravely interested in the iron fish hook, examining it, asking, "Where are the fish biting?" "Oh, downstream," said Caline, casually. Moving then through vines and briars and dodging a fringe of low-hanging sycamore limbs, Carter wrapped an arm about the full hips of the girl beside him. There was no struggle. But there was a fire blazing within Carter. The fire blazed. And then there was quiet.

As Carter lay upon the fine white-grained sand, resting, Caline began to cry. She put her hands about his neck, weeping. But Carter did not weep—perhaps if he had even then she might have spared him. But Carter did not cry, he was only restless. "It's getting late," he said, "I'll have to be getting along," and hurrying towards the road, he called back, "I'll be seeing you."

All this had taken place as Caline had planned. Lying that night in a feather bed in the cabin of her father, further down the creek, she reviewed the results of this day, saying "it's too late now to turn back." Getting up she lit a candle, studied herself in a narrow looking glass. Burning darkness distinguished Caline—oily black hair, shining brown eyes; her arms were very small and plump and her small waist was very narrow but there was this about her physique—this small upper body was set like a wedge into gross hips and legs of enormous proportions. Caline was half a mermaid, half a giant woman.

Caline met Carter the next Saturday afternoon by the side of the same creek, ran with him like a calf, allowed him to catch her in a patch of mud-caked weeds. She met him a third and a fourth time—this also was the plan. But on the fifth as the blazing sun was setting in the dazzling west, she put her head on Carter's naked shoulder, saying, "Mister Caldwell, there is something I've got to tell you." There was a subtle lessening of the passion in the grip of the arms that held her; a note of coldness in the voice that asked, "Well, what is it?" Beginning to cry, Caline said, "We'll have to get married."

Carter laughed. "Oh, for Christ sake," he said, "don't be foolish."

But Caline was grim. "We've got to get married," she said, "And I mean we're going to get married." Long conversation followed, fierce and intense and low, growing every moment more determined with Caline, with Carter more angry. Finally Caline announced that whether Carter liked it or not he was going to marry her. "I'm not so foolish," she said, "as your sister Narcissa."

Instantly, light blurred in Carter's blue eyes, rage swept over his reason and with all his strength he began beating Caline with his fists. In a few seconds she was lying sprawled on the clean sand, blood running between the delicate curve of her lips.

"Control yourself," Caline said, severely. There was no fear in her face. "Think what you are doing—I left a note sealed in a pillow at home telling the folks if harm should come to me that the man responsible would be Carter Caldwell of Keowee."

Only then did Carter realize how tight about a man can a woman wind her long hair. "You've thought of everything, haven't you?"

Caline was shrewd enough not to reply. She knew if she answered that it would become an answer that would never be forgotten. She said nothing and Carter in a new burst of rage flung sand at her bleeding mouth, handful after handful. Then he turned from Caline and ran through the canes and briars. Night had set in before he reached the Caldwell cabin. Without entering the house, he climbed the hill to the burying ground. "I killed Narcissa," he said to himself, leaning against the wall about Narcissa's tomb. "I killed her," he wept. "Now I ought to kill myself." But Carter knew he would not kill himself—he was the head of the Caldwell family, he could not bring down on them the final disgrace. For he considered suicide the greatest of the crimes; especially would suicide dishonor his mother. Also he considered taking one's own life an act of cowardice, and deep within him, there was the fear of the hereafter; he was afraid of the belief the wilderness had on this subject—there would be no pardon in Zion for self-murder.

"I can't kill myself," said Carter, "and I can't kill Caline." He considered killing her, but he realized it was one thing to kill a ruined sister, quite another to kill a woman one had ruined oneself. "I won't solve anything just by letting matters drift—for Caline will tell, it's what she wants—it will be to her advantage to tell. She will tell her father and her brothers, and either the Lotts will shoot me or I will have to shoot the Lotts." It occurred to Carter that the Lotts were a numerous family of men. All that night he wandered among the tombs, concluding in the end as Caline had—he would have to marry her.

So married they were—on the Saturday next.

Wet with stale sweat of a half day of hard work, Carter on Friday noon bathed his great-limbed body in the cold waters of the horse branch, and dressing in a fresh work shirt, and new breeches, said to his mother, "I'm going to town."

"All right," said Lucinda, unconcerned, "bring me some Cayenne pepper, some nutmeg and some mace."

Soon he was off, astride the saddle mare and riding hard, he reached in mid-afternoon the log cabin of Preacher McKay, who at the time of Carter's arrival, was sprawled full length on the piazza, his long and narrow head against a stick of firewood—having a springtime nap. "Brother McKay," shouted Carter, riding up to the edge of the porch, "I came by to ask you, please, to do me the favor of being at our house tomorrow afternoon at five o'clock." McKay never was able to gather his wits very quickly on being awakened suddenly, this time he was hardly conscious before his caller, turning about, was galloping through the grove. "What time, what time?" he shouted. "Five o'clock," cried Carter.

Riding into the drowsy square at Pendleton, Carter bought the things his mother had asked him to get and from Mister Aaron's store he went to Equal Sue's cabin in the cane patch. He stayed there that night, leaving the next day for the opposite bank of the creek, where he knew Caline would be waiting in the dusty road.

"All right," he said, pointing northward, "Get a move on; get going—we haven't got too much time; we'll have to hurry." He made Caline walk the entire distance to the Caldwell cabin, following her on his horse. She was sweating and dusty when they reached the cabin but without giving her time even to wash her hands, he called McKay and had the marriage service performed.

❧

When at midnight that night the Connecticut clock was striking, old Lucinda was listening, wide awake, thinking this marrying was the strangest of all the strange things a Caldwell had ever done. As she lay in her bed and the clock ticked, she was overwhelmed with worry. For she wanted her son to be happy in life; she wanted too for the family to bear a good name. "What will people say," she kept saying to herself, "How can we explain?"

Alone in another wide bed in the same room lay Caline, weeping silently, and all the time thinking now that he was her husband that she would work her fingers to the bone, do anything in the world to please Carter. She wanted passionately to rush to Carter's side, on her knees to beg him to forgive her, to explain everything, tell him over and over that she loved him, always had loved him—only him. On her knees, she wanted to cry, "Carter, I was a poor girl, I had no friend. there weren't many men left in the wilderness. And you wouldn't notice me otherwise, I had to scheme." She would plead as she never had before, and if he would forgive—if he would forgive!

But Caline did not go to Carter; she lay alone in the big bed and wept. And as she lay there, crying, Carter sat in the cook cabin before a low fire, brooding and staring into the heart of the flame. "Men before me have been through this," he told himself, "What they were able to go through—I can go through." Then he jumped up, wringing his hands. For before him appeared the swollen face of Narcissa. He ran outside, facing the night.

"God," he cried, "I can't stand it."

❧

Carter began to treat Caline as though she were a servant, a hired hand; sometimes he said to her that the day was a fine day or that perhaps it might rain; sometimes at the table he asked her if she would pass the biscuit plate, the butter. His conversation was conducted with his mother. Most of the time he discussed with her the progress being made on the new house. Soon it would be finished.

Often Carter would ask Lucinda to come with him to the top of the hill to see a door that was being swung in place, to look at a shelf, to tell him where a row of pegs should be placed in a closet. Turning once to Caline, Lucinda said, "Caline, you come with us."

"No," said Carter, instantly, and there was no doubt about the furious determination of his tone.

Many times in the late afternoon, in the flaming glow of the sunset, Carter would stand on the hill, his mother by his side, and stare long and silently at the house—already it stood for him as a symbol. They had built it with their own hands, it was their will. Already it seemed to him to belong there—like the old mountains and the thrush's song and the blue mist that hung over the far hills. With all these, it fit—it too was Carolina, the Carolina the Caldwells had opened up themselves and settled. It was such a stern and solid house—Forest Mansion would stand as long as the oak trees and the granite slopes of the mountains. And the implication of Carter was—the Caldwells would stand with it.

"It has character," he said to Lucinda.

Carter wanted to say to his mother that he must make himself worthy to live in such a house; he wanted to say, "I must become as strong and simple—as good." But he could not bring himself to express such words, they reminded him too overwhelmingly of his own darkness. He only thought these words.

Finally the day arrived. The last wooden peg was driven into place.

Forest Mansion was finished.

*

For eighty years the Caldwells had lived in cabins. Eight decades had gone by since old Narcissa had started into the fringe of frontier civilization from the quiet valley north of Philadelphia. And now in the midst of a southern forest, here stood the citadel she had longed for—the safety, the security. But it was not hers, it was the son's of her grandson. In the long chronicle of Narcissa's children, this should have been one of the poignant moments of rapture. And it was such a moment, but like most times of triumph the poignancy was tempered—so many to whom it would have meant so much had gone on.

And as for the living…

"Ma," said Carter quietly, "I don't feel like having any kind of a house-warming—not just now. I don't feel like any kind of a celebration."

Lucinda said, "All right."

So they moved into the new house. The graceful, homely furniture—the firm walnut tables, four poster corded beds, hickory and white-oak chairs, the curly maple cupboards and the clock were loaded into the oxcart and hauled up the steep hillside.

And the carved, chromed rooster was swung from the weathervane. As the arrangement of the furniture began, Carter made one stipulation—one bedroom must be set aside for himself, he would not occupy a bedroom with Caline. This scandalized Lucinda.

"What will folks say?" she demanded.

"They can say what they want to," said Carter.

Carter realized that he must come to some working agreement with his wife. This seemed to him to be the time to make an understanding. He came that evening into the kitchen where Lucinda and Caline were frying ham for supper. "Caline," he called out sternly, "You come with me—I have something I'd like to tell you." Drying her hands and looking half-hopefully, half in terror, at the tall figure of her husband, Caline followed quickly. She understood full well what was about to happen. The two made their way into the central room.

"Sit down," said Carter, pointing to a chair. Caline sat down and Carter shut the door. "Well," he said, "We can't go on like this and somehow we've got to go on; we've got to reach some sort of agreement." Nervously Caline ran her fingers along the seam of a blue apron. "This house is yours," Carter said, "You are free to run it but..." Suddenly Carter shrugged his broad shoulders. "Aw," he broke off, sounding a note of despair. "Why bother about trying to talk—what in hell does it matter." He left the room.

That night he burst into Caline's room, tearing away the bedclothes and her night-gown; his secret intention was she should bear child after child after child and finally if... well, that would be the will of God.

Instinctively, Caline guessed what was in Carter's mind. But she was unafraid. She was young then and strong.

"I won't die," she said to him.

Carter made no answer.

❧

Carter did not permit her even to name their children. For some strange woman's reason, Caline wanted more than anything to call her first son Lott—Lott Caldwell. Something told her, she had a feeling that things would improve between herself and Carter if only they called their first son Lott.

"Please, Carter," she begged, making one of her few requests. "Please, let me name this one—just this one."

"His name," said Carter, "is Stephen John." Carter wrote the name himself in the Caldwell Bible in deep blue ink. "Stephen John Caldwell, second of that name of Forest Mansion," wrote he. One day not long after that, Carter in a rage threw a pan full of scalding water on Caline; she picked up a kettle from the stove and scalded him. "I can be as mean as you can," she said. Later she crept into her bedroom and shut the door—bitterly she wept.

Chapter Seven

It was at this time that Queen Elizabeth came to Forest Mansion. Tall and proud and black, she was standing in the old slave market in Augusta when Carter first saw her—an immense figure poised beside a white column. Among a group of frightened Negroes, cringing and uncertain, Queen Elizabeth loomed triumphant. Seemingly an ageless being, above destiny, she broke into fine singing when the time came for her to climb the block. Her shoulders were flung far back and very white in her jet face were wide eyes and brilliant teeth. "Lord," she sang, "I'll fall upon my knees and I'll face the rising sun." The fearless physical beauty and the courage of this black woman entranced Carter. At once he began bidding, raising the price higher and higher. After a quarter-hour of haggling, she was his. He had bought her.

He brought Queen Elizabeth to Keowee and in the same wagon also he brought some cotton seed. Without even suspecting it, Carter was fixing the seal upon the misty uplands. "Yes, Lord, hallelujah," sang the Negro woman as northward rolled the wagon.

In less than a year Carter noted in his farm book, "Cleared six dollars an acre on wheat, eight on corn, thirteen dollars on the cotton." And also before that first crop of white cotton was picked from the heavy bolls in the red fields, he recorded, "A son was born to Queen Elizabeth—she named it Richit, nicknamed it Popcorn." Men laughed at the news that Queen Elizabeth at Keowee had become a mother. "How can that happen," they asked Carter. "A child without a father?" Carter did not reply; it was not humorous to him. For the child's skin was light.

The great figure of the Negro woman soon was familiar about the valley, she fitted readily into the scheme of things, and she brought with her a new spirit and a strange new richness of the imagination as her contribution to the dour valley in which the Caldwells had settled. She told great stories of mysterious things and of magic, she believed in charms and signs, and in her dreams she saw visions. Some of the things she saw frightened even the wisest men and women—for instance, she said she had a vision once in which the ghosts of women who were unfaithful to their husbands rose before her. She saw these men leaving their homes, saying they were going hunting or trading at Augusta, then suddenly she saw them returning quickly and without warning—at night. And terrible were the results. Queen Elizabeth said in this vision some of the men strangulated their wives, carved holes in their hearts. The Negro slave was well aware of the uneasiness this vision caused in the upcountry—so she told it as often as she could and as innocently, adding finally that she had almost been able to see the faces of some of those women. She would throw back her head and roar, "They seemed powerful familiar."

Queen Elizabeth brought the fantasies of the African animal kingdom into the Keowee wilderness—all the intricate and double-edged rivalries of Brer Rabbit and old Brer Fox. She enchanted the briar patch. And then there were her songs, the slow-moving wailing songs that she sang at the top of her great voice—songs of a world in which everyone did his best but always was beset by trouble; weary men marched through her songs on their weary way. "Oh, the children of the wilderness moan for bread," "I'm going to rest from all my labor when I'm dead," "We will all sing together on that day," "Look out there sinner how you tramp on the cross." Also Queen Elizabeth sang the hymns the Caldwells sang, slowing their quick tempo, changing them all into a weeping minor key, distorting their original rhythm into a new rhythm. It was a beautiful thing to hear her slow chanting of "Will there be any stars—any stars in my crown", and nobody anywhere ever sang "Sweet hour of prayer" with a greater richness of feeling. And many times when she was lonesome, she would sing songs of her own—bits of melody so filled with sadness and sorrow that like the note of the whip-poor-will and the baying of lean hound dogs at the moon and, long later, the lonesome sound of a train coming round a bend in darkness—once heard, they lived in Keowee forever.

Queen Elizabeth filled the world about her with all the mystery and ritual of her magic—nails, teeth, saliva, perspiration, dandruff, scabs meant mighty things to her. So did snakeroot, jimson weed, rusty iron, lizards, buzzard feathers, powdered brick dust, blue grass. Devil's shoe strings rubbed on the hands, she said, would give a man control over any woman the moment the rascal shook her hand. "And I mean control—CON-TROL. So," said she, to the women, "don't you shake hands with strange men," adding in her wise way an announcement of the fact that she spoke from experience; once she had shaken hands with a strange man—a powerful black buck from Edisto Island.

"What happened, Queen Elizabeth," she always was asked.

"Honey," was her answer, "I lost control."

In Queen Elizabeth's formulae of magic, women could overcome men with drops of blood and as proof of that she told of an old woman she knew on James Island—a colored woman, flat breasted and sterile, who dropped one drop of her blood into a young man's liquor cup and that man stayed on with that woman even after she had beaten him with a stick. "So help me, God," said Queen Elizabeth.

The wilderness never was the same again after Queen Elizabeth.

Carter was surprised to learn how lightly she controlled the great emotions, the will and the conscience and all those involved problems which gnawed at his own reason. Things were arranged simply for Queen Elizabeth—they were epic. To her the world was a hill, heaven was a hill, and between these two lay the fires of hell in a deep pit. The road she had to follow from the here to the hereafter was like a long tight rope, and onto this she ventured, a rope walker. She hung on as long as she could, then she fell off, got singed a little, and started over. Always the heart was willing with Queen Elizabeth, always the flesh was weak—that was the beginning and the end of human conduct. Yesterday was the long-buried past, tomorrow might never come—there was the living present. She never forgot that God was a merciful God, He would forgive her any time in the twinkling of an eye. So no matter what might face her, Queen Elizabeth was prepared, she was ready.

Carter soon began to visit Queen Elizabeth in the darkness of night. "Don't you ever tell a living soul—do you understand," said Carter the first time he crept into her dark cabin. "Mister Carter," said she, "I know things don't nobody know except me and Jesus— I know something don't even I know."

On the morning after that first trip to the cabin, Carter felt ashamed of himself. It startled him to hear Queen Elizabeth, entering the kitchen to start breakfast, to begin singing as jubilantly and freely as ever:

> "Oh they tell me of a home far beyond the skies,
>   Oh they tell me of a home far away;

Oh they tell me of a home where no storm cloud rise,
Oh they tell me of an unclouded day."

The deep voice rang, easy and filled with true religious devotion. The sound filled Carter with remorse, he was overwhelmed with the old aching feeling of again having done what he should not have done. Rising, he dressed quickly, determined to face Queen Elizabeth alone—to overcome his shame and embarrassment before Caline came in to eat.

"Good morning, master," said Queen Elizabeth exactly as before; there was not the slightest change in her manner, no degree of intimacy, no lack of respect. "The day is surely fine." Watching over a frying pan filled with frying eggs, she now began singing to herself in a low, humming voice:

"Oh the land of cloudless day,
Oh the land of the unclouded sky,
Oh tell me of a home where no storm cloud rise,
Oh tell me of an unclouded day."

A few minutes later, Queen Elizabeth turned to face Caline, who now was entering the room. "Good morning, mistress," she said, also exactly as before. Gradually Carter was to learn that the Queen Elizabeth who lay at night in a cabin upon a feather bed never saw the rising sun—this naked figure of the darkness vanished with the owls and bats.

Many times during this period of his life, Carter told himself he would not go another time to the black woman in the outer house but he lacked the will—again and again he went, reproaching himself bitterly at first, repenting in remorse, but as time went on the remorse became less remorseful. These visits became a habit.

And as many men need a woman to talk to, Carter began telling his secret plans to Queen Elizabeth—to a soul that existed only in darkness. One winter night after a bitter scene with Caline in the great room of the mansion, Carter told Queen Elizabeth about his wife—the whole story, told her he hated Caline. He reproached himself for this afterward but Queen Elizabeth seemed not to have heard a word. When day dawned that morning, a still clear day with the wind of the night dying down, Carter was awakened by a triumphant burst of song from the back yard:

"His eye is on the sparrow,
And I know He watches me."

"Good morning, master," Queen Elizabeth said cheerfully as Carter came into the kitchen. Queen Elizabeth did not remember. But Carter remembered, and it was on his high-cheeked passionate man's face that his wife read everything. Caline knew and she had known from the beginning. At first she would slip into her husband's empty bedroom and flail the empty bed. She would cry out to herself, calling Queen Elizabeth low, dirty names. "I won't stand for this," she told herself on many cold nights, "I'll drive the woman out of this country." Sometimes she thought of telling Carter but then she would say to herself. "What good would that do?" During the cold first winter of her married life, Caline discovered the desolate spiritual isolation of a wife of her condition. There was nothing she could do, Carter would only insult her; very likely he would say to her what difference did it make if a man's whore were black or white, she knew Carter was that cruel. Soon Caline saw this was an arrangement she would be obliged to accept. "Very well," she said, "then I will accept it, and I'll never let him know that I even suspect."

Bitterly unhappy, Caline turned for consolation to flower gardening. to the passionate mysteries of religion. She visited sick neighbors. helped the poor, with complete frankness and understanding turned over a cabin to an unmarried mother whom a family down the river had turned out of doors. Also she became fond of hounds, keeping at least a half dozen chained in the yards of Forest Mansion. "Dogs," she once said, "will never turn on you, no matter what happens, your dogs will still follow you." Caline planted the double rows of honey locusts along the sanded road curving down the hill into the holly ravine, she laid out the gardens of Forest Mansion that long afterward were to make her as famous among the Caldwells, as closely identified with them as Carter was. On the cool northern exposure she planted the celebrated yellow garden; on the warm south, the bee garden; this latter designed according to principles set down by old Narcissa in her herb book— "A garden should connect the solemnity of summer with the cheerfulness of spring, for it should be filled with all kinds of fragile flowers, as well wild as garden flowers, with seats of chamomile and here and there a peach." Possessing the great characteristic of the lonely pioneers—an utter unquestioning belief that the wilderness would remain their home through all the centuries of later time—Caline planted on the noblest scale. As the northern border for the yellow garden and the southern border for the bee garden, she set a line of brooding moody cedar trees and next to these she dug holes for a thick row of holly bushes and within this and also extending and forming the east and west borders of both gardens were the double tiers of formal boxwood, the boxwood that was to give to Forest Mansion its characteristic dry and pungent scent. Caline liked yellow, the sun color of life and love, she said, and she immortalized this affection in the yellow garden. Within this towering border of green, she planted only flowers with yellow blossoms, massed wild patches of blazing gold foxglove and partridge pea and from the fields brought frostweed, mullein, moth mullein, wild wood sorrel, the tiny yellow flax, beds of sundrops, primroses, buttercups, yellow star grass, dog-tooth violets and great gold beds of wild indigo and mustard. On arbors clung bowers of yellow jesamine and the sweet fly honeysuckle and about a shallow pool were yellow pond lilies, yellow lady's slipper and a wild fringed orchid. From March unto November, Caline kept this north garden a constant scene of shifting yellow shades—it was a wild and beautiful sight, quickly acquiring fame. In time people who once had come to Keowee to see the first window panes in the upcountry returned to see these yellow flowers, tales were told of Caline's garden from Charleston to the Tennessee.

Soon after Caline started the planting of her golden blossoms, she was converted to primitive Methodism by a young itinerant circuit rider by the name of Charles Clark. This young man, tall and extraordinarily handsome with light curling hair and a face clean and luminant with zeal, rode up one day on a fine horse, and dismounting began to speak to Caline of the tragic need of man for that gentle quality of godly surrender and rocklike faith whereby alone he could search for the only true way. Listening to these words, Caline concluded immediately that this man had been sent to her by God as a guide for her salvation in a time of loneliness and despair. His appearance in the time of her greatest need and confusion was regarded by Caline as a miracle. Quickly she invited him into Forest Mansion—a chair was put for him before one of the dark Carrara mantles and through an entire afternoon Caline listened, completely rapt, to the impassioned flow of his words.

"It's a divine message—I'm sure," said Caline, "I'm sure God has sent you to help me to find the way." Caline listened with such sympathetic and genuine attention, that soon the young man began to reveal to her the depths of his own lonely ambitions—here lay the vast wilderness, wild and unconverted, waiting, crying for the word, "The Lord has called me to the frontier for this duty," he said, a look of agonized intentness coming into his face.

"I am a flame." The boy bounded from the chair. "O, I must set this country blazing with the holy fire of God." Suddenly moved herself by a fierce desire to serve God, Caline burst out, "I am ready to help you." The young minister said, "Let us pray." Afterward he held his powerful hands over Caline's head, he quoted to her the strange words of Paul to Timothy that women adorn themselves in modest apparel with shamefacedness and sobriety, not with broidered hair or gold or pearls or costly array. "My sister," he said, "you must put away earrings and ruffles and rings and plumes." Caline jerked from her ears two thin hoops of gold, quickly a ring was slipped from her finger. "Welcome, my sister," said Charlie, clasping her right hand, "welcome into the tabernacle of God."

Caline insisted that the circuit rider make Forest Mansion his permanent headquarters while engaged in carrying the word into the mountain country, this invitation she held open even after Preacher McKay came one day to warn her that the young man under her roof was a false prophet.

"He beareth false witness," said McKay angrily demanding that Clark be sent away. "Brother Clark," replied Caline with icy fury, "is a devoted man of God." Laughing at her scornfully, McKay called to his horse. "Get up," he said, and turning to ride away, he yelled at Caline. But she out-yelled him, "He is inspired by the Holy Ghost sent down from heaven."

"He's got a mighty handsome young face—if you ask me what I think," cried McKay. "I didn't ask you," replied Caline, adding as a parting word, "You Pharisee."

Caline now was happier than she had ever been in her life—talking through the hours and clays with Charlie about God and the surrendered life and the guidance of God and the heathen frontier and the Methodist way. Often he counseled her, his handsome face very grave. "Envy," he said, "is a fell destroyer—how carefully should its first subtle approaches be checked or guarded against—how often has it broken the sweetest ties of Christian affection, shorn the mighty of their strength, caused talents to be prostrate." Soon Caline discovered this was a sermon that Charlie was developing, he had begun to think aloud in her presence, and this pleased her. "You inspire me, Sister Caline," he said, and Caline closed her eyes—no one ever had talked to her in this manner.

In the yellow garden one day Charlie said the time had come for Caline to stand up before the people in the brush arbor, among the unbelievers, and publicly confess her sins, to bear witness, to testify. This worried Caline. For urged on by the spiritual force of the young man, she wanted passionately to sweep her soul clean of the great troubles of the past, to seek release, yet she still was distracted by worried misgiving and doubt, she went through some anxious hours and sleepless nights, then timidly she sought the evangelist's advice. "There is a sin," she said, wavering in her words, hesitating and blushing in deep humiliation. But Charlie understood. "Sister Caline," he said, "reveal at a meeting of this kind but do not expose yourself." This sent Caline on her way, free and rejoicing; the spinning wheel hummed and for the first time since coming to Forest Mansion, Caline was heard to sing:

"The mountains holier visions bring
Than e'er in vales arise;
The brightest sunshine bathes the wing
That's nearest to the skies."

Appearing that Sunday at the brush arbor, Caline wore a plain black dress, a spectacular costume for one of her dark beauty; she made her public confession. "I have borne false witness," she said, "And I have been selfish, I have said things I did not mean to say…" She told of many safe little sins, witnessing for perhaps a quarter of an hour, then with black swishing, she settled herself on the hard front bench. Everyone began singing, "I have ceased from wand'ring and going astray, since Jesus came into my heart." While joining in the song, Caline was saying to herself, "Next to yellow I think black is my favorite color." Black was not for her the color of sorrow—it was mystery.

It was not long after that meeting under the oak boughs that Charlie saw a vision. The divine spirit appeared to him in a dream, telling him to prophesy. Accordingly he went out and threatened the destruction of the Blue Ridge Mountains by fire and sword unless the people in Kcowee Valley repented. Also in the midst of the fine sound of his voice, he shouted one clay in the brush arbor that God had made him as good a man as any man spoken about in the Book. "I have been called to bear witness," he shouted, "and I stand before you as good a man in my heart as Saul or Elijah or as the Prophet Jeremiah."

"Hold on there, brother." From a back bench, the long figure of a murderous-type Baptist mountaineer slowly loomed into view above the heads of this Methodist congregation. "Hold on—are you as good a man as Jesus?"

"Jesus was not a man," said Charlie, patiently. He was accustomed to being heckled, jeered at, questioned; sometimes even the most faithful of his congregation would interrupt him in the midst of a sermon to disagree. These were free times, this a free congregation. "Jesus," said Charlie, "was the son of God." A wild laugh came from the mountaineer who lurched against one of the tottering poles of the arbor. "Brother," he yelled in a thick voice, "You ain't as good a man even as those thieves they crucified with Jesus." It was evident that this man had been drinking, all were aware of it, all knew that his intention was deliberately to stir up trouble. Caline tried to motion to Charlie to ignore the man but the young man paid her no heed.

"I'm a better man than any thief that ever lived," Charlie shouted, anger in his words.

"Could you stand the test?" inquired the man insolently.

"Sure," said Charlie, striking the pulpit with one of his broad palms. A pitcher of water fell crashing to the floor. "Then just step outside, brother." Charlie walked into the open and the wild, half-drunk man said to a group of other mountaineers with him, "Boys, let's crucify him." They plaited a crown of swamp briars, putting it on Charlie's head, and they laughed and pointed their fingers at the young minister; but he remained meek and humble. He ordered his own followers to be quiet, to make no disturbance. "Have mercy upon these idolaters, Father," he said, "they know not what they do." A cross was made of two pine poles and Charlie was made to drag this up a hill, still he was meek. Then one of the boys, drunker than the others, spattered Charlie's face with some wet cow dung. Suddenly Charlie stood still, slowly he wiped the filth from his eyes and mouth. "Boys," he said, to his own followers, "take off this cross—this Jesus business has gone far enough."

This brought howls of laughter from the men. who pounded one another on the back and pointed their fingers at Charlie.

"Hell, boys," said the half-drunken mountaineer in his thick voice. "He's a false prophet sure as hell fire—he ain't even got the guts of the thief that was crucified beside the Master." Laughing louder than ever, the men walked away, leaving the pine sticks still tied together.

Charlie was humiliated and beaten. Bitterly that night he said to Caline, "I am strong enough—I am deluded." Caline gave him a drink of peach brandy, told him not to doubt, he was a true servant of God, must expect ridicule, brave persecution. Encouraged by her warm, tender sympathy, Charlie revived in spirit, was back again the following Sunday in the old pulpit under the oak leaf shelter—shouting God had given him the power to perform miracles.

Pointing his hands towards a cloudless sky, Charlie commanded the rain to fall on drought-burned crops. That very afternoon there was a shower. A few Sundays later in wrath at the sinfulness and unhearing of the people, he called upon the Lord to wreak his vengeance. On Wednesday, early in the morning, a high wind swept across the valley, knocking down hundreds of trees and killing cattle. True it was tornado time, but just the same many in Keowee began to feel uneasy.

Growing bolder after this, Charlie became convinced the end of time was near at hand, this old world was winding up—many were his signs, the summers had become like winters, the days as dark as night, and in Jerusalem as foretold in the Book an army was encamped. To prove that he knew of what he spoke, Charlie said he would go down into Keowee River and God would divide the waters. He waded into the stream with a hickory stick in his hands, calling on God to part the way. Finding the river to run on as usual, swift and clear, the multitude that had followed Charlie began to laugh. Charlie heard himself called fool and crazy fool—and not only by the lost Baptists but by Methodist brethren as well.

He wept, saying this time to Caline, "I am convinced of my deception—I have not heard the true voice of the Infallible Spirit—it has been the devil himself that has misled me." That night, he packed his things, flung them back of his saddle, and rode away without even saying good-bye.

Caline never forgave Charlie for leaving as he did, without a farewell, but neither did she forget him. His exalted face would appear in her memories; she still could hear him telling her, "I am a flame."

ᕫ

So Caline turned again to growing yellow flowers and raising turkeys, to attending weddings and funerals, to her lonely world of secret reveries.

And there were her little children to occupy her time—Stephen John the second who took after the Caldwells, his eyes being blue, his skin fair and his hair yellow; he was followed by Lucinda the second, a dark child like the Lotts but Lucinda did not live long, she died of the cholera morbus; after Lucinda came Artemissa the second and after her Carter the third, Temperance the first; then there was Unity.

On the night Unity was born, Caline in a fit of hard stomach pains begged Carter to send to Pendleton for the doctor.

"They charge too much," said Carter.

Although he still was bitter, Carter succeeded gradually in turning the great flood of his energy away from himself and his trouble and into that man's world of work which always has existed in a realm more or less remote from life in the house.

There was Forest Mansion, there was his father's plan—this plan for Carter became more and more absorbing, he determined passionately to make it live. First he would free Forest Mansion, make it self-contained, a refuge beyond the demand any power could make upon it except the tax levied by the state; he fertilized the fields, allowing all of them every seventh year to lie fallow, he built stone walls, planted fruit trees, scuppernongs and grapes, terraced the steep hillsides. He built the mansion's immense pine-beamed log barns, a smithy to sharpen his own plowshares, shoe his own horses; on the horse branch he built a grist mill, began grinding wheat and corn for everyone for miles around, taking one measure in every four for himself; he built a molasses mill, set up a saw mill. Then he built the covered bridge over Keowee River—Caldwell's Bridge, a beautiful structure, and from then on levied a toll on the long line of travelers passing by Forest Mansion on the way to the west. Carter was a builder and his days were filled, he found forgetfulness in his work.

Also he entered politics.

He was hard at work late one September afternoon, trying himself to pick three hundred pounds of cotton in a day, when a red wagon drove up before Forest Mansion— a delegation. "Carter," yelled the chairman of the group, and the valleys for miles about echoed. For it was Colonel Todd Bowen of Seneca Plantation, a famous possum hunter who knew how to shout. With the Colonel in the wagon were Preacher McKay and old Aaron Gadlock, keeper of the Pendleton store. The three carefully lifted themselves down, settled themselves importantly on the piazza while Queen Elizabeth ran to bring them a pitcher of cool water and a watermelon to cut.

When Carter arrived, his strong face streaked with sweat and red dust, old Aaron assumed a strange, dignified air, announcing that this was an official call. "The committee of the Keowee division of the Democratic Party, sir, now waits upon you."

"Mister Carter," said Aaron, folding his pink hands over his storekeeper's belly, "We have instructions to notify you it is our wish for you to consider going down there to Columbia for us."

"Carter," said the Colonel, "we want you to run for us for the Senate."

"Well, friends," said Carter, trying to appear as embarrassed, as overwhelmed as he thought it proper that he should. "I hadn't thought about it." But he had, often he had considered it. He wiped his forehead, stared a few moments toward the distant rim of the mountains. Then in his simplest manner, he said, "If you all want me to run, why I'll run, I'll be proud to."

And run he did. He sent word through the district that he would make a political speech the Saturday following at the town square in Pendleton and when the time came, he climbed onto a platform before the Farmers Hall, announcing himself a candidate for the Senate of South Carolina. Carter spoke awkwardly but without hesitation. "Folks," he said, "You all have known me all your lives and you know, I reckon, about what I stand for—but I just want to tell you to make sure. If you all think fit to elect me I'll stand down there in Columbia just as I'm standing here—for the same things in one place as in the other." Carter hardly saw the crowd gathered before him, the plain, hard-working men and women of the uplands. He was thinking, it was an emotional moment for him—into his vision loomed the wilderness road and on it were the frontier people, lonely, longing, spiritual craving marking their wasted faces.

"Folks," he said, "I believe in the ideals of the frontier—in the standards and principles of the lonely men and women who risked everything to open up the wilderness. I believe in freedom as they did and I believe as they did in the hope for a perfect world. And, brothers and sisters, I don't care who stands up to tell me—not even if he is the President of the United States, I don't care who stands up to tell me there ain't such a thing as a perfect world nor ever will be—I don't care, folks, even if I know myself that it will never be. Still I'm aiming at it and trying. I believe in the pillar of cloud and the pillar of fire and the star I have never seen. I've got faith in America and I'm for the America of tomorrow that has got to be a better place for our children than it has been for us."

A cheer rose for Carter, men and women clapped their hands and shouted, but Carter motioned for quiet. "I'm a plain man," he continued, "And I take my stand on the side of plain men." He was as serious now as a prophet. "I am on the side of the weak and the meek and the poor—I stand for those who have NOT against those who have. I believe the purpose of government is to prohibit the accumulation of great sums of money in the hands of the few. And I believe in change as against the status quo. Folks, I believe things have got to improve in this country and when they have improved they've got to improve some more." A roar went up again from the crowd. Acknowledging it, Carter added in a lower voice. "That's about all I wanted to say, I reckon—I believe I am my brother's helper—that's my general political philosophy and if you all see fit to send me down there to Columbia—why, I'll deal in that general way with whatever particulars that crop up."

The crowd closed in about Carter, dozens of men trying at once to shake his hand; many congratulated him, approving his views; time and again Carter was told, "You talk like your pa and your ma." Many spoke even of old Narcissa, the great-grandmother, "I knew Narcissa—boy, those were her convictions to a T."

On voting day, Carter was elected and from his first appearance in Columbia he became a character—a curious backwoodsman who in his first speech in the Senate announced that whatever Charleston stood for he probably would stand against. "I don't believe in Charleston," he shouted, beginning to stir to a new height of bitterness the feud that had existed between the uplands and the lowlands of Carolina since time had begun. "I come from the wilderness road," he said, "I am for small farmers with few slaves or no slaves at all and I am against landed gentry with hundreds of slaves—I'm for the Baptist and Methodist and Presbyterian way of living, I don't belong to the Protestant Episcopal Church."

Silently, disdainfully, the gentlemen of Charleston ignored the crude man from the mountains. But Carter was not to be ignored. He had not been in the Senate a week before he proposed that United States Senators ought to be elected by popular vote instead of receiving their appointment from the legislature. For Charleston could control a legislature more easily with its money, its powerful social position than it could the people's vote. "Besides," he said, "popular vote is more democratic—the popular vote would more closely represent the will of the people."

A severe figure suddenly arose from the Charleston side of the house. Deliberately, he waited until there was order in the Senate. Then in chill Charleston accent, this gentleman stated, "I believe the common people are too ill educated to be trusted with such responsibility."

Angered, not only by the words but by the man's superior tone, Carter answered with the inspired reply that was to make him a famous man in the western mountain rim of Carolina. "Hell, man, I believe that men educated in poverty and almost in ignorance of literature of any sort are yet capable of great achievements and of actions the most highly conducive to the prosperity and character of the state to which they belong." Passionately Carter cried, "I believe in equality."

"I hate equality," replied the fearless Charlestonian, quivering with fury. "I believe in justice." Then raising his long forefinger, pointing it at Carter like a pistol, the Senator called Carter "a cheap rabble rouser—a demagogue."

"I denounce you," said the Charlestonian.

"Who cares whether you denounce me?" replied Carter, angrily smiling. "I welcome your denunciation and I say to you—to hell with you and to hell with all like you, you and the aristocratic foreign city you all live in and the foreign sea from which you borrow your un-American ideas. I turn my back upon you—the tops of the Blue Ridge Mountains are my standing ground and my face from now on is towards the setting sun. It is in the vast western spaces that I look for my share of the world and its glory."

That night in the inn where he was staying, excited and unable to sleep, Carter felt that he had to write to someone at Forest Mansion about himself. He couldn't write a letter to Queen Elizabeth. So he did what he had never done before—he wrote to his wife. "I am doing fine, I think," wrote he, "Anyhow, I feel fine."

Returning home at the close of the session, riding horseback through the red hills of the uplands, Carter began to talk of intellectual things with Caline—he told her of the Senate, its scenes, outlining his speeches, his political hopes. But at night it still was to Queen Elizabeth that he went to unburden his secret soul, to ease his physical being.

But whether Carter was at Forest Mansion or away in Columbia, Queen Elizabeth bent just the same over the tubs at the washplace, cooked as humbly in the kitchen, sang with the same humble note in her powerful spiritual voice—"Rise and shine," "Death ain't you got no shame," "Oh trembling man, God going to hold you with a trembling hand." And the number of her children increased. After Popcorn there came serious-minded Shadrack and superstitious Gotheny, then Ninny and Lily Bell, very light, then Moses that died.

On the evening that Moses was to be born, Queen Elizabeth walked homeward through the flaming light of the sunset with young Stephen John the second—all day she and he had been hoeing cotton on the hill they called the dove hill, and as they came near to Forest Mansion, a whip-poor-will began its desolate twilight cry. The look of sudden terror that came into the frightened face of the Negro woman was one of the memories never to fade from the boy's memory. "Lord," Queen Elizabeth murmured, as the song was repeated, "Have mercy." Hurrying on, almost running, the woman whispered to Stephen John that it was a sign. "I don't like whip-poor-wills crying round my house," she added.

Melancholy, she sped on, speaking almost unconsciously. "One time a whip-poor-will landed on a windowsill of a house where I was staying—that was long before I came here to Forest Mansion—and a child died in that house; it came again and just hooted a time or two—and the woman's husband left her." Queen Elizabeth shook her head. "No, sir,

Mister Stevie, I don't like to hear whip-poor-wills hollering around me, I don't like that at all."

At ten o'clock that night Moses was born, he lived one hour and died. Afterward, Queen Elizabeth said to Stephen John, "I told you—it was a sign." And she wept so bitterly that Stephen John could never afterward listen to a whip-poor-will without a creeping feeling coming over him.

Two days later, Queen Elizabeth was back again in the same field with Stephen John, singing sad songs, hoeing cotton. The cotton was laid by, it opened white in the vermilion fields, they picked it with their skilled fingers, and then there was winter. The cold winds came and fierce gales flailed the bare trees against the stars, wild gusts tore through the hills, deep and roaring and desolate; across the savage sky fled the frightened clouds, driven before such tempests; the thrashing green blue boughs of the pines glistened in the moonshine with ice and, wild and lonely, like a glazed ship at sea, lay Keowee in the midst of the wilderness and the mountain rim and Christmas. It was during the blowing of these cold winter winds that Queen Elizabeth created a magic character at Keowee that took on actual life and, like the genie in old Asiatic stories, grew immediately beyond control. Coming in late one freezing December evening from a lone walk along the banks of the river, Queen Elizabeth caught a sudden glimpse of an old toothless white woman gathering pine knots and pieces of dry driftwood for her cabin fire. This aged being, alone in her old age, lived only a short distance from Forest Mansion in a cabin set in stony soil among blackberry briars, silver maples, weeds and a row of wild clingstone peaches. The wild wind was blowing her full skirts wide at the time Queen Elizabeth saw her crossing the steep side of a ridge. It was almost night and Queen Elizabeth was a little frightened. The sight of the old white woman made her uneasy. Immediately she thought, "Miss Sally Crossing is a conjure woman—sure as you're born, that's what she is." Frightened now by her own thoughts, Queen Elizabeth ran in a different direction. The next day she began spreading the story of what she had seen, making the account more filled with mystery every time she repeated it. "I saw her— I'm telling you the God's truth; I saw her coming home from the river field, it was almost dark—she was gathering old cow bones and twigs and things, mumbling to herself strange words. That's what she was doing and that is what she is—a conjure woman."

In time these whisperings reached Miss Sally herself and with the intuition of genius she decided to make the most of this dark background—she thought of it at first as a protection for an old woman living alone, it would do no harm for slaves to fear her. Walking with a great knotted hickory staff a few days later along the Keowee, Miss Sally came upon old reel-footed Harve, a red-eyed, blue gum slave belonging to the Hunter family. Squatting quietly beside the swift water, he was fishing for catfish. Suddenly Miss Sally whinnied like a horse and when the terrified Negro looked up she waved her hands in his face, shouting "Never die." Calling on the Lord's name, Harve fled through the canebreak, leaving at Miss Sally's feet a string of six catfish. So did Miss Sally at the age of seventy-five start upon a career. Her first meal as a witch was fish, dipped in heavy yellow meal, fried brown in butter. Crazily, she ate these fish, laughing and saying to herself, "Never die—never die, sure enough."

With the boldness almost always demanded of men and women of strength at the beginning of strong careers, Miss Sally risked everything now. She took a chance. With her old black dress beating about her long bones, an old bonnet over her head, she climbed the public platform in the town square in Pendleton, rang the public bell, sang a ballad and afterward predicted to the puzzled crowd that had gathered that a man in their midst was about to die. "Folks," she said, "the sands are running fast, he's sinking." She predicted when Jupiter came in conjunction with Venus, the man would die. Again she rang the bell and departed. Word spread quickly that Miss Sally had lost her reason but just the same the pages of many almanacs were searched that night for the ascension time of the planets—Jupiter would appear in conjunction with Venus on that following Friday. And on that Friday night, with the cold north wind blowing, racing down the valley with the edge of a blade, old man Rock Taylor, one of those who had stood that day in the square listening to Sally, turned over in his bed without a word and quietly passed away.

"Lord God," said Queen Elizabeth, her white eyes bulging in her ebony face on hearing of Taylor's death, "Lord God, Miss Sally is a conjure woman for true." Already Queen Elizabeth was in fear herself, afraid of the creature she had brought into being; the image of her frightened mind was growing.

Soon Miss Sally's life had become full of secret visits and prosperity—there were sacks full of sweet potatoes, peanuts, corn meal, there were smoked hams lining the walls of her house, a fire roared in the fireplace with knots brought in by strangers and at all hours of day and night, ignorant Negroes and the superstitious among the more primitive whites were calling for Miss Sally's advice. Soon Miss Sally whipped together a new page for the sorcerer's book—borrowing mysteries from each of the three races living in Keowee, she began to think highly of making a living as a witch. On a waning moon only, she said, could soap be boiled or corn put in the ground—a waning one would think the first, waste the ears of the second; the seeds of gourd should be flung carelessly over the surface of the ground to grow at will—to sow gourd in prepared soil would bring a family to disaster. Uttering strange words, speaking in parables, Miss Sally now began to reign over the crops and seasons and in time becoming more sinister she trafficked in charms, worked spells, haunted the conscience, making such statements as women dying in childbirth were being punished by God for their sins. Finally the sorcery of this aged woman swept her into that great current of tragedy in which the Caldwells lived. Wondering still who was the man who had known Narcissa Caldwell, brooding much about that mystery, and curious, Miss Sally decided in her crazy way to stir the mists about this secret. She was curious to know what would happen.

Getting up early one still morning in the winter, she tramped through the hoarfrosts and ice to the walled tomb in the burying ground at Forest Mansion. Short-sighted, she moved her old face over the granite slab, close to the letters, studying all she could see. Shortly afterward the whole upcountry was startled by an announcement from her that the face of the man who had not married Narcissa Caldwell was slowly making its appearance on the surface of Narcissa's tomb. Already, she said, a thin wavering line could be seen, this portrait would as surely as sin reveal in a short time the keeper of the secret. The man's features would stand out as clear as his face in the flesh. "O the man is lost," Miss Sally said, "He is living in night, for the forces beyond mortal control will drive him on the next anniversary of the crime to visit Narcissa's burial place—there is nothing he can do to save himself, his path is charted in the magic stars." The excitement stirred by these shrewd predictions was prodigious, the entire region began talking. Rapidly the word reached Carter at Forest Mansion, exciting him; it pierced the mulish ears of Preacher McKay in the sanctity of this manse, old Aaron soon heard it at his store; it was told to Jimmy O'Reilly during a drinking bout in the cabin at Equal Sue's. The young clock peddler had drifted in toward dusk with five other travelers of the wilderness, all gambling men at heart, willing to take a chance, kindly and friendly men of the backwoods who shot and carved one another with knives whenever they drank too much. They were sitting about a fire of blazing logs in the half-lighted cabin, drinking corn liquor from a jug.

"Did you all hear about Sally Crossing's latest raving," said Sue, who was baking some hoecakes in a pile of hot ashes on the hearth. Squatting for this work, she looked upward at the drinking men as she spoke.

"No," said Jimmy in a casual, friendly way. "What trouble-making is she up to this time?"

"She says Narcissa Caldwell's man is a goner—his face is appearing on her tomb." It happened that Sue at the moment had her eyes upon Jimmy, it was he who had asked her what Sally had said; Sue saw the confused look that spread over his tired features, also she saw that he nearly dropped the jug.

"Miss Sally says there's nothing the man can do about it," said Equal Sue, talking on, quickly. "The fates have taken charge." She turned again to care for the bread she was baking, turned automatically for she was very proud of her hoecakes, she baked them well. Besides she was startled by what she had seen, she wanted to think.

Sitting there with the jug half lifted to his mouth, Jimmy felt the old fear overwhelm him again, torment and terror; there was the old sense that he was being hunted, that he must be careful; somebody might suspect. There was a choking sensation in his throat, making him want to scream. Soon he rose, kicking back his chair, "Well, folks," he said, "I got some things I ought to be about—I'll be seeing you." Sue followed him to the door, watching him with a new sense of wonder. Once in the clear air of the dark night, Jimmy ran—half-drunk but running as swiftly as he could, madly fleeing from Sue's troubled eyes and words and from crazy Sally's warning. Flashing words raced through his alcoholed brain, vivid pictures of fever and fear, searing his cloudy mind—he said strange things to himself, muttering, "We know in our hearts, that is all—not here nor now but the memory lives, it's a fire, it's a scar..." He remembered being alone at night; there was the sight of powerful, falling stars, the feeling of the far away—"O years of trouble and solitude and searching for a way, O loneliness and sorrow and the long months of fear and the sight of the sun shining through a rag of cloud and a sudden coming of strength when everything seemed over...O mercy..."

Tormented, he flung himself face down on the crag of a granite rock and into the vast darkness of the lonely night he screamed—time and again, then he wept and this brought him momentary relief. Quietly, he began to think—a face could not flare forth on a bare stone, that was not possible, it was foolish but just the same he was afraid; the whole country would probe into this mystery again, this time with the hand that stirred it holding the powerful fan of drama. "I'm hounded, I'm hunted like a criminal." Violently, he protested. And over him came a new fear, greater, more gripping than any of the others—he was afraid some night he would drink and while drinking would not be able to keep himself from seeking the face on the tomb, he knew the unbearable power of that drive. Again his blurred senses wandered..."O God...God..." the clouds, the winds, the wild sky, there was stillness and the faint far-off glimmer of lightning and from the west snow gathered, silent and floating, it stirred the soul to watch a storm, he stood on a hill in spring and a frail flower bloomed, a strange white flower—O the flower of fear—he lifted himself from the rock. Now his decision was made, his final plan was finished. He would go this one time to the tomb, see it, see the line in the slab, the blurred marking of the face, then rush away, leave Carolina for good and all—he would never come back. Hurrying along the clay road, he walked a half dozen miles before midnight, and on reaching the holly ravine at the foot of the hill at Forest Mansion sat down on a log to wait for the cold winter moon to set. Sometime later while climbing the steep hill to the burying ground Jimmy paused a moment, a light had begun to shine through the cracks of the old Caldwell cabin. Turning about Jimmy crept to this house and looking through an unchinked slit between two warped logs saw the giant figure of an ageless, broad-shouldered velvet-skinned negress; it was Queen Elizabeth, warming her hands before a bright fire. As Jimmy looked, he saw a tenseness come over the woman's frame, he saw her whirl herself about—then he heard her scream. For she had seen his eyes watching her. "Lord God," screamed Queen Elizabeth, "the conjure woman is haunt me." Throwing open the door of the cabin, she started off toward Forest Mansion, shouting every step of the way.

Jimmy also ran—he ran long and as swiftly as there was strength within, then he fell on his knees, listening to the sounds, afraid of the wind in the pines, the footfall of the beaver. Lonely and beaten, he gave up the struggle. "God," he said, "there is no more purpose to my living—no more order and I can't live without order; I have come to the end of my bourne." And from that time forward, nothing mattered to Jimmy except the longing to confess, to tell everything and regardless of consequence to rid his conscience of its troubled burden. In his dazed groping way, he came the following Sunday into the stone meeting house, into the solemn simple church; slowly he bent his angular body into a seat; for an hour he sat there with an expression on his face like an idiot's—about him drifted the fierce words of Preacher McKay who was this morning spinning a sermon from a dream. The deep voice of the minister rose and fell—there was a weary traveler walking along an endless fence held up by posts with faces of suffering spirits stamped upon them. "My friends," cried the preacher to the members of the congregation before him, "I was that weary traveler—it was me and in this dream the faces of the posts reminded me as I went on my troubled way of all the wicked things I had ever done...'O you sinned,' cried the face on the first post. 'You bore false witness,' said the second face. 'You forgot the Sabbath Day.' 'Thou hast committed adultery.' Well, folks, when I could not stand this torment any longer I cried in a loud voice 'Have mercy' and they took pity on me. They said 'All right, brother, we will not torment you if you will do a certain thing.' I asked 'What in God's name is this thing' and they said 'Shake hands with a certain man.' 'Who is the man?' I asked and they told me—friends, he was a man I had stolen from. 'I will shake hands with him if I can,' I said and I went away and saw this man and I told him I was sorry for what I had stolen and he smiled and forgave, he shook my hand. And after that the voices asked me whether I wanted to remain longer on the troubled old earth or was I prepared to go on with them toward glory. I said I wanted to go. Well, my friends, they told me first I would have to tell everything I'd done in my whole life and I started in to tell—from the cradle to the grave. But I wouldn't have to speak before they'd divine me. Loud they'd wail. 'O sinner, sinner.' And as soon as I'd hesitate on any part of my life, they'd say 'Now he hesitates.' Well, all the time I was talking there was a mumbling sound like the rolling of chariot wheels and I felt the roaring of winds around me—I was riding through the air. Soon I saw a face I'd forgotten greet me and finally there was an angel—an angel opened a gold door and I saw a sight of angels and fine flowers and I heard great singing and everything in every direction was gold—solid gold. Then the angel closed the door and all became darkness again and in this void some voices about me began to tell me the journey was getting shorter. Far-off in the distance, I saw my mother, just as I used to see her, smiling and crying from joy.

"So I reached the place where all our friends were gathered; there a spirit told me to-morrow I should see God. And I shouted 'hallelujah' and everyone laughed for moments, they said, were counted where I was in thousands of years. During all this time, I was left alone with the dying, all gasping, and finally a voice shouted, 'Brother McKay, you'll be there tonight, throw away your possessions—your gold ring and all your money, shed your earthly raiment.' A trumpet horn sounded and the darkness broke and there, folks, in a blaze of dazzling glory, Paradise was before me—the sky blue with diamonds and through a great valley walked saints in clothes of purple and...O, friends, a wonderful sight loomed in the distance..."

Suddenly a cry rose from the back of the church. "Have mercy." Brought to earth by this cry, uttered with piercing anguish, Preacher McKay said quietly, "Unburden yourself, brother—tell us your trouble, you are among your friends."

Through all the telling of this dream, Jimmy had sat quietly on the back bench, all the time seeing himself on that same journey, meeting a splendid figure in fine crimson and over and over in his ears rang the words of this spirit—"You killed me, I will not shake your hand." The words roared and welled and the next thing Jimmy knew he had jumped to his feet, was shouting "Have mercy."

"Let us help you, brother, to find the way," said McKay.

Now with the moment at hand, Jimmy trembled. Fierce forces tore into his con-sciousness, raging like cyclones within his spirit. Fully did he intend to cry out his deep secret, scald for all time the fire in his heart—"I did it—it was me." But the words that the congregation heard were not these. They heard, "Folks, I've passed the blossom of my life and I want to unburden myself by confessing before you I haven't lived as I ought—I love good liquor and go in for having some fun but I hope it'll be well for me when I come to my final sleep. I'd like to ask you all to bear with me, pray for me. I want to tell..." Abruptly, Jimmy broke off, fierce tears filling his fiery eyes. "O, I'm a poor lost soul," he muttered and reeling down the aisle, he disappeared from the church. The droning song of a dry fly whirred through the stillness, a siren-like sound rising from the depth to a height where for nearly a half minute it quivered, full and sustained, then again its notes descended.

"Brothers and sisters," said McKay, lifting his bony hands, "let us pray for peace."

Deeply moved by Jimmy's burst of tears, this anguished demonstration of dark hid-den sorrow, Caline brooded. Riding home after the service, she said to Carter, greatly disturbed, "It was a strange way to act for a man seeking refuge in confession."

"You never can tell about the secret troubles of a man," said Carter, his eyes on the dusty road, "Maybe he didn't confess the trouble he came to tell about." The buggy wheels jolted over a rut, the shining horses' harness creaked, glinted in the sun; Carter and Caline drove on through a hot afternoon, both in deep reverie and in silence.

That evening as the sunset brought red and indigo into the clouds behind the Blue Ridge, spreading flame like heavy oil on a canvas, Preacher McKay stopped in a state of high excitement at Forest Mansion with the news—Jimmy O'Reilly's days in the world were over. "He hanged himself from one of those mimosa trees on the bluff over the river." It was the Hunter boys who had found him.

Startled and saddened, Caline and Carter for a long while said nothing—as the time wore away, the clock in the central room could be heard ticking the moments. Finally Carter said, "The clocks he sold were good ones."

"Poor Jimmy," said Caline, "he hadn't a home. A home and a good wife—that was what he needed." Folding her thin hands, lifting her careworn face toward the fading skyline, wondering what sorrow, what secret Jimmy had carried within his breast, what broken past he had buried. "Why," she asked herself, "Oh why?"

And in two other houses at that moment, two other persons were wondering also about the dark mystery that had risen within Jimmy to destroy him. In the old Gadlock house in Pendleton, Aaron Gadlock the storekeeper remembered the look that spread over his young friend's face the morning he heard Carter Caldwell had asked about him. And in the cabin on Eighteen Mile Creek, Equal Sue remembered another look, deep with worried trouble. But neither Aaron nor Sue said a word so long as they lived about these recollections. Jimmy was their friend, they loved him.

So the great forces of tragedy swept on in the wild wilderness—Jimmy's blue star had set and Caline's now was setting. She was tired and worn and through the months of this last summer she was growing bigger with the child that was to be named Lucy—the last of her children. Wasted and gaunt featured, Caline worked through the stifling days, hard at the full and vigorous tasks of a country woman's life—tending to chickens, turkeys, guineas, a group of growing children; she turned to her yellow flowers in the great north garden and sometimes she walked along the hilltops, seeing, hearing, thinking among all this richness—the great range of granite mountains, the old valleys filled with fine trees and growing crops, among all this, there was defeat only for her; she had failed for Carter would never really love her. After all these years, he had neither forgiven nor forgotten. And tramping these hills carrying high this last child, Caline was overcome with that final weariness that never finds rest—like the long wind from across the mountains she was mortally tired. So here in the vast quiet she turned for the last time to her symbols—the wild dazzling sunsets, the cloudless southern sky, the cross. Her halfhearted prayers now were listless. "God," she said on the Fourth of July that summer, "A woman's courage cannot last forever."

Then from the west, a wind rose, soughing with infinite patience in the pines, crying of the solitude and the lonely land, and that evening the sun set in a peculiarly powerful way, falling mysteriously, seeming to pull at Caline with its magnetic force, to lure her on also. A wild gladness filled Caline's heart and as she walked toward Forest Mansion, she said, "I am glad, so glad that God is calling me on."

That night Lucy was born and Caline died.

Caline lay before the black marble mantelpiece in a white shroud of satin, still in the final rest. The little hammers of the Connecticut clock hit the quarter hours, pounding a deep gong, a pendulum swung, ticking, tocking. The dead watching over the dead! The great paneled room, waxed and polished, was heavily scented with the dolorous fragrance of cape jessamine, the flowers of southern death; in piles they lay upon the cedar box and resting on the satin was Caline, a wax camelia on her breast, an odorless white camelia, it intensified the wax-like whiteness of her corpse skin, the rich thin skin that reacted so instantly to living wind and sun. Only weather ever gave to those pale cheeks a flushed color. The still eyes were closed, the nose tilted, the cheeks hollow and the cast of the head was forward and eager, of a fragile beauty, a piece of wistful sculpture.

"Beautiful, beautiful," said Abernathy Oaks, the Pendleton embalmer, hovering over the casket.

"A good job, brother," nodded he to a helper, who also smiled and nodded. "Yes, sir."

Quiet satisfaction beamed in the eyes of Abernathy as the long old hands of McKay rose over the jessamine and the satin.

"...and he cometh forth like a flower and is cut down, he fleeth also as a shadow and continueth not."

"A sight to see," murmured Abernathy, "a scene to remember." Keeping to their wilderness tradition, the Caldwells hauled the body of Caline to the burying ground on one of the oxcarts, stripped bare—one of the old original oxcarts that had brought them to Keowee over the wilderness road. As the season of freshets was at hand and hard rains had been falling, the heavy wheels of the cart mired deep into the red earth, leaving sharp tracks before the broad piazza. Dried and hard, these marks could still be seen when two months later Carter drove up to Forest Mansion with a second wife sitting beside him on the front seat of the Caldwell carriage. This quick re-marriage made all of Caline's children mad, it turned old Queen Elizabeth into a raging fury.

"The master must have cast his eye over the crowd gathered at the graveside," said the Negro woman. "Right there in the midst of the praying—there he was, just a picking and choosing." Queen Elizabeth flung an apron over her dusky face. "Lord, lord," she wept. For in spite of the strange arrangement of their living at Forest Mansion, Queen Elizabeth had long held her mistress in deep and full respect. Once in the secrecy of the kitchen, the Negress had said to Caline, "I is a slave woman and there's things that happen to a slave woman that is beyond her power and control." She gave Caline a quick look and after that there existed an unspoken understanding between these two.

Caline's children were eating breakfast in the kitchen the morning Carter drove away in the carriage early, without saying where he was going, and they were assembled there again, making an early supper on pancakes and syrup, when the father returned with the new wife, three step-children and a beautiful parlor harp. Furiously indignant, the young Stephen John the second offered to show his new step-mother about Forest Mansion, and at once he led the woman to the front piazza and pointing to the ruts in the sidewalk said they were left by his mother's hearse. Hating this step-mother, he began to call her "Old Ellen." Soon the others were doing likewise.

It was years later that Stephen John, mellowed by maturity and troubles of his own, began to speak of the second wife as "Miss Ellen" to command the extensive family, black and white, to do the same—an order that was obeyed in his presence by everyone except Queen Elizabeth. She refused to the end to speak either of "Mrs. Caldwell" or "Miss Ellen"—her compromise, intended as a subtle combination of respect with a certain disdain, was "Mrs. Ellen." Queen Elizabeth never was able to consider Carter's second wife as mistress of Forest Mansion.

CHAPTER EIGHT

Young Stephen John the second came running down the broad back steps of Forest Mansion, a rifle in his hand, shouting wildly to Silas the third, his younger brother, suggesting that they go into the deep woods north of the house to hunt for gray squirrels. This suited Silas; so they called Popcorn, the oldest of Queen Elizabeth's children, and the three started out at once over the bare March hills, pretending they were a band of the Cherokee Indians. They had only two bullets among them but that did not bother them as they did not care much whether they shot squirrels or whether they even saw a squirrel. It was the wide, mysterious, selfless world of boys that they wanted to wander about in and explore.

"I'm Chief Black Bear," said Stephen John, his blue Caldwell eyes glistening.

"I'm Chief Wild Panther," said Silas.

"And I'm Chief Crazy Wolf," said Popcorn, but Stephen John objected. "There can't everybody be a chief, Popcorn," he said, assuming his family's tone of command. "Somebody's got to be braves for the chiefs to be chief of—you've got to be a brave."

So Popcorn became a brave, following his chieftains, bringing up their rear, carrying the rifle. This band of marauders halted for a few minutes in a deep red gully to see whether the last rains had washed out any clear quartz crystals, but finding none, they moved downward to the moss banks of a small stream to inspect a skunk's hole, to look at the wild Indian turnips that just then were beginning to spring up in a patch of marsh. Further down this stream they stopped to carve the names of the two chiefs, Black Bear and Wild Panther, in the hard gray bark of a big beech tree, and there were some tracks that had to be followed along a patch of wet sand—they were tracks of a raccoon and a muskrat but the boys said they were a wild cat's, they hoped at any moment to run into this wild cat.

Suddenly Stephen John decided the little stream was running round the wrong side of a granite boulder so they brought dead logs and daubing blue mud over them forced the water to run in a different direction—they stood for a time watching the stream follow the course they had willed it to follow and this gave them a great sense of satisfaction. This was power.

They found the loose woven sticks of a dove's nest on the end of a pine limb, then they listened to the hollow drumming of a downy woodpecker's beak drilling a home in the decayed limb of a willow tree. Crossing a small swamp, the party stepped lightly over the heavy mud that remained from the winter freshets, here alders were breaking into bud, the red maple was blooming and they ran into a frightened drove of snowbirds, running to cover from a hawk. Beyond in the open, the wheatfields were green and wrens were singing—it was springtime in Carolina and about these boys everywhere were the signs of this vigorous season. The wild plum was sweet smelling and white in the wild hedge row, a thing of fragile and wistful beauty; blue forget-me-nots studded the pasture with the strong color of new hope.

The world was fine and warm and free, and the boys lay down on a high ledge above the river, content for the time to watch a lizard sleeping. Far below them ran the swift river, glistening in the afternoon light; a rag of white cloud hung over the sun, revealing a burst of light rays, drawing water over half a continent and over the great valley hung a fine blue smoke, filled with the honest and simple smells of woods burning and the earth of South Carolina warming.

"When I grow up," said Silas, his arms folded under his chin, "I'm going out to see the world before I settle down…I'm going to roam around and travel…I want to see the Mississippi flow and look at Texas and hear a coyote howl and watch buffaloes on the move and see the Missouri and the great plains and the Rocky Mountains and smell a dust storm coming…When I get out and get going I might even go as far as the Western Ocean…" Just then the sun broke clear from the cloud. "And when I find the right country, I'm going to settle down and live right and I'm going to make a million dollars" Wistfully and filled with envy, Stephen John listened as always he listened to Silas' restless talk of roaming and adventure, listened for Stephen John was the oldest son and he knew and he had known from infancy that he would be obliged to stay at home—he had to take care of Forest Mansion, be the head of the Caldwells. But staying at home was not going to interfere with his making a fortune, he was going to do that too, and also he was going to become a great man—he too was young and full of determination and high hopes; in his mind's eye even now he could see the page in the histories and encyclopedias filled with the life of Stephen John Caldwell.

From over the magic West, the mountain rim that seemed always to invite the young on, from over the west just then came a gust of warm spring wind and they forgot their dreams; for Popcorn had raised the rifle and fired. From the limbs of a hickory tree a squirrel toppled.

Many times in their boyhood did these two brothers talk to each other—lean and angular and reckless, they possessed in themselves many of the wild, rude qualities of their fathers as well as peculiar inherited cast of the family features—ruddy, high-cheeked faces, ascetic and passionate with deep blue eyes and yellow hair. They were curiously tender and kind and brutal, much like their fathers—Stephen John in his way was another original Silas, the third Silas another Carter. They were restless, even in childhood favoring the hard, driving life of action—they wanted to be moving, to be doing something. But at the same time both were given to contemplation and reflection. Like so many of the Caldwells, searching for a way, experimenting, they began very early to drink hard liquor, also they became undisciplined and self-indulgent in their secret passions. In addition, Silas concealed within himself a great feeling for beauty—Stephen John a sense of order that became more pronounced as he grew older, he kept certain things in certain places, he had begun already to plan every minute of his time. But both boys had the great western dream—each in his way followed the pillar of fire; they believed in the lofty star.

It was their recklessness that kept them close to the earth. This recklessness soon got Silas into trouble. When he still was a mere youth, he drove one evening from a church service with Matilda Hunter, who was ugly and older than Silas but she was a daughter of the oldest family of friends the Caldwells had and Silas should have considered this obligation—the Hunters had been associated with the Caldwells in every kind of venture from the very days of the wilderness road. But Silas did not stop to consider this—he was full of spirit, anxious to know things, to experience, to feel. So he drove the girl into a patch of pines and stopped the horses.

He enjoyed himself but he was not willing to risk the possible final consequences of the indulgence of his passions. At home alone he soon repented, prayed fervently that nothing would happen—this was not what he had planned to do with his life, this would trap him, tie him down in Carolina when he was determined to see the world. After a time he became thoroughly frightened, came one morning to ask his father for money enough to go away.

"What for? What have you done," asked Carter, alarmed. The boy blushed and suspecting him, Carter asked, "Has it something to do with purity?" The boy, burning with shame, nodded. Anxiously Carter began fumbling in a desk for his tinbox. "Son, don't tell me who the girl is—I'll find out soon enough—but tell me this," and he looked earnestly into the boy's face, "Were you entirely to blame?"

"Not entirely—she was as willing as I was." Suddenly the boy began to sob. "I don't want to marry her, I couldn't bear to marry her."

"Then don't marry her," said Carter, all but yelling the words. He thrust a handful of bills into the boy's hands. "Here," he said, "take this and leave while you can—go and don't ever let anybody make you marry anyone you don't want to—no reason is strong enough for that."

Silas left that very day.

"Well," he said, saying good-bye to Stephen John, "I'm on my way." Silas started out, excited and with high hope, on his long western journey, bound for the Caldwells living in Mississippi. It was freedom, escape—he had hardly a thought for Matilda Hunter.

It was not long after his departure that Matilda's father, Joseph William, in a state of great anxiety and worry, came to call on Carter and it was then that Carter learned for the first time that the girl was Matilda.

"Carter," demanded Joseph William, "Where is Silas?" Looking straight into his friend's eyes, Carter replied, "To tell you the truth, just now I don't know." That night Carter wrote to his son, telling him the Hunters claimed he had betrayed Matilda—that she had expected him to marry her, that Silas had given her his promise. It was weeks before Silas could reply. "Pa," he wrote, "I meant no harm—I only had a curiosity to know if she was an honest woman." This caused long laughing among all the Caldwells, the gusty women as well as the men, and when next old Joseph William, desperate because of so much delay, came to Forest Mansion, and was shown this letter, he was so angry that he shouted at them all, "You're a lot of unprincipled scoundrels—there isn't a shred of honor among you."

Fifty years before this, such a situation would have ended up in a shooting, but the half century had changed both the Caldwells and the Hunters; a little of the roughness had worn off. Now all that happened was that the Caldwells laughed. Joseph William Hunter turned and walked away.

A week later the Hunters decided to send Matilda on a visit into Kentucky, and after that the Hunters and the Caldwells did not speak to one another for eighty years.

Alone now at Forest Mansion, young Stephen John missed his brother—their long walks through the woods, their days working hard together, plowing the long corn rows, hoeing in the rocky cotton patches, their secret talks and drinks, and their drinking conversations.

Stephen John was lonesome. Alone, he climbed the hills beyond the mansion; it was a still summer day in which nothing moved—only light slowly circling the day, a pattern on quiet shifting shadows. Lying upon a carpet of brown pine needles, his tanned arms under his head, he saw a swift shadow darting, a powerful motion disturb this world of rest and in a pinetop above him there rose a scream, gray feathers began to flutter down—in the midst of life was death, a hawk was picking the bleeding meat of a sparrow. This was a shocking thing to witness in such a peaceful place—yet Stephen John admired the strong beauty of the murdering hawk, its exact precision. "Be strong," he said to himself, "strike when you have to—strike like a hawk."

He watched the wild fading sunset that evening, was moved by its vast free beauty—solid yellow, not a cloud to break the unity of its glory. But not this appealed to him most—not yellow, not the great red and indigo sunsets of southern spring or summer or the yellow suns of September. In cold gray winter were his favorite sunsets. On those chill evenings the gold disc sank in a pure sky of colorless color—pure light. "That's what I like," said he to the western sky, "the cold sun of December." Stephen John was acutely aware of these natural things—the glazed sun and the moon, the glittering light of the stars. Like the first Stephen John and the first Lucinda, this boy also was held breathlessly by wild flying mallards, moving between the immensities, the unknowns—beating their sure swift wings through the present. But there was this difference—where the uncle and the grandmother bowed their spirits in humility to the unquestioning flying of these great birds, their acceptance of their fate, Stephen John worshipped the power of their speed; already he was harder than they ever were—only energy counted with him, and beautiful were the strong.

Stephen John was strong, also he was not strong. He had the faith, the courage, the will but also there was within him that other side—brooding and melancholy, he had inherited the old austere asceticism, he was part an esthete. Lying there, lonely and sad, Stephen John began thinking of his brother Silas, fortunate, traveling, bound for Louisiana and Texas, bound for the Rio Grande. A fine thing—to see the world.

"Aw hell," he said to himself, restlessness overpowering him. But he shook off this mood, he hurried home, saddled his horse, galloped off to visit Unity Caldwell, his cousin. Unity was friendly and frank, also she laughed loud and often. A boy did not think about lonely hawks flying when Unity was around; he did not long so much to see the Mississippi River.

More and more often after that, Stephen John sought the company of this cousin—they rode, walked along the cliffs above the Keowee River, watched the mists rise in the valleys, danced the square dance in the farmers hall at Pendleton. One night he asked her if she would marry him, gladly she replied that she would. And for a few hours Stephen John was wildly happy. But later, riding homeward over the dark hills, he realized suddenly that it was not winning Unity that interested him most—it was the trying to win her.

Rising very early the next morning, at the first break of day, Stephen John galloped hard up and down the river, through the fields, and then flushed and sweating he burst into the kitchen which was warm and hungrily scented with the smell of red country ham frying. In the dusky pantry, lighted by one small window, was Queen Elizabeth, kneading dough and singing in her old wonderful contralto voice:

"Bear your burden, sister, through the heat of the day."

Dropping into a chair with his back to the fire, the boy flexed his firm arms over the chair back and soon into the kitchen swept Queen Elizabeth to fill a china plate for him with hominy, a heaping helping, gravy and ham. "Here, honey child," she said, "eat yourself some breakfast."

Slowly Stephen John ate. Frowning, he presently remarked, "Queen Elizabeth, do you think I'm too young to be getting married?" There was a look of uneasiness settling into his high unlined forehead. Quick to sense emotional trouble, the Negro cocked her great face, "What that you say," she inquired, stopping to look at Stephen John. She had heard what he had said.

"I don't want to marry," answered the boy.

The Negro woman was exasperated. "That's all I ever hear about this place—one half the time it's want to get married, the other half it's want to escape getting married." She slapped down a heavy pot on the stove.

"Well, I don't want to marry—that is, not right now."

"I know what you been up to," she said. "God, boy, what you mean—hugging and kissing that girl and one thing and another and then you come in here and tell Queen Elizabeth you don't want to marry—why God A'mighty, Mister Stephen John, I declare to God sometimes I say to myself that boy acts like white trash—like plumb good for nothing low down white trash too—and that's what I got a mind to say to myself right now."

Lightly scowling but ignoring the Negro's rebuke, Stephen John replied, "I could get along with the hugging and kissing and the one thing and another part of it but I declare I don't want to be tied down so soon." Changing tone, suddenly becoming grave, Queen Elizabeth sat down in a chair beside the boy. Pointing her fat hands at him, she said, "Now you listen right here now to old Queen Elizabeth." And she took hold of one of his hands. "You done gone too far, I suspect, to back out—and in that case, child, you ought to marry that girl—so you marry her, you hear, you marry her and get yourself content in your mind—there ain't nothing bad as living a discontented life."

Now Queen Elizabeth began waving her free hand directly in Stephen John's face, menace in her tone. She spoke in an accusing tone…"Looking after smack, that's what you are after, honey—want to drive wild round Pendleton and roll eyes at the fast girls. Well, you just get your mind off that thing, boy—there ain't one girl in the world got anything that any other girl ain't got and the sooner you learns that the better it will be for you—and also while I'm about it, you listen to me tell you this, too—you either controls smack or smack controls you."

"All right," replied the boy, impatiently, "I'll marry Unity, I've promised her and I'll have to go through with it—but just the same, I wish I didn't have to marry anybody for a long, long time."

Not long afterwards, he married her. Stephen John stood before the mantle in a great bay of green holly and lilies in the parlor at Hopewell Landing and, awed and frightened by the awful solemnity of the service that was binding him, he choked over the wedding vows. But somehow he said them and his embarrassment brought smiles into the gleaming eyes of Senator Carter Caldwell; into the eyes of "Miss Ellen." They mistook the boy's fear for bashfulness. Smiles hung also upon the cheerful faces of Unity's parents, Pisgah and Mattie Green Caldwell, and upon those of a crowd of other Caldwells gathered at the plantation on the banks of the yellow Seneca River—gathered there all the way from Pumpkintown and Ninety-six in Carolina to upper Alabama, Tennessee, and blue-grass Kentucky. For the members of this inland family always crossed mountains, forded the swiftest rivers, traveled over half a continent whenever another Caldwell was dying or about to take a wife.

Outside in the grove among the slaves—in a fine new calico dress that already had split in the shoulder seams was Queen Elizabeth, smiling in more triumph than anyone and fanning herself with a whole turkey wing fan.

҉

Unity, who by her marriage now became the second of that name in the Book at Forest Mansion, was tall like many of the Caldwell women, had the fragile-like great strength of the latter ones. Her lips were the quivering lips of the old Narcissa—the upper extending over the lower giving to her appearance that often sensitive and hurt expression. Her cheek bones were high, running prominently under her eyes, blue as the gentians. And her hair was the Caldwell hair, Caldwell thin and Caldwell yellow. Her hands were long like Narcissa's; very big were her feet.

There was no doubt about the Caldwell quality of this fourth lady at Forest Mansion. And sometimes this concentration of the Caldwell character frightened her—she had the same fear that Artemissa had. She feared this continued mingling of the blood. For so related and intricately inter-related was she with her young husband that her grandfather was also his grandfather; her husband was a second cousin and a third cousin and a fifth cousin—no matter in which direction she traced her family, Stephen John always appeared sooner or later as a cousin. Even her own parents were her cousins and now her children would become her cousins.

Always Unity laughed when attempting to explain to strangers the complexities of the Caldwell line of descent which more resembled a tree-trunk, she said, than a tree. But always in the dark night there hung about her deepest thoughts that great curtain that troubled Patrick's line—haunting her was a memory of "not quite right."

"Queen Elizabeth," said Unity one early morning to the Negress who was mixing pounds of things for a pound cake, "isn't it odd how the Caldwells marry the Caldwells."

"No'm," responded the Negro woman, halting a moment from her work, "it ain't so odd—for the Caldwells is proud folks. They is too proud to marry them sorry aristocrats that clutter up the low country, and up here in the upcountry there ain't nobody good enough to marry Caldwells except Caldwells." Chuckling to herself, Queen Elizabeth pitched back her fine kinky head. "It is marry theyself or die in the cold old virgin's bed—and there ain't many Caldwells doing that."

Into the kitchen at this moment came Stephen John, laughing, and insisting that Unity go with him for a walk. Together they climbed the early mist shrouded hills and entering one of the great cool pine groves, they suddenly decided to strip off their clothes, to run through the trees, wild and free—stark naked they leaped like frogs, chasing each other. Wild-eyed, Popcorn happened to come through this part of the plantation, returning to the house from his rabbit traps, and he saw Stephen John and Unity. Rushing to Forest Mansion, he told his mother.

"For God's sake, children," said Queen Elizabeth when the two returned sometime later to the house, "what in the wide world you all been doing?"

"Enjoying ourselves, Queen Elizabeth," said Stephen John, quite without shame, adding "we've been making ourselves contented—I never was so contented in my life."

"Thank God," said Queen Elizabeth, breaking into loud glad laughter: she threw her warm old arms about the boy's great shoulders.

Often Stephen John and Unity walked miles together—they hunted deer, rabbits, quail and fished with Popcorn in the swift Keowee for catfish; sometimes they even divided their work—he would help her awhile in the flower gardens, she would go with him into the field. Stephen John, no longer lonely, became graver now and more earnest—he began searching for himself, seeking for some pattern and purpose for his life, an aim. Gradually, more and more time was spent with his father, riding with him over the plantation, talking over the problems of farming, the prices of cotton, talking, planning for the future. And Carter during these last years made frantic attempts to instill in this son the ideal that his father had instilled into him—it became his constant theme, his deep voice preaching discipline and duty. Stephen John must resist the greatest temptation of his kin—the restless desire to go on, to see; in the midst of a world of motion, he must not move, he must stay at Forest Mansion; he was a Caldwell on a rarer plane, must realize the seriousness, the importance of his responsibility, must feel in the depth of his soul for this farm and this farmhouse, in its destiny, its purpose—for already it had cost lives, red blood ran through these fields and red gullies, the life of a great family had its being here, a part of a nation; there on the hilltop were those who had gone on, there in the sky hovered the unborn and unbegot. "We are responsible to them both—especially, son, to those who are to come after us; we ought to leave this a better place for our children to live in." And there were the old Caldwell commands—never sell a foot of the land nor mortgage an acre, in hard times do without, help all Caldwells who were in need of help, educate the children.

In his earnest desire to stir the fire in Stephen John's heart, Carter held back nothing—he even told this son the tale of himself and the boy's mother, making no attempt to defend either himself or Caline. Father and son were riding through the woods to the north of the house on the afternoon that Carter dug the details of this story from his bitter memory. They were riding through a forest of white oaks, marking great trees that Carter wished to be felled for timber; branding a giant with two sturdy strokes of a hatchet, Carter looked for a moment into his son's face and told him. And when he had finished, he gave his oldest boy this final bit of advice, the strongest, most embittered lesson he had learned to pass on. He warned Stephen John of the danger lurking for anyone who experimented with emotion, told him of the exorbitant price human beings had to pay for daring to taste the forbidden fruit, to sip the spiced milk of the white ass. "The taste," Carter said, sadly, "isn't worth a lifetime of sickness and grieving." Tears came into Carter's eyes. "Son," he said, "be good—be good if you can but if you can't be good, then be strong. And if you can't be happy, thank God for discontent and if you can't resist the forbidden fruit—well, pay the price without whining. And don't be afraid of tragedy. It's the hardest but it's the noblest of a man's burdens."

Just then, old lean flop-eared Red, a hound, jumped a rabbit from a pile of brush—through the woods bounded the dog after a tuft-tailed rabbit, yelping, and after the hound galloped Stephen John, shouting "sick him, boy…"

And sad and silent and perfectly motionless, old Carter watched the whole procession, moved deeply—he was alone, always solitary, even in experience, he was alone. Man of the wilderness.

A series of seasons soon passed at Forest Mansion, an autumn, a hard winter, and over them Carter kept watch with an almanac—Septuagesima Sunday came, the moon was in Apogee, wet and chilly and there were high winds and flying clouds and there was a fine spring and then the dewberries ripened and around again came laying-by time with the thermometer a hundred in the shade. In the half afternoon of an August day, a great thunderstorm rose in the west, and as it approached Keowee, Carter decided he would feed the pigs before the rain began. Slinging two cedar buckets over his wide shoulders, he started down the back path but the first swirling gusts came upon him sooner than he expected. Hurrying, he sought shelter under the tallest and thickest of the great pines that stood on the hillside behind Forest Mansion. Waiting here, Carter looked out over the miles of valleys, filling now with the storm; he began thinking of the first sight the Caldwells had ever had of this country—it was just such a day, he saw them, migrants on the wilderness road, reaching the high hill on that first morning. Faraway and long ago—and looking up now at Forest Mansion, strong and stern as the mountains, his heart was stirred with pride. He looked and a great crack of blue fire at that instant split the storm sky over the vast valley; there was a searing sound and a blazing blinding bolt tore down the pine under which Carter was standing, it struck Carter, who still was holding in his hands the iron handles of the cedar buckets. Standing in the open door of the kitchen, Queen Elizabeth saw the lightning fling Carter to the ground. Screaming, she ran and in a moment she was followed by Stephen John, running through the raging downpour. In a few minutes Carter came again to his senses but up one arm, across his chest and down his other arm, there was a line burnt deep into his flesh.

After that, propped in a chair, he became an invalid, seeming at first to improve but later slipping into a daze that gradually settled like a mist over his mind, a cloudiness that gradually increased.

So Carter died—"the head of the Caldwells, a Senator of South Carolina, builder of Forest Mansion, struck by lightning while swilling pigs." It was chiseled on his tomb.

❧

So still a young man, Stephen John inherited Forest Mansion. After his father had been buried on the hill, he took a drink of corn liquor, sent for everyone to gather in the central room of the house and when all had assembled, the black ones as well as the white, he bowed his head, prayed, and then read from the Bible, after which he made a brief speech. Calling for Queen Elizabeth at the conclusion of this speech, he said to her that by direction of his father's will she had become a free woman. Curtsying, thoroughly frightened, Queen Elizabeth said, "Yes, sir."

"Do you know what that means?" he inquired and Queen Elizabeth said, "yes, sir." But Stephen John saw that she did not comprehend. "That means you can do anything you want to, whenever you want to—you can come and go as you like."

"Yes, sir, that's right."

Turning now to the other slaves, a dozen in all, Stephen John gave them a promise that he would never sell any of them nor would any new slaves be brought to Forest Mansion. "Twelve slaves is enough," he said, a new graveness marking his appearance as he began dictating his first mandates. Swiftly and surely and without embarrassment Stephen John spoke—land thereafter on the place would be rented to tenant farmers, on the shares; if slaves so wished they also would be permitted to rent a few acres. Also the slaves were not to call Stephen John master for he did not like the word "master." "It is abolished," he commanded, "and also I don't like the word 'plantation'—it is abolished also; from now on Forest Mansion is a farm."

"Yes, sir; yes, sir," sang the Negroes in chorus, bowing, backing, and repeating aloud their instructions. "Master isn't master, the plantation is a farm."

"Do you all understand?" inquired Stephen John.

"Yes, sir, master," said Popcorn, already forgetting. Furiously, Stephen John shoved the Negro through the door. "Not master."

"Yes, sir, Mister Stevie."

Alone again in the study which he had made of Carter's bedroom, Stephen John poured himself another drink of corn liquor in a tumbler, began planning a rigid schedule. First for a half hour he wrote in his diary…"My first duty is to keep this place self-contained—Forest Mansion must keep in step with the changing times." And so under his administration did it continue; from all over the world he began to bring in new plants and curious seeds—New Zealand spinach, lettuce, salsify, Switzerland chard, Guinea squashes, Spanish radishes, mazagan, Windsor beans. Popcorn was sent to Pendleton to study blacksmithing under a master smith and on his return was set to making hinges and mule shoes. Gotheny was made head of the grist mill, made to grind flour and meal on a regular schedule, soap machines were set up in the backyard, candles were poured, a special spinning room was built, even silk was spun now at Forest Mansion—a splendid heavy silk woven from cocoons brought round Cape Horn from China in a Baltimore clipper ship. A grove of mulberry trees were planted for these expensive worms to feed on and in searching for a dye to use in staining the silk, Stephen John turned again to the old herb book of great-great-grandmother Narcissa.

More cotton was planted and more cotton. New grounds were cleared for still more cotton.

And Forest Mansion prospered. Already rich, Stephen John became richer. And the richer he became the more autocratic did he grow. He took everything and everyone in charge—named the horses, cows, even the pigs, decided which were to be killed and how and when; how many vines, shrubs, roots, bulbs were to be set out and where they were to be set; he fixed the time for going to bed and getting up, decided what was to be eaten at each meal.

Finally he began telling Unity which dresses to wear. This made his wife wild with fury but like everyone else, she submitted. So with everyone and everything in hand at Forest Mansion, Stephen John began to consider bigger fields. He convinced himself it was his duty to run for Congress.

He ran and he was elected.

On the Sunday before he was to depart for Washington, he attended church at the old stone meeting house and returning home he drank half a tumblerful of corn liquor and called the Caldwells to dinner—they ate for an hour, then for an hour they retired for a nap. Another half tumblerful of corn liquor was gulped by Stephen John and then he read aloud to Unity for a half hour from the lonely meditations of Marcus Aurelius, the stern old Emperor being one of his favorite writers. Closing the pages of the thin volume exactly at the moment the chimes of the old clock began ringing out the half hour, Stephen John said to Unity, "Now we have thirty minutes that I have not planned." Getting up and starting to his study, he remarked, "I will put it to use writing letters," and he suggested she might compose an essay on spring—"for practice, somebody might want a piece on spring sometime for an album."

Flaming with anger, Unity suddenly rebelled. "Jesus Christ," she said and turning her back on her husband she left the house. "What a life," she said, kicking the deep red dust in the dry road that led downward into the holly ravine. Soon she heard Stephen John behind her and a few moments later, humble and worried, he had his arms about her, apologizing. "I'm sorry." In an instant then he became his old self once more, was laughing and suggesting that they forget everything. Talking to her tenderly. "I couldn't live a day without you, my darling," he said, "not even for an hour."

O happiness! O love and happiness! Unity felt the fine feeling and her spirit soared and in her heart burst a glad song. O voluptuous, beloved, chiefest among ten thousands—his eyes were as the eyes of doves by the river of waters, washed with milk and fitly set; his cheeks were as beds of spices, as sweet flowers; his lips like lilies, dropping sweet smelling myrrh, his hands were as gold rings set with beryl, his belly as bright ivory overlaid with sapphires, his legs as pillars of marble, set upon sockets of fine gold. Lovely…

Enraptured, Unity pulled her strong young husband to herself, her soft hands held his thighs.

"Beautiful, sweet…"

In Washington, living in a little brick house with a fine fan door beside the canal in Georgetown, Unity took up water coloring, painting flowers and fruit and foliage, and in the vast pile of marble on the top of Capitol Hill—vast and lonely in its location, isolated like the people it stood for and as free—there Stephen John sat through the days in the hall of the House of Representatives, listening to speeches and making them—about the west, always about the west. The deep pride of his mountain fathers stirred within him as he heard lean, angular Congressmen from rowdy, unlettered Kentucky and Illinois rise to fight for roads and canals and other great western improvements—he supported them all, even the most fantastic. For like old Carter and old Silas and even old Narcissa, he believed in the country beyond the mountains, was willing to risk everything—a gigantic public debt, even the future itself on the western venture, the great America—inland and remote and protected, a thousand miles from any sea!

Once in order to raise public funds for the building of a canal across Ohio and Indiana, Stephen John proposed a higher tariff for revenue and brought upon himself the intense anger of every great slave-holding cotton grower in the Congress. Furiously from the center of the room rose one of his fellow Carolinians—one of the aristocrats of the low country, Charles Pinckney Rand of Charleston.

Traitor," shouted Rand at Stephen John, "You're a traitor to the South."

"Order," shouted the old Speaker of the House, rapping hard with a gavel.

"I'm no Southerner," Stephen John shouted back. "I'm a Caldwell of Keowee and you know who the Caldwells are—we're founders of the West."

"Order, order," continued the Speaker.

"Rabble rouser," yelled Rand.

Filled with pride and satisfaction, Stephen John walked that afternoon through the dusky corridors of the Capitol—one of his favorite strolling places for already it had become for him a sanctuary of the wild free spirit, the fathers had walked in these halls, Washington and Jefferson and Monroe and Madison, here already was hanging the Thomas Jefferson of Thomas Sully, the contemplative Washington of Gilbert Stuart; Stephen John loved the purple tiles, the marble stairs leading upward to the Senate, the plaster stars and the eagles, the burst of Virginia sunshine through the windows…"O shrine of the plain and common man!" This afternoon, he gloated greatly—he had succeeded in Washington in stirring again the bitter Carolinian feud which since the beginning had divided the men of the red hills from the feudal lords of Charleston.

"We'll lick them yet," said Stephen John, leaving the Capitol by the flight of steps upon which the Presidents came to take oath as Presidents of the United States. "We're getting along, by Jesus; we're on our way." Walking across the broad open square, he entered a saloon. At once he was surrounded by an admiring group of rough Westerners.

They took him home at midnight, unconscious in his own vomit.

But at sunup, Stephen John was riding southward in a stagecoach. With Unity beside him, he was on his way to Forest Mansion to preside over the formal family reunion that he had summoned to assemble on the second Tuesday in August.

❧

Under the white oaks in the yard behind the great house were two hundred gaunt, lean men and women, mostly with high cheek bones, deep blue eyes, thin and yellow hair. Among the thin featured women, whole lonely expressions somehow conveyed a hidden hungriness of the spirit, were ladies in fine satin and lace, talking in the friendliest way with women in linsey woolsey and sunbonnets. There was a judge among the men and a Tennessee preacher and a man who had shot another man.

Free to travel at this season of the high summer, their crops laid by, the Caldwells had come into Keowee in oxcarts, carriages, in wagons pulled by mules, on horseback—and some had walked in, barefooted. They were drinking liquor and laughing and talking and enjoying themselves under the trees where the women had loaded long rows of tables with victuals—cold fried chicken, fried steak, venison, fried pork, whole boiled ham, roast duck, boiled guinea, baked turkey, cold veal, hard boiled eggs, lemon tarts, cheese straws, bowls of high-seasoned chow-chow pickles, peach preserves, brandied peach pickles, apple butter, blackberry jelly, pound cake, chocolate layer cake, marble cake, fruit cake, corn on the cob, fresh grapes, cold watermelons, cantaloupes, musk melons, pomegranates. To drink there was fresh hard cider, blackberry wine, sweet and deep purple in color, dry wine from scuppernongs, muscadine wine, elderberry wine, a little of which would intoxicate, dandelion wine, clover blossom wine, the most exotic of all, persimmon and locust beer, jugs of peach, apple, and wild cherry brandy, sweet milk, buttermilk, cold spring water, corn liquor, pale and old and fierce as fire. At noon Stephen John led the procession of young people to the burying ground to decorate the graves of the dead ones with wild flowers—the hardy wild rose, the wild mountain laurel. Halting the children at the stone to old Narcissa, he began lauding her memory—"She was old and afraid but she came on anyhow over the wilderness road; at over eighty years of age, she started out into the lonely country beyond the frontier; she knew she would never be able to come back but she didn't give up to despair, she didn't surrender. So she sleeps or in this wide open space, under these trees, in the west wind; she rests, buried, conquered and slain, immortal for that reason…she learned to listen, to see, hear the birds sing, see the color of the flowers…"

Stephen John offered a prayer, then he had the children sing and as their voices rose he was overcome with feeling for all those men and women, dead and gone, the lonely fathers, who had come into the wild country and driven out the Cherokees and enslaved Queen Elizabeth and planted cotton among the ghostly forest of rung trees, fought, wept, stolen from each other, killed their enemies and themselves, repented in poignant remorse, longed for some quality of repose, some degree of spirit they had never found. With the veins in his livid face bulging, he cried out, "Children, here is the spirit that made us." Stephen John tottered against the wall about the tomb of the third Narcissa; he had been drinking again.

Returning unsteadily to the mansion, Stephen John presided at dinner; excitement began as he announced the first set of a square dance. Quickly a group of fiddlers and banjo pickers, all Caldwells, began playing the swift screeching music of the wilderness; there was roaring and shouting and Pisgah Caldwell of Hopewell began to call the set:

"S'lute yer pardner, let her go!
Balance all an' do-se-do."

Sweating and breathless, they halted at the end of this lively dance to listen to Stephen John; he was pounding the table with a gavel. Suddenly they saw a look of bewilderment come over the Congressman's inflammed face—Stephen John collapsed and they laughed, continuing their dancing. The head of the Caldwells was carried to his room by Queen Elizabeth's Popcorn and Gotheny. "The Caldwells," said Popcorn, as they lifted Stephen John up the stone steps of the mansion, "sure is got a lot of ways of amusing theyselves—they preaches awhile, they prays awhile, then they breaks down with the liquor jug and fiddle."

The dancing went on until sundown, then the journey homeward was begun. But after that the Caldwells gathered at Forest Mansion on the second Tuesday in August for a hundred and three years.

※

One afternoon in the autumn, twenty years after that first family reunion, Stephen John was walking through the fields—in a deep thicket a thrush sang, raising its superb sweet voice, again and again; Stephen John listened and then he saw a flock of blackbirds, flying south, a sure sign of cold weather; soon there would be frost and the bumblebees and butterflies seemed aware of it, so madly were they dashing from one last flower to another. Grasshoppers seemed in a panic—they aroused Stephen John's sympathy. For grasshoppers were adventurers, wild and free, and their reckoning day—the day that he knew came for all adventuring spirits was at hand. Returning to Forest Mansion, Stephen John shut himself in his study and became again the head of a family whose business extended now from Keowee to the canyons of the Pecos.

Stephen John had the Texas fever. It was in the air everywhere. Rumor had reached Forest Mansion after rumor, one extravaganza following another, all telling of the immenseness of the fertile plains and the wealth to be had there, the utter inexhaustible richness of Texas. There were no poor folks there, everybody had money in Texas.

Reaching into his desk, Stephen John brought out a jug and poured himself a drink in a tumbler. Gulping this down, he sat back in his chair and closing his eyes, folding his hands, he pictured to himself the wild procession—from Carolina, Georgia, Tennessee, Kentucky, Indiana, Illinois, Missouri, Alabama, Mississippi; he saw the wheels rolling and the dust flying—there went the Caldwells, dozens and scores. He could not go himself, but he could help those who could go, and as payment he would take land. "I'll make a million dollars," he said to himself.

Roused by this thought, Stephen John turned to the pile of letters on a table before him. A cousin in Kansas whose crop had failed in a drought wanted to borrow two hundred dollars in order to move on to Oregon. "Here is the two hundred," wrote Stephen John, "I'll stake you—will take it back in real estate when you get able but why don't you try Texas instead of Oregon?" From another cousin there was a business proposal—a lawyer, this cousin wanted Stephen John to lend him « thousand dollars to form a company to speculate in Texas land, suggesting that he, Stephen John, and two other Texas cousins, one a rancher and the other a railroad official, buy lands in areas where railroad extensions were scheduled for construction. "Cousin Ted, being a railroad man himself," wrote this lawyer cousin, "can find out beforehand what routes the extensions will take—we can't lose, we'll make a fortune." "I'll take the chance," wrote Stephen John, pouring out another glassful of liquor. And from a cousin who was a contractor there was a request for three thousand dollars…"All these new Texas towns will have to have schools and churches and jails; let's form a company and build them, with luck we ought to clean up a hundred thousand…"

Unlocking an inner drawer in his desk, Stephen John now drew out a thick black book, the diary in which for years he had written the secret, often passionate and lyrical thoughts of his scheming mind. Now he wrote: "We're really getting somewhere at last, but we've only started, we've just begun. For there never was such a land as our land is—the great protected western refuge, a continent, and it's ours—it is personal with us, a part of our life, it is our blood. For already streams bear our name, a city is called after us, more than any others, we are responsible for the creation of those western states. And we've only begun—there is no limit to the things we will do in the future…"

There was a light knock on the door. Unity came into the room to remind Stephen John that it was time he left for Pendleton to keep an appointment made a week previously with his old friend, Colonel John Simpson. "But I don't want to go," shouted Stephen John, a thick note in his voice. "Hell, why should I go to Pendleton when I don't want to? Ain't this a free country?" He made no attempt to move from the heavy chair in which he was sitting. Unity closed the door.

And Stephen John reached for the jug.

❦

And brighter and brighter burned the fire of this Texas fever.

Stephen John's daughter Caline, the second of that name at Forest Mansion, was married that winter and on the day of her wedding left for the Lone Star country, going with her young husband, Habersham Wyatt, his father and mother, his three brothers and their wives.

And a few days after their departure there arrived at Forest Mansion from Mississippi a fever letter from Brother Silas, who long before this had forgotten his past in Keowee, had married a Mississippi girl, settled down to farming in the delta. But the Texas fever was too much for Silas. He wrote:

"Dear Stephen John:

"Just a line to tell you we are pulling up stake, leaving for Texas. We have just heard from Cousin Caldwell Evans and his folks at Two Tree and they say they are wonderful pleased with the Texas country. There is the cheapest land there they ever saw and a man can make a better living there with a third less labor than here. Good land can be had for about $14 to $16 an acre. We are going to start tomorrow. I will try to rent 226 acres of the finest bottom land as a starter. Cousin Will Caldwell has left for the Oregon country but I think Texas is better. Will commence writing soon as we get settled."

Weeks, then months passed. Then Stephen John began to receive long accounts from Texas—heaven itself. First there was this one from Mary Caldwell, one of the daughters of Brother Silas.

"Two Tree, Texas.

"Dear Uncle Stephen John:
"Well, here we are and well pleased I reckon but I thought when I first arrived here that if all Texas was mine I would not have it—I have never been a visiting anywhere out here yet except a Mrs. Clark's about three times and I miss visiting. It's a hard country. I like to visit Mrs. Clark though as she has always lived in a town or city and is extremely highfalutin and finical. Still I like her amazingly. I enjoyed myself very much traveling. I like to look about, see the country, but in New Orleans I relinquished the idea of ever marrying a Frenchman. New Orleans looked just like a city would look except for Jackson Square, the French Cemetery and the park. Heard many folks talking French. I don't know why myself but don't think I could ever get fully adjusted to everything being French.
"Tell the girls that when we went to Austin, we spent a night at a mansion house with some folks by the name of Johnson. Their folks came to Texas when Mister Johnson was a boy so they are old residents—had a brother killed by the Indians. He is one of the aristocracy, if there is any here, had a splendid house, magnificently furnished—to be short, is rich, has thousands of acres of this fertile Texas land—AND NOT A CHILD—has been married twenty years and no prospect. Now, don't you know I wish they would adopt me or his old fat wife would kick the bucket. I would do some grand maneuvering to become mistress of his wide domains—but I am digressing.
"If only we had our own folks out here with us, we would be as happy as birds. But, oh, we sadly miss our friends and relations and sigh for some congenial companions. Come, you all, and stay with us. I will promise the girls a good horse and saddle and we will mount them and grow as wild as the mustang ponies. This is a wild country and no mistake but wildest of all are the young men. I never saw nor read of so much dissipation—though there are a few reliable ones and I must give them credit. Pa and ma send love.
"Love,
"Mary"

Soon afterward there came this word from Caline:

"Honey Springs, Texas.

"Dear folks at home:
"We are doing pretty well out here but this country isn't home to us and to tell you the truth we are eating out our hearts, we are so homesick for Carolina. We talk about home all of the time and every day we say we are going back there next year on a visit. Don't say a word about it, for it's uncertain, but if nothing happens to the crops we are coming in the fall.
"I am much better satisfied than I thought I ever would be but do not feel willing to remain in Texas forever. Hold on to a ham and smoke it good for I feel like I could eat all of one myself. If I had written only a few days ago I could have sent you a bouquet of tube roses and geraniums. This is the soberest looking country in winter, imaginable, not a vestige of green to rest the eye upon, and O how I long for a sight of the dear old mountains and does

my mind wander back to lovely Keowee valley. You all don't appreciate the beauties of home and the dear Blue Mountains until you come to the flat monotonous woods and prairies of Texas—though they too have their attractions.

"Don't forget, you all always are welcome at our western home, which is comfortable if not luxurious."

⁂

At the end of a day, among the deep shadows—with this letter and the jug before him, Stephen John sat for a long time, drinking the pale yellow liquor and thinking, dreaming of Narcissa, who grieved in Keowee for Pennsylvania just as Caline was grieving in Texas for Keowee. Ah, Narcissa—lonely and lost in the silences of Carolina. The Caldwells had gone a long way since she took that first step in Pennsylvania. Forgotten now was Pennsylvania, it was Carolina that was home and the time would come, Stephen John reflected, when the granddaughters of the granddaughters would yearn for the wide plains and the bluebonnets—Texas would raise its own branch of the traveling Caldwells.

Texas would and the Oregon country would. Maybe even California.

⁂

Of course California would and sooner than Stephen John expected.

For on the very day that Stephen John was sitting in his study, musing in the world of reverie—on that very day was gold discovered in California. And the greatest drum that ever was beaten in America began to sound. The great wind itself seemed to carry the magic music—there was gold in California and there was California fever. California had taken the place of Texas.

And among the first to go were the Caldwells. Soon Stephen John was receiving the word—Will Caldwell was riding overland through the high plateau passes of the Wyoming country, some of the Missouri Caldwells had started before Will Caldwell; Cousin Taylor was leaving. Silas and Habersham had left from Honey Springs in Texas, had gone to New Orleans, had sailed in the Barkentine Flying Spray, departing in the midst of the hurricane season into the Caribbean, choosing the jungles of Panama and the Pacific as the shortest way.

Even Stephen John, when he received this last letter, was stirred, even he would have liked to start out for the gold fields. Walking over the red hills and the old fields to the rock, he sat down and thought of the old days—he thought of Silas, planning, dreaming of travel. Far below him the swift river was flowing, the sun also was shining, the west wind blowing but Stephen John was not conscious of these now. He was thinking of Silas, sailing on an ocean; he was thinking the thoughts of the one who must stay at home, envying the footloose and free.

"You'll have to see them for me, Silas," said Stephen John, "See the fine things and the beauty."

⁂

And down on the Caribbean sailed Silas. The sky about him also was filled with sunlight and over the sea the west wind also was blowing. Silas was sitting in the prow of the Flying Spray, on a coil of rope, watching the blue tropical ocean and the sea birds and feeling the sting of the salty air—and his secret spirit soared for at this moment he was living. This was the passionate life for which he longed.

There he sat—halfway between Louisiana and Panama—dreaming, his mind and his soul filled with the lyrical rapture that stirs in every man's secret heart…facing a wind that blew with solemn sustained power, like a strain of deep music, a melody persisting through a great wind symphony, exalted, inspired…his secret spirit soared, he thought of all the impatient men, gathered in the Flying Spray, here for a time, going on, earnest and anxious and restless…soon gone. Here was a new generation of the wild new world, passing where the old ships had passed, where Columbus and Pizarro and Drake and all the other pirates had passed, here now were they…and he thought, we live and leave no record of our hopes, the cry in our hearts…it is like the wake a ship leaves in the water, it is not there. But beautiful…beautiful is the sea, so deep and awful is its power…its solitude. Faraway is home, faraway on a continent where it is summer, a silent afternoon, hot with bees buzzing…the endless doing nothing of passengers on a ship, sitting, sleeping…alone, always alone, Americans are alone, it is the winding road for us, the path of a star…sometimes I cannot bear the loneliness…I am a seashore worn always by the sea…

And then a fresh wind blew and Silas shifted himself on the rope…and free in space is spirit, memory that has no time; he began thinking of his own past, Stephen John and he and Popcorn were sitting again on the rock…and there lay the road, the years…how often had he pictured the way ahead, dreamed of it, but the actual way never had been the dreamed one, it was another road, harder and richer and the sights that he had started out to see were not the ones that he remembered…not the view of the cathedral lived…it was something else, the sudden and unexpected…not the great famed thing but the mist, a look of sorrow on a face, a whisper…O the secret! It is the fragile creations of a moment that never die, that one remembers on and on through a lifetime…the lines of mountains lie in the mind, a sunset never fades, a peach blossom never shatters…the light of a star shines on and there is the dim glimmer of distant lightning and the harm that one has done, the evil. O the poignant regret that never dies.

Said Silas there is a cloud over my conscience, a shadow that I cannot endure, I must endure it…riderless horses and windshod feet and the fear of fire at sea…I am the specter…who was young but is no longer young but the passing of youth is not to be regretted, I shall not regret old age, age is a time of understanding…and sympathy is better than joy, more enduring than pleasure, the first voyage is for fame, fortune, the promise…but the second journey is made for mere travel's sake, for the enjoyment of the ride…

From out of the depths of blue light rose a star.

And suddenly over Silas came a great forgetfulness, he forgot his wife and Texas… sailing the vast lonely Caribbean, Silas had become happy, he had left some place and had not yet arrived at some other place…he was on his way and that was what Silas liked, these were the circumstances and the circumstances only that brought him complete joy…he was on his way and while on that way his deep-seated restlessness, the yearning, found a moment of repose.

Pure light, pure water, pure star, violent clean merciless sea…the sailor's stars, so far… grieving winds, the sad music of the sea…its waves, its skies were the angels' home, its deeps the den where evil flourished in darkness, rank, obscene…O evil flower of the night…

Seared, purged, cold, clean…a symbol.

"God," said Silas.

So days passed on this trip, weeks passed, and Silas did not care if the voyage were never over. But Habersham became more impatient with every passing hour. He walked the deck, up and back and back and forth over the teakwood, fretting and fuming, whistling for wind and more wind, cursing the luck.

"We're never going to get there," said he a hundred times to Silas.

But eventually the low brown hills were sighted, the course was changed, sails re-set. One morning very early, they came into San Francisco. And excited, exhilarated, belonging indeed for the time among the mystics, Silas rushed ashore, into disordered streets. His first act was to climb the high rocks overlooking the ocean—from the westernmost hill in America, on the rim at last of his continent, to gaze upon the Pacific. Facing the strong wind, his yellow beard spattered with sea salt, Silas stretched his arms—at the end of the road, this was his salute.

"For Christ sweet sake," said Habersham, pulling at Silas' coat tail, "What in the hell are you doing?" After the weeks lost in inactivity at sea, cramped, Habersham was burning to start immediately for the gold fields; not another moment was to be squandered, it might cost them their fortune. "Jesus God," he shouted, his voice carrying through the strong wind. "What do you think we've crossed half the world for?"

Silas did not reply. Before him in the streaked mists, gray-green, sailed a ship, moving swiftly into the sun, a trail of scud behind it; low swept the gulls. This was glory. Two centuries of hard western travel, a thousand lives were behind him and here at last was he—at the western goal. Far away in the vapors of thought, he saw the long line behind him, the lonely ones on their way, lifting up their voices, weeping at night, men of wild joys and acquainted with grief—restless, wandering, hoping, searching yesterday and tomorrow for the dream, dissatisfied always with the present, camping for a night and moving on, expecting to find what they sought beyond the next mountain, in the next territory, surely in the next river valley. And here was he at the end and what was he saying?

"It isn't here, we haven't found it."

This was the victory.

Far away in the vapors Silas heard the cry, saw the lost restless procession, the lonely hungry men of the passionate secret life, eating cornbread and fried ham, their eyes like the Indians' trained on the farest valley. And about them was the fragrance of sassafras and sweat and prairie dust, a people speaking a dialect of their own with rudeness and vigor, talking in a way that no amount of living in foreign lands would ever change. The sound of storms in Texas was in their ears, the note of the Idaho coyote howling; with the smell of cedar, the rustle of corn stalks in their recollection, new world music—continent men, one with the American sun and the wind and the western sky. There in that wilderness, they were born again, cleansed and scoured in the heart—changed by the turn of a western hawk's wing, the cry of a western bird, the fall of Ohio water. And all of them in the secret heart, dreaming, searching for the way, driven by the small voice to seek the valley where life might be lived in the noble way, where they would accomplish the great things they had wanted to accomplish, amount to something and become somebody...turn their backs forever on the mean and petty. Find rest. Live at peace.

In anguish Silas cried out to himself, "Are we destined always to this loneliness? Must we always be restless wanderers? Never come to a home?"

He asked himself the question and what was his answer—the west wind blew and the Pacific Ocean pounded itself against piles of rock. Long did Silas stand there dreaming. Then turning to Habersham he asked, "What are we looking for anyhow in this country, what do we hope to find?"

Looking at Silas as though he were crazy, Habersham yelled in exasperation, "Gold, you damn fool—what else did you think?"

⁊⋌

Before starting that night for the gold hills, Silas and Habersham sat down by California lamplight, hurriedly wrote letters back to Texas; mailing these, they started. They wrote to Texas and from Texas was relayed the story of their far western experience to Stephen John at Forest Mansion. Wrote Caline on the same night that Habersham and Silas landed in San Francisco:

"Dear Pa:

"I have not heared from any of you in so long a time; I hear from Habersham who is thousands of miles away twice to your once; he or Uncle Silas has written every two weeks but we have not heared yet whether they have reached California, they set out safe from Panama. Aunt Sarah is very uneasy, she has grieved so much she has become unhealthy. She said she never was so weak before and I don't know any other cause without it is living exposed to the cold winter. She said after Uncle Silas left she could not get warm all night. I do not see any use of her staying in Texas as she will have no stock when she gets her hogs fat and kills them but one lone cow and calf, one sheep, one sow—and I don't think she will have any pigs soon. But she stays on. Well, we are waiting for news and while I'm waiting, I will start this letter and keep adding on until we hear...

"I went to the Methodist church last Sunday. Three persons were to be baptized, one of them was not prepared. They went to the creek to baptize them, one of the candidates knelt at the edge of the water and had the water dipped up in a pitcher and poured on. The other went in the water and knelt and had it poured. The minister said straightway come up and out of the water. The third one was to be immerst had she been ready. I went to Two Tree Church that night to hear Rev. Reid preach. He did not attend—I do not know any cause without it is the report that has got out about his becoming lonesome at a late hour when he should have been at his own house sleeping—he got lonesome, they say, at a California widow's house. This has caused more laughing than anything I have heared since I been here but I can't write it, I will have to send the word about it by the first person going to Carolina.

"I have concluded I will not close this letter until the California mail comes, even if I have to hold it a month—My littlest boy is not well. He has the summer complaint that is common among children. I think some of the grown persons were troubled with it last Sunday, they kept going out while the preacher was talking. Habersham wrote the boys to study their books but the boys say they are confused, they can't study the book nor nothing else much. Aunt Sarah said she hopes she will not have to go back home for a support. I told her that she has a plenty and is said to be the most industrious woman in Texas. She canned two bushels of peaches in one day and had the back door trots besides, very bad. I tried to get her to quit work but she said she would not until the men comes in from California.

"You all ought to come out and eat peaches and watermelons with us. We have a great deal of fruit. I would like to have some of your pears and apples as they will not grow in this part of Texas. If nothing happens maybe I will come to see you this winter or spring—that is, if Cousin Dock and his wife get in their crop without anything happening. They say I can count on the trip sure—his wife says she can hardly wait, they are going to see her folks in Georgia and that will be my chance to see you. Cousin Mary says tell ma if she was back there as she was and knows as much as she does she would come again to Texas sure—if she did have the chills. She chilled two or three months straight along but is stout as ever now. Some of our kinfolks wanted to know if Cousin Dock and Cousin Mary did not wish themselves back on the same old place just as they were. Cousin Mary says earnestly that she does not but will not humor them far enough to tell them one thing about it. If you see any of Cull Parsons' family tell them Cade, Jane, Emmer and Sarah are all doing well and are going to have increases in their families this summer. Tom Hunter and old Sally Hunter are dying of fever whether they are worthy of writing about or not.

"Well, I think of a multitude of questions to ask…

"The California mail has come sooner than expected. I have got a letter from Habersham today which was a great satisfaction to me. He wrote that he was well, he wrote he had the mumps on the ship but was well of them. He said there is a good deal of stealing going on there. He said there was a Negro stole five thousand dollars from a Mister Martin of Tennessee, a merchant, who was keeping store about three hundred yards from where he was living. He said the Negro was caught but stood out from telling where the gold was until the rope was around his neck. He said the Negro was told then if he would tell they would let him off. So with that he told and they hanged him anyhow. And a white man was hanged the same evening for stealing one hundred ounces of gold and another one has been hanged for murder. He said he has heard of many such scrapes as that. I have not got time to write it all down for the letter must start shortly. He said he was doing tolerable well. We have not heard from Cousin Caldwell Evans and the Kansas boys—whether they all got there safe or not. We have just heared from some others that started overland at the same time. They have had a rout of it. No more at present. Your daughter,

"Caline."

Other letters followed, filled with high hope and adventure, and then came one with a postscript that caused Stephen John to walk the hills and spend a long time in reflection. "P.S.," it said, "Habersham and Uncle Silas say they are not doing as well as they had expected." That was all there was, this was the only inkling, but it struck deep into Stephen John's wisdom. He was not surprised soon to learn that Habersham and Silas were returning to Texas by the overland trail, was not surprised at all to receive word they had arrived again in Texas, ragged and almost barefoot and without a penny in their pockets. They wrote him for a little money and he sent it to them, then Caline wrote that times were hard in Texas, they would return the loan as soon as they were able. But no word at all came for a long time from Silas direct, only rumors reached Forest Mansion, then finally a letter came in from Mary Caldwell, Silas' daughter who had married a tall, rangy cattle man, a Texan by the name of Raney. Mary wrote and in her letter, between the lines, clear and evident, came the story that deeply worried Stephen John, that filled him with grief and sorrow.

For it brought, in failure and defeat, an end to a life that had started with great spirit and enthusiasm. It meant Silas had not succeeded, Silas had lost the way. Mary wrote:

"Two Tree, Texas.

"Dear Uncle Stevie:

"Well, I suppose you have heard some wonderful tales about us all. I will tell the truth about it all. I suppose you have heared Pa had to come and live with us to get his living which is not so. Mr. Raney bought this place. It took all the money we could scrape together to make the last payment which was $1,000. We then had neither meat, bread nor money. We had been boarding, had that to pay. Pa and Ma had meat and bread but no home—what else could either of us do but join. You have heared Pa had run through and drunk up everything he had. Uncle Stevie, tell me how could he do this when he had nothing—he never has had anything much since he left Mississippi. When he left Mississippi he had about $200 and Cousin Caldwell James had the same amount and when we all got to Louisiana Pa didn't have a red cent. He borrowed $20 of Cousin Caldwell and when he landed in Two Tree, Cousin Caldwell had fifty-three dollars in specie, 13.50 dollars in greenbacks, Pa had 10 dollars, which he had borrowed, and he had two mules and the old mare. The mare died. He sold the mules for $150. He bought provisions with half of the money and the other he paid the freight on Sam, Fred and Watts Caldwell's baggage and he never got one cent of it back. That is why I am going that far back for now the worst word Sam, Fred and Watts can say about Pa and mother they say it—I can't imagine why they say so much about him drinking and getting drunk so often when there is not one of them but will get drunk and loves whisky just as well as Pa.

"I have heared that Sam wrote back and said I was dissatisfied with Texas. I am well satisfied. Mother and all the rest that came in our crowd are satisfied—and even if they weren't they wouldn't never let on. We all went to work when we got here and had plenty to divide with the others when they got here—that Sam Caldwell lived in the house with Pa for a year and never put in one bite of provisions, then would curse at table because they did not live better.

"And as for those other boys—well, Fred Caldwell was owing sixty dollars for his rations, he said he was going to stay in one place as long as he could get credit, then move again. It wasn't long before the whole of Texas was on to that fellow's tactics. Uncle Stevie, tell me what room has any of them to say such things?

"I will tell you another trick Sam Caldwell done on mother. Mother, Cade and Emmer made them a separate cotton patch which made three parts of a bale. They all went to town to trade out their cotton. Mother took up all of hers but one dollar as there was no bed cord, coffee nor black pepper. Emmer took up all hers but $2.15. Sam goes to the clerk, says he would take up that money of Mrs. Caldwell's and Emmer's...so when the goods come, Mother and Emmer sent for their things and the word came back Sam had taken up that money and was to settle with them. When Mother named it to him he said it was not so but guilty conscience needs no accusing.

"Uncle Stevie, I expect you believe all you have heard but I think you will believe me. And if you could be here just a little while you would see that all the above was true. This and what you have heard before is the both sides of it. So will say no more on this subject. Take it as you think best.

"This leaves us well. I will send you my little Tommy's picture so you can see how pretty he is—mother and pa send their well wishes to all the family and wish them to write. You must write soon and give us all the news there afloat. All the connection are all well so far as I know.

"With love,
"Mary Caldwell Raney."

This letter took Stephen John back through the years into the far past, back to the red fields and the deep woods of the long before, and through these he moved again, a boy, and with him was Silas, also again a boy, and their ideals still were high and their ambitions boundless and they both of them were going to become great men, do something noble with their lives, and make a million dollars.

Suddenly a feeling of overpowering sadness came over Stephen John.

"Failure," he said, "it's failure."

So in the fable of the Caldwells an end came, and a beginning. The powerful five-rayed star, the pillar of fire that had guided them for so long was fading, the pillar of cloud was falling into darkness, fast disappearing, and far from the goldfields of California and the plains of Texas—in the sky of Carolina, a newer star, smaller, less splendid, was about to rise, become a new guide for those at Forest Mansion. The long era of the westerners, their search through the vast territories of western space, was over; for the next seventy years the Caldwells were to seek within themselves for an answer. They were to remain at Keowee—become local, a family of southerners.

PART TWO

The Southerners

CHAPTER NINE

Like crabapples and turnip leaves which grow sweet on the blasts of frost, so did Stephen John become kinder as he grew older, trouble ennobled him; he grew deeper. Plain and proud and still common, he had much to face in his old age—a storm and flood and constant foreboding and finally war. Death swept through Stephen John's family between the first battle of Manassas and Appomatox Courthouse, took off Caldwells for a cause they had opposed in Columbia Statehouse and in Washington for a hundred years. Charleston had won and they had lost; Charleston's war was upon them, "the rich man's war and the poor man's fight." Only after many of their men had been killed did the Caldwells become embittered with the Yankees.

Added to all this for Stephen John was personal bitterness and private despair. For Stephen John looked upon his life as failure—he never recognized the part he played as counselor and banker and friend to that long western procession, the band that moved on. In his perspective of his secret self, Stephen John saw vertically instead of laterally—as a Caldwell in the line of family descent and not as one guiding a family into western space. His yearning was for another kind of distinction—to become a father of great children. The time had come, thought he, for Caldwells to create beauty, for them to make a place in the spheres of culture. And in that deep ambition, his sons and daughters—every one of them, failed him. He regarded them as having failed him. He complained bitterly to God of his children. For a long time Stephen John had no children at all; try as he and Unity might, they conceived no heirs at all. They worked, exercised, they rested without result; they made attempts during waxing and waning moons, during autumn, winter, spring, summer, Sunday, Wednesday night, Saturday afternoon, upon feather beds, in the open on the grass.

"We've tried everything—still no sign of a baby," Stephen John said in despair one day to Queen Elizabeth as the two sat before the log fire in the still kitchen. The young man was rather angry too about this failure. "Think of something," ordered the boy sharply, "You ought to be able to tell us something we can do—God knows you have had enough experience." He then mentioned an obscene word.

This enraged the old Negress and turning upon the young man she said fiercely, "You shut your mouth, Mister Stevie. I may be born a black slave, bought and paid for, but I am a respectable woman in my heart and I don't allow talk like that from nobody." It was the boy's tone of speaking, rather than the sound of the speaking to which Queen Elizabeth objected. "You get right up from that chair, sir, and you get out and you stay out of this kitchen until you can find your manners…" There was a blaze of real fury in her staring eyes.

The boy left the kitchen and at once the old Negro woman relented—she turned to her stock of magic. A few minutes later she disappeared, returning hours later with a combination of charms—the sperm of a goat, some woman's red fluid, sassafras buds and wild cherry bark. These she whipped in a bowl with the yelks of four turkey eggs. "Here, children," said she that noon, handing to Stephen John and Unity high glasses filled with this yellow drink. "You all drink this down—it's good for what's ailing you."

Curiously and skeptically, Unity picked up the glass. "What's in it," she asked. "Never mind, ma'am," said the Negro woman, positively waving her fingers in the girl's face. "Don't you come in here asking old Queen Elizabeth what is it. You drink it, ma'am." And Unity drank and in nine months was born the first of their children. It was a girl, strong with the deep blue eyes of the long line of the Caldwells.

"What'll we call her?" whispered Unity.

"Do you mind if we call her Caline," said Stephen John, seriously tender, concern showing on his glowing young face.

"I think it's a wonderful name," Unity said. So the baby was named Caline for the mother of Stephen John, whose secret spirit he had watched wither. Many times when his mother did not know that anyone knew she was in her room crying, Stephen John had known. Sometimes he had cried himself—so sorry had he felt for his secretly troubled mother. He had wanted to put his arms about her, tell her he loved her but somehow after he began to grow up there was too much restraint within him. He never told her.

Soon Caline the second of that name was followed by another girl, then another— Frances and Unity who was to become the third. Then one day in June there was great excitement in the mansion house, the bell in the yard soon afterwards was clanged with walloping frenzy—Miss Unity had given birth to a fine son. Once again did Stephen John honor his mother. Lott was his name for the heir. Stephen John wrote the name in the Bible on that same June day, boldly in the biggest letters on the page, "Lott Caldwell."

"Heavenly Father," said Stephen John, "make him everything that my mother wanted me to be."

Five boys followed Lott—Lafayette, Warren, James, Richard, the fourth Silas. And a strange generation this was—a vivid and varied group of lusty individuals, searching in their desperate ways, forever asking themselves the old question—what is the nature of life. All of these boys, except Silas, were to die before they were thirty years old; but the girls were to live to be more than eighty.

Only Caline and Silas were to marry. He did not approve the match which Caline made; and before Silas had taken a wife he was dead. But he would not have approved Silas' match had he been living. He yearned richer unions for both of them than either of them made.

His first blow was Frances. Frances was a peculiar looking genius. She was tall as a poplar, thin as a rail, her beeswax skin was smooth as candle tallow. Not even Stephen John ever said that Frances was gifted with beauty. Yet he insisted she possessed wit and he said wit was to be prized more in a woman than any grace or virtue—it was more rare. His dream for her was to marry well—that was all a father could expect from any daughter. But somehow Frances did not take to the kind of men that Stephen John thought she should, and when her twenty-fifth birthday came around and found Frances still unmarried, Stephen John stopped thinking of Frances' future. His disappointment in Frances was a disappointment but it was not a very deep one—he turned simply to the younger children, began dreaming for Unity and for Lott. Stephen John in a way ignored Frances after that, and Frances detected this change that had come over her father. It made her sensitive. She quit sitting down at mealtime—the first of the eccentricities she gradually developed in her attempt to protect herself, to give herself a shadow of importance. Instead of sitting down, she began to pace the floor, plate in hand—pretending at first that she was too busy to sit down, that she would be needed at any moment in the kitchen. Whenever she wanted a piece of fried chicken, a slice of ham, a hot biscuit, she would pause, stab the food with a fork, continue her walking. Soon this was a habit that had grown upon her. Once when she was twenty-eight, her father in a burst of anger called her an "old maid" to her face and Frances wept. But alone in her room that evening she faced the situation, admitted that she was what she was—a spinster. Also she admitted to herself that she was desolately lonely and in an attempt to keep her mind from this loneliness she began diligently to study French, teaching herself and pronouncing the words as though they were Anglican. When she had acquired a reading knowledge of the French language, she began to study German, then she studied algebra and geometry—all her life she turned to books in an effort to escape from herself, she studied calculus when over seventy. Also in her old age she began to smoke strong, home-cured tobacco in a pipe which she carried in a black satin pouch. To women of extreme religious convictions, she said her smoking was to ease a chronic catarrh, and having said this she would cough, sniffle and reach for the pipe

There were things that Frances knew that Stephen John knew nothing about—he thought when he saw her gazing sadly off toward the ridge of blue mountains that it was disappointment that was troubling her. All his life he thought it was this that was her problem—nothing did he ever know of the inner fury that blazed for many years within the being of this daughter; he never knew of the hesitations and impulses—of the battles she fought, of how she decided finally that will and discipline were the way for her—the only escape.

Stephen John never knew how strange, or perhaps it was how deeply human, this warped daughter was. She rigidly denied herself, disciplined her life, and yet when she was an old woman she passionately regretted the choice. When her niece, a young girl named the fourth Narcissa, came to her hesitantly to ask advice, she gave the child an answer that was completely filled with personal repudiation.

"Aunt Frances," said the girl, "if you wanted to do something you were not sure about—yet at the same time you wanted worse than anything in the world to do it, what would you do?"

Cautiously the old woman stared at the anxious face before her searching its lines "Has it something to do with your virtue," asked she. Blushing, the girl nodded.

"Then do it," Frances said, all but shouting. "Do it—be human and weak where love is concerned-run all the risks, take all the chances; don't let yourself dry up as I have." The look that she gave the girl was anxious and pleading. "Somehow," she said, "discipline isn't the way."

Stephen John gave up hope for Frances but he was longer giving up the ambition he held for Unity. For Unity did have beauty—she had flashing eyes and spirit, manners of distinction. Surely, said Stephen John Unity will find herself a wealthy husband. It always puzzled him that she never did.

Unity never in her life had but one adventure. She allowed the son of a former tenant farmer to call upon her at the great house of the Caldwells. He was a handsome young man, full of gaiety, and Unity drove with him several times about the country, attending all day singings and square dances. One night the boy put his arms around her, told her he loved her. Unity smiled and kissed his smooth face but she did not tell him about what she was thinking—he was too poor for her, his chances of succeeding in life were too small.

Unity like many women was ambitious. The future she dreamed of lay faraway in great cities, and in this picture she moved—one of the great ladies of the world, wife of someone that was rich and famous. So when the boy kissed her, fervently in intense earnestness, she smiled and was silent.

But Unity at the same time was curious and she was daring. She was burning within to know the feeling of being completely loved so she allowed the boy to lead her away in the moonshine, into a clump of alders, and there she learned some of the things she had wanted to know. The tender and gentle boy, more innocent than she, regarded their new relation as holy. Tenderly kissing Unity, he said, We must marry." Unity said he must give her a few weeks to consider. When the time had passed and she felt nothing was happening to her, she told him curtly "no" and in the dark of that night, the boy cried. Then he went away and within three months married another girl. Unity never forgave him; she thought that he should spend the rest of his life alone in passionate despair. The boy married and became father of a family, while Unity, alone at Forest Mansion, waited for her dream man to appear. He never came. Those were the hard days following the war when there were more women than men So before Unity knew what was happening, life had passed her by as it passes many men and women. She had aimed higher for herself than even her father had aimed for her—that was her trouble the target at which she was shooting lay beyond the reach of her spear. On the day of her fortieth birthday, Unity padlocked her bedroom door, afterward carried the key wherever she went. She did nothing special in this secret room, sometimes she prayed, "God give me rest"; she read the Bible in this room, committing to memory the lascivious songs of Solomon, wrote in a diary, lamenting the hard dull days, the desolate procession of her life through a barren, wasted territory. But the locking of this door intensely excited the people of the uplands, it became one of the consuming subjects of conversation—why should Miss Unity let no one into that room, what was she guarding there, what did she do during all those mysterious hours spent in that chamber by herself. They imagined many weird answers.

One day Windy Bill, a grandson of long-dead Queen Elizabeth, asked Unity. "Miss Unity, ma'am," said he, "what is it you does in that padlocked bedroom by yourself." Crisply the Negro was informed, "I dance naked, Bill, before the mirror." Unity laughed, a high excited cackle, and she wondered why in the world she had given him such an answer. Bill went right out and told what she had said, his story creating a tremendous sensation. There were many in the up-country who said without a doubt Unity Caldwell was crazy—but she was not crazy, she was lonely and she wanted somehow to be noticed, she wanted someone to say something about her. In the beginning, it was for love that she yearned, then it was for a cause that she sought—some work in which she could lose herself. After Appomatox she found neither.

So she grew old and knit things and went every evening at sundown to the spring branch, solemnly washing her hands in the cold water; she would pull on a pair of gloves and after that would touch nothing with her bare hands until morning. She grew to be very gaunt, a wrinkled old woman who wore the same sort of flowing black dresses regardless of changing fashion. Once every twenty years, she said, her clothes became very stylish. Unity tended the hives of yellow Italian bees in the bee garden, grew rows and rows of the old time red roses called the Star of France, also she liked wild tiger lilies. And she waited forty years for death.

Stephen John's ambitions burned with a bright flame for his sons' success. Determined that they should place the Caldwells high in the world—in literature, in the sciences, in anything so long as they rose on a pedestal, set the name Caldwell glowing with a fadeless light. He sent all of these boys to study at Carolina, but to none of them did he ever send enough money to live on. It was one of the father's curious traits—he who poured hundreds and thousands of dollars into the hands of western relations and western friends, was always stingy in his dealings with his own sons. He sent them next to nothing and sent that only after their letters had become more and more urgent. So, one by one, the boys, tired of trying to make ends meet on so little, quit the college, and Stephen John could never understand why lack of funds should be the excuse they gave him for quitting. Excuse was the word he used. Finally only Warren remained. A burning inner fire strengthened Warren. Even in a cold room, he still held to his ideal—he was determined to secure an education, determined to become a great physician, one of the great men of his time—nothing should stand in his way nor stop him. He made a plan for his life, set out to live the plan. Once to his father, with determination in his eyes, Warren said, "I'm going to amount to something—I'm going to be somebody in this world." And so delighted was Stephen John with this statement that when Warren had received his degree at Carolina, he sent him on to New York to continue his medical studies. Warren nearly starved in New York—literally, he nearly starved but he worked hard, the record he left there was brilliant. Warren was considerate and good—going on Sundays to church to please his mother, writing his mother every Sunday evening, telling her what the preachers had said.

One day one of his professors, a grave man with a heavy red beard, told Warren and his classmates a great epidemic of yellow fever had broken out suddenly in a crowded slum district of the city. "Medical volunteers," he said, "are needed." Warren was among those offering himself for this duty. "I must tell you, young men," said the professor, "you know it is a dangerous undertaking—I warn you, some of you won't come back."

Warren was not afraid. He felt the great destinies had sent him into the world for a purpose, to accomplish great things. He trusted in his star. He believed in his earthly role even after falling ill himself—death was almost upon Warren before he doubted. In a clear lucid moment in the depths of a night, with the dead and the dying all about him, the boy suddenly realized there was no hope. Suddenly and swiftly, the conviction came over him, and burning with a passionate desire to live, he clenched his hands. "I can't die," he cried, putting the whole strength of his soul into the protest. "I can't." He fell soon afterward into a coma.

Warren was buried under the snow in Brooklyn, on the cold slope of Greenwood Cemetery—dead among the Yankees and during the bitter years of the war, nothing grieved Stephen John more than that his son should lie so far away—far away in the North, covered by cold Long Island earth.

After Warren's death, none of the Caldwells visited New York for sixty-two years, then a number of them, tall and lanky, appeared there together—come to attend the unveiling at the Hall of Fame of a bronze statue to the original Carter. And from those ceremonies, held on a high hill in the Bronx, these southerners started immediately towards Brooklyn with flowers for the tomb of Warren. They did not forget.

After Warren died, Stephen John turned to Lafayette. Lafayette's gifts were a fine willing mind, a fine body and all the warming ways of charm. People were attracted to

Lafayette and noticing this, Stephen John said to himself that Lafayette would succeed. This son, thought he, was strong; he never suspected that in Lafayette, fiercely bound, were all the dissatisfied passions of the Caldwells for travel and adventure—he thought Lafayette wanted to go west to make a name for himself in business. This was what Lafayette had told him. "There's opportunities in the West," said Lafayette. What Stephen John did not know was that his son was going because he wanted to be going, that he wanted to know and see things, to experience the varieties of life, that more than anything he feared being overtaken by life in some backwater; he hated the trivial.

"He'll succeed," said Stephen John on the day that Lafayette left Forest Mansion. He beamed and waved a handkerchief and from the foot of the hill Lafayette also waved. Lafayette visited among the relatives in Georgia and Alabama and Mississippi, finally he came to the city of Vicksburg, and there for the first time he saw one moonlit night the great river—flowing forever, endlessly moving, strong like the country it drained and flooded. Through half a night, he watched the Mississippi and thought, watched the steady surge, listened to the almost silent sounds of one of the greatest forces in the world. He listened and he looked and within him spoke the voice of rapture, saying "O this river, this great river—free, living as I would live." It moved him as nothing had before.

The Mississippi became his wandering home. For drifting into New Orleans, he learned to gamble; caught on so quickly and so well that he was taken in by the restless band who lived on the river boats by their wits. He was taken in by the crowd working the flotilla. He drank hard, played hard, dared, took risks, acquired skill even at cheating. Always he was a traveler after that—Vicksburg, Memphis on its hill, St. Louis became familiar places, even Little Rock and Cincinnati. These were fine places and he liked them all but it was the river life that he loved—the great restless, eternally moving Mississippi. He watched it, listened to it; sometimes he wrote ecstatic impressions of the Father of Waters, the Old Muddy, he copied these down as they came into mind, sent them to his father. These fragments arriving at Forest Mansion from far places puzzled Stephen John. He did not know what his son was doing and had difficulty following his movements. For in all his letters, Lafayette was very vague. Once from Cincinnati, he wrote that a fever had brought him north from New Orleans, a few weeks later it was a real estate proposition that had taken him clear to Independence, Kansas. Stephen John began to suspect what he would not admit. Chance had become Lafayette's fortune.

Sometimes Lafayette had thousands of dollars in his pockets and there were times when he had nothing. So more and more, he came to live for the moment only, to enjoy to the full the present—the food and good drink that were before him, the scenery and the people about him, a song, a conversation. Casual as a cloud, he went on—becoming almost the only Caldwell ever acquiring patience. Lafayette learned even to be ill, to spend days amusing himself with trifles, watching flies, sun shadows. Hiding out, he never tired of studying the ever-changing flow of light on the muddy water. It had become the love of his life—the Mississippi.

Children liked Lafayette; he listened to them with attention, told them wild stories of his great-great-great-grandmother who had the frail name of Narcissa and who was scalped by the Indians, of his great-granduncle who disappeared without a trace. Many times in winter he whispered to the children, traveling on the boats, that if they looked into the fire in the stove hard enough and had faith they would see little dwarves. Always the children would look and they believed, they would stare and stare but they could not see. "Then you do not believe hard enough," Lafayette would reply, saying, "Look again." Once a solemn little boy searching the flames suddenly shouted, "I see them." Pointing into the red coals, he cried, "I see a whole army of them riding blue horses and at the head of the army is a green dragon with fire in his mouth." Handing the boy a quarter, Lafayette said, "Jimmy, someday you'll be President of the United States."

For several years, Lafayette lived exactly as he had dreamed as a boy of living—furiously, relentlessly, without any restraint. He gambled and drank and traveled; also he had his way with women. Like Carter his grandfather, Lafayette tried to regard the lust act as only a natural force, a vapor collecting, spirit demanding release, a physical situation, an exercise; and as sunny days and storms vanish from the memory so did many of the companions of his bed disappear from his memory—of some only faces, only hands were remembered, some were recalled only as parts of bodies, a circumstance, a position, a perfume, only that and nothing more; some of the sweetest remained in memory as the vilest, some of the streetwalkers as the most modest. Soon Lafayette lost the exalted meaning of love, that ethereal value which another's arms can give, that satisfaction. Women became only a womb; he wanted change only, new wombs.

So did Lafayette wander, deeper and more dark, venturing into the depths of the rejected. Periodically, he was overcome by remorse. That other force which drove into the consciousness of the Caldwells—that longing to fall at the feet of God, to renounce the world, to quit wickedness. Lafayette would drop on his knees, try with all his will to do better. He would reproach himself for the selfishness of his life, crying in lonely anguish, "O God, what do I mean to anybody, whom have I ever loved, what human being has ever received any help from me?" Lafayette would determine to do good, he would rush into the churches, bow down in prayer, raise his once clear tenor voice, singing the beating rhythmic hymns, "Glory to His name," "Jesus is tenderly calling me home." One time tears rose in his eyes when from a thin, beaten looking little man with a radiant face, he heard the triumphant words from St. John: "He that cometh to Me shall never hunger; and he that believeth on Me shall never thirst."

"Heavenly Father," he prayed, "have mercy." He longed for that inner life, that ecstasy that sustains the human soul against all the troubles of the world.

But that very evening he was about his old haunted way. There was no turning back now for Lafayette, for he had gone too far; too many accounts awaited their payment and there was more than anguish to be dealt with, more than remorse and regret. For one thing, he had been scourged by Venus. Prowling one night in the dark, Lafayette followed a woman whose face he could scarcely see. He went with her into a shack in one of the alleyways of New Orleans. This woman was almost toothless, there were hairs upon her breasts. After a time the voice from this vile body spoke, "Well," it said, "how do you feel now." "I feel better," said Lafayette.

"You'll sleep tonight," she said, turning him into the street. And he did sleep, like one heavily drugged. Hours later on waking in his room, he remembered her parting words and they alarmed him. Instantly, he sensed in them a sinister warning and it was a warning all right. Lafayette in a few days more said if ever he met that woman again he would kill her. He was that angry. But he did meet her and he did not kill her. When he saw the form, cold under an arch—coughing, he turned into another street and ran. He blamed only himself—"when one lies down with dogs, one must expect to get up with fleas."

Near the end, he wrote to Warren, whom he loved more than his other brothers, "All of us must choose, brother, between passion and self-denial; I have chosen and I have seen the sights, I know the answers—but there is nothing left now for me to stand on, the sand is quick…for God's sake, brother Warren, profit by my failure and lead the plodding life… Routine is the thing, restraint and discipline."

In the end, Lafayette was deserted even by the gamblers. One day in Canal Street, ill and almost penniless, Lafayette met the closest of his friends from the flotilla. "Hello, Curly," said Lafayette, smiling. "Hello," said this friend, stopping and very formally bowing. Then quietly he said, "I'm glad to see you, Lafayette, but I'll have to ask you after this not to speak to me in public."

So it had come to this—for a Caldwell of Forest Mansion! Lafayette turned, stunned, into St. Louis' Cathedral; sitting there through an afternoon, seeking, searching in the gloom; he looked down the narrow aisles into the choir where the white pure lilies stood on the altar among gold and red velvet and from out of the darkness the music poured into his ears, like wind moving through the sky. "Behold your God, behold the glory of the Lord is risen upon thee." And there came to him the voice of a priest, saying slowly, "We are pilgrims, my friends…pilgrims on our way through the valley, on our way unto the Kingdom of God…this hard life, this trouble, it shall soon pass…so labor and live nobly, stand up against the trial, face the test…do something with life, and if we die, we shall have earned our death, our reward shall be in heaven…"

"Oh," said Lafayette, "I am lost. I live in night, in the ghastly light of the moon."

He wandered into the darkness, stood for a time brooding over the river; then he made his way into a criminals' meeting place and there in a gambling game he deliberately cheated. He was detected, and there was a quarrel and a man shot at him. Lafayette was wounded mortally. And at Keowee, Stephen John in his pride and grief covered the circumstances of his son's dying. He said Lafayette had been taken by the galloping consumption. He raised a marble stone to the memory of this son. For Stephen John was a Caldwell and the Caldwells forgave the Caldwells in death, granted to them all a claim to their graveyard, the good and righteous, the wicked, and nothing but good was written on the stones.

Stephen John was silent about Lafayette's failure to find the way. "He's gone."

James, Stephen John said, was taken by pneumonia. James had always wanted to write, and when he became a journalist he became at the same time the secret hope of his father. This assured Stephen John that James would be the one who was to become the great Caldwell—a great writer. James borrowed a little money from his father at ten per cent interest and with this fund started a newspaper, a four-page journal that violently supported Bell and Everett for President and Vice-President of the United States, favored the prohibition in America of the sale of whiskey. James himself drank heavily but being unable to overcome this passion, he longed with fervor for the day when no person anywhere would be able to buy a drop of whiskey. He spent hours dreaming and drinking. Between these times he wrote all the copy for the columns of his paper—bitter political editorials, long denunciations of the evil of drink, various other items. The remaining space he crammed with dozens of little essays about the hottest fires he ever sat by, the coldest beds he ever slept in, pieces about mad dogs, runaway horses, Carolina sunsets, signs and dreams and premonitions—many things. He reprinted old Narcissa's herb formulas for making dyes, also he wrote and printed a poem—a verse about the song of the woodthrush whose lyric seemed to inspire so many of the Caldwells. He called his poem "a hymn for the angels" and it delighted his father. James possessed a quality of unprediction, Stephen John said, that delighted his subscribers; they never knew what to expect next. One week, instead of the usual article denouncing alcohol, there was a gargantuan recipe for making wine. Many in the mountains were accustomed to doing a little brewing, to making wine in medium quantities—a gallon of blackberry wine, a gallon of pale scuppernong, perhaps a quart or so of muscadine, a heavy sweet wine barrel of good new cider and five gallons of prime peach or apple brandy add a bushel of sweet grapes. Let them stand together until they work or clarify—then rack off into clean jugs and try to let it stand—the longer the better." The readers of "The Presage," including Stephen John, laughed and wondered; they never knew what despair had caused this tormented young man to print this recipe. In a desperate attempt to gain control of himself, James decided one day to go for twelve hours—for just twelve hours—without drinking; he determined with all his spiritual power to carry out this purpose. And he failed. In desperation, he tore into bits an article he had prepared for that edition—an account of the way drink ruined character. To take its place he flung the recipe at the printer. It was symbolical for James, it represented final defeat. Never again after that did "The Presage" refer in any way to liquor as a problem.

"The Presage" was well received but it did not live long; James had no talent for making collections; when he could run the paper no longer, he moved on into the heart of the Blue Ridge Mountains into North Carolina and there with a little more money, borrowed at twenty per cent from his father, he started "The Opland Courier," which also favored the nominations of Bell and Everett.

Sometimes James worked very hard on his editorials and essays but often for days at a time he would forget them entirely—he would ride off into the mountains or drink himself into unconsciousness at the hotel where he boarded; then his printer, protecting him, would fill the columns with anything he could find and under the masthead, the proud peacock emblem of the Caldwells, would insert:

"Indisposition of the Editor:

"The editor has been very unwell with the Bloody Flux, for the last 10 or 12 days, so much so that He has been unable to prepare any editorial at all. We hope that He will be well enough to get the next issue out, when He will have many things to attend to."

Seized by unrest, James would ride through the deep valleys, climb the granite peaks; he would scribble fragments of thoughts, words, disconnected phrases that appealed to him, packing his pockets with these odd inscribed pieces of paper…"The still pools…the frogs crying, the brooding winter woods, soaked by the long rains…still and sad and quiet, resting…O to feel the sun shining, to know the joy of the vast quiet and the dark shadow." And sometimes he would cry out, filled with anguish and longing. "The restlessness and the road on which there is not turning…the whirlwind and the ragged cloud and the poisoned flower…is there no response in the world, no place to rest…"

James kept these bits of paper on which he had written. Some day he would sit down, pour out his inner soul, weave together all these things and many other things, compose a picture of these wild and lonely mountains and the high western wind and the solitude and silence and his own wandering in his own country, searching for a way…more than anything in the world, this was what he wanted to do but he would never get it done and one night he admitted to himself that he never would, he lacked the stern discipline and the will and perhaps he lacked the power…it was a bitter hour in his bitter life.

Shortly after this, a friend of James' named C. W. Gillespie, a lawyer, wrote two letters to Stephen John at Forest Mansion. In the first,'he said: "I saw James this morning and I am happy to report he was looking sober as a judge and has promised to stay sober from this time forth. He thought he would stay sober sure this time for he had been at the point of death when we sent him off that last time. I do believe if we hadn't sent him off he would have killed himself. But at the present his prospects are better than any time in my recollection. There is no paper in the county now but 'The Upland Courier' and but one other in western North Carolina, the 'Baptist Telescope' having died out."

In the second letter, following the first by a few weeks, Gillespie wrote: "I feel quite sure James will hardly ever drink any more. He says he will not and he has been put to the test once or twice since he got sober but he has resisted with complete success. I know that he won't drink while he is within reach of me but I fear if he was 40 or 50 miles off and with a regular drinking crowd the temptation would be stronger. But I hope he will be able to resist even that before a great while. He seems to be firmly set against the evil."

James' next bout of drinking was his last. And Stephen John at Forest Mansion grieved more for James than for any of his sons except Lott.

Lott was a young man with a powerful body and a depth of perception and feeling about which few knew. For Lott concealed his inner thoughts—only his closest companions in the Confederate Army understood him, certainly Stephen John never did. Lott never wrote his father about those things he felt or thought, he filled his letters home with description of things, with action. "About the 15th of July we were ordered 10 miles down the river and on Saturday the 20th we were informed that General Scott had left Washington with his well-equipped army of many thousands. General Evans, commanding, thought best for us to fall back to Bulls Run, a distance of about 10 miles, giving other Confederate forces time to join us for the fight pending. We crossed Bulls Run just before sundown at the stone bridge, forming a line of battle on the south side of that stream—it is a muddy slow moving stream. After holding ourselves in readiness for battle through the night, on Sunday a.m., just at sunrise, General Scott opened fire on us from the opposite side of the stream with his artillery from an elevated position at a distance of 1 mile, his purpose being to attract our attention while his army was crossing the stream one mile above us. By 8 o'clock we discovered that his army had crossed the stream—the war had started. Two companies were left to guard the bridge and the rest of us had no more sense than to go for them at a double quick pace—we soon found ourselves forcing the enemy in an open field where the battle was on in earnest. Cousin Taylor Caldwell was killed in the very first volley. Elisha Ferguson fell mortally wounded. It was soon discovered that the enemy was endeavoring to surround us. At this juncture, General Bee made along our lines as apparently cool as if nothing serious was on hand, giving orders to fall back to the Henry House, a distance of 800 yards where we could continue the fight. General Bee was killed before we reached the Henry House. By two o'clock in the afternoon if we had known anything about war, we might readily have concluded we were in on the eve of a massacre—but we didn't know. We don't know much yet and still we do know a great deal—a man learns a lot about war in a single day…"

"Fredericksburg…We were exposed to fire today but not engaged, we held a position that was not attacked by the enemy, exposed to cannonading only. We were in plain view of the fight between the enemy and our forces…our troops were lined up against the bluff of the bottom land that was near a mile wide from the river. We could see the enemy as they formed their lines along the river, watching them as they moved on our troops. Our men held their fire until the Yankees were almost on them when they opened fire on them…the slaughter was desperate. I passed over the field of battle a few hours later and the dead were so numerous that many were being placed in the same grave…so much for today…"

And so much for many things. Only the soldiers knew of those deep feelings and longings, the hope and courage that were the real and secret Lott. Only they heard.him say he considered Taylor Caldwell a lucky man—to be killed in the first volley of a war, heard him express the fear that when his own time came he would not be killed but would be left mangled and alive. Only a few men of the Seventh South Carolina Rifles ever heard those things that a man tells when the end of a day has come and he lies down in a quiet place to rest, quietly to talk, to speak of experimenting with living, of trying to find one's way. They knew Lott. Knew that he had tried license as had his brother Lafayette and extreme discipline as had Frances, his sister, and gradually through trial and error had rejected them both. Some of them were with him the day when he found quite by accident in the great Book of Ecclesiastes the verse that was to shape his road…"To everything there is a season, and a time to every purpose under the heaven. A time to be born and a time to die; a time to plant and a time to pluck that which is planted; a time to kill and a time to heal, a time to break down and a time to build up; a time to cast away stones and a time to gather stones together; a time to embrace and a time to refrain from embracing, a time to love…"

"That makes sense," the soldiers heard Lott say. And afterward they said to one another that had he lived he would have been a happy man, for there was in him an emotional balance that sinned and repented and that refrained from sinning and then did not refrain. But Lott did not live. In Pennsylvania, marching north toward Gettysburg there came for him a premonition, and he wrote his last letters and prepared and on the long ridge behind the peach orchard on the third day, the Yankees killed him. He was a part of the guard that was to cover the Confederate retreat, and it was during a lull that a stray bullet hit him—he was thinking of home, the swift river and the blue mountains where the mulberries grew, the whip-poor-will, the red glare of columbine, the old December earth, holly and chinquapins and cedars—"never cut a cedar, save a cedar"…and there was a red bird singing. He was thinking of the song of the red bird, its note…

The word traveled south and in South Carolina, all the Caldwells traveled to Keowee for the memorial service that was held in the section of the burying ground in which the Caldwells had begun to bury dead soldiers—Stephen John raised a slab to Lott between the slabs to Silas the second who died among the patches of goldenrod at the battle of Kings Mountain and John Caldwell the nephew who, wounded, died of thirst, a corpse under the beautiful clouds of Mexico at El Molino del Rey.

The hard battles were fought around Chattanooga and among the granite boulders on the north slope of Lookout Mountain, high above the bend in the Tennessee, the

Yankees killed Richard—the last but one of the sons. This was more than Stephen John could bear. With all the old men about him dying and all the young men dying, with the causes for which he had stood already defeated, Stephen John began now to pray for the only victory—for final and merciful and blessed death. He pleaded with God, beseeching Him, "do take me." Passionately, he wanted to go on, to escape, he could not bear to be still among the living when that inevitable day should arrive, when word would come that Silas too was dead. Silas the fourth, now his only son—"O have mercy, God save Silas." Old Stephen John would wake at night, crying out from dreams in which cannon roared and fire and shell poured about Silas. One day Windy Bill came in to wind the old Connecticut clock with the twisted pilasters and the engraved face. It had stopped running. "It's tired," said Stephen John, "Let it rest."

Worried, discouraged, filled with grief and ill, Stephen John walked that afternoon into a sleet storm—down into the holly ravine and along the banks of the dark freezing river and into the woods, forests of glass in which dead leaves hung from the trees like fine pieces of porcelain, glazed with ice. Returning to Forest Mansion from this long walk, he went to bed and when pneumonia came upon him, he died.

CHAPTER TEN

For nearly two years after Stephen John's death there was no white man at Forest Mansion—only the Negroes and the white women, the two Unitys, the first and third, and Frances. All of them thought Silas the fourth must be dead. It had been so long since any word had come from him. They knew he had been in the Shenandoah Valley with the Army of Virginia, knew he had been listed as missing. But as months merged into a year, then two years, they gave up hope. Silas too was dead.

But Silas was not dead and one day a long time after the surrender at Appomatox he returned home. It was late of an afternoon in the autumn. Tired, worn by hard travel, ragged, he stepped into the yard. Immediately there was a great commotion. The dogs began to bark and Windy Bill, the grandson of Queen Elizabeth, began shouting at the top of his voice, "Gracious God," he yelled, "If here ain't come home the Captain." Bill dashed across the yard to the great bell. Soon the whole countryside was filled with the sound of curious clanking. Within a few minutes everyone on the place had gathered.

They could hardly believe their eyes.

Silas grinned in a hard, sad way. Soon he was explaining what had happened to him. Shot in the chest during the battle on the bank of the Chickahominy, he had been pitched by some Yankee soldiers into a tent among a pile of soldiers who were so desperately wounded that they did not think there was a chance for any of them. He had been left to die and would have died, but some nuns came and cared for him. One of them had dipped a swab into a bucket of iodine, and thrust this into the gash in his breast. Seeing that he still lived, these nuns took him on a stretcher to a field hospital and later the Yankees had removed him from there to Philadelphia, where after a long time he had recovered. Then he was sent on to a prison camp on the far northern waters of the Hudson River. Six months after the surrender he had been released. With nothing he had started south, walking down the face of the continent he had come—from New York to Carolina.

So Silas was again home. And he and Windy Bill the very next morning began planting some winter wheat. They hitched an ox to a plow.

Thus did a new era begin for the Caldwells at Forest Mansion. One civilization had collapsed about them, another had to rise, so they started. They began with the only things they had left—a scythe and a sickle and a plow and a pair of oxen and their hands and their strong backs and their old will to live. Also there was the land and the mansion. So they turned to the wheatfields and to the cotton lands, but they were not in their hearts as they once were. After that they could never understand what Northerners and Westerners were talking about when they spoke of America as young. For over them had come the tired feeling of age, it had settled also over their great south country—the south was old and they were old, they felt they had lived within the shadow of the Blue Ridge as long as the west wind, they felt as worn as the granite mountains. Time was long for them, flowing in both directions, and in this stream they formed only a link. They were merely the present.

They thoroughly understood their position—they had but barely escaped annihilation, only a remnant of the family still remained. A full century would have to elapse before they could hope to recover their old strength. And it would be a century, they knew, in which it would take all their energy just to keep themselves alive, to keep ahead of starvation. They need plan nothing else for their lives—plowing cotton, digging potatoes would keep them busy. Times would be hard and they would have to do without. For no matter what happened, they were determined to keep their hold on their land—they would not sell an acre, they would not mortgage a foot of their property.

There would be no more western migrations from Forest Mansion for there was no one to migrate. Those who would have been the migrants already were buried, many of them in one grave, on the battlefields. And as for the ones who had taken up lands in Texas, the Oregon country and California—they would have to take care of themselves. Forest Mansion could no longer lend them a helping hand. For Forest Mansion's influence was gone. Its dream of the west had vanished.

The Caldwells were soon an embittered, long-remembering, provincial family. They looked backward, grieved over the lost past. They turned within themselves. At the family reunions on the second Tuesday in each August, they recited the family tree from the time the first Caldwell landed in Pennsylvania; they were told what Senator Carter Caldwell had said the time he took the stump in the square at Pendleton; they heard again and again why the first Silas feared the adoption of the federal constitution; Frances always repeated the tale told by the first Carter about the star that appeared in the west when Narcissa was scalped.

They were THE Caldwells and they thought constantly about it. It was a beginning, an end for them, a full wheel, a cycle. The Caldwells were the Caldwells, prouder and still more proud. Still they were restless. The blazing sunsets beyond the mountain rim, the bending out of sight of the swift river, a curving road, an unclimbed peak still stirred them—they remained travelers at heart. Still they were searching, seeking.

Many times, particularly during the last of the winter months, the sound of wind rounding a corner stirred the old trouble, they got to wondering how things were getting along in other places. Then the old fever would tug worst—they would get the going blues. But now instead of riding away to Tennessee or Texas, they traveled around Keowee Valley—they became great travelers within the bounds of a single county. It was "going" that had always interested them, not so much where they were "going." They kept constantly moving during this period in a forty mile circuit—visiting the kin folks. They had to work so hard during the spring and summer that they kept their rudeness and their vigor.

Silas rose before daybreak, he was a hard worker. With Windy Bill, he split rails and patched the fences, pitched rocks into the deepening red gullies; the two sowed sorghum, cowpeas, wheat and oats, sawed wood, re-covered the barns with hand-hewn shingles, they even painted Forest Mansion with some Charleston paint found in a corn crib—left over from the days before the war. And during the third winter, Silas remodeled the front of the mansion, he tore away the two low rooms and the small piazza, built a great southern colonial porch with tall pillars. This enraged the entire Caldwell connection but there was nothing they could do about it.

To all their protests, Silas replied, "I always said if I ever had a house of my own I'd have columns if all I had was columns and a kitchen." Now the house was his and here stood the columns. And that was that. One day Frances, in a fury, said to him, "It's a damn cheap Charleston way to buy magnificence." Frances despised Silas and did not pretend that she did not. Once on one of her tours of the valley, she announced to a family gathering, "It's my settled conclusion that the survival of Silas Caldwell through the Civil War is the very finest proof that a war cuts down the noblest youth of a nation and somehow spares a lot of scalawags and rascals to inherit the earth."

Silas was shorter than most Caldwells but he had the blue eyes and the high cheek bones, the thin hair. He smoked twists of home grown tobacco, very strong; chewed pressed tobacco plug, drank peach brandy by the quart, and hating free niggers, treated them as though they were cows or pigs. He wheedled, cheated, and soon ran off the place every poor white tenant he ever had except one—old man Tob Nally who was as mean as he was. Silas showed no mercy for his family, begrudged them every penny they spent. In time Silas added a new kind of pride to the varieties of pride that the members of his family all possessed—he began bragging about his crops. Nobody grew crops as he grew, nobody raised so much corn, had better stands of cotton. Soon it was discovered that he was pouring fertilizers onto fields that bordered the roads—his tallest and thickest crops grew where people could see them.

"Cheap, cheap," roared Frances, who at the time was at Hopewell Landing, visiting. "Yes," added she, gulping down a glassful of blackberry wine and shuddering momentarily from satisfaction, "Yes, if times had stayed normal—why, we'd have been rid of dear Silas; we'd have sent him packing off to take up new lands for himself in Texas—then Texas would have had to put up with Silas and things would have gone another way at Forest Mansion."

Frances sighed. For times had not remained normal and there was Silas, fourth heir at Keowee. "Eating," she said, "liked a starved pig, stuffing handsful of food and spitting bones and tough pieces of un-chewed meat into his plate. Belching is a habit." Frances raised her angry voice. "He's a human volcano," she said. "Soon he'll have to sit with his legs far apart to make room for his belly."

Silas married Patience Noble, his second and fourth cousin through Stephen John's side of the house, his fourth and fifth cousin through Unity the first. Patience Noble as a young girl was known for the flair of her stylish clothes. Often she sat up half of a night weaving yards of extra cloth for trains for her dresses. Once she made herself a corset from canes cut in the Keowee bottoms. Up the aisle of the stone meeting house she walked, so proud and full of spirit, and then something happened, the canes slipped and she could not sit down. She was obliged after her marriage to give up her fine clothes notions, and sometimes for ten years had to appear at the church in the same black dress, the same bonnet. Silas always told her he had no money to throw away on women's silks and laces.

Because Silas constantly nagged her about being wasteful and extravagant, Patience Noble became very niggardly, miserly in frantic attempts to save. It was whispered fifteen ounces made a pound in Patience Noble's butter mould, rumored she put water in the sweet milk that she sold. She played the organ at the meeting house in her later years, sang hymns in a thin soprano voice, holding the high notes, quavering, and once or twice a year moved by a sermon she would jump up from the stool and in a desperate way shout "save me."

During the first six years after her marriage to Silas, she became the mother of four children—the second Lott, States Rights who died in infancy. Sunshine who also died while quite small, and the fourth Narcissa. Patience Noble's yellow hair turned gray soon after the death of States Rights.

Often Silas spoke sharply. He was hard to deal with—Silas spoke insolently to many people, yelling at Negroes and sometimes flailing them when very angry, and he was forever involved in some sort of dispute—often he appealed to the technicalities of law, suing neighbors over a foot of land, disputing with everyone on principle. He entered suit in Texas against the Texas Caldwells over some of the property claimed for his father, but he lost. For the Texans appeared in person at the courthouse to defend themselves while Silas was a thousand miles away, and besides the judge was married to a Texas Caldwell. After the lawsuit the Caldwells of South Carolina and the Caldwells of Texas refused to have anything to do with each other for more than fifty years.

Silas sued the Baptist Church over a stand of timber, sued the state, the county; for twenty years he wrangled with a faction that opposed him in Pea Ridge School District. But his longest and bitterest feud was carried on with his daughter Narcissa. This lasted a lifetime. It had its beginning so:

On a dull Saturday, sulking and impatient, in one of his worst moods, Silas drove alone to the crossroads store to swap some hard butter cakes and guinea eggs for a bucket of lard, some rice and ten pounds of Louisiana sugar. Reaching the store, he saw a Negro suddenly dart from among the crowd of laughing black men. It was only a glimpse that Silas had but it was enough.

"Stop there, nigger," he yelled, furious and reining in the mules. The Negro stopped, yanking from his head a worn hat. It was Windy Bill. "God damn you," shouted Silas, his sullen face puffed with passion. "What the hell you doing here?"

Apologetic and humble, Windy Bill said he was doing nothing.

"Why aren't you at home chopping cotton," roaded Silas.

"Captain Silas, this here is Saturday afternoon."

"What's Saturday afternoon," demanded Silas, "Saturday afternoon's the same as Monday afternoon and Wednesday afternoon. The Book says six days shalt thou labor. It doesn't say anything about Saturday afternoon." Silas raised his fat legs over the side of the wagon, lowered them to the ground. "You get home and you grab a hoe," he said to Windy Bill.

"Yes, sir," said the Negro.

In the crowded store, Silas pushed his way forward, scowling, and turning about to leave after finishing his trading, he came face to face with Mary Belle McCord. He hated Miss Mary Belle, she hated him. She had hated Silas since the Sunday of her fainting spell years before at the stone meeting house. Her glistening jet wig had fallen from her head and Silas from his seat in the next pew had reached into the aisle, picked up the wig and placed it on her bald head, back side before. Always Miss Mary Belle believed this had been deliberate; she retaliated by saying often and loud that Silas treated Patience Noble like a dog.

"Well, howdy," said Miss Mary Belle. Silas only stared. It was a way with Silas—he spoke to persons if he felt like speaking, if not he glowered. "It looks like rain," said Miss Mary Belle. Still Silas said nothing. Then Miss Mary Belle said she had seen young Narcissa at the all-day singing the Sunday before on Glassy Mountain. "Sure looked fine, Captain Silas—mighty fine and in a fine singing voice, I tell you—fine voice." Narcissa had gone to that singing with young Miles Crossing as escort—Miles whose mother Sue Crossing was the widow of a great nephew of Sally Crossing the conjure woman of Queen Elizabeth's day. Miss Mary Belle did not believe Silas Caldwell knew that his daughter was appearing in public places with a Crossing; so to annoy him, she told him. "Made a fine looking pair, I tell you—Miss Narcissa and that boy."

Silas' face turned red; breathing heavily and angrily, he kicked open the door, hurrying out. Miss Mary Belle gave a gay whirl to her parasol.

Unmarried, over forty, Miss Mary Belle led a dull life—it was dry routine, without much reason. At six o'clock every morning she rose from her feather bed, rose from the side towards the window, always she slipped on her left stocking before the right, she kept soap at the left of the bowl on the washstand, folded the towel so the ends were exactly even; at seven she always ate breakfast, at twelve she ate dinner, she ate supper at six o'clock. Between times she visited, read papers, worked for the church. Like a mouse she seemed always to be looking for something, she tipped along when she walked, timidly. She jumped at unexpected sounds, was afraid of the dark and spiders and snakes and dogs and thunderstorms. At night she went about her house locking windows and doors, then trying the locks to make certain they were holding. Her little pleasures were few.

That evening at Forest Mansion a bowl of steaming water-ground grits was set before Silas at the head of the Caldwell table, also a yellow bowl of gravy with fried fatback, a plate of hot biscuits and peach preserves. At Silas' left sat young Lott the second, tired from plowing all day in the field; in the dim glimmering lamplight at the foot of the table was Unity the third; Frances walked the floor, a gaunt lonely figure, spiritually starving; in the kitchen were Patience Noble and Narcissa who never ate until Silas had eaten—Silas said it was their duty to wait. The heavy voice of Silas echoed through the two rooms, reading before the evening meal from the twenty-ninth chapter of Ezekiel, "In the tenth year, in the tenth month and in the twelfth day of the month, the word of the Lord came unto me saying, Son of Man, set thy face against Pharaoh King of Egypt and prophesy against him and all Egypt..." This reading from the Bible meant nothing to any of them. It was an old custom they had inherited, one that having lost its original spirit, had become mere rote. Then came the mechanical blessing, mumbled quickly, "Lord make us thankful..." The rest was too low to be heard. A wooden spoon lurched into the grits. There was no conversation, there often was none when the Caldwells ate alone. Five minutes later, Silas wiped his wide loose lips, belched. Suddenly he shouted, "Narcissa."

In the kitchen, filling a pitcher with warm night's cow milk, Narcissa answered; soon she appeared in the doorway, standing lightly, wiping her long Caldwell hands with a dish cloth.

"I hear," said her father, staring angrily, "that you've been to Glassy Mountain with old Sue Crossing's boy." Narcissa said nothing. Scratching the beard under his chin, again belching, Silas added, "I don't ever want to hear anything like that again—hear. That's the last of that." There was a tone of finality in his voice.

Narcissa whispered, "I hear."

"That boy is a lazy, shiftless nobody," said Silas, raising his voice, his face flushing. "He's poor buckrah, white trash and his folks ain't nobody but tenant farmers, always drinking, cutting one another up, getting into trouble. I tell you right now there's not one of them fit to be seen out with a Caldwell and you know it—or if you don't you ought to. I won't have a daughter of mine running around with a common plow hand, a cotton chopper." Growing more intense, Silas shook his fat hand at the girl. "And while I'm on the subject—I don't want to hear of you running around with anybody else—not for a long time yet. We need you around here awhile, we need you to help."

Silas got up; there was the sound of his heavy shoes, squeaking through the rooms; soon the squeaking of Lott's shoes followed; slowly Unity sipped cold coffee from a saucer, her hands gloved; Frances walked the floor. In the kitchen Patience Noble said, "Well, Narcissa, I reckon we better get on with the dishes." Her quiet voice sounded tired. Narcissa rinsed drinking glasses in soft soapy water. "Ma," she said, despairing, "I don't see anything wrong going out with Miles—this is a free country and I like him." Patience Noble dried a glass, a blue one. "You heard what your father said, he thinks the Crossings are nobody—they're all run down."

"And what are we," asked Narcissa, turning bitterly upon her mother.

"We," said Patience Noble, drying another glass, "we are the Caldwells."

That night Narcissa was a long time washing her feet in the tub at the well; for a long time she sat there, her head resting against a cedar post, looking into the brooding southern night. It was one of those August darknesses, streaked now and then with the glimmering heat lightning, with the heavy air hanging hot over the hills, a fine night for the cotton crop. Katydids chirped in the sycamores and postoaks, and from the tall grasses, the wild rose bushes in the pasture, came the lonely cricket chorus.

On the wide piazza, beneath the white columns, sat Unity, Frances, and Patience Noble, also hearing the lonely country sounds—listening to the disturbing and far off rumbling of a train, a somber echo rolling through the restless hills; they stared into the dark. Somewhere in a distant valley, someone blew on a hunting horn, a low vibrant note that for some reason caused the chickens to stir uneasily on the roost, the Nally's dog to bark. O the loneliness of the night, the women were thinking, O the disquiet and the foreboding—the unrest!

Narcissa slipped off her thin dress without lighting a lamp and in the darkness in the next room Frances listened to the child, still so young and already crying. Once she thought of trying to offer comfort but she changed her mind. "There are times," she said to herself, "when there is no comfort—we had better learn to face those times by ourselves." She lay awake a long time, herself disturbed, and in the other room Narcissa lay awake. Nor did Patience Noble sleep.

Before day broke, Silas reaching from his bed beat the floor with a heavy brogan shoe, waking everyone in Forest Mansion with the noise and shouting, "Time to rise." Soon the household was up and about—Lott was feeding the horses and mules, milking the cows; Narcissa was carrying corn to the pigs; by the firelight in the kitchen Patience Noble was frying ham, stirring cream gravy. At breakfast, Silas opened the Book to the ninety-first psalm, reading, "He that dwelleth in the secret place of the most high shall abide under the shadow of the Almighty." After that the meal was eaten in silence—nobody spoke a word.

On washing the breakfast dishes, Narcissa disappeared into the pasture; hurriedly she followed the spring branch, walking in the level paths of the cows, she smelled the primeval scents of tangful old Carolina, the damp molding earth, the purifying stench of polecat stale and the vigorous resin smell of the pines and the dry fragrance of the muscadine, and she listened to the quiet buzzing of gnats and sweat bees and the harsh jay birds and the shy woodthrushes singing so pure a song, so filled with contentment and peace—she felt exalted. She thought the thrush sang finest, better than them all, better than the mocking bird or the liquid song that the vireo sang—sorrow and infinite patience were in the thrush's song, she understood the thrush's singing. She looked in the still pools, .at the star-shaped leaves of the sweetgum, at the bright green mosses, empty shells left by squirrels, spiders webs, the green wings of the snake doctors, turning blue in the glinting sunlight; she felt the warm west wind and watched the sun shine and the white clouds drift. These were the scenes of home.

Narcissa crossed the little swamp, jumping from grass tufts to logs, dodging briars, then climbing the hill beyond she sat on a jutting rock, looking at the rolling range of mountains, the soaring blue wall, shrouded with a thin curtain of a still finer blue. Looking, lying flat in the warm sunshine, Narcissa mused—Bald Knob, so blue, Miles had climbed Bald Knob—he had been there hunting; Yellow Mountain, Pine Mountain, he had been there gathering chestnuts; Nameless Valley, King's Gap—Miles had stood at King's Gap, too—at the top of the world, seeing east and west, he had told her; he had seen to the vast end of space, he had stood alone in the glory. She thought always of Miles—Strange and playful and full of spirit and feeling. O love, she cried, holding out her arms to the empty air; he was illiterate and poor, it was true, but there were other things; she loved him for the other things, for the things he understood, for the tales he told her. There were so many things he knew to talk about other than weather and the crops and the price of cotton—there in that valley southward from Rabun Bald ran the stream called Toccoa—a little river, he had said to her, no bigger than the horse branch, but it was famous in Georgia. Narcissa gazed into the west, a smile coming on her face—"Toccoa" was his name for her; in Cherokee, he said, it meant "The Beautiful." "And on that little river there was a high precipice of rugged rocks, a hundred and eighty-six feet high," Miles had told her, "and at its foot lay a pool, so still, and on all sides were tall granite rocks and shady trees. All was so restful, so full of peace and over this cliff came a softly falling stream that broke into a heavy spray—a river drifting away in a mist." There was no stunning noise of crashing waters at Toccoa, "only a pattering into a pool." Often in speaking, Miles used the beautiful lyrics of illiteracy.

O his eyes, his fine face, O his strong hands!

"A blue day is Monday," said Narcissa. With Patience Noble and Unity the aunt, she washed; they scrubbed clothes in tubs at the spring branch on an outcrop of solid granite. They battled the blue shirts the men wore with battling sticks and dropped the pounded garments into an iron washpot to boil; the men's clothing was very soiled. This was hard work but the smell of fat pine burning was a good smell and Narcissa liked to watch the blue smoke of the wash fire rise and blow away, and in the afternoon with all the wash on the line, satisfied with a day of work that was done, she liked to gather the little red, yellow and pink flowers that grew in cracks in the sheath of rock. Symbols, these flowers—they gave her courage for growing; where other plants died they bloomed brighter than the flowers in the garden. Narcissa dropped into bed with the early dark, very tired.

She turned the next day to drying apples; with Patience Noble and Unity she sat on the quiet back piazza cutting the fruit into small pieces. One time every hour, Narcissa would take the pansful into the vegetable garden and spread the apples on long strips of boards to evaporate in the sunlight. In the cornfield at the foot of the hill, Queen Elizabeth's Margit, her blue dress wet with sweat, a blood red rag bound about her head, was hoeing cotton and singing with fervor, "Lord, I'm trying to get ready for the judgment day." On the porch, Narcissa, Patience Noble and Unity also began to sing, "Yes, trying to get ready for the judgment day." Then for nearly an hour they worked in dull silence. Suddenly Narcissa stood up, apples and apple peel falling in all directions. The girl's face was flushed, her yellow hair moist. "I'm sick and tired," she cried, tearing off the apron she was wearing. "I want to be somebody, to amount to something—I don't want to spend my life peeling apples." About to burst into tears, she ran away. She ran through the cotton field, kicking her shoes in the field dirt, red and rich dust, smooth as velvet. Stopping at the spring she drank with her lips from the chill pool, stooping over far; she lay on her back under an oak in the shade, in the dark still shadows; she cried for a while, then she listened to the zooming of a wild fly, a high note of a mosquito, a dripping of water. Not a leaf was moving, not a breeze; the only sounds in the world were a fly's and a mosquito's, the only action a water's drop. O the loneliness, the vast silent immensity of this country, the monotonous hard drab lonely existence it forced upon her. Narcissa was overwhelmed; again she cried. The shade under the tree now was not cool, it was hot and oppressive. So getting up, Narcissa looked at the clouds, she saw that a thunderstorm was making up.

Quieted by this brief period of rebellion, her burst of emotion spent, Narcissa returned to Forest Mansion. Without speaking either to Patience Noble or Unity, she tied the apron again about her middle, again began cutting apples. Soon a low rumbling stirred in the west, a trembling warning, but the three kept on with their work; the storm did not stop them until there was a sharp searing crack of lightning, followed directly overhead by a crashing peal of thunder. Then Narcissa darted to the garden, sweeping into her apron the fruit that was drying.

The first heavy drops of rain, scented with dust, were already falling when she returned to the kitchen. For an hour, Narcissa and the two women sat serenely, their arms resting on a table while the wild storm winds blew and the rain poured and—crashing and roaring the southern elements wore out their fury. There was a blinding bolt of light, a crash. "Struck somewhere near," said Unity. One of the trees in the yard had been hit but they were not frightened—they were southern women, accustomed to thunder and lightning.

Wednesday was warm and hot; Narcissa ironed. She moved a heavy flatiron over shirts, plain dresses, heavy sheets; occasionally to slicken the rubbing surface she rubbed the iron with beeswax and cedar sprigs. In the kitchen was her mother making jelly from the apple peel left from the day before, nothing was wasted at Forest Mansion. While ironing, Narcissa watched Patience Noble, bending, walking between the wood stove and the table, her face covered with perspiration. In a corner, knitting, was old Frances, sipping red wine, talking about the Caldwell family, southern kind of talking.

"The first Ross Caldwell of Caldwell," she said, "married a Gilstrap and they settled on Crow Creek." She clicked the needles. "That's right," said Patience Noble, pouring brown New Orleans sugar into a boiling pot of water.

"And they had four girls and six boys—first there was Essie," continued Frances, "Essie married a Cooper and moved to Georgia; Ella married a Roper and went to Tennessee; Elizabeth died; Rebekah married one of old Bill Taylor's sorriest boys and moved to Texas; Aaron, the oldest boy, was killed in the war; Washington married one of Cousin Willie Caldwell's girls and kept the homeplace; Thomas was captured at Spotsylvania Courthouse and died in a prison camp in the North; the second Ross went to Texas and on to California during the goldrush; then there was their Warren—now, let's see, what happened to Warren? Patience Noble, whatever became of Warren?"

This conversation was interrupted by Nora Nally, wife of Nally the tenant. Bustling and noisy, Nora came into the kitchen, smiling, wiping her honest face with her apron; she had come to bring a letter.

"Miss Patience Noble," she said, "I saw Miss Becky Caldwell at the crossroads and she gave me this note there to give to Miss Narcissa." Hearing her name mentioned, Narcissa came into the kitchen. Nora Nally sat down by the door, wearily, beginning to fan herself vigorously, waiting for the excitement. Aloud Narcissa read:

"Hopewell Landing.
"Dear Narcissa:

"Mr. Knox, the trustee of our school district, wants to know if you will teach school over near his house. He sed if you will teach, write the articals and send them over to him and he will make up the school. You must send me word tomorrow or the day after and I will let him know right away. Also send all the news. Clarissa is still mending, she can walk over the house and hopes to attend preaching by the third Sunday. She is doing well, I reckon, but she still grieves over the babe. Tell Cousin Patience Noble I have got those bonnets. I have not done anything to my dress yet; there was a marriage at the church, out of doors, last night—Miss Ellinberg and Mr. Victor, just escaping disgrace by a few weeks. Let me know, sure.

"Your cousin,
Becky Caldwell."

For a moment, release from all this lonely monotony and routine loomed in Narcissa's mind, she became wildly happy, her spirit soared—here was the chance, to earn money, a new scene, new things to do. But then she thought of her father. "What will he say, ma?"

"I don't know what he will say," said Patience Noble. But she did know and so did Narcissa know. "I'll go and ask him." Soon she returned. "He said he won't have it." Shrugging her shoulders, Narcissa pitched the letter into the fire, it had been only a straw she had grasped at.

"A dirty shame is what I call it," said Nora Nally, sipping a tumbler of Unity's wine.

Back to the ironing went Narcissa, working through a long afternoon scented with beeswax and cedar and sweat; then came the lonely dusk. She rested on the cold slab steps of the front piazza, her back against one of Silas' white columns; lonely and tired she watched the pure green light of the radiant western star, thinking Miles' name for it was Nagoochee—for Miles' mother, like the first Carter Caldwell. had heard from the Cherokees the old legend and had told it to her son. The night wind, rising in the west with the sunset brought the fine perfume of pennyroyal from the pastures and a few late crows, hurrying, flying over the red fields on their way to the dense pines before dark night caught them; from somewhere in the southern distance there drifted the mourning piercing cry of the whip-poor-will, so tired, so sorrowful that Narcissa shivered.

From the deep darkness of the porch came a strong tobacco smell and the deep sound of her father's voice—talking restlessly with lean Nally, the tenant, about the Civil War—Lee and Jackson and Gettysburg and the Bull Runs. "Mr. Nally," sang the heavy bass, quiet and steadily pitched, "It was about this time during the thick of the engagement that I became lost from my own detachment—I found myself among the Louisiana Tigers, wild men, Mr. Nally. The Louisiana Tigers were the damn-dest fighting-est soldiers there were in the whole war; they were such fighters they fought among themselves when they couldn't fight Yankees. Why, I heard a Kentuckian say once he had seen Louisiana Tigers chained to trees in their own camp just to keep them from killing one another, and a lady in Virginia told me when she heard the Louisiana Tigers were coming she started to leave home—even Virginians were feared of the Louisiana Tigers. But, sir, that lady told me they were the gentlest and kindest things around a house ever she laid her eyes on—she told me she'd rather have Louisiana Tigers camped about her than almost any other Southern soldiers." On and on talked the voice, on and on. Listening, Nally the tenant clung to the edge of the porch floor, one foot on the floor, the other on the ground. Said Nally about once in every five minutes. "Well, I declare." He was not listening to Silas.

Alone in one of the small rooms off the great central room was Patience Noble playing the small parlor organ, singing frantically "Patiently, tenderly Jesus is calling." Her frail soprano voice quavered. And alone on the back piazza was Frances, smoking in a small black pipe a twist of tobacco as strong as Silas', wondering and thinking—thinking of the still things and the quiet things and the little things, the beauty of the little bloodroot and the anemone that had the courage to bloom before anything in the spring and the trickle of water in the spring branch that was without power to hurt anything and yet was the source of power and of the quiet breeze; thinking of the great things, the storms and the winds, the water dashing over the rocks…a lifetime was like that, like years of the weather…

And with her hands gloved, the door to her room secure, strange Unity had retired for the night; on her knees, she was praying with passionate fervor, "Blessed Jesus, hold me…"

They were all alone at Forest Mansion.

Next morning on finding the sun unclouded and hot, Narcissa worked in the garden among the old-fashioned knot-like tomatoes, vermilion and pure brilliant yellow, the emerald green peppers, eggplant rows splashed with cochineal and true purple, all the beautiful vegetables which Narcissa regarded as massed color—not as form at all; she planted a long row across the garden of string beans, the variety called the Kentucky Wonder; broke with a heavy hoe the earth crust formed by the recent beating rainstorm. Then she turned to pulling weeds from the beds of lavender, mint, life everlasting, catnip, gray old sage. Hoeing, bending, far away from the rich garden in thought, the girl was startled by a close voice whispering, "Miss Narcissa." It was Windy Bill, standing beside her, a red cedar bucket in one hand, a smile on his dark unworried face. "I got something to tell you," he said. "I was at the crossroads store last night, ma'am, and young Mister Miles Crossing—he was there too and when he sees me coming in after a can of sockeye salmon, he says to me quiet so no one in the store will overhear—he says Windy Bill I got a favor to ask of you. What's that, Mister Mills, I asks back, What it is that old Windy Bill could be doing that'd be a favor. Well, he says to me, Windy Bill, you tell Miss Narcissa that I says I'll be at the rock under the tree tomorrow afternoon, rain or shine—And I says Sure, I'll tell her. Mister Miles, but what rock is you mean and what tree. And he says It don't matter, you just tell Miss Narcissa I'll be there from right after dinner until black night. And, Miss Narcissa, I says to him, Mister Miles, I'll tell her that for sure."

"Well," said Narcissa, staring angrily at the Negro, "I won't meet him there—I can't meet him."

"Yes, ma'am," said Windy Bill, putting on his hat.

But Narcissa changed her mind. As soon as she had washed the dinner dishes, she reached for a bonnet and left, no one in the house seeing her leave. Patience Noble and Unity were rummaging in a rag bag in the garret, Frances and Silas were asleep. But from the woodpile, where he was chopping fat pine logs into stove lengths, Windy Bill saw the girl hurry through the bee garden, force a quick way through the boxwood hedge and disappear down the locust road. He laughed to himself, and lifting an axe he started a slow song, "O I got to walk to those gallows." On the down stroke of the shining blade, he shouted, "Wham" and up came the blade. "With the preacher man by my side." And again down and "wham". Bill muttered, "Lord, this world—this troubled world." It seemed a part of his song.

Climbing the hill beyond the swamp, Narcissa knew Miles already had arrived at the meeting place for the warm wind brought the fine sound of his fiddle music; under the smooth bark tree she found him, lying in the grass, his long unkept hair blowing about his sunburned forehead—laughing. Miles was wearing a torn blue shirt, a pair of yellow cotton breeches tied about himself with a cord. His feet in clodhopper shoes were slung over a boulder. He did not stand when Narcissa appeared, he merely began singing to the tune of his fiddle. "I got a girl that lives at Letcher, she won't come and I won't fetch her." Looking up at Narcissa, the boy wrinkled his face, sang "ring dang dooly day." Then he threw down the fiddle, jumped to his feet. Miles was tall—taller than Narcissa and she was tall. His fine hands, his arms were about her and like the clouds the hours of the afternoon drifted away.

Narcissa leaped the barbed pasture fence, she ran through the darkening swamp and scarcely noticing the bog holes or sweet briars, she stepped lightly along the cow path, enraptured, inspired—in the whole world there was love only—nothing mattered but love. Love's way was the way.

Silas was waiting in the deep chair beneath the high white columns. "Where have you been all afternoon—neglecting your work," asked he, violently angry.

"I've been on the beech tree ridge," said Narcissa, without much show of fear or of respect.

"Doing what for God's sake for so long?"

Narcissa told him, "I've been talking to Miles Crossing." She looked her father full in the face, hiding nothing. "That's what I've been doing and you might as well know it right now, Pa—I'm going to marry Miles."

Beating the arms of his chair with his brutal fists, Silas shouted, "What?" He had heard but he hardly believed. He screamed the word "what" so loud, with such fury, that it was heard by the Nallys in their cabin over two hills, and Windy Bill tieing beans to canes in his new ground heard it. So did Lott in the long field by the river.

"What did you say?"

"I said I am going to marry Miles Crossing," replied Narcissa, quietly and firmly.

The fine facial features of the Caldwells set in the molds of Silas' gross flesh turned livid; hatred, intense and uncontrollable flared in his eyes. Suddenly bending over, reaching for the gourd dipper in a water bucket at his feet, he dashed a dipperful of water into his daughter's face.

"God damn you," he cried, "get out of here; get off this property." Then in a rage of new fury, he threw the bucket, gourd and all at Narcissa.

So Narcissa left Forest Mansion. She walked quietly without a backward glance. She was young and she was not afraid—she believed in the future and because she loved a young man and he loved her, she did not doubt that all the rest of her days would be happy. At last, she had escaped and that was enough; loneliness was behind.

A hard man that never wavered, sure that the consequences of disobedience were full upon the one who disobeyed, Silas read at the supper table that evening from the sixteenth chapter of Matthew, "The Pharisees also with the Sadducees came and tempting desired Him that He would shew them a sign from heaven..." And then Silas ate—a great plateful of grits. But alone that evening, with the mocking birds, the owls and the swifts, Silas sat on the wide piazza in the darkness and unknown to anyone, he wept. But before retiring he struck Narcissa's name from the old Bible in which the Caldwells had kept their records since Narcissa the first in 1699 married in Pennsylvania.

"I disown her," Silas said to God.

Patience Noble cried, her head upon the kitchen table, and she cried until she could not weep another tear; then she sat for a long while staring through a narrow paned window. An almost full moon, about to set, was shining, lighting her pale wet face.

"Frances," she said, "I fear for them—he's fine and handsome and he has charming ways but he's illiterate and he's never done a full day's work in his life. Miles at heart is a fiddler, a shuffler—a rabbit and possum hunter. And Narcissa is a Caldwell."

The lead hammer of the kitchen clock drew back, striking a half hour, another of those quivering old notes from Connecticut, that for a hundred years had rung out the time at Forest Mansion. Patience Noble breathed deeply. "The world," she sighed, "is so queer and sudden."

"I'm glad," said Frances. "I'm glad she had the spirit."

CHAPTER ELEVEN

The swift night of the south had settled by the time Narcissa reached the crossroads store, and oil lamps were burning, ham was frying, coffee boiling in the country kitchens. In the dim-bright doorway of the store she saw Miles, leaning on one shoulder, loafing, laughing, talking with one of the Hunter Negroes, Bigfoot Bill. Startled, Miles came running. "What are you doing out here after dark?" he asked, and Narcissa began to cry.

She told Miles what had happened and taking the girl by the hand Miles started toward the store. "We'll get married right now," he said, "right here and right now."

"Mister Ed," called Miles, speaking awkwardly, "We'd like to get married." Behind a counter—baldheaded, spectacled and old—was Ed Newton, the storekeeper, and justice of the peace who during sixty years of emergencies in the upcountry had married hundreds of men and women in a hurry—poor boys and poor girls, old rich men and young women, young men and old rich women, old fat-chested widows and fat fathers of many children, sometimes pregnant girls and frightened boys. Ed never inquired—all that he asked was whether they had living another husband or wife.

"We'd like to get married, Mister Ed," repeated Miles.

Mister Ed glanced up from the ledger in which he had been entering accounts and he was astonished—it showed on his face.

"My God," he said, dropping his pen which a moment before had been used to charge a pound of coffee beans to Miss Mary Belle McCord. "You and Narcissa—why, Miles, what in the world are you talking about…" Miles then told Mister Ed what Narcissa had told him. "Mister Silas ran her off the place, Mister Ed, he threw the water-bucket at her."

Listening angrily—he never had liked Silas Caldwell—the old storekeeper lifted the kerosene lamp in his palsied hands. "I'll marry you," he said, positively and without hesitation, "Sure, I'll marry you—young folks, you all just follow me." He led the way through a stack of lard buckets, plowshares, sacks of feed and harness to the wing of his home which adjoined the store.

"Mattie," he shouted, calling to his wife, "A wedding for the parlor."

"All right, Mister Ed," came a sweet voice from the far back of the house. The smoking lamp was placed in the center of a table of Jamaica mahogany; the room tightly closed smelt musty. "You all just stand there by the mantelpiece," said Mister Ed, "and soon as Mattie Lee brings me in my Sunday coat, we' marry you."

"Mattie Lee," he shouted once more, insistently.

"I'm coming." Soon with a black coat in her hands came Mattie Lee, a large woman with very large arms and breasts. Behind her came Miss Mary Belle McCord. The two women took one glance and became highly excited—they had expected to see some mill hand or tenant farmer, some mill hand's embarrassed daughter. "Why, Narcissa honey," said Mattie Lee, throwing the black coat at Mister Ed. "Why, child, whoever'd thought it—you running away, getting married at the crossroads store." Windows were thrown open, furniture dusted; dashing into the yard, Mattie Lee grabbed the pale death-like blossoms from a row of cape jessamine bushes. "A bouquet for the bride."

"The lord bless my soul," Miss Mary Belle was saying from the leather sofa. She was thinking, "What a sensation!"

※

Like children, Miles and Narcissa walked that night down the vermilion dust road, hand in hand; Miles in a mood for teasing, his spirit high and free—but not Narcissa; already grave and anxious, she was in the midst of the here and now, worrying already about tomorrow. From the moment of her marriage Narcissa was changed, she was old, restless and uneasy.

"What'll we do," she asked, "how will we make a living?"

Miles stopped, he kissed Narcissa. "This is our wedding night, Narcissa—isn't that enough to think about for the present?"

"Yes," said Narcissa, smiling nervously, "it is."

A chill summer night mist had settled in the shallow valley through which Yellow Creek ran, muddy among the willows, on its brief way toward Keowee, the mists clung to the swamp vines, the alders, the willow trees; Miles hugged Narcissa.

Farther along the clay dusty roadway, about a mile, they turned at a mail box, climbing a cabin path through fresh-smelling vines. Soon there was a small light from a window, an upcountry voice began singing, nasal and high pitched, "I think when I read that sweet story of old." It was Sue the herb woman singing, the fat, friendly middle-aged mother of Miles. Besides prescribing decoctions of resins, roots, wild medicinal plants for diarrheas, fevers, mortifications, colds, dysenteries, cancer and consumption, Sue also pierced women's ear lobes for earrings, sticking straws into the fleshy wounds until they healed—many women in the upcountry, including Sue herself, wore gold hoops in their ears. A strong, strange woman, Sue dug in the swamps for roots, like a man, hunted for possums and squirrels, fished in the river for catfish and carp. From many Negroes and stray Cherokees she had gathered wild tales and superstitions. At the hour of low twelve, she said, witches entered houses through keyholes—witches that could be killed only by a silver ball. Strung about her fleshy, sweaty throat on a gold chain was a crude stone crucifix—a fairy stone, she said, very old. She said the news of Calvary was brought to Carolina by a band of weeping angels who dropped as memorials a lot of little crosses such as hers.

Like the old Narcissa, Sue made scarlet, green, even purple native dyes; also she possessed elements of other information about which women came to her in private.

Miles whistled, a powerful shrill greeting; the door of the cabin opened, Sue's form appeared in the light.

"Guess who's with me," cried Miles.

"Who?"

"Your daughter-in-law and my wife."

There was a moment of silence, then there was a quick, hurried movement and down the path came Sue; without even seeing who Narcissa was, Miles' mother in the darkness said, "Welcome, daughter, to our home."

Inside the low-ceiled house, Sue gave no sign of surprise nor did she ask either for a word of explanation; always Sue allowed persons to tell her what they chose when they chose to tell it; this was one of the reasons many came to her cabin in time of trouble; old Sue knew how to sit still and listen.

"We'll get together a supper," she said, filling the stove with fire. In a short while, the three were sitting about a bare pine table, eating crisp pork bacon, hot hominy; also there was coffee, hot biscuit, white salted butter, apple jelly. Then after they had eaten old Sue stood the lamp on an iron-bound chest in Miles' bedroom.

"Goodnight," she said.

Quickly Miles closed the creaky door, kicking it shut with his foot; with one great breath he blew out the lamp flame and he grasped Narcissa, unbuttoning, undoing hooks; then bounding into bed, he pulled the girl after him and fiercely felt her pressing herself against his body. "This is wonderful," she said.

Miles later slept but Narcissa did not sleep. She lay still, exultant one moment that beside her lay the man who loved her, uneasy the next—no land, no money. She listened to the wind in the pines, smelt wood ashes, some sage that must be hanging near to dry; long afterward she heard a bird calling and soon after that day began to break—there was light to see by. A set of fine dogirons, home forged, stood in a fireplace and there were waxflowers under a glass on the mantel, and also in this room were two hickory chairs, over one of which lay her yellow dress, Miles' blue shirt. On the bare floor were his yellow breeches. Oh it was wonderful—she drew in her breath.

Quietly, she raised herself, dressed, tiptoed barefooted from the house; up the steep hill extending above and behind the cabin, she climbed, birds singing, the sun about to rise. Below in the clearing was the little house, three rooms of pine plank with clematis vines thick on the low porches, a beautiful place, she thought, vital as though it had grown like the trees from the field. The yards, beaten hard, needed brushing, she observed; she admired the sunflowers and hollyhocks, wild splotches of yellow and pink-blue; there was a small barn, a corncrib, a garden filled with weeds, an arbor loaded with small ripe grapes that needed picking, a peach tree on a terrace drooping with small peaches that were ripe—she would gather them, she decided.

And then surely and slowly up from the east came the sun, the wild red ball of summer; in the dazzle of the first rays the whole clean world glistened, all filled with hope, she thought, and with courage. Now in a moment it seemed so simple; her fine young husband was strong, she herself was able. There was good land, thousands of acres of it to be rented; they would work hard and save, soon buy their own land, start out themselves, from nothing make something of themselves—Miles and Narcissa Crossing!

Slowly taking her time, Narcissa returned to the cabin. For three hours she waited restlessly before either Miles or Sue stirred from bed. It was nearly half past eight before Sue came from her room.

"Good morning, Narcissa," said Sue, ignoring the blush that spread over the face of Narcissa—now a new wife's face. Sue began bustling about, talking, combing her hair, poking the fire.

"We're sort of late this morning," she said, pitching flour, pouring buttermilk into a bread tray. "We get up whenever we like to around this place; we got no rules nor regulations; we just get up when we want to and we go to bed when we want to go to bed and when we feel like working we work and when we feel like resting we rest." Old Sue added to the mixture a cup of flour, heavy dark flour, ground from hill-grown wheat at the Caldwells' water mill.

Boisterously, a few minutes later Miles burst into the kitchen, singing. "Howdy," he said, laughing and sousing his face in a pan of cold water. He dashed with a tin bucket to the pasture, fed, milked the small black cow; returning, fresh and vigorous, the boy sat down with old Sue and Narcissa to eat breakfast—it was nine o'clock, the latest Narcissa ever in her life had eaten that meal. Miles and old Sue drank the milk the black cow had given a few minutes before; it was still warm, animal warm.

"Have a glassful," said Sue. "No thank you, ma'am," said Narcissa. They did not drink warm cow's milk at Forest Mansion; milk was cooled twelve hours at the spring house before the Caldwells drank it.

Miles wiped butter and red jelly from his mouth. "Folks," he said, standing astride the breakfast chair and reaching for a straw hat hanging on a nail in the wall above him, "it's a fine day for fish to bite; let's go fishing."

"Suits me," agreed old Sue. Turning to Narcissa, the older woman inquired, "How about it, honey? How'd you like to catch a nice bait of blue cats?" Never had Narcissa heard of anyone dropping work on a fine summer work day to fish, her real thought was of the peaches ripe on the terrace in the cotton patch; these should be preserved or dried, the grapes in the garden should be jellied—fish always swam in the river but these sweet wild peaches and grapes soon would be too lusciously ripe to handle. But she nodded.

"I'll wash the dishes," said Narcissa, gathering knives and forks. "Law me, child," said old Sue, "We'll leave them until we get back." Miles dug a few earthworms from the rich soil of the garden. Off the three started—down the hill to the mail box, down the maroon road to the river; they moved along the wet bank, through canebrakes, jumped drift logs; they came to a still pool, here they dropped their lines and patiently sat down to wait; they relaxed—Miles leaning against the rough bark of a sycamore, completely at rest, old Sue intently gazing at the unbroken surface of the water, at a waterglider; Narcissa regarding them both, utterly amazed by the depths of their repose, their peace.

After a time there was gay mixed laughing and soon there appeared a group of Negroes in blue overalls, barefooted. "Howdy, Miss Sue," said they all, bowing. "Howdy, Mister Miles; Miss Narcissa, ma'am, howdy." On they went, dodging the low vines, the thick matted canes, talking to one another, laughing loud. Narcissa, Miles and old Sue sat on the mudbank, hardly stirring until noon by the sun, then with five blue catfish on a twig, they returned to the cabin in a high mood. Old Sue dipped these fish in water-ground meal, fried them in butter, an extravagance that Narcissa noted, and at one o'clock the Crossings ate their dinner. It was a drowsy, hot day; so they all lay down to sleep—but Narcissa did not sleep, she disapproved sleeping during the daytime—it was time wasted, she said to herself.

Later in the afternoon, Miles and Sue decided they would cut a watermelon. "We believe in enjoying ourselves," said Sue. As they sat in the cool shade.of the porch eating the red heart of a great melon, the carriage of the Claytons drove into the yard. In the driver's seat was Windy Bill and sitting in the back in her Sunday taffeta dress was Frances. Her face was beaming.

Narcissa kissed Frances' wasted cheek. "Your mother sends you her love," said Frances, "and she's sent you these things." In the carriage were dresses, other clothing, shoes, hats, twelve patchwork quilts, dishes, cans of fruit, a ham, a miniature of Patience Noble painted by Unity the first; also there was that Caldwell treasure, the precious sugar bowl with the gold band that had been brought over the wilderness road by the first Narcissa. While old Sue helped Narcissa and Windy Bill unload these possessions, Miles ran to the spring after more watermelons. Bringing back the two biggest and best, he ripped them open with a butcher knife, eyeing them with appreciation—the melons were red, rich and ripe.

"Here, Miss Frances," said Sue, "you help yourself to a piece of heart." They sat on the porch, eating the chilled melons. Then to leave Narcissa alone with Frances, old Sue hurried into the kitchen to tie a bundle of lavender and mint as a gift for Patience Noble; Miles walked into the hard yard to talk with Windy Bill.

"I'm glad you did it," said Frances, grasping Narcissa's hand. A stern look came into Narcissa's face. "Well," said Narcissa, "I've made my bed and whether I like it or whether I don't like it—no one will ever know."

During the next few days, Narcissa dried the peaches, she made the grapes into jelly, she swept the yard, pulled the garden weeds, planted Kentucky wonder beans, declined twice to go fishing, scattered a pint of fine turnip seed over a bed that old Sue had intended for some herbs. "We ought to have some turnips," said Narcissa. Old Sue said nothing. One afternoon behind the clematis vines on the porch, Narcissa told Miles it was time they looked for favorable land to rent. Miles, lying easily on the floor, his arms under his head, was startled. "Rent land!" he exclaimed, "what do we want to rent land for?"

"Why, we've got to get a place of our own," said Narcissa firmly. "We'll raise a crop on the halves, we'll save and pretty soon we'll be able to start buying land for ourselves."

"But what do we want with land," said Miles, "I'd rather be free to lie here like this when I want to than to own the biggest house and the biggest farm in this country—than to own Forest Mansion. Besides we've got a place—we are welcome here with ma."

"We can't live off your mother."

Miles got up. Alone he walked through the deep, still woods, among pines and dogwood and sourwood and patches of orange milkweed and wild hedges of sassafras and ripe maypops, along the steep ridges in the shadows of oaks that never had been cut—never in the whole of time. For a long while, his lean face burning in the sun, Miles sat on a rock—a married man, older already and more settled, thinking.

Reaching the cabin in the evening, Miles kissed Narcissa. "Narcissa," he begged, "let's don't ever become tenant farmers—let's go to the cotton mill; it'll be easier there to save money—we'll have a pay check coming in, cash in hand every Saturday night." There was a beseeching look in his eyes. He took her hands, asking her to "think it over." She agreed. But she mistrusted this move. She was afraid of the mill and its implications—the leaving the rich, free fields to go into a narrow town to work by the hour for someone whom neither she nor Miles had ever seen—to live in a house belonging to a stranger; Narcissa sensed to the fullest the significance of this change-even the sound of the word wages was shocking to this daughter of the land-owning Caldwells—two and a half centuries of living in one's own house were behind Narcissa. But Miles was insistent. "Just as soon as we save enough to buy ten acres of land, we'll leave the mill—that oughtn't to take us long." "All right," said Narcissa, and smiling again in a teasing mood, Miles played on his fiddle.

So Narcissa and Miles moved to Isundiga on the wild rocky gorge of Yellow Creek; they arrived in a rain, moved into a two-room shack built into the side of a steep hill, facing a winding muddy road; on every side were many more two room shacks, facing winding wet clay roads, a hard, heartless looking place, it seemed to Narcissa—very poor in spirit.

Hardly anyone grew a flower, there were only paths, hard back yards, weedy gardens and there were no curtains over windows. Lean black-eared dogs wandered about the houses, many of which by day were deserted, since children as well as men and women worked in this mill. A rising whistle blew every morning at half past four—at six work began. Six to six was their shift. Often in the winter the hands went long before day to the mill, a bare oblong of red brick and rows of windows with a conventional brick tower; the sun had already set, the last light died in the sky before they left the looms in the evening.

Narcissa and Miles arrived at Isundiga in the afternoon early; in their house among the rafters they saw the mud cells of dirt daubers, there were several wasps' nests in the peak of the pitched roof. Narcissa scoured the bare board floor, washed windows, scrubbed the granite hearthstone; Miles built a fire in the open fireplace, and when coals were red, cooked supper. He and Narcissa made their first meal as factory hands on fine spoonbread and coffee.

The rain slacked long enough for the sun to set, pale red, among the aqueous water clouds; looking through a window, Narcissa saw new clouds gathering over the long ridge, mists in the valleys—a clean, water washed sight; again she took hope, perhaps living at the mill would not be so bitter after all; she determined she would feel encouraged.

Narcissa jumped from bed, startled, awakened by the scream of the rising whistle, a powerful merciless sound, full of terror. "Worse than pa beating on the floor with his shoe," she said, half awake. Pulling the sheet over his head, Miles grunted. With the bellowing sound still echoing through the hollows, Narcissa lighted a fire; when the hominy pot had boiled and the pan of biscuits browned, she called Miles, "Rise and shine!"

That morning Narcissa walked part of the way toward the mill with Miles, watched him walking on through the mists and the trees; he went on that first day alone, as they had decided Narcissa would not work the first week with things at the house still to be settled. Working at home, Narcissa boiled string beans with fat pork and potatoes in an iron pot slung over the open fire from a crane; she fried peach pies, pulled weeds from the garden patch at the rear of the house, began also to spade that area. For there was time still to sow turnips and turnips would be something with which to face a winter. Miles came in at noon when the whistle blew, and again when the whistle blew he left for the mill. Going in the afternoon to the company store to buy some low-country rice, Narcissa saw a woman slap a sallow cheeked child that had picked up a red stick of cheap sugar candy from a counter. "You fool," shouted the woman, "keep your dirty fingers off the storeman's counter." The child, knocked nearly over by the hard blow, began crying. Without thinking twice, Narcissa hurried across the crowded storeroom, over to the woman, whom she recognized as one of the former tenants of the Caldwells of Redhill.

"You shouldn't have done that," said Narcissa.

"You tend to your own damn business," said the woman. Narcissa turned away—she was bewildered. But she made up her mind that instant that she did not like the place, that nothing should keep them there a moment longer than was necessary.

That night Miles was discouraged. "It's hard money, honey," he said, dashing cold water over his face in his old carefree way, "it's a cage."

Stirring hominy in the iron pot, Narcissa said, "It's new, maybe it won't be so bad after you get used to it—to the routine."

"It's been like a hundred years," said Miles, running a comb through his dripping hair.

Eating, Narcissa suggested they divide their time from then until spring into periods of six weeks, perhaps that would help the months to pass more quickly; they would count days until mid-October, then until December, the first month of winter. "We can stand anything for six weeks and whenever we get so blue we think we're going to break—we'll just say to ourselves everything must come to an end—everything has an end and a piece of string has two. It's going to be hard but we can stick it out."

"What kind of a way is that to live," said Miles.

They fell early into bed, forgetting for a time everything but each other. And in no time it seemed the whistle again was blowing, the second day had arrived. Narcissa was beating the feather bed with a stick that morning when there was a knock, a firm rapping at the front door.

"Mrs. Crossing," sang a friendly, fiat-toned upcountry voice.

"Yes," answered Narcissa, straightening her apron, brushing back her thin yellow Caldwell hair.

A strong young woman, broad shouldered with big capable hands, stepped hesitantly into the house. She held a small glass of purple jelly. "Mrs. Crossing," she said, smiling, "my name is Mrs. Richards—Marthy Richards, and I thought I'd like to welcome you to the mill hill—I live next door and I'm not working myself just now—I'm expecting."

Smiling, thanking the visitor for the jelly, Narcissa accepted the gift. Simple, unassuming, the visitor sat down. "My husband is Pete Richards," she said. "He's a spinner in Mill No. 2; we moved to the mill a year come November; Pete's one of old man Charlie Richards of Mile Creeks' boys—maybe you remember old man Charlie, was a tenant once of your Cousin Pisgah Caldwell at Hopewell Landing. I'm a mountain girl, myself, Miss Narcissa—I'm going to call you Miss Narcissa—I'm one of the Rupeses of Joccassee Valley." Marthy shifted herself, straightening the blue dotted dress over her swollen belly.

"How do you like living at the mill," said Narcissa, sitting down, the jelly jar in her hands.

"I don't like it at all, ma'am; it's a sorry place for white folks," said Marthy, disturbed. She told Narcissa that many of the men and some of the women were hard drinkers, some spending more than half their wages on whiskey. Pointing across the road, Marthy told of a drinking man living in one of the houses there. "His baby died in convulsions and he was out drunk—they couldn't find him." Now his wife was about to die, and again he was missing. She had pellagra, said Marthy, her legs were swollen.

Again pointing across the road, this time to the shack opposite the Crossings', Marthy said there lived an old woman with a cancer. "Slowly, Miss Narcissa," said Marthy, "she's being eaten away. It was only in the right breast a few months ago but now it's consuming the left one; someday it will hit an artery and the old lady will die out like a light." The old woman was a Gassoway who had come to the mill with her son from the headwaters of the Toxaway; this son, a hard worker, was spending every cent he could raise for salves and cures.

"Once a week, a high-priced doctor comes from Greenville to dress the old lady's breasts," said Marthy. "He don't do much for her—can't do much, but I know how they feel about it—they want to do all they can. But it's just pitiful, the old lady sits over there by herself all the day. She's afraid to die."

Marthy sighed with regret, Narcissa threw some wood onto the fire, gave the boiling beans in the pot a stir.

"Miss Narcissa," said Marthy frankly and with a puzzled worried look, "I been having trouble with my husband and I don't know anybody around here to turn to and I got to turn to somebody." Quaintly familiar in the presence of Narcissa, and simple and certain of sympathy, Marthy began telling her troubles. "Pete don't want to get up in the morning when the whistle blows. And he don't want to go back to the mill when he comes home for dinner. Half the time I have to take his hat off the peg and hand it to him and say, Pete, you just got to go." She said sometimes he would pretend his head ached or his back was strained; sometimes he would not work more than two or three days in a week, and sometimes for a week he would not work at all. "I am afraid, Miss Narcissa...I am afraid some of these days the foreman will tell Pete to clear out and stay...and with the winter coming on and me expecting, I ask you where in the world would we turn?" Anxiously, fearfully, Marthy looked to Narcissa for an answer.

"Couldn't you go back to your folks?" asked Narcissa.

"No'm," said Marthy, shaking her dark head. "There isn't any place to go back to—all my folks and all Pete's have done just what we're done—they've given up their places and moved to the mills."

Narcissa was frightened, alarmed from the depths of her being; suddenly within her rose the warning sounds of the long centuries of pioneer instinct, the old legacies from the old Carter, the old Silas, began surging into protest—this was thin ice, red was everywhere, every sign screamed danger; this was not the old precious road to the land where all should be equal lords of living, at home in a free house, safe in a refuge. This was pure terror to the spirit born in the immense solitudes among the vast, sheer spaces.

Marthy was still speaking; she hated to drive Pete as she had to drive him, it hurt her always to have to nag him on. "Because I know what it's like," she said, "to have to stay all day long, from daylight to dark, inside of a house, at one place, doing one thing over and over and over. It's a dog's life—it's not a fit way to live for man nor beast, and it's because of my feelings that I don't drive him from the house often as I should. Miss Narcissa, I don't raise hand nor voice when Pete tells me he can't work because of pains in his head or about his heart."

"Marthy," said Narcissa with grimness in her voice, "don't you and Pete stay here one minute longer than you have to."

"With God's help," said Marthy, "we'll leave in the spring." The shrill siren ended another hundred years and, hot and very tired, muscles sore, Miles came back to Narcissa; he smiled, ate greedily, then slipped off the blue shirt and the yellow breeches; almost immediately he was asleep. It seemed only a short moment until again the summons was screeching and here, dreaded, was another day.

The last September sun was shining full and ripe upon Isundiga, the long west dusty wind was blowing and Narcissa crossed the road to visit the old woman with the cancer.

A dark shawl of fine blue was about the woman's shoulders; she sat propped in a chair on the piazza.

"Howdy," she said to Narcissa; Narcissa replied, "Howdy."

"My name is Narcissa Caldwell Crossing," said Narcissa, accenting the Caldwell, "I'm a neighbor."

"I'm pleased to make your acquaintance...I'm especially pleased to know one of the Caldwells," said the old woman, her silky rocklike face showing grayness like a weathered board, like the ghost of a dead chestnut tree standing grim in a green forest, years after it has died. Her hands were very thin. She smiled, held up to Narcissa a sheet of paper.

"I'm writing a few lines for my little granddaughter's album," she said. "My little granddaughter lives in Texas and she wrote to me and said, 'Grandma, send me a few lines for my album.' So I'm writing them for her. A few lines on spring—it's my favorite time of the year. Old and heavy things seem so light in spring, like the old apple tree covered with blossoms. Things don't seem to have anybody at all in spring—there is only beauty and spirit."

Soon across the road came Marthy Richards with a bowl of hot potato soup. "It ain't much, ma'am," she said, putting the bowl on a table beside the old woman's chair. "But it's something hot."

An hour later while stirring cabbage in the boiling pot, Narcissa stopped, still in a bending position, to listen to a song. It was a frail weak voice, uncertain and old and filled with frantic anguish:

> "Hold thou thy cross before my closing eyes;
> Shine through the gloom, and point me to the skies;
> Heaven's morning breaks, and earth's vain shadows flee,
> In life, in death, O Lord, abide with me."

Narcissa felt so sorry for the old, waiting, patient, frightened woman, she cried. Nothing seemed to exist, she said to herself, nothing seemed to exist in this whole village but long hours of work and worry and trouble.

On that Saturday night, laughing loudly, a noisy group of Miles' friends came rushing into the house; it was a surprise party, a welcome to the mill hill.

"Howdy," they roared, great smiles on their thin faces, white from long work indoors—gaunt ill-looking men and women; Pete Riggins, a former tenant at Hopewell Landing, his tall dark wife Essie; Wash Roper, tall, stooped son of a former tenant at Forest Mansion, and Rachel his wife; and there were several others, including a stray woman, who came alone, a little drunker than the others. Pete and Essie and Wash and Rachel were somewhat shy and embarrassed at first in the presence of Narcissa; they called her "miss." But as soon as Ike Abernathy arrived they became easier in their manner—Ike brought a five gallon cask of liquor and a guitar.

"Howdy," shouted Ike, laughing and dropping the wooden barrel on Narcissa's table. He pulled the wooden plug from the bung hole, inviting all to gather round. "Folks," he said, "don't be bashful, I made it myself." At once he was surrounded; the powerful, oily-yellow, crude whiskey was drunk in long gulps by the visitors, the potent qualities of its rough spirit making them glow and quiver. Only Narcissa did not drink, and Miles, watching his wife, drank only a little. Soon there was general excitement, loud wild talking, laughing, and singing between many visits to the keg.

Sitting in one corner on the floor, her legs spread before her, the stray woman shouted to Essie, "how you been getting along, Essie?" Essie, leaning against the mantel, said, "Not so good."

"Hah, I know just how you feel," shouted the woman, her voice high above the others and piercing. "I ain't been getting much myself lately." The woman doubled over, laughing. This was ignored by Narcissa. Narcissa lined the walls with the few chairs, meal was sprinkled on the floor, and with his fiddle, Miles began calling sets, Ike accompanying him on the singing guitar. "Salute your partners," sang Miles. There was bowing and backing and reeling; flushed and sweating, the visitors turned after the first set to the cask again, gulping new throatfuls of the liquor, rapidly becoming very drunk. Soon Narcissa saw Pete and Rachel, Wash's wife, slip into the other room. Following them, she found the two already on the bed, Rachel with her shirtwaist loose, Pete fumbling over her with drunken hands. Bursting with anger, Narcissa ordered them to get up. "And get out of here," she said, pulling roughly and with fierce strength at Pete's suspenders. "Get out of my house this minute."

A strange, sudden quiet came over the group—the power of Narcissa's stern command cowed them all. "Get out," she repeated, shoving Pete and Rachel toward the door. The others followed, Ike grabbing the keg. "Aw, come on folks," said Ike, "we'll go to my house." "Yeah," yelled Essie, "we'll go to Ike's," and out the door they stumbled.

In less than an hour all this had happened, they had come like a whirlwind and had gone, and weeping Narcissa now turned to Miles. Miles took his wife in his arms, doing so without speaking. Narcissa wept. "I hate this place," she said.

The quiet waiting weather of October came, the long days, centuries long, following the speeding nights of rest, then November. Now Narcissa worked too at the mill, attending a machine sixty hours a week, thrusting out a hand over and over. Sometimes it seemed physical energy was all that counted in the whole world, only strength—at first Narcissa envied those with sufficient reserve strength still left them to be able after working all day in the mill to cook and wash clothes; but gradually she found this extra strength; she cooked, washed, sewed, scrubbed at night—on Sunday afternoons she dug among the turnips and green collards in the garden. For Narcissa was strong, also this was not an end, this way of living—it was a means to an end for her; she was working there for a certain period of time, with a purpose and a plan.

"We can stand it," she kept saying, "We can stand it until spring."

Then one morning Miles did not get up when the whistle blew. "Narcissa," he said, "I'm sick—my back hurts." Two days later he did not report for work after the noon hour. "I've got an awful pain in my head," he said. Narcissa hurried on. Again that morning she said to herself, "I despise this place."

November sped on, cold, hard with frosts, then December with gloomy rain. One Saturday at dusk, hanging a towel to dry on the rail of the back porch, Narcissa glimpsed a boy, still in knee breeches and very young, and an older girl, hurrying into the Crossings' outhouse in the back garden. She saw them stepping furtively, glancing about quickly, then slipping through the door. In this brief glimpse, Narcissa recognized them: Rhiney Ellis, a thin, prowling girl who lived in one of the houses in the next upper row; a reedy, idle boy from the house beyond the house of the old woman with the cancer—Jimmy Lawrence. Several times Narcissa had seen Rhiney standing at night on dark corners. The boy she saw on Sunday afternoons, lying on the porch of his house, sleeping in the sun. Narcissa reached for a broom and opening the outhouse door she struck blindly into the dark. "We're looking for a hen nest," said Rhiney, and Jimmy ran.

❧

It was Sadie Rose Lawrence, Jimmy's mother, who was singing as Narcissa came into the dim lighted Lawrence home. Glancing at the whey-faced boy sitting before a wobbly bare table, eating apple pie, Narcissa started to speak admonishingly to him. But Jimmy spoke first. "I know what she's come for, Ma," he said, thrusting a rude thumb toward Narcissa. "She's come to tell on me for getting a piece of tang."

Sadie Rose dropped a pot on the table. "Who you been messing around with this time, for God's sake?" she said, a troubled expression showing on her tired passion worn face. The boy bit deeply into the pie, unconcerned.

"It wasn't that Rhiney Ellis, was it?"

"That's who it was, Ma—it wasn't nobody else."

Sadie Rose dashed to the cookstove, grabbing the steaming kettle. "Surely, son, it wasn't Rhiney." Jimmy nodded. The boy was jerked by the shirtcollar across the room. "Here," said Sadie Rose, pouring boiling water into a pan. "You wash yourself right now— just as hot as you can stand it. And use plenty of soap."

The mother began calling the boy vile, vulgar names; then furiously Sadie Rose turned upon Narcissa, staring deep into her face. Narcissa, frightened, ran. "Oh," Narcissa wept, "this is a wicked place."

❧

Miles had pains in his back again on Monday. "Terrible twitch, right there," he said, putting his right hand over his left shoulder blade. Through that long winter morning he sat in the bright sun, resting in a straight chair on the porch, the chair tilted against the wall. On the floor, his head at rest against a post, sat Pete Richards and sprawled on the floor was one of the Ramsays from one of the houses up the road. By the hour, they talked, idly smoked tobacco, and laughed.

This particular ache of Miles' continued for three days. At the end of the third day, Narcissa coming home late from the mill found the table upturned, a chair broken, pieces of dishes on the floor. Miles lay across the bed, his arms outstretched, his face flushed. There were whiskey bottles in the grate. Also ten dollars was missing from their tin box on the mantel.

Brooding despondently, Miles said late that night to Narcissa, "I'm sorry about the money." He buried his face in the pillow—filled with shame.

"It's all right about the money," said Narcissa, gently but taking advantage of the occasion to speak her own mind. "We're going to leave this place," she said, "we're going back to your mother's." So they left Isundiga, early the next morning, hiring Randall Jones, the delivery man, to haul their furniture to Sue's cabin.

Soon afterwards Narcissa and Miles became tenants on the Taylor plantation, whose owners for two centuries had been friends and distant relatives of the Caldwells of Forest

Mansion. Solemn old Alfred Taylor rented out thirty of his richest and best situated acres of farm land to Narcissa and her husband. Narcissa liked the quiet of this new home, a firm clay-daubed cabin, very old and very beautiful, thought Narcissa—even if in a slattern sort of way. It stood soft and fine-lined in a south valley among poplar trees and green pines; there were cardinal birds, pure vermilion, in its thickets; thrushes in the evening sang their peaceful lyrics; the red clay of the fields was fine for growing cotton, it was rocky and rich. Narcissa would have stayed on at Seneca but Miles became impatient. He heard of a farm where more cotton could be grown with less fertilizer and work; so when the first crop had been picked that October from the fields they moved across the county—renting that year from the Lathans of Oolenoy.

Autumn after autumn after that, Miles and Narcissa moved, becoming wandering restless tenant farmers, always poor, never able to buy any land of their own as something always seemed to turn up—there was a drought or fertilizers were high and ate up the profit or the price of cotton would drop. On and on, they moved, Narcissa each time gathering together the household goods, the chickens and cows, reckoning every three moves equal to a fire. Finally they came to the Bennett Plantation, settling in a long clapboard house in a stretch of bottom land, narrow and muddy, where the waters of Twelve Mile flowed into the Keowee to form the Seneca.

"Miles," said Narcissa, rebelling finally at their roving ways, "I'm never going to move again."

"All right," said Miles, "all right."

Already Miles had started drinking again, more and more he was living the free careless life that he always had preferred in his secret heart—was living less according to Narcissa's driving way. He raised hound dogs and hunted possums and rabbits and fished in the rivers and fiddled for square dances. Miles was happy.

Then came the accident that made him a cripple. Working one winter with the railroad section gang—one cold morning in the deep cut above Keowee Station, Miles was struck by a steel rail that fell from a hoist, a glancing blow. After the accident, he never again pretended even to look for regular employment; he hobbled about on a crutch and from then on, he frankly set out to enjoy himself. Narcissa took the indemnity money he received from the railroad and bought the house they lived in and four acres of land. And that became their compromise—Narcissa had the security she sought—she had land of her own, a home at last; Miles had a free way of life.

Alone most of the time after this, Narcissa often tramped the woods, beginning to find what rest she was ever to know in the contemplation of nature—in the exalted quiet of the vast silence about her, it brought her a measure of peace. And the sight of the looming mountains began to lift her inner senses—like the mountain rim and the worn valleys, she became quiet and calm, learning sympathy from solitude, learning not to fear defeat or sorrow. Defeat and sorrow were of the earth like her body. And her body was bound to this mute earth like the great mountains and the oaks. But her spirit was not bound. It soared through time and space, free as the wild wind and the sunshine. For her body she would accept a lifetime of work and hardship. But for her spirit..."No," she cried out to God. So as Narcissa lost hope for herself and Miles she began living again for her two children—Caline who was daring and undisciplined and Caldwell who was sensitive and withdrawn and was developing into another of the family's brooding dreamers.

Sometimes Narcissa turned to the past, not so much to grieve over lost glory, as to seek a lesson for the present. Often in her thought loomed the memory of the old woman for whom she was named—the old first Narcissa; she would say to herself that after living for eighty years her great-great-great-great-grandmother considered her entire life a failure, yet there at Forest Mansion was her tomb—a refuge for her descendants through two centuries, a place for them to retire to when they wanted to think. "So little," murmured Narcissa, "do we know of the value of our own lives—so few of us ever see our lives whole, lying dissociated, like a map behind us, like a field." This thought always gave her courage. Perhaps there was some reason even when no reason was evident.

And now like the first Narcissa, the fourth Narcissa turned to religion. She began to see herself also as a pilgrim on the way—on the journey through the troubled valley of this world, bound for the Kingdom of God—which was her true home, the place of final rest. All this about her would pass and she would stand before the right hand of the throne. She began to lift up her eyes to the hills—the Blue Ridge Mountains to which her mother and her grandmother and the grandmother of her grandmother had in their day lifted up their eyes when in trouble. For like God, the eternal mountains also gave strength. The mountains were ageless old to Narcissa; they had been, they were and they would be; in their serene strength they bound her both to the beginning and the end of time. And they were more than that to her—they were beyond even time, they were immortal.

჻

Watched also by Silas was this rim of mystic mountains that rose—a wall separating Carolina forever from the vast western refuge. Through all the years that Narcissa wandered from farm to farm seeking with Miles for that something that neither would ever find, Silas sat at Forest Mansion—in the deep chair on the porch behind the white columns in summer, beside a window and a fire in winter, and he gazed into the deep hills and the valleys within the valleys, his mind filled with worry and grief. Sometimes he listened to the harsh cry of the blue jays, sometimes to the catbird's call, and he saw the blossoms of the dogwood, the red judas tree bud and blossom and die, and he smelt the fragrance of muscadines and persimmons and the honey locust and the fuzzy pink mimosa. And it filled him with loneliness—he was a lonely man.

Often in the silences of the summer day and long winter nights Silas would think of Narcissa and he would wonder, sometimes wanting with all his soul to send for her to come home, to tell her he loved her, wanted her to visit him; but he never sent the word—something within him would not let him, his daughter had been willful, she had disobeyed. So instead of sending for Narcissa, Silas would send for old Nally the tenant, and instead of talking to his daughter about love he would talk to Nally about battles in Virginia and Tennessee—the memory of the Civil War became his escape.

"I'm a Jackson man, Mr. Nally—Lee was a great general, a very great general. But General Jackson was greater."

"Yes, sir," said Nally, sitting on the porch ledge, one foot on the ground.

"Jackson was a miracle man, a genius—Jackson understood human nature…Once Jackson whipped the Yankees with soldiers armed with nothing but sticks."

"Well, sir…well, I declare."

❧

When times began to change again and the people decided to draw up a new constitution for the State of South Carolina, the citizens in Keowee chose Silas as their representative in the constitutional convention, and once again a Caldwell was to find himself riding down through the red hills of the uplands to attend to public business in Columbia.

And down there in the marble halls of the war-marked Statehouse, inspired in the presence of the painting of old Senator Carter Caldwell, looking somberly down upon him, Silas felt a deep new feeling sweep over him. He awoke. Suddenly within him was revived in all its old vigor the vision of the frontier dream—the founding of a land where all should be equal and free. Rising unexpectedly, Silas began to speak. He lost all consciousness of those about him, forgot that he was not a public speaker; he began to pour forth a passionate appeal for more rights for the common man. He began to recite Carter's old speech—the address he had heard repeated at so many of the family reunions.

Breathing heavily, he pointed towards the country he came from, the uplands, the Piedmont region and the mountain rim; dramatically, he cried, "There it lies—the hope of the New World in that poor mountain country, in the hearts of the poor man, in his dreams. Idealism is still his goal and it must become ours again. We must plan for a better world."

So was the mountain voice of a Caldwell heard again in public debate in Columbia and the response to this speech astonished Silas. He was startled to find it had the same moving effect Carter's words had had in the same hall many years before. It established a reputation for Silas. It made the delegates from Charleston uneasy.

Late one night, a Charleston delegate arguing in the midst of a tense session said, "The gentlemanly way would be this…" Angrily, Silas interrupted, "Who gives a God damn about the gentlemanly way?" Pitching his great arms, he shouted, "God forbid that we in this country should ever become gentlemen…I hope the day never comes when anyone dare call me a gentleman…I'm no gentleman; I'm a plain man, a farmer…I'm rude and vigorous and free…" Silas glared. And across the aisle on the low country side the Ravenels and the Rhetts glared. But on Silas' own side, the O'Reillys and the McKays cheered and whistled and beat their workmen's hands.

Again were the men from the hills impressed with the words and the spirit of Silas. They held a meeting the next morning and on the next afternoon they sent a delegation to call on him. They sent the mayors of the three hill cities, Greenville, Spartanburg, and Anderson, to ask Silas if he would become the upcountry candidate for Governor of South Carolina.

"Captain Silas," said a gaunt, plain looking man—W. O. Jenkins, long the mayor of Greenville, "we've been bossed in this state for two centuries by those damned Charleston aristocrats—and two centuries is just two centuries too long. At last we've made up our minds to break for all time the hold Charleston has always had over the common citizens of this state. We've organized and we want you to head our ticket—you'll have every political organization in the up-country behind you."

Silas was astonished. "Why, W.O.," he stammered, "you'll have to let me think it over."

"Sure," said Mayor Jenkins, "think it over, Silas—take a week."

So in high excitement did Silas start that very evening for home; he wanted to walk in the burying ground before announcing his decision, sit on the porch at Forest Mansion, consult the valley mists, the mountain ranges. From Forest Mansion, he would issue a manifesto.

But changing trains that night in the station at Spartanburg, hurrying down a flight of great steps, Silas was struck down by a tired heart. An interne and three assistants from the city hospital brought him, a great hulk gravely ill, on to Forest Mansion slung in a heavy canvas stretcher. And from his bed there, Silas sent to Pendleton for his two closest friends, Colonel Simmons and Captain Billy Mann, to hurry to him. And when these two arrived he asked them to hold his hands for a minute. Then he began drawing up his will. He remembered the district school, the old stone meeting house, the Baptist orphanage, the Baptist board of foreign and home missions, the upcountry branch of the Democratic Party. All of his old feuds but one were forgotten. To his "dear and only son Lott" he left Forest Mansion and all other properties and possessions. He hesitated a moment, then spoke of "his willful and disobedient daughter Narcissa." To her nothing was to be left. "Nothing," said Silas, but as an afterthought he ordered Forest Mansion in proper time to provide for the higher education of her children.

He signed his name and a great stillness came over the old place. "I wait," said Silas, "to be gathered into the garner of God."

So Silas died and he was buried and a month afterward he was followed to the grave by Windy Bill, the last of the Caldwell slaves. A wild tail end of a tornado swept through Keowee Valley, dipping and twisting and filling the air with pieces of trees and houses and great stones and animals; it blew down Windy Bill's cabin and the chimney, flying into the air, fell on Bill. The family gathered for Bill's funeral and that was the last time but one that they ever gathered anywhere in such strength. For times already were changing in Carolina. They came once more to Forest Mansion a few years later to be present at the burying of the second Lott.

Chapter Twelve

Forest Mansion was an old house now—both the look and the feel of age were about it. The chrome rooster on the weather vane was worn and even the boxwood in the garden, an inch at a time, had grown old and unkept, the holly trees and the cedars were in need of pruning, and mosses hung from the wasted limbs of the old locusts that grew along the drive. Even the smells of the place by their survival suggested another time, another age—there were dry musty fragrances of sage and lavender bushes and the garden box. And the red terraced fields, planted for a hundred years in cotton, seemed as worn now as the mountains. Forest Mansion was the fathers' house, it had begun to stand as a symbol for the past.

The second Lott, fifth proprietor of the homestead, also stood for the past. His first act was to tear down the great piazza with the tall white columns that Silas his father had set up; Lott did not trim the dense hedges, but he restored Forest Mansion—he brought back the stern and simple lines of the frontier. This became the most absorbing interest of his life—the preservation of a time that had vanished. In the great central room, he even placed the furniture—the Connecticut clock with the engraved face, the drop-leaf table, the chair—exactly where they had stood in the time of his father's grandfather. He searched the first Silas' sketches to make certain.

This Lott was tall and handsome in a thin, wiry way—he had the blue eyes and the yellow hair of the four men who preceded him, and in other ways he was the son of the fathers; he was plain and simple in his manner but he lacked their rough readiness. He was gentle. When he went walking through the forests he liked to take his two small children—the last Stephen John of Forest Mansion and the last Lucinda—with him. Holding the boy by one hand, the girl by the other, he would talk to them endlessly of the days gone by; deliberately he turned their attention, after his, deep into the well of departed glory rather than into the bright southern sky. And all of the time he did this unconsciously. For he never once suspected that he was deliberately making his life into one long lament, a second-hand affair. No one ever told him he was. Many southerners were never told.

"Children," he said to them more than once, "gaze about you." And he would sweep one of his thin hands over the hills and the red fields. "Children, this is the land of the Caldwells and you are the Caldwells—before you are anything you are first Caldwells. Next you are Carolinians and after that you are citizens of the United States—it was we who gave our consent to the formation of the federal union. Never forget it." Another of his favorite sayings to them was, "By the grace of God, you had the honor to be born in South Carolina."

Sometimes Lott walked with these children among the Indian mounds on the hills to the south of Forest Mansion; he would tell them on these trips of the time DeSoto in his travels passed northward through Keowee Valley, and how in the bottomlands below those south hills, the Spaniard found Indians living in towns that were very old even then. On these walks, Lott completely forgot everything but the hills and the fields—he too reckoned his spirit as speeding backward in Keowee Valley through the Cherokees and the Creeks into the ancient mists of time.

Lott taught his boy and girl to admire the beauty of the flaming orange milkweed and the yellow butterflies and the song of the wood-thrush and the sight of the looming mountains. Also he was determined passionately that his children should acquire culture.

※

One afternoon on the small restored piazza, Lott was sitting. About him were a pile of books and papers, carefully writing... "Dear Cousin John, as you know I am compiling the genealogy of the Caldwells of the entire United States and I have learned that your great-grandfather was Benjamin Caldwell who married Frances Beeland and that they moved from Virginia to Walton, Ga., in 1804, but Benjamin's father is a blank—can you help me fill in this gap?"

The gathering of this vast and intricate family tree had become Lott's absorbing hobby. It took him back over the trail of the Caldwells from Pennsylvania, down the southern mountains to Keowee, and then westward all the way from Texas to Oregon and California. For the first time in half a century Forest Mansion was again in communication with far places. It gave Lott a great satisfaction to see the letters pouring into the house. He wrote hundreds of letters trying to complete his tree. He even wrote to the Caldwells of Texas.

People were always telling Lott if he kept delving into the past he would find some day that one of his ancestors was a horse thief and Lott would laugh, pretending it was very funny. But his faith in the Caldwell name was too great to be disturbed—he knew about Tobias Caldwell and the second Carter Caldwell, but somehow theft and even murder when committed by a Caldwell did not seem to him mere theft or the taking of a life. They all bore gleaming names in his anthology.

"...Dear Cousin Ella, I am trying to trace the family of Cousin Pisgah Caldwell after they left north Alabama for west Texas...any help you could give me would be appreciated...," Sealing this letter, Lott glanced away for a few moments, toward the distant ranges. Picking up another sheet of white paper, he turned again to his writing. "Dear Cousin Charlotte..." He had been writing for an hour when he was interrupted by a young woman who placed one of her hands lightly on his shoulder. This was Naomi, his wife; she was a granddaughter of the step-daughter of Carter Caldwell, the great-grandfather of Lott. Glancing up, smiling, Lott took the hand in his and for a moment there came over both their faces a deep solemnity. For both of them were thinking of the same thing—the dark shadow of death that hovered over Naomi. She was ill then of diabetes and any time her hour might arrive. Someday soon, she knew and Lott knew, she would fall into a coma from which there would be no rousing—for there was no escape in those days from diabetes. Lott took Naomi's hand and she smiled and kissed the top of his head.

"Dear Governor," wrote Lott, "as you know I am tracing the history of the Caldwells..."

There was the sound of the pen scratching the stiff paper. And in her bedroom, fallen on her knees, Naomi was fervently beginning a prayer, "God, allow me to live until my little children are old enough to remember me."

※

It was toward the end of that year that Lott visited New York. A generation had been born that had found in the original Carter Caldwell all that the frontier had stood for—the star of hope and the pillar of fire, the principles and the standards, the dream. Books were beginning to be written about his life and now a bronze statue was to be unveiled to him in New York at the Hall of Fame. Carter had become "Carter Caldwell—-the founder of the Tennessee."

Stephen John was to pull the cord at the unveiling ceremony, Lott to deliver an address. It was a great period of excitement for Lott. Naomi was unable to make the journey but Lott and young Stephen John went. And on a hillside in the Bronx, a crowd gathered, a band played and Stephen John gave a red silk rope a tug. And Lott spoke. Only instead of speaking about Carter, he talked about Clarissa. "None of those early Caldwells," he said, "would have been more surprised than Clarissa that Carter would be destined for fame." He said that Clarissa considered herself more practical than most of the Caldwells, the axe and the plow meant more to her than journeys over mountains; she never saw the white cloud that Carter saw, the mists, the wistfulness of beauty. "Clarissa never forgave Carter for the crops he left her to make. To the end he was a poor provider."

Lott's picture appeared in the newspapers—a thin man in a costume: a cocked hat, a powdered wig and colonial waistcoat and knee breeches. "A great-great-great nephew of Carter Caldwell," said the papers. It was the happiest day of Lott's life.

❧

So in a state of rapture, Lott returned southward, and not long after he decided to visit his sister Narcissa—he would tell her he was sorry for the wrongs he had done her, ask her to forgive him; he would tell Narcissa that she and he were all that was left of the numerous family of Forest Mansion—so why should they live in enmity. Was this not a feud between Narcissa and their father more than between himself and her? One morning very early he hitched the horses to the carriage and drove down through the red hills to the Twelve Mile bottoms. "A pleasant place," thought he, as he came upon Narcissa's house and saw the scrubby grove of pines and the sassafras and wild plums and the mimosa and hedges of red crepe myrtle and jessamine that all but engulfed it.

His heart pounded wildly within the walls of his ribs as his sister came to the door in answer to his knock. "Narcissa," he said, "I've come to ask you to forgive me for all I've done." He held out his hands—but Narcissa, with hate in her blue eyes, replied, "No." Lott pleaded but again and again Narcissa's answer was "No." She was defeated now and bitter about it. Sorrowfully, Lott climbed into the carriage and drove back toward Forest Mansion and, sorrowfully also, Narcissa climbed into a one-mule wagon and headed in the opposite direction—toward Jefferson to peddle butter and buttermilk and the produce of her garden. Late that afternoon, Lott sat on the porch at Forest Mansion, gloomy over his failure and dejected. Picking up a great sheet of paper he began to copy onto it a collateral branch of the genealogy on which he was busy, "Richard born 1682 married Sarah, John born 1684 married Martha…"

Returning homeward—a thin straight form under a canvas umbrella, Narcissa sat on the spring seat of the wagon saying to herself she had done wrong, she should have forgiven Lott, have asked him also to forgive her—she wanted to forgive him but she would not permit herself to. The past was too long and hard for her to forget. Again she said to herself, "No." He had never done anything to help her.

And as Narcissa urged the mule on, calling to it and hitting it a lick with a hickory switch, Miles was lying in the shade of a great wateroak tree, telling stories to a dozen

children. Still slightly crippled from the railroad accident, Miles mended chairs now whenever he felt like it and whenever he needed a little money, and sometimes he wove chair
bottoms and made fish traps. He picked tunes on a banjo box and fiddled. "Yes, sir," he
was saying, "the Indians gave out of tso-lungh." The group of children, all of whom knew
that tso-lungh was tobacco, listened in wonder. They came as often as they could to hunt
and fish with Miles and listened to his great stories. "The Indians knew that the country
where it grew best was located faraway on the great waters; also they knew that the gate-
way to that country was a mighty gorge guarded by a great army of spirits. But they must
somehow get some tso-lungh. So the Cherokees called a council. While discussing the
dangers of the journey a young man stepped forward. 'I will go,' said he, proudly. He left
and never came back. In great sorrow, the Cherokees called another council. Now a great
magician rose. 'I will go,' he said. And he turned himself into a mole and bored his way
into the fragrant country of the tso-lungh. But pursued by the spirits he had to flee. Next
he turned himself into a humming bird and again succeeded in entering the tso-lungh
country, but he was unable to bring much of the weed back with him—a humming bird
is so tiny. Flying home this time, he found a larger number of Cherokees on the point of
death on account of their yearning for a smoke. The magician, alarmed by this state of
affairs, placed a little of the precious tso-lungh in a pipe and blew gently upon the braves
and they soon recovered. 'I will try again,' said the desperate magician. This time he turned
himself into a great western whirlwind and swept through Hickory Nut Gorge, stripping
the mountains of vegetation and frightening all the guardian spirits. In this gorge, the
magician found the bones of many braves. Turning these bones into men, he returned to
the Cherokees with great loads of God's tobacco."

Miles laughed and the children, all delighted, clapped their hands. Miles laughed
again—a deep, long laugh. Narcissa heard this peal as she drove up into the yard and it
annoyed her. She said to herself, "Miles gets sorrier and more no account all the time."
Bitterly she admitted, "He'll never make anything of himself."

In the yellow garden at Forest Mansion, there was a song. It was Naomi, working
among the foxgloves, that sang.

PART THREE

The Americans

CHAPTER THIRTEEN

Miles was a great broad-shouldered lusty man, free from the complicated legacies woven through the generations of his wife's tormented family, and the strange characteristics of Caldwell Crossing, his son, caused him concern. Caldwell would not tramp the woods with the rowdy boys, nor would he listen to the stories that Miles told them, nor did he like to hunt. He sat on the porch talking to his mother and sometimes he played quiet games with his sister Caline, but most of his time was spent alone. This bothered Miles. Once when Caldwell was five years old Miles found him playing with an old rag doll, carrying it in his arms. "You're a big boy now," said Miles, laughing at the boy, "and big boys don't like dolls." Miles leaned over and taking the doll from Caldwell, he flung it into the fire, laughing and expecting his son to laugh also; but without moving or saying a word, Caldwell watched the flames; tears came into his eyes. Miles could not understand this, he was baffled.

And one day when Caldwell was about eight, Miles witnessed a scene that caused him poignant sorrow. He was cutting canes for fish poles in the thick canebrake on the east bank of Twelve Mile and he heard a group of boys' voices shouting "sissy." Pulling back the canes toward the outer edge of the brake, he was able to see what was going on—it was Caldwell who was being derided and the boys who were harassing him were the boys who often hunted with Miles and fished. This angered Miles and his first impulse was to rush out upon them, thrash them, but he changed his mind—it would do little good for him to force these boys to pattern their conduct toward Caldwell; a boy has his own hard way to make in the world, even one's own son—the force and the will must come from within. So Miles stayed where he was and listened. "Sissy," he heard. And he saw the boys grab Caldwell's hat and school books and throw them into a tree and he saw them throw Caldwell down and take off his shoes. Then Caldwell was struck in the face, all the boys laughing. This made Miles furious and then he became furious with his son. For Caldwell did nothing, he quietly allowed himself to be slapped.

Later that afternoon, coming upon his son at home, Miles started to sit down beside the boy and talk to him, but he did not. "What would be the use," Miles asked himself; he felt the contempt that some men have for those who will not strike back. So he was silent; and Caldwell retreated into the world of solitude—lying on rocks, Caldwell heard in the great orchestra of the wind the high note, the lonely song of the wood thrush, and he was filled with bitterness…O to retreat, to escape, to be able to run away!

To amuse himself, the boy began building secret cities—faraway in the fields and in the hidden thickets he plastered mud on stumps and laid out streets and set up government buildings and railway stations and hundreds of homes—all from sticks and mud and pieces of broken glass. In the largest of these cities, he built a temple to the sun, setting an altar before it, and here at sundown he would burn offerings of cotton soaked in oil. As the smoke rose, he would beat on a sheet of metal and chant a song. He surrounded these cities with walls and heavy forts, launched a fleet of a hundred barrel-stave ships for their protection. Then suddenly he would turn on these creations of his loneliness and patience. Standing away in a rage, he would shower his cities with rocks, bombarding them until all his palaces, congresses, courthouses and museums were in ruins. The sight of all this pillage and defeat would make him feel important and very happy.

And from the ruins he would presently build again—bigger and better cities. One day when Caldwell was about fifteen a whey-faced boy named Jimmy Thompson started a rumor that Caldwell was a "morphidite." He whispered the rumor about the schoolhouse in Jefferson.

"What is a morphidite?" asked Jack Hunter—one of the Hunter boys to whom no living Caldwell had ever spoken, for the Hunter-Caldwell feud was still in existence. Jimmy told him and this created a sensation among the boys at the school. Deciding they would know about that for themselves, they took Caldwell that afternoon into the woods and stripped him. Then feeling ashamed of themselves, they tied all Caldwell's clothes in knots and run away.

Sitting down on a pine log, naked, Caldwell considered his situation. Intelligent and self-taught to reflect deeply, he found suddenly springing into being within him the power and the will. Deliberately he decided he would change his character. "God," he said, "help me from now on to be like other boys—make other boys become my friends." Caldwell dressed himself and next morning he forced himself to ignore all the past. "Hi, Jimmy," he forced himself to shout at Jimmy Thompson, laughing at him, and Jimmy's face flushed crimson. That afternoon, Caldwell hit Jack Hunter in the eye when Jack slapped his cheek, and when his hat was snatched, he snatched another hat. He fought and came home bruised and beaten but he did not mind. Already he was beginning to learn. He hunted squirrels after that and went fishing, and one day he told the boys about his secret cities. He took them to his capital in a deep laurel thicket on the spring branch. "This is the great city of Alabu," he shouted, adding with pride, "and I'm the King of Alabu." Then he lit the oil-soaked cotton and beat on the metal and the boys thought the whole thing was wonderful.

He went to the swimming hole and was embarrassed, pulling off his clothing. But soon he found that the boys paid no attention to nakedness—Jimmy Thompson taught Caldwell to dive. He played football with them and baseball and felt fine.

And then all these things were changed again. The country went to war. One April morning, the teacher at Jefferson told them all they must remember that day—the United States had gone to war. Soon the drums were beating outside the school window and the flags began to fly and Caldwell remembered—the apple trees were blooming and the dogwood was white and a mocking bird was singing in the rain. And after the rain fell the sun shone. He looked into the west and closed his eyes, saying "I must remember." Before many weeks, heavy trains rolled day and night over the tracks that ran beside the school-house—toward the east, always toward the east, car after car filled with mules, cannon from the western forts, food and supplies, then soldiers began traveling on these trains—thousands of them from Mississippi and Louisiana and Texas, the great western plains, the far western mountains. On and on, filling the great south with their rumbling lonesome echo. And at the school and on Sunday at the church everyone began to sing "Keep the Home Fires Burning" and the great battle hymn of the republic.

And with his lusty voice Caldwell sang with them. "He has died to make men holy, let us die to make men free." Those words burned in his mind, burned and burned. And one evening when they were burning particularly deep and he was walking through the main street of Jefferson, he met a giant of a man, a recruiting sergeant.

"Hi, buddy," said the sergeant, stopping the boy under the oak tree in front of the bank. The man was friendly, greeted Caldwell as though he were a comrade in arms. "How old are you, friend?" asked he.

"I'm twenty-one," said Caldwell, looking the sergeant in the eye and trying to look four years older than he actually was.

"Fine," shouted the sergeant. And Caldwell joined the army.

He put on the khaki uniform and took the gun in his hands and his young heart throbbed within him—he was a man now, a man accepted by men as a man. He sat down to pour out his feelings in a letter to his mother. He was a soldier!

"A soldier," said Miles, reading this letter with pride. "Yes," said Narcissa, as proud of her son as Miles was.

The boy's letters began arriving regularly in the house in the Twelve Mile bottoms, almost daily they came, telling with glowing enthusiasm of the routines and duties and of the fine new friends. And after a time they began to come from more distant places, Newport News, then there was a break, followed by letters arriving in batches—from Europe. Sometimes brooding now and filled with deeper quiet, these later letters were more reflective…"the wind is fair and calm is the sea…dear mother, here is the beauty men have been trying since the beginning to describe, it is a fine thing to stand at the stern of a ship, watching the wake of a vessel vanish, vanish like our lives into the vastness…it is there and in a few minutes it is gone…dear mother, I have been to dreary, dismal St. Paul's, it is like a barn, so very bare…and I have been to St. Sepulchre's church to the tomb of Captain John Smith, he isn't the first American, I decided…if he were he wouldn't be over here…Worthy Master Hunt and those others at the ruins in Jamestown in Virginia, they are the first Americans…how surprised, mother…walking through London in the mist I came upon a fat figure on an iron horse and the words I saw were KING GEORGE III; I couldn't have been surprised more had they been Pontius Pilate or Judas, but I'm learning…Burgoyne and Cornwallis have statues in London and maybe somewhere if I get far enough I will come someday to statues to Pilate and Judas. I had thought in all the world that George III was a man without honor…Up early and off from Victoria Station to Canterbury to see the beautiful yellow cathedral with fine windows filled with stained glass…I came to a plain stone chair standing on stones before a great stained window—the chair in which all the heads of their church have been enthroned for a thousand years—since St. Augustine's time, and standing there I felt that through this rock flowed the spirit from Calvary and the Cross, straight from here across the Atlantic. I looked down the narrow aisles…it was the anniversary of the murder of blessed Saint Thomas à Becket. And in the evening I sat far in the back, in the dark, listening to the choir and the chanting of the mass, the organ pouring its divine song through the centuries of time…beautiful, it was beautiful…the deep purple and the green of the windows in the north transept built for pilgrims who could not read, telling them in great pictures the story. 'Pilgrims,' said the sign where Thomas was murdered, 'pray for peace.' And I prayed. The choir came down the steps as Thomas himself came that winter evening…when the sun was setting. They sang, 'Ah, St. Thomas, pity our helplessness, rule the strong and lift up the fallen…' the voices rose, 'pray for grace that we may be better men, guide our going in the way of peace!…Outside were the rooks, mother…and fog and feeble northern light, so far from our new world sun and so far from home…I am so far from home, mother…I think of you and the red fields and our cotton patches and the walks we used to take…I can see ourselves and the sun shining on us and in the west there rise the Blue Ridge Mountains…"

With these letters in her hands, Narcissa prayed. Three times every day she went to the high bluff over the river and among the strewed granite she would lift her eyes, interceding for Caldwell. But as time went on she seemed to sense something, there was the premonition, a feeling that became acute as the newspapers announced a concentration of American troops before St. Mihiel. The First Army of the United States, half a million young men, was moving into action under the command of General Pershing.

"At dawn after a heavy bombardment by a great mass of heavy artillery, the main attack jumped off, covered by a rolling barrage of artillery fire…"

"Oh, God," prayed Narcissa.

"…little resistance was encountered, the advance was rapid…the battle was characterized by the most intensive artillery bombardment and the largest concentration of air forces ever seen on the western front or in the world."

Narcissa could scarcely bear to read the blurred words. "Dear God," she prayed desperately.

"…losses were comparatively light…less than 7,000."

But among the seven thousand was Caldwell. There a few days later was his name in the casualty list. Narcissa saw it herself and dropped the paper; she screamed.

Chapter Fourteen

Slowly Narcissa had to rebuild for herself a new reason for living; she who first had lived for herself alone, then for herself and Miles, then for her children, had now to learn to live for the sake of living itself—to endure and if possible to enjoy the present time and the moment. Narcissa had learned the bitter lesson—the uselessness of resistance. So she said to herself: endure and obey, resign to the will of God...watch and admire and accept the blazing sun and the wild bees and the clean fragrance of the flowers and the wind and the cold richness of winter—work and offer prayers for mercifully no one must live forever. Narcissa began piecing a quilt from bits of rags and silk—the old design was her favorite, the wandering lonely Road to California. She stitched and one day, stitching, she thought how little does one know of a human being, how many are the things that a man tells no one, that he hides a lifetime in his heart and never breathes a word to a soul, how like a stone a man looks, his face like a slab of granite, his mouth saying words about the weather when within are the noblest thoughts of creation, a dream of eternity, a spirit without limit, a smothered and buried cry...

"God," she wove that day in red thread in one corner of this quilt. "Thou art God and Thou always hast been God and when this world is swept away still wilt Thou be God."

"In the end," she said, pushing the needle, "there is only the land, the warm, fine land—the fields about us and the seasons...and there is faith. And faith's way is the way." Narcissa had surrendered.

In time the government sent home the coffin of Caldwell, wrapped in a flag, and quietly and in private and at the wish of Narcissa, the boy was buried in the burying ground at Forest Mansion with Lott the first who died at Gettysburg and Richard who died at Chattanooga and Silas who died on Kings Mountain. And Narcissa Put up a stone:

> "Sacred to the Memory
> of
> Caldwell Crossing—Killed at
> St. Mihiel."

And in small letters at the bottom of the stone, she also had chipped: "King of Alabu."

Stephen John stood beside Narcissa at Caldwell's grave during the funeral service—Stephen John who was the last to bear that name at Forest Mansion. He placed on the red earth a wreath woven from the yellow flowers that still grew in the wild, unkept yellow garden. And when the benediction had been said, he turned to his aunt. Directly he said to her, "Aunt Narcissa, I want to go home with you." Violently Narcissa began to weep. She took his hand. "All right," she said.

So Stephen John drove that afternoon down through the hills to the house in the Twelve Mile bottoms. For two weeks he worked with Narcissa in her vegetable garden and rode in the wagon with her to Jefferson and he sang the old songs and talked and went swimming in Twelve Mile River.

Idly watching him, digging potatoes one day in the field below the house, Narcissa saw the boy suddenly halt for a time and standing erect stare away steadily, lost in contemplation of the range of misty mountains. And watching him, Narcissa sighed. For to her it was the sign—wandering and restless and searching and seeking for the way.

The boy turned again to his digging. But Narcissa brooded. He was so young.

⁂

Returning at the end of the fortnight to Forest Mansion, Stephen John plowed in the corn and cotton fields for the rest of that summer, working beside wide-eyed black Bubber Joe and powerful T.M., grandsons of Windy Bill. The sweat poured from his body, streaking his dusty face and his blue cotton shirt and yellow breeches.

"The monkey going to get you, Stevie," said Blubber Joe about once every hour, laughing at the sweat that rolled down the boy's strong face.

"Not me," said Stephen John, also laughing. He drank deep from the bucket when the waterboy came round and he plowed a straight furrow, and the feel of the wind was fine and he sang with the black boys—"I don't care where they bury my body, just so my soul's at rest," "I'm on my way to that land where I'm bound..." He and the black boys hunted the wild red foxes, riding mule back in the chase, and he hunted the red squirrels, trapped muskrats and polecats, studied the birds, learned the names of bloodroot and Indian pink and the robin plantain and anemone. Stephen John liked this wild free life—the cloudless skies with their stillness and the remoteness of the winds that blew from beyond the mountains and the wild ducks flying. But all the time Stephen John felt deep within himself that he was biding time, waiting to grow up, that on becoming a man he would move on, see for himself. For he sensed that the great current that once flowed so swiftly through Forest Mansion had moved on and he intended to find it, he intended from the beginning to live where the great river flowed fastest—he wanted to struggle in the fullest stream.

And it was not of the western distance that he dreamed. For times again had changed. He turned northward in his flights—to the steel towers of Manhattan. It was New York that rose at the end of his road. Always it was New York City.

⁂

One winter day Stephen John was sitting beside his father before the log fire in the central room at Forest Mansion. "Daddy," he said, seriously in a sudden burst of concern. "I want to learn—I want to become an educated man. I want to get the plainest, soundest education that any American boy can get."

"I'm glad to hear you say that," his father answered, quietly continuing to look in his lonesome and lost way into the firelight. Impulsively Stephen John grabbed his father's coatsleeve. "Daddy," he asked, "Can I go to Harvard?" The boy was afraid this request would take his father by great surprise—Harvard was so far away from the red hills and it would cost so much money to study there and it was northern—none of the Caldwells had ever gone there. But his father instead of showing surprise asked "Why do you wish to go particularly to Harvard?" and Stephen John replied, "I think it is the place for me to learn the things I want to learn."

This was one of the sadder moments in Lott's sad life. He continued to watch the fire. All his life he had tried to stop the flow of new forces about the homestead of the Caldwells but he had failed in this fight and he had just reached the mental state in which he was willing to face the facts and to admit his defeat.

For ten years he had opposed the tearing down of the old stone meeting house. "It's the pioneer church," he had cried out at meeting after meeting called by the old congregation. "It's our fathers' church—it's stood for everything the frontier ever stood for. For a century and a half our people have gathered in it on every great occasion—they came to the stone meeting house to pray before starting into the western wilderness, taxation without representation was discussed here, and here the Declaration and the federal constitution were considered. Our fathers met here to debate nullification and secession...my friends, we can't tear down this church, it's this country."

He had fought and fought and he had lost. "All that is the past," Lott had been told by young Charles McKay who announced the congregation's decision. "We can't live in the past. We've lived for too long already in the past—that's been one of the things that are wrong with us. What we want now is progress—we want it and we're going to have it." So the old stone church, soft in outline but enduring as the hills, had been torn down and in its place in the red cottonfields of Carolina had risen a gothic fane with vaulted Norman windows. Lott had shuddered.

His next battle had been to keep the old covered bridge that the Caldwells a hundred years before had built over Keowee from beams hewn by their own hands—a structure so strong that the storms of a century had not dislodged it. Lott had fought the tearing down of this bridge in every court and finally as a last resort had appealed personally to the Governor of the state. But again "progress" had won and he had lost. The state highway department had removed the bridge and over Keowee had built a soaring span of poured concrete, a structure as splendid as an arc of Georgian marble. It was beautiful, Lott had had to admit that, but so was the covered bridge beautiful, and it had been a landmark. And the red dusty road also had had to go. And with its going Forest Mansion had lost its old atmosphere of leisure, its quiet. For the old road had become a national highway, paved eighteen feet wide, its curves graded, and along it at high speed whirred the motor cars and trucks of forty states.

The church had been lost, the bridge had been lost. And lost was the great genealogy over which he had labored for so many years. There were so many gaps in it that he never would be able to fill. It had shocked Lott to realize that among the Caldwells even there had appeared a generation who did not know who was the father of their grandfather. They neither knew nor did they care. Many of them had not even answered his letters. Lost, lost.

Lost also were the lands—the fields about Forest Mansion, wasted and worn and unmended while Lott had pondered over the line of the family descent, had fought his battles to save the past. But this Lott would not admit—he said hard times had caused the decline of Forest Mansion, the low-price of cotton.

Of all these things he was thinking, sitting there before the great fire, when Stephen John so suddenly put to him his question. He startled the boy by the rapidity with which he gave his answer.

"Yes, son," said Lott, "you can go to Harvard."

"But the money—it costs a lot of money to go there," said the boy.

"We will raise the money," said Lott. And raise it he did. He sold the timberlands which originally had belonged to Carter Caldwell the first—the fine pines and the oaks and the hickory trees that the Caldwells had never cut. Stephen John was to grow many years older before he was to realize how revolutionary and catastrophic a decision that was for Lott to reach—a man who with all the intenseness of his nature worshipped the way of the past forced now to violate all the advice and tradition of a hundred and fifty years.

It was the bitterest day of Lott's life. But he did not hesitate. "I must equip Stephen John," he said, "for life in an era that has paved the road."

⚹

Tears came into Lott's eyes on the day that he drove silently down through the hills to the station at Jefferson where Stephen John was to board the northbound train.

"Son," he said, looking deeply into the boy's face as the two stood on the station platform, "Son, don't forget—you're the last of the Caldwells."

The boy laughed. "Sure," he said, "I won't forget." He spoke the words lightly.

"Well," said Lott, sadly, a resigned expression on his tried face, "remember also the words of Carter Caldwell—if you're going to dare at all, dare a lot; risk everything, be willing to take all the chances."

Stephen John smiled, he shook his father's hand. Quickly and with boundless joy he swung aboard the long, green, southern train.

⚹

And Lott was lonelier than ever, for Stephen John never after that spent much of his time at Forest Mansion; his was the passion for travel. During his first college vacation, he shipped to sea from Boston, signing on a cattleship as a deckhand. Through the second vacation he followed the reaping machines northward over the immense wheatfields of Kansas, sweating under the intense blaze of the prairie sun, feeling for the first time in his life the feeling the westerner never loses—the great sense of inland continental security, a thousand miles of America stretching from him before reaching any sea. He picked prunes in the great valleys of Oregon, walked in the rain forests through the deep filtered lights that seep downward through those gigantic treetops. Sometimes on his journeys, he thought of the old days when the country was young, he thought of the frontier, the pioneers, living their hard full lives. Sometimes lying in soft berths on trans-continental trains, he visioned the pioneers, on horseback, in wagons, the great procession.

Fathers of the fathers, moving on, restless of the earth. Fathers of the fathers who never turned back, travelers upon the long, lonely desolate journey, moving through the far past. Elemental in their qualities, belonging among the strong, the eternally lonely. They raised their voices in the darkness, cried out in their solitude. But they kept on. It was the place beyond the place that they sought, the valley wider than secrets of sorrow where at last there would be no restlessness, only stillness and peace.

They moved on, continentals from the beginning, equipped for distance, for living in great territories, their clothing tough and rough, hob nails in their boots—strong leather, shining and waxed. Fine to them was the feel of good leather and coarse good cloth, they loved it better than silk, beauty was in that very roughness. So was beauty in the catbird's song, the hawk's flight, the glowing trunk of the sycamore tree bare in the winter. Far away in the wilderness, they created their own beauty—in lonely hearts, from plowing great red fields, from feeding pigs and cattle, from standing on the far rims of mountains, looking, seeing far, miles away a lone house, a tree, a duck flying—the lonely road always theirs, the high trail; brooding loneliness crept even into their ballads and their poems, the wailing note was their cry, their lament, always has it lived in the depth of the New World soul.

And always there ran the road, winding, and in their ears was the sound of swift water flowing and in their hearts was the faith, and in their eyes the vision of the future, vast, swept by the forces. So, on they went, ravaged but still believing, their souls lying like the great fields, unprotected, eroding, melting away but they never turned, on and on—the procession. A strange race, dissatisfied, never quiet—but looking and searching, seeking always for a way. "It must be found; God, let us find it."

Over a great land…a lone American man and an American woman, tramping alone, looking at a swollen river, watching a sunset from a hill, listening to the swaying sound of sweet gum leaves, a hard rattle, a cold wind. Like the stars and the cross…high was it all and faraway.

Three times in those years Stephen John crossed the United States in model Ts, camping out, sleeping in tourist camps. He saw roaring Niagara and the Grand Canyon of Arizona, and once he stood for a long time watching the Mississippi River, thinking of Lafayette Caldwell and the way he had spent his days on the Mississippi. At Gettysburg he walked among wild onions and daisies along the ridge where Lott had died and at the battle monument on the saddletop of Kings Mountain he stopped once to read Silas' name. In prairie Texas, that somber land, he visited Two Tree and Honey Springs and one time in San Francisco he walked along the cliff where Silas had walked. He stopped among the rocks, gazed into the Pacific, held rapt by a shining sun and a wild wind that whipped the waves into frothiness. And above him circled a fleet of gulls, mottled, crying like hawks. He gazed long and long—at the end of a road.

Stephen John was stirred to his deepest depth by the sight of the Pacific Ocean beating so ceaselessly upon the Californian rocks. The infinite swelling of that sea quieted him, the still voice within him began to speak—to clarify great issues to him, to define himself to himself.

Who am I, asked the voice? What am I? And then it asked Stephen John, am I grieving over things past, am I beginning to live in the long ago? Never in his life had Stephen John been so shocked. For he realized that losing himself in the past was exactly what he was about to do—it was the unconscious southerner in him, the latter-day Carolinian, the influence on even an upcountryman, finally, of the old poison of Charleston. And he realized this was not his intention at all, it never had been—he did not regret the passing of the old days, it was the present that concerned him, the living of a life. Old Carter and old Silas and old Stephen John and Narcissa—they had lived lives in a great way and, by God, he was going to live his.

And then the voice asked him, what do I think of the past? And Stephen John began to search for a reply. Why, the past, said he—it means a secret obligation and a responsibility to me, it is my inspiration, I must stand as firm for the revolutionary principles and standards in my time as Carter and Silas stood for them in theirs; I must be as ready as they were for emergency, must renew myself as they did, find strength and new strength, be willing and glad to change as times change—take a part myself in forcing change.

And then the voice asked Stephen John what do I think of my name? Stephen John saw instantly the necessity of forming an immediate answer to that question. And in drawing up his reply, he found himself going beyond the southerners, he went back to the frontier to one of the speeches of Senator Carter, from out of the past that lived there came to him the words: "Family pride is as good and useful a motive controlling the acts and lives of men as it is ridiculous when constituting their stock in trade; to wear an honored name worthily or to illustrate the good lineage a man comes from is a splendid ambition, but to base a claim for consideration of favors on an accident of birth is opposed to American tendencies and the spirit of our institutions." Suddenly Stephen John said to the voice within himself, "I am a Caldwell, and I am proud I am a Caldwell, it is an inspiration to put my name among the other names; but also I am not one whit different from the last Polish peasant who has come to the United States and I am proud I am not one whit different."

With that a great satisfaction welled into Stephen John; he turned his back on the Pacific Ocean—it was a symbol, he faced the east and after that the east was to him the future.

Finally when his college education had been acquired, Stephen John found a job in a law office on the fortieth floor of a New York skyscraper, a great mass of stone and steel, stern and austere. The wide windows of his office looked down upon the spire of Trinity Church and in Trinity Churchyard he could see, a marble speck, the tomb of Alexander Hamilton. Always the sight of this tomb would rouse the ire of the frontiersman that was in Stephen John. Once looking down on this tomb in the churchyard at the head of Wall Street, he said aloud scornfully. "It is where it belongs." And at once he began to think of Thomas Jefferson who lay buried far away in the heart of a continent on the top of a mountain with vast valleys and mountains stretching away into distance, with winds blowing and a feeling that the air was free. "I believe in Jefferson," said Stephen John, "and rowdy Andrew Jackson and the working man and the boisterous Democratic Party." And that day he felt that he should leave this law office in a high tower in a city, he should go back to the worn cotton fields and do something about the upcountry—it was home and always had been home, it always would be home. It needed him. Often did he have such thoughts. But also there were other thoughts. Another part of him always replied "Why should you go back, what for?"

Death decided this issue for him. His father died. A telegram came, calling him back to Forest Mansion.

And again there rose before Stephen John the procession.

Riding southward, through Philadelphia and gleaming Washington, covered with rain, and on through still Manassas, deep in sleep, and through Charlottesville, still the shrine of all he stood for, Stephen John thought of the long line that had gone before him over this same great roadway—the great procession, dreaming of a land without a king and a church without a bishop, facing the wilderness and the solitude, the immense loneliness, and there rose out of the night the cry and the tornado and the flood and still there lived the dream; he thought of old Narcissa and of Silas planning the house and Carter building the house; and there was the house itself, stern and austere, filled with the things they had made, the chairs, the tables, the beamed ceilings, the portraits of Senator Carter, Congressman Stephen John,

Caline the first, the second Unity, and there were the marble mantles from Carrara, the Confederate flag hung on the wall by the fourth Silas. He ought to stay.

He thought of his lonesome grieving father and his mother who had died before he was old enough to remember, and he thought of the cotton fields and the red hills. He ought to stay. Time told him so, tradition told him, so did a part of his spirit.

Of all these things he thought. Also he thought of the span of concrete over Keowee and of the paved road, the long strip of cement that was a road and more than a road. He thought of that stretch of Carolina highway, lying like a ribbon over the hills, and it moved on, and moving on it took him with it. He thought of the rocks of Gloucester and the maritime streets of Salem and wild desolate Montauk and Fire Island and there also was the paved road, and Annapolis rose in his memory, simple and heartily provincial, and so rose the marble capitol in Washington and the high plateaus of New Mexico, the roaring Kootenai River, the great curved bay at Monterey.

Boston, the Kansas wheatfields, Oregon.

The great green train blew its whistle, the lonely sound echoing through the miles of mountain Virginia, and lying aboard it, wrapped in a brown blanket in a pullman, was Stephen John at his crisis.

"Danville," he heard a muffled voice saying, the train was stopping. And he turned over and slept, he had reached his decision.

A few hours after reaching Forest Mansion, Stephen John drove to Twelve Mile bottoms to ask Narcissa for his sake to attend the funeral. And when she had agreed, he said to her quietly, "Aunt Narcissa, we're not going to bury father at the burying ground at home."

"Why not," said Narcissa, startled.

"Well," said Stephen John, "it won't be long now before family burying grounds will be a thing of the past—with the roads paved and everybody scattering it won't be long before family graveyards will be forgotten and neglected. We're going to hold the funeral from the stone meeting house and bury him in the churchyard."

So, covered with a blanket of cape jessamines from the old gardens of Forest Mansion, Lott was carried into the new gothic church and choir investments tried to chant Gregorian music. They did not wish to sing the old-fashioned hymns the Caldwells always had sung but Stephen John insisted—he had the hymns lined as in former days when there was only one hymn book in the congregation and when, also, there were Caldwells who could not read. The hymns were lined and sung line by line: "Abide with me," "Lead kindly light."

And as the coffin was wheeled away, the shuddering organ sounded the favorite song of a hundred years of evangelical Caldwells:

> "I'm a pilgrim and I'm a stranger,
> I can tarry—I can tarry but a night."

And the hard red clay fell into the deep grave and the Caldwells drove away in their automobiles, and as they departed there was still the thundering music pouring from the pipes.

"Going home, going home."

❧

Rolling north that evening through the red upcountry hills, moving through the cotton fields, sped a long green southern train, the Piedmont-Limited, bound from New Orleans, Birmingham and Atlanta for Washington, Baltimore, Philadelphia and New York. Aboard, looking through a window at the worn southern lands, red gullies and patches of splendid pines were the last Stephen John and the last Lucinda, children of Lott, grandchildren of Silas, great-grandchildren of Stephen John, great-great-grandchildren of Carter, great-great-great-grandchildren of Silas, great-great-great-great-grandchildren of Carter, great-great-great-great-great-grandchildren of Stephen John and old Narcissa, great-great-great-great-great-great-grandchildren of Charles Carter Caldwell of Pennsylvania. Also traveling with them was young Aurora, daughter of Azalee, granddaughter of Dazarene, great-granddaughter of Ninny, great-great-granddaughter of Queen Elizabeth.

"Hot ziggidy damn," said Aurora as the train pulled out of the station in Charlotte, "I'm heading for Harlem."

A few days later in the Bronx, these three, Stephen John, Lucinda, and Aurora, stood in the high colonnade at the Hall of Fame. Silently they put three sprigs of green leaves at the feet of Carter Caldwell, founder of the Tennessee. They stood there staring long over the northern rocks of Manhattan, looking toward the basalt palisades and New Jersey.

"We must make something of ourselves," said Stephen John, earnestly, passionately. "We must be somebody."

❧

At the same time that they were standing there—faraway at the house in Twelve Mile bottoms, Narcissa was reading in "The Greenville Piedmont" the news that Forest Mansion, the home of the Caldwell family for generations and one of the great houses of upper Carolina, was to be sold at public auction. With tears dulling her eyesight, she was learning for the first time that Stephen John Caldwell of New York, the heir, had found himself unable because of his work to make his residence at the old homestead, and being himself unable to be there was unwilling to keep the place as an absentee landlord.

"On Friday next the sale will be held…"

Narcissa could read no further. A great feeling of despair swept over her—it was as though someone else close to her had died and gone on, and she began to weep for Forest Mansion as she would have wept for any of the Caldwells.

But Narcissa had little time for this grief. She had the present to consider. It was immediate for Miles had suddenly changed his way of living. He had become another man. Bald-headed now and almost without teeth, still crippled, he had quit mending chairs, wove no more fish traps, he no longer bothered to fish. Miles was seldom at home any more, often he came and went in darkness, sometimes he would stay away two or even three days without sending Narcissa any word, sometimes he arrived home in almost a drunken stupor.

This new Miles frightened the children, who for so long had been his friends; they no longer came to see him and in their place there came now a lot of wild men and women, all of the volatile riffraff of the county—old Ira Jackson, who drank heavily and whipped his wife; Tom Smith, a half-witted shoemaker's helper who once had raped a colored girl;

Democrat Griffin who did nothing, lived off his wife—and there were factory hands and Negro hands with chaingang records. Then early one morning Lizzie Springs added herself to this list—she was Jefferson's prostitute, a beautiful sort of charmed profligate whom men could not leave alone. She came into the yard in a thin yellow dress, so long it touched the dirt, carrying over herself a red parasol, and there were splotches of red powder on both sides of her pale face.

"Miss Narcissa," said Lizzie, embarrassed, "please, ma'am, could I speak just a minute to Mister Miles."

Angrily Narcissa shouted, "You get away from here and you stay away—you hear me." Narcissa slammed the door in the woman's face and this riled Lizzie's temper. "I'm trying my best to be polite," said Lizzie. "Get away," shouted Narcissa.

Thoroughly aroused now, Lizzie said, "With a husband as low down and good for nothing as that man of yours, Miss Narcissa, I'd advise you to hop down off your God damn high horse." There was no reply to this. So Lizzie threw a chair against the closed door, knocked a flower pot off the steps. "Tell him when he comes Lizzie Springs said for him to see her before night—or else." Lizzie turned over a chair and went away.

Inside the house, Narcissa lay on the bed, crying. "Things can't go on like this any longer," she said to herself. "Miles and I will have to have it out." In the clean, scrubbed kitchen, Narcissa after a time poured a little coffee into a blue cup but she did not drink it, she sat by the window, the cup in her hand until the coffee was quite cold. When the old clock on the mantle hammered eight, she rose quickly, gathered an armload of dirty clothing, started down the hill toward the spring branch. She stalked through the woods without once shifting the bundle off her bony hip, she moved on rapidly, walking like a man. There was now a mole on Narcissa's nose, a bruised vein lay like a red fan on her right cheek, gold hoops hung in her ears. She was so bony lank and cadaverous that her body resembled hickory poles in a dress.

The path led through a thicket where scrubby blackgum and blackberry briars grew. At the foot of the little hill, at the spring, Narcissa dropped the clothes on the dry leaves and from the force of years' habit, pulled open the creaky door of the low log springhouse to see that the milk buckets were weighted properly in the cool pool of water. Scooping up a little of the water in her thin hands, she poured it over her brown face; then swinging the clothes over a shoulder, she walked to the wash place. It was not far from the big road; it stood among some tall sycamores near the junction of the spring branch with the river.

Narcissa had been washing hard for an hour when down the red road astride a half-starved mule came Democrat Griffin, slump-shouldered, a weaseled man with a stubble beard. A frazzled straw hat with a shoestring band was on the back of his head, his old shirt was blue, his breeches a beautiful, faded deeper blue.

"Miss Narcissa, ma'am, howdy," said Democrat.

Narcissa despised Democrat, not only because of the way he treated his wife, but also because he drank and gambled—she hated drinking and gambling. The only crop he took the least interest in growing was watermelons, he could not grow a bale of cotton on four acres, he was that trifling—Narcissa also hated him because of that.

Narcissa said, "Good morning."

"How you, ma'am?" inquired Democrat, dropping the rope reins, worn out plow lines.

"Oh," said Narcissa, indifferently and continuing to wash, "I'm mortal tired." She wrung soapy suds from a tablecloth.

"Where is Miles this morning, Miss Narcissa?" asked Democrat, cautiously.

"What do you want to know for?" said Narcissa, blazing with fury.

"No reason in particular," said Democrat quickly. "Just happened to be passing—I'm on my way to cut a load of canes for bean poles and I allowed as long as I was in the neighborhood I'd pass the time of day."

"Well," said Narcissa, positively and sternly, "Miles isn't here."

"No harm done," said Democrat. He clucked to the mule and casually, without moving a muscle, Democrat jogged on. He had never cut a load of canes in his life and Narcissa knew it. The clatter of mule hooves came from the loose board bridge.

Narcissa filled a tub with cold, clear branch water; turned it brilliant blue with three pinches of bluing. The sultry sun was rising high, a bumble bee buzzed, symbol of all those long summer days of drowsiness to Narcissa. She began rinsing.

She waited for Miles through the afternoon, a sleepy day; she sat on the piazza which was long and wide; there were clematis vines and morning glories, fragile extravagant flowers now drooping, which shut out the quivering glare. Sundown came, then night and on the piazza, her long legs crossed, still Narcissa waited. It was another of those deep southern summer nights, streaked with the smell of the earth, with heat lightning; the air lay heavily over the cotton fields, and north and south the trains sped, whistling long and weirdly—a sign of rain. The town clock at Jefferson had struck eleven, a muffled slow echo, before there was another clatter of hooves on the Twelve Mile bridge, followed by a rumble of wagon wheels.

Narcissa heard "whoa" spoken softly, a crunching sound on gravel, a mule stopping. She heard Miles drinking from the gourd at the well, the light from the lantern making him a mile long in the shadows; at the steps she saw him slip off his shoes; then he saw Narcissa.

"What you're doing still up?" he said, annoyance in his voice.

Excited and uneasy, Narcissa put her hands to her throat. "You've got to quit it, Miles," she said hysterically. "It's not honorable, it's not right—it's against the will of God."

Miles said quietly, "Those are strong words, Narcissa—against the will of God."

Narcissa began to weep.

Annoyed still more, Miles pulled up a chair and sat down. "For the hundredth time let me try to explain my side," he said, patiently, slowly. "My folks have always made liquor, Narcissa—for a hundred years they always made whiskey and they made good whiskey, the best corn liquor in this country—they were proud of it. They hauled it all the way to Augusta in bullock carts in the old days and nobody ever accused them then of doing anything wrong..."

"Times have changed," said Narcissa, imperiously positive.

"Not for me," immediately replied Miles. "No, by God—not for me."

There's a law against it now—you're breaking the law. You've got that to consider."

Miles groaned. Narcissa stood up. "I'll give you just six hours," she said, "to make up your mind whether you're going to quit this moonshine business or whether you aren't going to quit it." Walking into the house, Narcissa slammed the door.

Miles went around to the back. In the kitchen, he ate some bread and molasses. He raised the liquor jug high also and drank. Then he fell into bed and slept.

❧

It was sunup and across the yard to the barn came Narcissa, a red hat, a light shawl in her hands. Miles was hitching Big Nell, the mule, to a wagon.

"Well," said Narcissa.

"Narcissa," said Miles, gloomily, continuing to work with the harness. "Narcissa, I can't give it up—I got the chance of my life to make a pile of money and I'm going to make it."

"All right," said Narcissa. She put the hat on her head, wrapped the shawl over her shoulders. "All right."

"What are you going to do, mother," said Miles, curiously, looking at his wife.

"I'm going to do my duty," she said, "I'm going to Jefferson and I'm going to tell the U. S. marshal my husband is running a still."

Miles leaned over, looked directly into his wife's blue Caldwell eyes. He kissed her suddenly on the forehead. "Just tell him it's in the Long Cove a little above the place where the ivy grows down to the edge of Visages Creek—me and Democrat Griffin will be there all day."

Miles climbed into the wagon, called to Big Nell and drove away, not looking back once. Narcissa reached for the stable door to steady herself, her head dropped forward, there she stood until the wagon had rattled over the bridge. Then slowly she returned to the house. The hat and shawl were pitched on a table. Narcissa sat down, again she began to cry.

She saw little of Miles during the weeks that followed, often Miles slept at night at Democrat's house; there were great rows when he did appear. Narcissa nagged and denounced him, she wept. Miles drank all the harder, bought her a blue silk dress which she flung out a window, bought her a set of china with red rosebuds. Narcissa sent the dishes back to the store.

One morning she was sitting in the kitchen, churning, when she heard sharp, staccato raps on the front door and going to answer the summons was faced by Miss Mary Belle McCord, now very old but still a power of energy, fat Mrs. Joe Wade, president of the ladies' missionary union of Jefferson, the weak Widow Adams, an asthma sufferer, and Lily Mae Sanders, chairman of the Jefferson ladies' committee for the Enforcement of the Eighteenth Amendment.

"Why, good morning, ladies," said Narcissa, wiping her long hands on her brown checkered apron, "you all have seats."

"Yes, all right—we'll sit down," said Lily Mae, at first a little undecided; she cleared her throat.

"We have come here, Miss Narcissa," said she, "about a serious matter. Sister Crossing, we don't want you to take personal offense at what we feel like we're obliged to say." Lillie Mae, nervous, opened and shut the clasp of an alligator hide purse that was in her lap; she was conscious of the intent eyes of all the women upon her.

"We want you to know the purpose of our visit grieves us as much as it surely must grieve you—also we want you to understand we have come only as a last resort—Sister Crossing, duty has brought us here this morning."

Standing in the doorway, still rubbing her clean red hands, Narcissa listened. Suddenly, dramatically, she saw the lines of Lillie Mae's face drawing hard. She heard Lillie Mae saying, "Miles is making liquor and we all know it. Well, us women won't stand for it in this community—not from nobody, not for one minute."

Up glanced the eyes of Miss Mary Belle curious to note how Narcissa was bearing the blow; she saw all the color except the red in the crushed vein flow away from Narcissa's troubled face. Narcissa looked very old and tired, she put a hand over her eyes.

"We can't have mercy, Sister Crossing, for those who break the Eighteenth Amendment in this country—so we've come here this morning, an official committee, to tell you if Miles hasn't quit this business within twenty-four hours, we're going to take things in our own capable hands."

The women stood, all rising together. "This is a warning," said Lillie Mae. Quickly the four walked away.

The light morning air echoed the wild quit-quequeeo of a warbler, a solitary vireo sang, its voice like a pipe, a weak reed, and in the yard the fragrant cape jesamine, rotten flowers of death, were that day bursting into full blossom; there was the sad wood thrush, the full vermilion cardinal, the lustrous blue peacocks—Oh, remoteness and sorrow, said Narcissa—stretching on and on through the years, the loneliness and defeat.

"Living is so bitter."

It was dark, a moonless night. Staggering drunk, Miles fell upon the bed.

"Why, hell, Narcissa," he said, thickly, unevenly, "Your own folks have distilled liquor in their day."

"The Caldwells never sold it and you know it," said Narcissa, coldly and furiously angry and severe.

Suddenly Miles could stand this no longer, all the troubles of a lifetime, roaring, burst like a tornado into his senseless memory; with an effort he raised himself on an elbow. "God damn the Caldwells," he shouted, wild, with all the intense feeling of his being. Over and over he repeated the curse.

Narcissa reached for the red hat and the light shawl. "This time," she said, "I mean it." She hurried from the house. And stumbling, fumbling his way along the dark wall, Miles reached upward with his long, sure mountain fingers; he was groping for the shotgun.

So for the time being an end came to the fable of the Caldwells in Keowee valley. Under the intense light of their own sun, they had vanished momentarily like the wild winds that blew among the tombs where, white ones and black, they lay buried on a hilltop that the Cherokees before them had used as a burying place for the dead.

They had disappeared from Keowee but in other places there were Caldwells.

And there was their living spirit. On the day that Narcissa was making her last decision, the old weathervane of Forest Mansion was attracting attention in New York City. Silas' carved and chromed rooster, which like Narcissa's sugar bowl had survived wars and the hazards, and had been placed on exhibition at a great show of American native art and folk sculpture. With its long flowing tail and long spurs, all re-colored with new chrome and ochre, there it stood in the center of an immense room preserved like some costly treasure under a case of glass. And on its mahogany stand, inscribed, was "Formal rooster carved by Silas Caldwell of Carolina, brother of the famous Carter Caldwell—this weather vane with its superb restraint and severity equals anything we have produced in American sculpture; it is an important product of the American mind in the making."

Forest Mansion's weathervane had been loaned to the museum by Stephen John, but on the afternoon that the exhibition was opened Stephen John was not present. It was a fashionable event and Stephen John did not take part in fashionable events. On that afternoon he had turned his broad back on the crowds and steel spires and towers for the wild desolation of Montauk. Among the bleak moors, among the gorse and struggling salt-sprayed oaks, he was staring out over the brittle green Atlantic—into bright sparkling water. And staring, silent he was not conscious at all of an ocean. Before him were steep red hillsides, a far range of granite mountains; he was thinking of cotton, bursting white over miles of upcountry lands…of still autumn sunshine, southern sunshine, and great pillows of cloud in deep blue sky. In his mind the narrow leaves of sourwood trees and dogwood were turning crimson, hickories were blazing yellow, and above them all loomed pines… red on yellow on green on white on blue…and a swift river flowed and wild ducks flew, a catbird called, a thrush fluted its quiet song…

Stephen John muttered to himself. "A man," he said unconsciously, "ought to have himself a piece of land—a man ought to be all right if he had some land to go to."

Suddenly dashing down a sand dune, Stephen John overcame this mood. Undressing quickly, he ran across a narrow strip of wet sand and dove into the chilly sea. Fiercely, arm over arm, he swam outward—a long way, moving with strength and endurance. He turned swiftly, shouted a wild shout; then he started toward the shore.

1. "Gneiss" (p. 2). Gneiss is a banded or foliated rock, usually of the same appearance and composition as granite.
2. "A wild flower in Keowee like fire" (p. 5). This wildflower is most likely one called Fire Pink and is common to the area; it is actually a brilliant red in color.
3. "pennyroyal" (p. 8). Pennyroyal is a perennial belonging to the mint family and is said to be one of the plants the Pilgrims introduced to North America Its pale purple flowers are set in whorls. Like most of its near relatives, Pennyroyal is highly aromatic but its flavor is more pungent and acrid than Spearmint or Peppermint. Pliny named it Pulegium for its reputed power to repel fleas and mosquitoes. It was also used in ancient times to terminate unwanted pregnancies, a use still noted by Nicolas Culpeper in his famous *Culpeper's Color Herbal.* There he notes, "The herb, boiled and drank, provokes women's courses and expels the dead child and afterbirth. If taken in water and vinegar mingled together, it stays the disposition to vomit. Mingled with honey and salt, it voids phlegm out of the lungs and purges by stool. Applied to the nostrils with vinegar, it revives those who faint and swoon." He also noted that crushed and put into vinegar it was good for cleansing "foul ulcers and takes away the marks of bruises and blows about the eyes and burns in the face" and was "an excellent remedy for flatulence and colicky pains in the abdomen." While its use in cooking fell into disuse, its medicinal and household uses continued and early settlers in colonial Virginia used dried pennyroyal to eradicate pests. Pennyroyal's essential oil is now considered highly toxic to both humans and animals.
4. Narcissa's dyes (p. 11). Narcissa's dye book, written in "her wavering handwriting," contains such secrets as: "Blue-derived from the inner bank of the ash tree; yellow very pale-from the root of the nettle; yellow beautiful and deep—from yellow root; red-from the bastard saffron blossom, from the juice of nightshades, from poke boiled in rainwater and set with alum." Stinging nettles are boiled and used as dyes; bastard saffron blossom refers to the wild crocus blossoms; the nightshade is an annual plant growing about a foot and with broad pointed leaves and white flowers followed by greenish berries which go black as they ripen, hence their name; and poke refers to the berries of the pokeweed plant native to eastern United States.
5. "Cibola" (p. 13). Noting Carter's decision to lead the Caldwells to new land, Robertson describes Carter's state of mind: "Gradually he drifted in the spacelessness of the mind into regions far beyond Keowee; he saw himself crossing mountains, coming to a long sloping land of plains, watered by rivers flowing west, always west; finally he came himself in that distant land, beyond the plains and the canyons, to the very walls of Cibola itself, the golden cities of Cibola. He dreamed." Cibola refers to one of the legendary Seven Cities of Gold the Spanish Conquistadors heard stories of from natives.
6. "the leather-bound Shakespeare book" (p. 13). The book has not been identified but its proud possession confirms the Caldwell family's dedication to learning.
7. "There were tracks of swamp animals in the narrow pathway which curve among dark-growing briars and elder bushes, the tangled vines of the bitter foxgrapes. Later Carter led them onto higher ground into a white drift of plum trees, all

in a burst of blossom, among budding dogwood and yellow jasmine and jewel weed and Indian pipes and turnips" (p. 14). This passage is typical of Robertson's knowledge of the region's flora and fauna. *Elder bushes* are the elder or elderberry, a flowering plant cultivated for its ornamental leaves, flowers, and fruit. The fruit or berries have medicinal uses and from which a familiar wine is produced. *Bitter foxgrapes* are one of many grape cultivars, including Catawba and Concord, native to eastern North America from which wine is made. In contrast to the European variety is the characteristic "foxy" musk of the grape though despite its name it has nothing to do with the fox. *The white drift of plum trees* indicates the plum tree's abundant white flowers. *Budding dogwood* refers to the dogwood trees native to the American South from Virginia southward, and *yellow jasmine*, sometimes called Carolina Jessamine and the state flower of South Carolina, is a yellow flowering vine that grows in the woodlands of the South, all parts of which are poisonous so it has no medicinal uses, though historically it is said to have been used as a topical to treat skin eruptions and measles, tonsillitis, rheumatism, and headaches. *Jewel weed* is a wild plant widely used for skin irritations. The plant's delicate, long oval stalked leaves end with a few rounded teeth; the upper leaves are alternate, the lower ones opposite are water-repellant, so they look like they're covered with tiny jewels after it rains. Native Americans used it to treat poison ivy and other rashes. *Indian pipes*, also known as ghost plant or corpse plant, are so named because, lacking chloroform, they have a ghost-like appearance. They grow in shady woods and are often found near dead stumps which provide them with nourishment. Native Americans used the plant's stem juices in the preparation of a treatment for sore or inflamed eyes, as a topical ointment for warts and bunions, and for aches and pains. Early colonists adopted these uses and extended them to the use of the powdered root of the plant in the treatment of a number of ailments, particularly as a sedative for a nervous or restless condition.

8. "Milkweed" (p. 15). Common milkweed has flowers that are pinkish-purple and in clusters; its fruits are green pods which turn brown before bursting open with fluffy seeds. Milkweed flowers bloom from June to August and are visited by many species of moths, butterflies, bees and other insects. While its sap is poisonous, insects and some animals are not affected. The Cherokee drank an infusion of common milkweed root and virgin's bower (Clematis species) for backaches, and they and the Iroquois and Rappahannock used the sap to remove warts, for ringworm, and for bee stings.

9. "Wild yellow azaleas" (p. 18) are one of seventeen native azaleas that grow in the Southeastern United States. The azaleas mentioned may well be the Oconee Azalea (Rhododendron flammeum) which blooms in April and May, or more likely the Piedmont Azalea, often called Wild Honeysuckle Bush for its yellow to orange-red flowers and fragrance.

10. "Painted trillium" (p. 18). One of the most beautiful woodland wildflowers, it is found from Ontario in the North to the Carolinas; this particular variety is white with red center markings. In the South it grows in a narrow band in the Appalachian Mountains from West Virginia to the high mountains of Georgia.

11. "Solomon's Seal" (p. 18). Solomon's Seal is a medicinal herb that has diverse

healing properties. It can be used as an herbal salve, tea, or supplement. As a salve it gives relief to injured joints, tendons, ligaments and the like; as a tea it soothes gastrointestinal inflammation and menstrual cramps and is known to lower blood pressure, relieve dry coughs, and increase mental concentration. Solomon's Seal has a rich history as an herbal remedy that goes back a long way.

12. "Wild American jorees" (p. 19). The Towhee or joree is a strikingly marked, oversized sparrow of the East noted for its cheery call, a two-parted, rising chewink, tow-hee, or (in the South) joree, made by both sexes. The call can vary in tone geographically from clear whistles to hoarse or nasal sounds. They are more often heard than seen as they inhabit brushy pastures and wood edges and scratch around the brush for their food (www.allaboutbirds.org/guide/ eastern _towhee/ sounds;wildlifehabitatcr.com/images/newsletters/March_2013_newsletter.pdf). See also G. R. Mayfield's recollection in *The Migrant* (1945) of hearing the bird's song which he had known and admired as a boy in North Georgia. He recalled: "His song is cheery and continuous from dawn to dusk, from February to September except for the molting season in August. These notes lingered in my memory vaguely until they came to a vivid reality in June of 1910. The incident took place on the bank of the Swannanoa River opposite Black Mountain Station in North Carolina, where I was engaged in some post-graduate studies. In the midst of my writing I became conscious of a new and exquisite bird song some hundred or more yards below my cabin on the mountain side. As I listened, these notes awakened childhood memories but I could not recognize the bird by the haunting sounds. Laying aside pencil and book, I rushed down to the lower side of the brushy clearing for fear the singer might cease or vanish from sight. But he was still there and in full view on top of a low bush—my boyhood Joree singing with all his heart and soul. Ten years later I began a serious study of bird songs and I found that individual Towhees vary widely in their songs, though all have enough in common to make them easily recognizable. Beethoven himself, master of variations for the same theme, would have reveled in the melodies of the Towhee" (www.tnbirds.org.Migrant Online/v0164-005.pdf).

13. "Wild blue anemones" (p. 19). The common names for anemones include woodflower and windflower. The plant contains poisonous chemicals that are toxic to animals, including humans, but it has nonetheless been used as a medicine. In the wild anemone flowers are usually white but may be pinkish, lilac or blue.

14. There are many passages in *Travelers' Rest* that indicate Robertson's knowledge of the flora and fauna of the region and his attempt to convey the Appalachian scene as his ancestors (here the fictional Caldwells) might have seen and experienced it. Typical is this passage of their travel through the Carolinas (p. 20): "They crossed great hills, forded wide yellow rivers, gathering dewberries and early purple blackberries, resting at night in dark groves of oak, hickory, chestnut; moving on through a rich, various south country, seeing the big-eared bat, cottontail rabbits, red squirrels, sometimes glimpsing a fierce lynx, a panther, a swift-fleeing frightened chipmunk. And in the moonshine at midnight, the brazen mocking bird, a tout, sang its mimic song." Towsend's big-eared bat is a species of Vesper bat so named for its extremely long, flexible ears and is seen where caves or abandoned

mine tunnels are available, hence they were a familiar sight in Appalachia. The Virginia big-eared bat is a medium-sized bat, pale to dark brown on the back and light brown underneath, and inhabits eastern Kentucky, eastern West Virginia, southwestern Virginia and northwestern North Carolina. Most of these wildlife are still familiar to southerners, particularly the North American panther, often called a cougar or mountain lion and familiar enough in the Carolinas if only for the name of the professional football team named for them.

15. "Alderbushes" (p. 21). Native Americans used red alder bark to treat poison oak, insect bites, and skin irritations. Blackfeet Indians used an infusion made from the bark of red alder to treat lymphatic disorders and tuberculosis, and recent clinical studies have suggested it can be effective against a variety of tumors. Many sources suggest that Alderbushes are a nuisance and are less concerned with their medicinal properties than how to get rid of them.

16. That Narcissa was especially adept at folk remedies and understanding of nature's bounty is indicated in the description of her herb book (p. 21): "Use birch for baskets and hoop poles, ash for plows, wagons, spokes of wheels, tool handles; use chestnut whenever possible for building purposes—many of the oldest houses in Pennsylvania are built of it; it is good also for tubs or vats for liquor and never shrinks after being seasoned; a decoction of the bark of the candleberry myrtle is good for dropsies as a substitute for Peruvian bark in the cure of fevers and mortifications; a decoction of bark of black cherry is very good for dysentery and consumption." Similar medicinal "receipts" are found in many early American cookbooks, most handwritten like Narcissa's herb book.

17. "Hornblende" (p. 22) is a dark-green to black mineral of the amphibole group.

18. "home of the sumptuous cape jesamine with its deathly sweet odor, a flower that corroded on touch, home of the passion plant, the rattlesnake, the bald turkey buzzard that fed in secret on carrion and floated like an angle in the sky"(p. 22). . The cape jesamine is known today as a gardenia, notable for its dark green foliage and creamy white flower and strong, sweet smell and the discoloration of the flowers when touched. Robertson's depiction of it is therefore appropriate. The common name of the passion plant is "passion flower." The plants are sometimes vines and their flowers come in a variety of colors.

19. "here a south sun shone and here were snakedoctors" (p. 22). Snakedoctors, or Snake Doctors as they are known in the South, is another name for dragon flies.

20. The specifics of the Western Carolina foothills through which the Caldwells passed is indicated by this passage (p. 22): "In this wild windy country, under this rough and ragged sky—this was their America. As they looked, seeing the growth of the land as far as the sight could reach, Carter began telling them the names of domes and crags and peaks, pointing to Glassy Mountain, small and glistening with igneous rocks, long Pine Mountain and Hogback and Rabun Bald beyond swift Tugaloo River." These names are still in use today.

21. "song of the catbird" (p. 24). The gray catbird (Dumetella carolinesis) is a medium-sized perching bird often mistaken for a mockingbird because of its similar cry. Its name suggests its identification with the Carolinas.

22. "milk fever" (p. 26). Milk fever is an inflammation usually brought on by an

infection from breast feeding. It is most common in the first six months after birth. Formerly believed to be caused by lactation, it is now held to be the result of the infection which causes the fever.

23. The description of Narcissa's burial place near the location Silas had selected for Forest Mansion contains a number of familiar wildflowers (p. 30). Yellow mullein refers to the biennial that blooms, a few flowers at a time, from June to September; the plant has a long history of use as an herbal remedy and Native Americans used the ground seeds as a paralytic fish poison. Saw briars are vine-like briars found in forests, old fields, and along roads; they get their name from the saw-like feeling one gets when brushed against or stepped on. Wild eglantine roses are a bright pink wild rose, one of the natural roses of North America. Wild eglantine roses are one of the most widespread species and called Rosa Carolina; they are common in thickets, hence why they are sometimes called pasture roses.

24. "June bugs" (p. 41) are beetles commonly seen in May or June.

25. "Tumble bugs" (p. 42). This is another name for a dung beetle.

26. "Corpse flower" (p. 42) is also known as the stink flower because of its rotting fish smell; it blooms, but rarely. Because of its rarity and more familiar location in places like Indonesia, one wonders if this could actually have been a flower the Caldwells would have seen or smelled, though Robertson himself would have been familiar with the plant from his Pacific travels and time as a reporter in Java.

27. "Watergliders" (p. 42) are a common insect often referred to as water striders, waterbugs, pond skaters or skimmers and found in almost every pond, river, or lake.

28. When Carter comes back from Tennessee (p. 51) starving, feverish, and begging for help he is given "dogwood tea and black cherry decoction." Dogwood Tea has been found to be beneficial in bringing down fevers and relieving body chills; it was also used to induce vomiting and relieve anxiousness in sick people. Black Cherry decoction is an herbal remedy made from the root of the black cherry tree and given for cramps, as a gargle for sore throat, and for cholera in infants as well as a disinfectant wash.

29. "Bed of arbutus" (p. 69). The Arbutus is a small tree with red flaking bark and edible red berries that resemble strawberries, hence it is often known as the Strawberry Tree. The bark and leaves can be used to create medicines for colds, stomach aches, and tuberculosis.

30. "Caline's yellow garden" (p. 90) consisted of the following: gold foxglove, partridge pea, frostweed, mullein, moth mullein, wild sorrel, tiny yellow flax, sundrops, primroses, buttercups, yellow star flowers, wild indigo and mustard. Foxgloves or digitalis bear flowers on tall spikes in various colors, including yellow, and are poisonous. The sleeping plant or partridge pea is a wildflower with large, showy yellow flowers that attract bees and butterflies and whose seed pods are eaten by gamebirds and songbirds. Frostweed is a member of the sunflower family and blooms in late fall and attracts butterflies, particularly monarch butterflies; it is sometimes called white crownbeard or ice plant. Mullein, also known as velvet plant, is a tall biennial or perennial with yellow flowers. Wild wood sorrel or sourgrass is a medium-sized edible plant, of the genus oxalis, found throughout most of North America; it has a lemony taste and yellow flowers blooming from May to October.

Tiny yellow flax is a biennial notable for its large yellow flowers. Sundrops or the evening primrose is a perennial with clusters of large, bright flowers and blooms in the summer. Primroses are spring-blooming flowers in a variety of colors, the yellow being particularly bright. Buttercups are wildflowers with bright, silky flowers; they have single blossoms as opposed to yellow star flowers which have clusters of yellow star-shaped flowers. The wild indigo referred to here is native to South Carolina and has yellow flowers; the plant was used for a blue dye. Wild mustard grows nearly everywhere (even in the Arctic) and produces on long stems clusters of yellow flowers.

31. "Freshnets" (p. 103) refers to a sudden overflow of a stream caused by heavy rains or the rapid melting of snow and ice.

32. "Mazagon" (p. 112) refers to plants or trees or Indian origin, known for their colorful seeds.

33. "Alders" (p. 151)are trees or tall shrubs that grow near streams and whose wood and bark, reddish or pale rose, are used in dyes and tanning.

34. "Red Judas Tree" (p. 162) is commonly known in North America as Red Bud. The tree is also known as Judea's Tree and supposedly the tree Judas Iscariot hanged himself from after betraying Christ. The trees bloom in early spring with pinkish-red flowers.

35. "Flaming orange milkweed" (p. 166). Milkweed is named for its milky juice and some species are known to be toxic. Milkweed is the sole food of monarch butterflies and its flowers produce a strong fragrance.

36. "the names of bloodroot and Indian pink and the robin plantain and anemone" (p. 177). Bloodroot is a perennial herbaceous flowering plant native to eastern North America and used to cause vomiting and to treat croup, hoarseness and sore throat. Indian pinks are a perennial flower, really bright scarlet in color, pollinated mainly by hummingbirds and common throughout the South. Plaintain is a large and troublesome family of weeds of which robin plantain is one of the many varieties.

37. "The light morning air echoed the wild quit-quequeeo of a warbler, a solitary vireo sang, its voice like a pipe" (p. 185). The description here is of the song of a warbler. There is a similar descriptive phrase in Bradford Torey's *A World of Green Hills. Observations of Nature and Human Nature in the Blue Ridge* (Houghton-Mifflin, 1898), a book with which Robertson may have been familiar. A vireo is a songbird.

CPSIA information can be obtained
at www.ICGtesting.com
Printed in the USA
BVHW031253150719
553489BV00001B/58/P